I0608131

Waiting for a Song

Naomi's Story

Other Books by the Author

Stone Trilogy

The Distant Shore
Under the Same Sun
Song of the Storm

Coming Soon

Stone Series

The Rosewood Guitar: Jon's Story, Fall 2014

Sunset Bay Series

The Nobody Girl, March 2015

Waiting for a Song

Naomi's Story

Mariam Kobras

Buddhapuss Ink LLC ❖ Edison NJ

Copyright © 2014 Mariam Kobras
Published in the United States by Buddhapuss Ink, LLC, Edison, New Jersey.
All rights are reserved. No part of this book may be reproduced or utilized in any form or by any means, electronic or mechanical, including photocopying, recording, or any information storage and retrieval systems without permission in writing from the publisher.

Cover Art *Reverie* ©2013 Eric G. Thompson
Author Photo by Sarah Fulford
Cover and Book Layout/Design by The Book Team
Editor, MaryChris Bradley
Copyeditor, Andrea H. Curley
Library of Congress Control Number: 2014936449
ISBN 978-1-941523-00-1 (Paperback Original)
First Printing June 2014

PUBLISHER'S NOTE
This is a work of fiction. Names, characters, places, and incidents are either the product of the author's imagination, or are used fictitiously. Any resemblance to actual persons, living or dead, business establishments, events, or locales is entirely coincidental. The publisher has no control over and does not assume any responsibility for authors, the authors' websites, or for third-party websites or their content. The scanning, uploading, and distribution of this book via the Internet or via any other means without the permission of the publisher is illegal and punishable by law. Please purchase only authorized electronic editions, and do not participate in or encourage electronic piracy of copyrighted materials. Your support of the author's rights is appreciated.

To contact the artist Eric G. Thompson or learn more about his works, go to:
www.ericgthompson.com

Buddhapuss Ink LLC and our logos are trademarks of Buddhapuss Ink LLC.
www.buddhapussink.com

For my dearest friends:

Wera Bartels
Bunny Hipps
Shaleeta Bihari
Virginia Hjalmarson
Pea Murell
Sue Farrant
MaryChris Bradley
Jeannette Schmid

You rock!

Chapter One

A BIRD WAS singing.

Naomi could hear its sweet warbling through the open window, carried in on the scent of cherry blossoms and coffee.

She was lying in bed, her quilt pulled up to her chin, trying to ignore the sunshine on her face, and wondered why humans thought birds sang. It wasn't as if they had deciphered the language of birds. It was an assumption, and nothing more, and that bird in the cherry tree, maybe he was just shouting at his wife for not having cleaned up the nest. Perhaps there was nothing romantic about it at all.

From downstairs she could hear her mother's voice and the clinking of plates.

Breakfast. They were having breakfast in the conservatory today to stay out of the way of the people getting the house ready for her birthday ball.

The mere thought of it made her burrow even deeper into her pillows and pinch her eyes shut. She wondered if she could sneak out of the house without being noticed, and hide somewhere until the day was over and all guests had left.

A ball. Her father's idea of a birthday party. They'd come all the way from Geneva to the Carlsson estate outside Toronto for this. She had argued and begged, saying she wanted to spend the day with her friends, Fleur, Manon, Giselle, and the others; but no. Your special day, he'd said, the day you'll be eighteen, when everything changes for you. It had to be celebrated at home, in Kleinberg, where all their friends were.

Eighteen. She didn't feel eighteen. She didn't feel like an adult, and she didn't want a ball.

Carefully, she opened one eye. The dress was hanging on the door of her closet. It was a pretty dress. A grown-up dress, a couture dress, made especially for her by a famous Italian designer.

She'd wanted black, a slim black silk dress with a back bare and a slit up the side to show her leg when she walked. Even her mother had been scandalized by that suggestion, and her father had looked at her as if she'd been eating live worms for lunch.

"Of course not," he'd said, and given her mother that short nod she knew only too well. "See to it, Lucia. Not black. And no skin." Which, after a sip of coffee, he had amended to "Shoulders, yes. Strapless is okay. But that's all."

Strapless. How she despised strapless dresses. Too often she had seen women fumbling with them, pulling them up for fear they'd drop off their busts. Of course, a well-tailored gown wouldn't do that. It would stay put. But that was the shame of it: You could always see who'd been saving on their clothes. For Naomi, it was the same category as clip-on bow ties. They were vulgar, she agreed with her father on that, just as vulgar as strapless dresses that slipped.

So here she was: no black silk and no naked shoulders. Her birthday dress was rose chiffon, which was the next-best thing to black silk, and it had little, puffy sleeves made of polka-dot lace. She could live with it. especially since it had a broad silk sash that tied into a big bow at the back.

Her father had been enormously pleased when he saw it and promised to buy her jewelry that would go well with the color.

"Diamonds?" Naomi had asked hopefully, but he'd again given her that icy glare he was famous for and replied, "Your husband will give you diamonds. Fathers don't give their daughters diamonds. That's as close to incest as you can get, my dear. No, I'm thinking pearls. Pearls will look lovely with that dress."

Naomi was certain that she could think of things that were closer to incest than diamonds, but as always, she didn't contradict. Pearls were better than nothing.

THE door opened.

"Aren't you going to get up, dear?" Her mother, Lucia, impeccable as always, not a hair out of place in her tightly knotted bun. "We're waiting for you! Cook made fried mushrooms especially for you. Come on, get up!"

Naomi pulled the quilt over her face. "I don't want to. It's nice and cozy in here, and I don't want to get up."

Her mother stepped inside and closed the door behind her. "Naomi, don't be ridiculous. It's your birthday! You should be excited and happy!"

That made her throw back her covers and sit up. "So if it's my birthday, why can't I stay in bed all day?"

Lucia sighed. "You're acting like a child. Come on; out of bed you go, and dress properly, will you. No jeans. Here." She opened the closet, letting her hand drift over the gossamer silk of the ball gown. "What a lovely dress. You'll look like a princess. Your father will be very proud." Hesitating a moment, she picked out a blue summer dress. "This will look nice on you today. I'll send up my maid to do your hair."

"But I want to go riding later." It was a feeble protest.

Naomi knew she'd lost when Lucia put the dress down on her bed. "There hardly will be time for riding today, my dear. The first guests will be arriving before lunch, and they expect to see you."

Birthdays. She'd been to birthdays where people ran around in shorts and had a big barbecue in the yard, where the men hung around the fire with beer bottles in their hands and the children splashed in the swimming pool. No one had worn a silk dress, or had a maid do her hair. Those parties had been relaxed and fun, and she'd enjoyed them.

Not here, she thought, not for her. Never for her. As far back as Naomi could remember, there had always been a new gown, always a grand affair with more adults than young people, and everyone had always been in formal clothing.

The Carlsson family, everything was always about the business. The gifts she received were meant to impress her father and not just to give her joy.

Most of them were locked up in the family safe or had wandered into her trust fund. A few smaller things she'd been allowed to keep in her room: a fine gold chain with a garnet pendant, a pair of earrings with sparkling opals, a silver bracelet inlaid with turquoises, allegedly handmade by a Navajo chief, especially for her.

She'd been twelve when a banker friend of her father had given her that heavy bangle, and she'd imagined an old, wizened man chanting over the stones while he put them into the bracelet. He even had a horse, a beautiful palomino, with feathers knotted into its mane. It had taken all her teenage willpower not to put the box that held it up to her nose in hope of smelling the wild scent of grassland, buffalo, and horse.

Her father had given it a disgusted glance and told her she could wear it, or lose it, for all he cared. It wasn't "real" jewelry at all, he'd said, just a trinket for a child, worth nothing.

Naomi had taken it to her room and slipped it on her wrist. It had been much too large, as if it was meant for a man's arm, but it had been hers, a talisman with the whiff of freedom.

"DON'T fall back asleep." Lucia pulled off her quilt. "Out of bed with you, and off to the shower. Would you like to know who's here already, waiting for you?"

"Not really." Naomi had a very good idea who it might be.

"Who knows, there may be diamonds for you yet today." Picking up the blue dress, Lucia added, "Maybe not this one after all. Maybe it should be something more festive."

"Mama. Please." Slouching off toward her bathroom door, she watched her mother rummage in the drawer with her underwear and pick out a red bra.

"What? You're eighteen now! I have a feeling Seth might propose today, and nobody would be happier than your father." She pulled a red dress out of the closet. "Here. This one."

Naomi closed the door and sat on the rim of the tub, rubbing her heaving stomach.

"Wouldn't that be something? Wouldn't it be exciting to get engaged to Seth on your birthday?" The door didn't deter Lucia. "Seth is the best possible match for you!"

"Not if I can catch a crown prince or something," Naomi shouted back.

That made Lucia pause. Then she replied, "Well. Haakon is only seven. That would be awkward. And Prince Charles is engaged to that Diana girl. Gustav is married to that German commoner, and Frederik is twelve or thereabouts. I don't think there's anyone available right now."

Naomi groaned. "What about the Netherlands?"

"Oh dear, no. You don't want to live there, do you?" Lucia laughed. "I think you'll have to settle for Seth."

It wasn't that she didn't like Seth. She did. She liked to go riding with him or sit in the library and talk about books. She was even okay with walking through the halls of the McMichael Collection with him and discussing Canadian art. But there was no way she could imagine kissing him, or worse.

"He's so old." She tried not to make it sound like a complaint but like a concerned, adult statement. "He's almost eight years older than I am."

"Yes, and he's been waiting for you for so long. He's a good catch, Naomi. Now hurry. I'll send the maid up in fifteen minutes. Breakfast is waiting."

Yes, and she'd successfully managed to dawdle away a good part of the morning without having to face her father and his glowing pride and, even worse, his plans for her future.

Standing under the shower, Naomi muttered, "You'll be such a success, Naomi. So pretty and so bright, and with the right husband, you'll rule the world. Just imagine, one day you'll be the owner of the entire family business—so many hotels, so much real estate—and you, heading it all. The Carlsson empire, run by my daughter."

She knew the words by heart. He said them so often that they felt like her second name, like a label she would have to carry around with her until one of them died.

"I'm not going to marry you, Seth." Rehearsing. It would be good to know what to say and not stumble into any kind of trap. "Not now, not next year, not ever. You're short, ugly, and a redhead. There's no way I'm going to marry a man with red hair. Just, no. Walk away, Seth." Which, of course, she could never ever say to him. Their fathers were too close for that, and there was too much money involved.

The best she could hope for was to win time, and maybe a chance to escape.

That was it. Her heart felt as light as a snowflake with the insight. She'd not turn Seth away. She'd bat her eyelashes at him and tell him that she needed time to grow up, that she wasn't adult enough to get engaged and she was afraid of leaving her home just yet.

He would understand. He'd be his old, kind, boring self and pat her shoulder and respond that of course he understood and to please take as much time as she needed.

Or maybe not. Dread clenched her stomach again. Maybe he'd not understand. Maybe he'd tell her that he'd been waiting for her to grow up for years, always with the knowledge that someday they'd get married, and here he was, twenty-six years old and more than ready for a wife.

Naomi's glance strayed to the window. Two floors up, and there was not a chance in the world for her to escape. She'd end up right on the glass roof of the conservatory, where her entire family was sitting right now.

She was trapped.

Chapter Two

HER FATHER, OLAF, rose from his seat at the head of the table when she walked in.

"Ah," he said, "Here's the princess now. Happy birthday, my dear."

They were all there: her mother, her uncle Carl, and Seth and his parents. Like a big, happy family they were sitting around the table, drinking coffee and chatting, and they were all looking her way. Her mother frowned. Naomi had decided to wear the blue dress after all.

There were flowers on the table, big bouquets of roses and peonies in all shades of rose and pink, and a couple of gifts, wrapped very nicely, near the only free chair, which was, of course, next to Seth.

Cook was standing in the door to the stairs leading down to the kitchen, a smile on her face and a dish of fried mushrooms in her hand, and nodded a greeting her way.

"Thank you," Naomi said, to no one in particular, and dutifully let her father kiss her cheek.

"I have a birthday present for you," he said, and picked up a jewel case of purple velvet with a famous name embossed in gold on it; she knew that name very well. "Something I'd like you to wear tonight, for the ball."

More jewelry, and more of the kind she wouldn't be allowed to keep.

"Open it," her father urged. "It's yours. A special gift, for your eighteenth birthday."

It was a circlet, and a very pretty one, set with pearls and garnets like tiny flowers in a wreath of golden twigs and leaves.

Naomi ran her fingers over it. "Thank you," she said again, her voice trembling a little. "It's so beautiful!"

Her father smiled, pleased. "Here." He removed the circlet from the case. "Why not try it on now."

She had refused to let the maid do up her hair, arguing that it would have to be redone for the ball anyway, and was wearing her long, black locks in a braid as usual; but she stood still as her father placed the circlet on her head. It was a perfect fit.

"There." He stepped away from her. "You look like the princess you are. Very nice. And it will look lovely with your dress tonight!"

"Naomi." Seth patted the chair beside him. "Good morning and happy birthday!" His red hair shone in the light, and his pale skin looked even paler in contrast to the freckles on his nose. "I was hoping we could go for a ride later?"

It was the only thing he could have said to make her smile. "Yes! I'd love that! Let me have a cup of coffee, and we can go!" She held out her cup, and he poured for her.

"You may find a surprise in the stables," Seth said, taking her hand in his. "And it may have four legs and a mane."

Blood rushed into her throat. Naomi opened her mouth to reply, but no words came.

Seth smiled, pleased. "I brought my riding breeches. Hurry up; eat your mushrooms."

She nodded like a child and helped herself when the maid offered the dish. "Say thank you to Cook for me," she whispered, and the girl nodded.

"You didn't buy me a horse, did you?" Her voice sounded raspy, excited, and she hastily took a sip of coffee.

"You'll see." Smug, he smiled smugly, with the air of a patient, loving adult. "I know the way to your heart is through the Carlsson stables."

Naomi blushed. "That's not true. I love horses, but I also love music. If you'd write me a song, Seth…"

"Ha! Sorry, no. No songwriting from me. Ask me to write something legal, draw up a contract, and I'm your man." His light-blue eyes shone like aquamarine. "Maybe a marriage contract?"

Everyone was watching them: her father with great interest, her mother with a fine smile, and Seth's parents with the same smugness he had on his face. Suddenly, the mushrooms tasted like straw and the coffee like bitter poison.

"There would have to be more in it for me than a marriage

contract," Naomi replied, waving him away with a flutter of her fingers. "I've been told to expect diamonds with a proposal. So maybe you'll have to drive downtown and find a jeweler instead of going riding with me."

She was pleased; it had come out flippantly enough to make her father stare and her mother cough into her napkin.

Seth, though, leaned back in his chair, giving her a bright smile that showed his small, even teeth. "Well, Miss Naomi. What if I did that yesterday, after work? You're playing with fire."

Returning her attention to her omelet and mushrooms, Naomi answered, "Don't be vulgar, Seth. You can't propose to me over breakfast, with our parents present. Try and be a bit romantic, will you."

Her father laughed; and that was something that didn't happen very often. "Here," he said, stretching out his hand to her. "Give me that circlet. I'll keep it for you until tonight. You look like a princess anyway, crown or not."

Regretfully, she handed it over. But the regret didn't last long. She'd go riding after all, and that was better than any jewelry could ever be.

FOR a moment Naomi thought their parents would escort them to the stables.

They were standing around in the big hall of the manor, Seth's father and hers with cigars, their mothers discussing the flower arrangements for the ball, when she returned in her riding clothes.

But Olaf only said, "Be back in time for lunch. There will be more guests here by then."

"Yes, Papa." There would be no time for a long ride. She had battled with her riding boots for nothing.

Seth was standing in the open door, his back to them, talking to his father. His breeches didn't look good on him; they made him look thicker and stockier than he really was. He reminded Naomi of a dwarf, one of the dwarfs in The Lord of the Rings: sturdy, strong, and ugly. She wondered if he'd grown a beard in the time she'd been changing. A red beard, to match his mop of red hair and balance out his missing eyebrows.

Lucia came over to her. "Don't be late. Just a short ride, and do let the stable boys look after the horses. No grooming today!"

"Yes, Mama."

Getting into Seth's car she wondered how they could tell her she was an adult now and in the same breath give her instructions on how to behave, and where to be, and when. It didn't make her feel very grown-up at all.

"So." Seth threw her a smile. "Finally eighteen, and finally a woman. I've been waiting for this day for a long time. It wasn't easy to be patient, you know."

"Oh come on." Her stomach decided to try out a very complicated barrel roll. "Don't tell me you lived like a monk, Seth. I mean, don't even try. No one would believe you anyway."

There was a narrow gravel road that connected the Carlsson mansion on the hill to the hotel at the other end of the grounds. It meandered across the golf course like a dry riverbed, following the contours of the countryside. A couple of times it dipped into the forest that separated the land from the lake and took them into deep, green shadows.

Naomi loved the forest. She loved the cedars and maples, and how they looked so different from each other and yet shared the space like old friends.

"I don't know what to say." Seth was staring at the road, his hands tightly clamped around the wheel. "This is not a discussion I want to have with you, Naomi."

Flustered! She'd flustered him, and she had to bite her lip to not laugh out loud. "Do tell, Seth. Do you have a girlfriend?"

The car swerved onto the meticulously kept lawn.

"I don't have a girlfriend!" Seth's face was turning red. It was an interesting red, not blotchy, as she had expected, but a uniform, dark red, almost the color of a pickled beet. "Not now, at least. How would I be able to propose to you if there was someone else? It would be so wrong."

"That's true." It occurred to her that he'd never, not once, told her that he loved her. "So are you going to propose to me?"

He laughed. "Nosy and impatient! But I'm pleased! You seem impatient to marry me."

The hotel complex came into sight. Like a mirror of the family manor, the main building sat on a knoll, overlooking the stables, several smaller houses, and the golf club. There were quite a few golfers on the greens, enjoying the lovely weekend weather.

Naomi had never figured out why people played golf. Her father had tried to teach her, tried to share his enthusiasm, but it hadn't worked. It still felt like a long, boring walk to her, and definitely designed for older people.

"I'm not really impatient to get married." She jumped out of the car when they stopped in the stable courtyard. "It feels to me as if my life is just beginning. I'd really like to finish college."

"Oh, not a problem! You can do that as my wife, Naomi. I'll support you in that! You'll want to study business and management, I assume." Seth had stopped walking and turned back when she didn't follow.

"No. Not really, no."

His invisible eyebrows came up. "No? What then?"

Like a kid, Naomi hid her hands behind her back. "I was studying piano, and singing. I'd like to go on with that." Her throat was dry, and swallowing hurt a bit. "At least for a little while."

"Music." He said the word as if he'd just heard it for the first time ever. "Now that is something I'd not have guessed. I know you play the piano, but I always thought that was more part of a lady's education than a real passion. Like riding and dancing. You know what I mean."

"Yes. I know." Somehow, for some reason she couldn't really name, his reaction disappointed her. "But that's not how it is. I really love music. I love singing." She pulled up her shoulders. "I don't like accounting and business. It's boring. And very uncreative."

"Well. I'm surprised. I always assumed you were looking forward to running the family empire. It's a huge thing, being the heir to all the Carlsson hotels. A lot of responsibility."

"I know." Once again she felt the heavy knot of dread in her gut.

"That's why I want to do a few semesters of something fun now. There won't be time later."

Seth gazed at her, slapping his riding gloves against his leg in a slow rhythm. "Music. I never knew that about you. How strange. We've been friends for so long now, actually since you were born, and I never knew you loved music that much."

"Yes, well…"

There hadn't been a hint of accusation in his words, and yet it felt like one, as if he was less than happy about her sudden revelation and had to adjust to it.

"Your parents," Seth said, "expect us to live here, at the Carlsson house. They expect us to take over from your father. My parents are very happy about that. The old thing, you know. Money marries money, land marries land. That way, you know that no one is after your wealth." He turned, looking back in the direction of the manor. "We could rebuild the south wing so it would be more secluded, like our own apartment, to give us more privacy, if you want that. But I think your parents are thinking of moving to Italy when your father retires." A flash of teeth in a brief smile, then: "But that's far in the future. I guess they'd like to see a few grandchildren before that."

Her fate, he was laying it out for her. Suddenly, that circlet with the rubies didn't seem quite that exciting anymore, and the ball even less.

Naomi was wondering if there was a way to hide in the woods all day, sneak a book out of the library and spend the hours sitting under her favorite tree down by the lake instead of dancing with strange men and smiling at birthday presents from people whose names she didn't even know. Maybe she could grab a piece of cake from the kitchen before anyone noticed and then run.

Run. What a delicious idea that was—run, leave all this behind: the duties, the expectations, the cumbersome weight of her inheritance.

She turned her back on Seth to take in her surroundings. Everything around her, as far as she could see, belonged to her family. Even if she sneaked away to the lake she'd still be in their territory, and there was no way she could leave it without at least a bicycle or, even better, a car.

Only she didn't have either. Bicycles, her father stated, were too dangerous for her, and there was no way she'd drive anywhere on her own. There was always at least a chauffeur, and most of the time a guard.

She was their precious heir. The one and only. The princess with the golden shackles.

"Come on." Seth tapped her arm to get her attention back. "Your birthday present is waiting!"

Chapter Three

OWEN WAS THERE, sitting on a bale of straw, polishing a bridle. He hardly looked up when they entered the stable alley. He gave her a brief nod, his eyes hidden by the cap he had pulled low over his face.

Naomi had never seen that bridle before; it was pretty, made of red leather, with tassels and tiny silver bells attached to it. They made a soft, sweet sound when Owen rolled it up.

"Happy birthday," he said, and it came out gruff and clipped. "I have a gift for you." He held out the bridle. "Thought it would look good on Apollo."

Her heart did a little flip. "It's so lovely! Owen, it must have cost a fortune!"

He shrugged. "Nah. It's okay. It's just a gift."

"What is it?" Seth had come closer; he was looming behind her, peering over her shoulder. She could feel the warmth of his body, nearly touching hers; and she shifted, stifling the impulse to move away.

"Oh, nice." He took the bridle from Owen's hand and inspected it. "Looks like the ones they use for the Arab horses, doesn't it? Pretty workmanship there!"

Owen lowered his head to hide a blush. "It's for Apollo."

"Apollo? That big black beast you like to ride, Naomi? That stallion with the attitude? I hate to see you on him. He's too tall for you, and you can't control him. Here." Taking her arm, he dropped the bridle into Owen's hand and pulled her away. "I've talked about this with your father, and he agrees. Apollo is not the right horse for you. So after consulting with him, I've bought a sweet little mare for you, a pedigree Arabian. If you want bells and tassels, put that bridle on her!"

"It's for Apollo," Owen repeated, jumping up, "Not for your tiny thing of a horse."

Naomi slapped her hand over her mouth to stop the giggles that were bubbling up in her.

They were facing each other, Seth in his expensive riding breeches and handmade boots, the riding crop in his fist, staring up at the tall young man, Owen, just a few weeks older than she, his mouth set in a thin line, his chin up. He was in ragged jeans and a faded shirt, his feet in muddy boots; but he wasn't afraid of Seth.

"Naomi picks her own horse. She's no coward."

"Being careful doesn't mean you're a coward, my boy," Seth replied, "And we can't risk her having an accident with that mean-eyed stallion, can we?"

"You're afraid of a real horse. Apollo is a real horse. Yours is puny and timid."

Her heart bled for Owen. Naomi stepped forward to stand between them. "It's okay, Owen." She laid her hand on his, prying the bridle from his stubborn fingers. "Come. Let's put it on Apollo and see how it looks, shall we? And then we'll saddle him up, and I'll take him out for a short ride."

"Child, I don't want you to do that."

She thought she'd misheard.

"Naomi, child, listen to me. I'd prefer to see you on a horse with a gentler soul."

She couldn't swallow past the lump in her chest, stuck somewhere between her lungs and throat, let alone talk.

His hand was around her arm again, tugging, directing, ordering her to move away.

Naomi drew a deep breath, fighting the pain. The scent of the clean, well-kept stable filled her nose; there was the dry dust of hay, the sweet aroma of oats, and the warm smell of horse, all of it mingling into memories of many happy hours spent here, away from home, away from anyone telling her what to do.

She closed her eyes. Of all days, this one was the worst ever to get into a fight with Seth. He would get away unscathed, with her father's sympathy, both of them bemoaning her stubborn soul; but she, she would be locked up in her room, and there wouldn't even be a piece of her birthday cake brought up.

Or worse, they'd make her attend the ball; and she'd spend the evening wedged between them, unable to breathe, and unable to dance with anyone else.

Three deep breaths. Slowly, she inhaled, breathed out again, and forced her shoulders to relax.

It was her day. She wouldn't ruin it for herself by fighting with Seth.

"I'd like to see my birthday gift, Seth," she said as sweetly as she could. "Now you've made me really curious." And added, to Owen, "Please saddle Apollo for me? It would break his heart if I didn't take him out for a ride, even if it's only for a few minutes." She leaned into Seth's shoulder as she said that, forcing her body into softness, and felt his grip on her weaken.

"She's right here." He led her toward a box stall at the other end of the stable, well away from the other horses. On their way, they passed Apollo's stall; and the stallion, catching her scent, stuck his head out over the partition and neighed softly.

"My baby." Of course she'd thought to bring a treat for him, and now she held out the carrots and apples.

Apollo took them from her outstretched hand delicately, his teeth never touching her skin.

"You're such a good boy," Naomi crooned, rubbing his soft nose and scratching his forehead.

Seth was shaking his head, his fists again on his hips. "Look at that beast! You can't even see over his back, Naomi! How do you get up there? Do you use a ladder? Who saddles that brute for you? Not even Owen is tall enough for that."

"I am tall enough. I've taken care of Apollo since he was born." Owen was standing behind them, the saddle on his arm, the tack around his neck. "Naomi raised him from the moment he popped out of his mother. There isn't a gentler or friendlier horse in this entire stable, and that's saying something. He thinks Naomi is his mom, and he's always respectful to her." With a grin, he shrugged. "That means he won't let anyone else ride him. He loves only Naomi, and me. Now make room, please, so I can bring him out."

"Oh hell, I don't want to be anywhere close when you let that monster out!" His hands up in defeat, Seth stalked away.

He looked like an insulted schoolboy after a lost playground fight, trying to keep his dignity by turning his back on his foes.

"Come on," she said, giving Apollo a friendly slap. "Move, you beastly monster. Let Owen put a saddle on you!"

The straw in his stall rustled when the big horse moved forward. Sunlight rippled over his glossy back, the long mane fluttered, falling over his eyes.

"You are so beautiful. What a beautiful boy you are!" Her hand ran down the sleek curve of his neck, feeling the muscles under the black coat.

"Naomi!"

He was shouting for her. Seth was shouting for her, impatiently, with authority, as if he had a right to.

Again that big rock of resentment turned in her chest, and she pressed her hand against her ribs to still it.

"I'm coming, Seth. No need to scare the horses." One step, then another in his direction, away from where she wanted to be.

IT wasn't easy to conjure up some kind of praise for the dainty Arabian mare.

She had never cared for the breed, hating the way they held their tails like dogs and how their nostrils always looked too large for their narrow heads. This one, a dappled yearling, was no different. She moved around her stall nervously, her black eyes rolling. She looked like a poodle.

Seth was explaining that Naomi couldn't ride her yet, of course; she was only a filly, she needed to grow and be trained, and he was sure Naomi would love to do that herself. He broke off, gazing at her, his eyes narrowed in speculation.

"Of course, when you're pregnant you'll have to stop riding and hanging out in stables."

It was too much.

"Even more reason to do it now!" She threw Seth a brilliant smile and turned to Apollo. Ignoring Owen's hand, held out to boost her up into the saddle, she swung herself onto the horse's back.

Without waiting for Seth, she let Apollo walk out of the stable and drove him into an easy canter as soon as there was grass under his hooves.

"Run, Apollo," she called, standing in the stirrups. "Run like the wind!"

The powerful muscles stretched, exploding into a headlong sprint across the golf course and up toward the forest that ran along the the perimeter of the Carlsson estate.

This was her routine: She would circle the land that belonged to her family once a day, measuring out her heritage in the long strides of her stallion. Without Apollo breaking stride even once, without stopping at the lake or visiting her parents on the terrace, it took them two solid hours to stake out her claim.

The wind in her hair, the rhythmic drum of her steed's hooves beating on the soft ground, she was free. For a short time, for a few heartbeats, Naomi was herself, the girl her soul wanted to be.

When she came up to the big iron gate that separated the Carlsson grounds from the road, she reigned in Apollo. It stood open to admit the caterers and limos with the first guests, those who'd flown in for her ball and would stay at the house: family, close friends of her parents, important people.

Right now though there was no one. It was just an open gate, a beckoning, open gate, singing to her, luring her into freedom.

Apollo shook his head impatiently, snorting, feeling her impatience; and Naomi patted his neck.

"No, we can't go that way, sweetie," she mumbled. "They'd never let me near you again."

The gravel path to the mansion wound away between the tall trees. She'd done the run down its length to the house so often, Apollo's hooves had made a trail in the ground right beside the narrow road.

She'd gotten some grief over that from the gardener who had been trying to cultivate flowers along the driveway, but her father, for once, had taken her side. He'd waved him away and told him to leave it—he liked to see his daughter ride beside his car when he returned from a business trip; it made him feel as if he was home.

He always made his driver slow down and then lowered his window to tell her where he had been, and what he'd brought her; and then a slow, spare smile would blossom in his ice-blue eyes, and he'd say, "And someday, you'll be doing this. Someday, this will all belong to you!"

Only, the things that made him smile turned her heart to stone, and with it her laughter.

Naomi shook off the moodiness. "Home, Apollo!" she cried. "Let's see some speed!"

And they followed the path toward the Carlsson mansion, racing along the slight decline and back up again to the house, where she saluted her father with her riding crop before turning her horse back toward the stables.

There were some golfers out, and they looked up as she rode past, her big, black horse trampling the hallowed green; but they kept silent.

She was the princess. She could ride across the golf course and damage the smooth ground. No one would dare to stop her.

Chapter Four

IT WAS AWKWARD; somewhere along the way she'd lost Seth.

He wasn't at the stables when she returned, and Owen only shrugged his shoulders when she asked. The car was gone too, which meant she'd have to walk back to the mansion.

The morning had turned into a baking hot summer day, the sun pouring heat liberally across the golf course. The undulating area simmered under the unrelenting light.

"But did he say something?" She handed the reigns to Owen. "Did he say he was going back to the house? I thought he was going to come after me as soon as you'd saddled a horse for him…"

"Gone," Owen mumbled, and walked away with Apollo.

Naomi stood in the open stable door, gazing across the landscape. She'd be hot and exhausted by the time she got home.

There was always the option to go over to the hotel and ask them to drive her home in one of the golf carts; but that would mean defeat, and she wasn't going to show weakness even if it meant breaking her ankle in one of the bunkers.

"I'm leaving," she called after Owen, and he raised his hand without turning back to her.

Out in the courtyard, she stopped.

"Owen."

This time he did turn.

"Owen, leave it. Don't unsaddle Apollo. Ride with me to the house, and then you can bring him back to the stables. Are you up to a race?"

The boy's face lit up. "Of course! Can we ride down by the forest? It's lovely and shady down there."

"Sure! Hurry!"

Apollo neighed in surprise when she got back in the saddle, feeling her excitement, feeling the sudden joy.

It took Owen only moments to put a bridle on his favorite steed, a dappled mare. He didn't even saddle her but swung up on her bare back.

"Go!" he shouted. "Go!"

Side by side, they raced down toward the forest line along the lake, winding in and out of the shadow, letting the horses find their own path, letting them run.

Naomi had pulled the rubber from her braid and let her long hair fly in the wind. Beside her, Owen was shouting, urging the mare to run faster, overtake Apollo, run, run, run; but it was hopeless. The large stallion shook his head in irritation and stretched himself to thunder up the slope toward the house and the big lawn behind it.

There were people on the terrace, sitting in the lounge chairs, standing and gazing out at the lake, champagne glasses or coffee cups in their hands: her parents, Seth's parents, her uncle Carl and his wife, and Seth. He was no longer in riding breeches but had on nice tan chinos and a light-blue shirt, an adult among other adults.

They were watching her: a tableau of humans, caught in that one instant when she and Owen had broken from the forest and became visible to them. A still life, a bubble in time, insects frozen in amber, that's what they looked like, and it made the laughter bubble up in her and break out; and that's how she arrived at the bottom of the terrace: wild hair flowing around her face and shoulders, her face lit up in mirth.

Olaf had put down his cup on one of the small tables and come to the stairs leading to the lawn, his face like thunder, ready to give her a tirade. Their eyes met, and something happened. Even though his lips were still in a tight, white line and his stance spelled anger, a spark of amusement softened his eyes. It traveled down to his mouth and made its corners twitch.

"You're ruining the lawn," he said. "Get off that beast and let Owen take him back. Here's some coffee for you."

She slid off Apollo's back.

"Thanks, Daddy," Naomi replied, and brushed a kiss on his narrow cheek.

"I can't believe your rudeness," Lucia said. "I can't believe you just rode off and left Seth standing there after he's given you such a wonderful present."

They were back in her room. Naomi knew there was no way she could get away from her mother, not even for a much-needed shower, not even through a closed bathroom door.

"I told Owen to saddle a horse for him," she called back, rubbing shampoo into her hair. "How was I to know he'd change his mind?"

"Naomi, you can't treat Seth as if he was a boy. He's a grown man; he deserves some respect! He asked your father for your hand today, and you, nowhere in sight! The engagement could have been announced an hour ago!"

Soap was running into her eyes, but it didn't sting as badly as Lucia's words.

"He can't ask father for my hand before he's asked me, can he? Now that is rude."

There was a pause, and so she pushed the shower curtain aside to look at her mother. Lucia was sitting on the edge of the tub, a towel in her lap, gazing out of the window, lost in thought. She had changed since breakfast, into what she called an afternoon dress. Naomi loved this one on her mother. The dark-red silk made her black hair shine and her skin seem even whiter than it was. As far back as she could remember, Lucia had upheld the rule of changing at least twice a day; and on weekends, when they had houseguests, there would be evening clothes for dinner, just as if they were stuck in the last century.

"But, darling." Lucia's hand wandered over her hair and checked the fat knot of braids at the back of her head. "I thought all that was settled and Seth asking your father a mere formality, a gesture of politeness. I know he was going to propose today, so what happened?"

She didn't give Naomi the time to reply though and went on. "But of course it doesn't really matter. He has the ring, and I believe he's only waiting for the right moment. And you're right, of course; the stable wouldn't have been a good place."

"Mama. Today is my eighteenth birthday." It sounded like a sad litany, as if saying it made the day more bearable. "I'm really not sure I want to get engaged today. I'm not even sure I want to marry Seth! I don't love him at all."

"Oh dear. You can't mean what you're saying, darling. Of course you love Seth! It's not the head-over-heels kind of love, I know that, and how could it be; you've been friends since you were a toddler! But it's a solid base for a successful marriage, Naomi. Trust me! Seth knows exactly what he's getting into, and you know you can always rely on him. There's nothing better."

"Is that why you married father?" Naomi knew it wasn't, but she wanted to hear her mother wiggle out of that one.

"No, that was different. But I'm not you; I'm not the Carlsson heiress. And of course my parents were delighted with my choice! Besides loving your father, I was marrying into one of the wealthiest and most powerful families in Canada and Norway."

Naomi rolled her eyes at the shower tiles. The same old song, and every time there was a line about the importance of the Carlsson family.

"So you see, there's really no comparing my marriage to yours. You're special; you're important. The man who marries you will find that the Carlsson hotel empire comes with his new wife, and that's why we must make sure you pick the right one."

"Yes, Mama." With a sigh, Naomi turned off the water and angled for the towel Lucia was holding out to her.

There was no sense in debating the issue.

"So if Seth proposes to you later, during the ball, you'll get a really beautiful ring, darling." Lucia rose, straightening her skirt. "He showed it to me while you were still out riding. It's gorgeous, a huge diamond. You'll love it!"

"I'm sure."

THE maid was waiting for her in her room, the curling iron and the box with the circlet in her hands.

"Miss," she said, "we'd better get started on your hair. Your father told me how it should look, and it will take a while."

Wrapped in her towel, Naomi sat down on the bed. "I haven't had lunch," she said.

Lucia smiled, her hand on the doorknob. "I'll have something brought up for you. Of course you can't come down until the ball starts. You're the star of the evening."

Naomi's heart did a little skip. "That's okay," she said, trying to sound cool and detached. "I'll take the time to rest and get ready."

The door closed softly behind Lucia.

Alone. She'd be left alone while the house filled with strangers; no one expected her to greet them and smile while they handed her envelopes or gifts for her birthday. There would be a lot of digits on those checks and pretty jewels, purses, and hand-embroidered cashmere shawls in the packages—maybe even a rare, leather-bound first edition of a book or some useless but very expensive knickknack no one ever needed.

"Your dress is so pretty, Miss," the maid whispered. "It will look fabulous on you."

Naomi moved to the dressing table and sat on the stool. "Thank you. I wanted black silk..."

Seeing the raised brows of the girl, she clamped her mouth shut and stared at her image in the mirror.

"Have you ever been in love, Louise?" she asked instead.

There was an array of cosmetics lined up on the table in front of her, most of it put there by her mother, including some brand-new lipsticks. Naomi never used makeup. She couldn't see the sense in it, couldn't understand why anyone wanted to paint her face. It seemed to her as if she was putting on a mask, like hiding from the world behind a pretty facade.

"Of course!" Louise's reply shook her out of her morose thoughts. "I have a boyfriend. He works over at the hotel as a bellboy during the summer. He's a student at York University. He'll be a teacher someday. And then we'll get married and settle down."

"How old are you?" Rude again, but Louise didn't seem to mind.

"Nineteen last month, Miss. When Reuben, my boyfriend, graduates, I'll be twenty-two; and that's a good age to start a family. My mother was younger than me when she got married."

"Yes. How nice."

She couldn't do it.

Opening one of the lipsticks, one with a lovely rosewood tone, Naomi realized that there was no way she could marry Seth.

"I always thought falling in love was something wildly romantic, take-my-breath-away exciting," she said in a low voice to no one in particular. "I've always dreamed of meeting the right man and knowing instantly that he's the one. He's the one I'd give myself to; and it would feel as if we're one: one soul, one heart, one breath. I thought falling in love was like the sky opening and pouring bliss over me, and music filling the air."

Louise laughed. "I think that only happens in romance novels. I think it's a pretty dream, a very pretty one indeed; but I don't think that's how it works."

Naomi dropped the lipstick.

Chapter Five

TALL, DARK, AND handsome.

Coming down the stairs, Naomi scanned the crowd filling the entrance hall for someone who'd fit this description; sadly not one of them did.

Slowly she descended, stopping on every step, wishing with every breath allowed by the tight bodice of her gown that there would be someone, some miracle man, to snatch her away, pick her up, and take her away to a different life—a carefree, sunny life where she could walk on a warm beach at dawn or hide in a forest wilderness when life became too much.

She'd run away with him to that new life taking nothing with her. She'd follow him and turn into a different person.

Maybe he'd take her to balls and dances just like this one, and no one would know who she was; no one would ask. He'd let her hide behind him, and protect her, and never spill her secret. He'd be tall, and dark, and handsome—her prince, her secret lover. He'd understand, and rescue her.

But first he'd dance a waltz with her. He'd push Seth aside and claim her, swing her onto the dance floor, his arm securely around her waist, smiling, gazing into her eyes, seeing only her.

Her hand pressed against her heart, Naomi stopped halfway down the stairs.

That was it. That was the thing she wanted above all others, more than anything else.

"Someone to love me," she whispered. "Someone who'll love me, only me and not the Carlsson estate."

The insight almost made her stumble. She gripped the banister and took a couple of calming breaths.

There she stood, a statue, turned from human flesh into stone in less than a heartbeat, and no one saw.

All those people, the guests who were here to celebrate her birthday, didn't see her.

She was less than a statue to them: a ghost from another dimension, the imprint of a girl in a rose chiffon gown seen from the corner of the eye then gone, a memory forgotten before it even happened.

HER father noticed her first.

He smiled up at her, his eyes flying over her to check that everything was the way he wanted it, and nodded, holding out his hand.

"Very lovely, my dear," he said. "You make me very proud tonight."

"Thank you," Naomi replied, blushing. Praise wasn't a thing she earned very often.

"Look at you," Olaf went on, leading her toward the ballroom, "All grown up and a pretty young lady. Seth will be so happy to see you groomed and dressed up."

Just one sentence. All he had to do was speak one sentence to destroy her moment of joy.

"Papa," Naomi said, "Papa, can I talk to you? Please, can we go to the library and talk for a moment? I really don't think…"

"Ah, and here he is." Olaf waved toward Seth, who was coming their way. "Later, darling. We can talk about whatever it is tomorrow, when the guests are gone. It would be impolite to retreat now. Here's your fiancé!"

And he laid her hand in Seth's and walked away.

"Well." Seth smiled, but it looked awkward. His face was blotchy with a failed blush, either from the heat or excitement, but she didn't care. He looked like an oversize penguin in his tux and shiny shoes, and it took all her willpower not to gaze down at them expecting to see a huge egg nestled between them.

"Well," he repeated, squeezing her fingers between his. "Come with me to the terrace? We need to talk, and I have something for you."

Dread settled in her stomach. The tight bodice of the dress didn't allow her to draw deep breaths, so she stood there, her mouth open, to get some air.

"Okay." There was no way out of it.

"Okay? Just okay?" He shook his head at her. "Today is the big day, this is the big moment, and you say okay? Ah well, I guess it's a remnant of your teen language. Come then!"

It was cool on the terrace. There was no one else there, as if they'd all been given a secret signal to avoid that space.

The sky wasn't totally black yet; it shimmered in that dark, translucent blue that came just before night, when the stars seemed as elusive as jellyfish floating in the open sea, their sparkle no more than dreams of themselves.

From the forest—down where it met the lawn—came the secret, hushed sounds of the wilderness waking up: the endless song of cicadas, the questioning treble of a nightingale, the murmur of raccoons wandering down their paths to the lake. The air smelled of roses and dry grass, of lavender from the terra-cotta pots lined up on the terrace wall, of pine needles baked by the summer sun.

The moon had risen over the trees, their tops cutting sharp contours into its golden face, giving it a crooked smile as it watched Seth pull a small, black box from his pocket.

"Of course," he said, "it's only a formality, since your father has agreed already. So here's your ring, the one you asked for this morning over breakfast. Let no one say I'd propose to a girl and not have a ring for her."

Without waiting for her response, he pushed it on her finger.

"There. Now it's official! We're engaged!" Seth took a step back to look at her, nodding, pleased with himself. "Olaf is waiting; he wants to make the announcement. I know he must be hopping from one leg to the other in anticipation, so let's go inside and celebrate!"

Naomi opened her mouth to reply, but he had already turned toward the beckoning door.

No kiss, no fiery embrace, not one word of love, no promises of a glorious future, of happily growing old together.

"Come, Naomi! They're all waiting for us." Again that imperious tone, and this time without even looking her way.

She closed her eyes, her face turned toward the moon, and imagined being in someone's arms, someone who had his lips on her hair and his hands cradling her back, someone who whispered love words to her and offered an eternity of happiness. The yearning was so strong, it felt like a knife in her throat, exactly in the place where the tears were waiting.

"Do you love me, Seth?" She could hardly say it.

Surprised, he came back to her. "But you know I do! I thought that was clear! Did you think I'd give a pedigree horse to someone I didn't love? Or a ring like that? It cost me a small fortune! You cost me a small fortune! I think that spells *love*, doesn't it?" Seth raised his eyebrows. "I'm doing everything the way your father suggested, the way he said you'd like it!"

"Seth."

"Let's go inside, Naomi. It's really rude to let them wait this long." Taking her arm, pulling it through his, he tugged; but she didn't move.

"Seth, I feel too young to marry."

That made him stop and look down at her. "What do you mean? When do you want to get married? We haven't talked about a date yet, so yes, we can discuss this. Of course, our families need to be involved."

You've never said you love me. You've never even said you desire me. She swallowed against the unsaid words.

"I want to go back to Geneva with my parents and do the next term at university. I've enrolled already, and it would be an enormous waste of money if I dropped out. I don't want to get engaged right now. This…" She had to think, and quickly. "Today is my birthday, and I don't want something as important as getting engaged to you to happen as an afterthought. I want it to be a big party, a huge ball. But not today."

"Ah, yes." Pondering, he looked past her into the darkness. "That makes sense. I can see why you'd want an extra event for our engagement." His eyes sparkled like watery stones. "So when do you think is a good date? We need a lot of preparation time if we do a huge party for it. I'm sure half of Europe's nobility will be invited by your parents. What about the New Year's Eve ball? That would be a nice setting, with the fireworks and all."

"Yes! Yes, Seth, that's brilliant!" Her smile was genuine for once when she pulled off the ring and returned it to him.

Seth carefully set it back into its box. "All right then, go back to Geneva until Christmas."

Naomi almost laughed, but it was too sad really.

"Okay then." She smoothed down the chiffon skirt. "It's settled."

And somehow, now that she'd won another seven months of freedom, she was actually glad that he hadn't suddenly turned into an ardent lover. That would have made it so much more awkward.

SHE was like a bystander, like a favorite piece of art that was changing owners.

There they were, her father and Seth, shaking hands, toasting each other, celebrating an engagement agreement in which she seemed to be playing a minor role. Even when Seth planted a brief, dry kiss on her lips, Naomi felt like a block of ice carved from an ancient glacier, something that had forgotten how to melt, something that had never seen the sun.

"So the wedding will be sometime next year," Olaf said. "Is that what you have decided? I have to say, I think it's a splendid plan! It will give us enough time to organize everything. Of course, the ceremony will be held right here."

"Yes, of course," Seth replied without waiting for her to speak up. "We'll have to talk about a date." He smiled at Naomi. "I think you should go collect your birthday presents, my dear. People want to sit down for dinner."

Naomi wandered through the ballroom, stopping to accept congratulations and presents until she couldn't hold all the envelopes and gifts anymore and Lucia rushed over to help her before she dropped something. There were a number of telltale little light turquoise blue bags that made her heart flutter a bit. She had a soft spot for jewelry, and she hoped there might be something in them that she would be allowed to keep and wouldn't just be locked up in the safe.

She'd argued with her father, saying that no one could enter the Carlsson house without being noticed, her room was as secure as the safe in his study; but Olaf hadn't budged. Her mother's jewels were there, and Naomi's would be kept there as well. Even her argument that Lucia knew the lock combination and could get at her things any time she wanted while she had to ask her parents wasn't accepted. Olaf had raised his eyebrows at her and asked, "So what's wrong with that? Once you're the lady of the manor you can change the combination and do as you like. But as long as I'm the master here and you're my daughter, things will be done as I wish."

"How wonderful, a New Year's Eve engagement party," Lucia whispered to her. "You're one lucky girl to be so loved by everyone. Smile, Naomi!"

And she did. She smiled her way all over the dance floor, collecting her birthday gifts, the lovely daughter of the Carlsson family, finally of age, finally old enough to be married off.

At last Lucia guided her to the dining room, where her birthday table had been set. The cake was there too, a four-tiered dream in pink, decorated with marzipan roses and tiny sugar leaves.

"I'm so proud of you, darling," Lucia said, her eyes gleaming. "You're so beautiful tonight, and so poised! You're everything your father and I dreamed you'd be, Naomi. I know his heart is bursting with happiness. And so is mine!"

At least, Naomi thought, smiling at her mother, at least someone was happy.

That had to be a good thing.

Chapter Six

THEY WERE SO happy.

She'd rarely seen her parents so happy, almost exuberant. Over a late breakfast, they watched as Naomi opened the envelopes and presents.

Lucia, sitting beside her, meticulously noted each name and every gift so they could thank the giver appropriately.

"It's a nice rehearsal for your wedding," she added, "because we'll be doing the same thing then."

For a moment, the joy of opening Tiffany boxes paled. Naomi let her hands sink into her lap, the pearl earrings she'd just unwrapped in them.

"The wedding won't be before next summer, or later," she said.

"Of course not, darling." Lucia touched her shoulders lightly. "Your wedding needs careful planning. I was thinking of suggesting next September, if you two can wait that long. The weather is more stable in September, and it won't be hot either."

She held out her hand, and Naomi dropped the earrings into it.

"I want a Christmas wedding."

Surprised, Olaf put down his cup. "You want to skip the engagement and just get married? That would make people talk. I really don't think you should rush things quite that much. And it would be impossible to organize. Naomi. Really, I think it should not be before next summer."

It took her a couple of seconds to put on a convincing pout. Then Naomi said, "But I want it. I want my wedding guests to arrive in sleighs; I want sleighs with bells coming up from the resort, and torches lining the path. And I want to wear a white fur cape, and I want mistletoe wreaths in every doorway, and a huge red-velvet wedding cake with silver sparkles and icing that looks like snowflakes. And a huge, sparkling Christmas tree in the hall."

Lucia stared at her. "But what a wonderful idea, darling! You're right; it would be spectacular!" And added, turning to Olaf, "Yes, let's do that! This year would indeed be awkward, but I guess Seth can wait until Christmas next year, and that gives us ample time to prepare! It's settled then! A Christmas wedding it will be!" She held up the earrings. "Aren't these the prettiest little things ever? Here, let me put them on for you, sweetheart."

Obediently, Naomi let her put them into her ears. It didn't hurt one bit. Nothing could possibly hurt her just now.

"I'll return to Geneva with you," she said, "and go back to university, if it's okay. I don't want to spend a year hanging around here without you. Can I?"

"Of course, Naomi! That's just what I wanted to suggest!" Lucia smiled at her.

"Poor Seth," Olaf mumbled, opening the newspaper. "He'll have to wait for you a pretty long time. Wonder if he'll be able to cope."

"Don't worry about him, Papa." So sweet. It was so sweet to drop those words into their joy. "He said he has other women. He doesn't need me for that. At least, not right now."

The coffee landed on Olaf's silk tie, and Naomi hid her glee behind a grimace of pain when the earring poked her ear.

STRANGELY, her father didn't suggest she put any of the jewelry she'd been given into the safe, and he didn't even ask how much money she'd received.

Back in her room with her armful of loot, Naomi sat on her bed and spread it out to inspect it.

There were gold bangles, pendants, a beautiful silver locket on a chain with a tiny diamond on the front, a very sweet garnet ring, and a silver comb set with turquoise and pearls.

Someone had given her a journal. It was lovely with heavy, cream-colored pages and a thick red leather cover, her initials imprinted on the cover in heavy gold letters.

There was money too, a lot of it. Most was in checks that she'd have to cash, but there were some bills, which she hid in her bedside table. She'd made almost thirty thousand dollars by being the pretty birthday princess.

And, of course, there was the horse. The most senseless and

superfluous birthday present ever. Naomi wondered if Seth would be angry if she called the little mare “Poodle” instead of using her fancy Arabian name, and that made her giggle.

It was almost an insult, giving her that thoroughbred, when he knew, when he'd known for a long time now, that she loved her tall Frisian.

Riding Apollo made her feel like a queen. She could put away the world, forget about the rigid routine of the big house and her life, and pretend she was a fairy, a transient being unfettered by restrictions and rules, someone outside everything: time, place, boundaries of any kind.

Apollo, and she had given him that name. Curious, Olaf had asked why she'd name a horse after a Greek god; and she, puzzled by her father's density, had replied that he wasn't named for a Greek god but for the spaceship, for the rocket that had taken man to the moon. It meant exploration, adventure, excitement, and, most of all, freedom.

She knew she'd never ride that new horse, and it made her sad.

They tried so hard, all of them, to bend her life in the directions they thought would be good and proper for her, but they totally forgot about her dreams and desires while they were making their plans.

NAOMI went over to the small, round table that stood under her window and sat in the chair next to it.

She loved this spot; from this chair she could look out over the lawn and trees behind the house, and a glimpse of the lake beyond.

She'd spent many long afternoons sitting here, during the winter, watching the snow fall, watching how it settled on the trees and wrapped around their limbs like fluffy coats. It had a music all its own, that thick, Canadian snow. A silent, gentle song of sleep and forgetting, and if she listened long enough she could hear the words hidden in that song. Like gossamer strands floating among the flakes, like a fragile satin ribbon that wound around and along the snow to embrace those heavy cedar branches, humming a last, dying note.

The open journal on the table before her, she unscrewed her pen.

That first page, its empty, cream-colored expanse, seemed like a mirror of the silent snow she'd been thinking about.

It beckoned, and yet it sent terror into her heart; once she put down a first word it would be destroyed forever, would forever bear her imprint.

There had been a card with the journal but no sender. All it had said was "Write from the heart." She'd turned it over and over, examined the envelope, and even shaken the book itself to try and find a hint; but the giver remained a mystery.

Write from the heart.

She didn't even know what to write. The only thing that came to her mind were a few phrases, some words about the wind in the trees and the loneliness of a wandering soul, and the pain of yearning.

"Lay me down on a bed of leaves."

She hadn't realized her hand was moving; her hand had been faster than her brain, and now she stared at that line, whispered it, felt the rhythm on her tongue, felt the slow melody behind the words.

"Lay me down and close my eyes."

Her fingers shook with the terror of discovery.

"Lay down my dreams and count the griefs."

That last line bothered her. She went over it again and again, but nothing better came to her.

"Hold me in your arms and drive away the night…"

Those words made her halt, and blush. Her eyes flitted to the door, but it was firmly closed, and there was no sound from outside.

"Love me, make it last forever."

There. She'd written it, and again it had been her hand, the naughty thing, and her brain hadn't rebelled.

Quietly, as if she didn't want to trigger another outburst, she put down the pen and closed the book.

Fresh air; she needed fresh air, and a ride through the forest.

That would wipe away the dense and sultry thoughts that were sneaking through her mind like tendrils of flesh-eating orchids.

"WE leave in three days," Lucia called to her when Naomi came down the stairs. "You need to start packing. Your father has to get back to work."

"Yes, Mama," she called back without stopping. The van was standing on the gravel out in front of the house, the keys lying on the driver's seat.

Naomi didn't have a driver's license; but she'd learned to drive on the narrow road up and down to the resort; and once, only once, her father had let her drive his big Mercedes to the gate and back to the house. It had felt like a malevolent beast pulling at its restraints, unwilling to obey her tentative touch on the wheel.

The old van though, he was a good friend. Her uncle Carl had taught her how to handle the shift stick and pedals, and how to make the clutch obey her; and now, driving over to the hotel, she made the car speed over the dirt road in a headlong run.

A golf ball flew past just in front of her about halfway to the stables, and she stepped on the brake, skirting onto the lawn with the rear wheel, throwing up dirt.

"I'll have your hide for that," Naomi muttered, trying to make out where the ball had come from. "Just wait until I'm back, on my horse."

OWEN was there, as always.

She smiled at him when he jumped up, waving, shouting, as if he'd been waiting for her since the day before.

"Take me riding with you?" he asked, breathless, and she nodded.

"Of course, Owen! You can come."

Her anger at Seth's rudeness toward the boy boiled up in her.

He was supposed to be a grown-up, Seth; and yet he'd treated Owen as if he was nothing, just a minor nuisance, even though he knew very well that Owen was special—different, slower—and that only the stable and the company of the horses made him happy.

And there was the fact that he was family, not very close family, but a part of the Carlsson clan anyway. The stables were his refuge, the one place where he could be left alone, and no one need worry about him. His mother, Henrike, worked the desk at the hotel. Owen was never far away from her.

"That baby horse is ugly," Owen said. "Looks like a dog."

Naomi had to hide her mirth behind her riding gloves. "Don't say that, Owen. I'm sure it's a very expensive horse."

Undaunted, he shrugged. "Some expensive things are very ugly, and only expensive because everyone wants them." He opened the door to Apollo's stall box. "Like oysters. Oysters are expensive, and they taste like cold snot."

"Owen!"

"It's true!"

APOLLO'S hooves sounded like thunder when he came out into the stable alley. Owen had braided his long mane again, and tied off the single braids with red ribbon. The black stallion looked like a circus horse.

"So pretty, Owen!" Naomi ran her hand down Apollo's neck. "That must have taken hours!"

Owen shrugged. "We were bored. All the lights and music from the big house, and the fireworks, and Apollo knew you'd be dancing with the ugly red-haired man. He was unhappy. I wanted to cheer him up."

Her heart danced.

She had won so much time, Naomi could hardly believe it. Nineteen months, and many things could happen in nineteen months. Seth could fall in love with someone else. The world might collapse. The sun could explode. Aliens could invade Earth.

Or, and this was the best version of all, she could meet someone else and fall in love herself.

Standing there watching Owen saddle her horse, Naomi wondered what it felt like, being in love. She wondered if it felt special, different, and if she'd know when the moment came. And who that man might be.

Chapter Seven

THE DRY, MEDITERRANEAN air hit her as soon as she walked off the plane.

It was hot in Geneva, hot in a way it never was in Kleinburg, at home on the family estate.

The wind blowing down the tarmac seemed to be coming right out of a furnace; it carried the scent of pine trees and lavender, and the stink of kerosine. Flying in over the lake, the high, snow-capped mountains had greeted her like old, familiar friends, like sentinels who'd watched the city for her while she was gone.

"We should try and get tickets for Bregenz," Olaf said, watching as their luggage was transferred from the jet to the limousine. "I'd really like to see that stage in the lake; it must be spectacular for opera. I wouldn't mind the *Magic Flute*, or some Verdi."

"I'd love to go; let's do it! Are you sending the plane back home? It would be nice if we didn't have to drive to Bregenz." Lucia hooked her arm through his, and Olaf smiled at her.

"No, we'll keep it here. I need to run down to Naples next month, and to Oslo. You could come, and we could stop in Paris or London if you want to go shopping or something." He turned to Naomi. "And maybe you want to start looking at wedding gowns? That should be exciting!"

As exciting as bird shit on her favorite purse, as exciting as being run over by a car.

But she nodded, and smiled, and replied, "That would be fun."

If the price for going to London was stuffing herself into an exaggerated, heavy, and uncomfortable white dress, she could do it. Easily.

"And I'm sure you wouldn't mind shopping for a purse or two," Lucia added, a grin hiding in the corners of your mouth. "I know my daughter. She's like me in that way."

Olaf came over to them and laid his arms around their shoulders. "I love to see my girls well dressed, and with everything they could possibly want. If purses are your wish, well, that's easily done. I'll take you to Milano, and you can fill the jet with them."

Driving toward the town, Naomi wondered why it had to be that way, why her father could be so kind and giving, so generous, and yet at the same time force her into a marriage she didn't want without batting an eye.

"I wonder if Seth will take you traveling."

They had reached the center of town. Naomi lowered the window to catch the sounds and smells of Geneva: coffee, fresh bread, flowers, and the tang of the lake. It was a very special scent: slightly moldy, mossy, as if it were a very old, very mystical beast that had come to rest here among the mountains and covered itself with water so it would stay hidden until the day it decided to fly away to the stars again.

Her family owned an apartment in one of the grand buildings along the lakeside, with a perfect view of the fountain and the town. Her room looked out to the street. It had taken all her charm and wiliness to convince her father that she needed that room so she could have the sun to wake her in the morning and look at the moon over the lake at night.

She'd told him she was scared of the backyard, afraid of being seen, with the next building so close; and that had at last changed his mind.

"Someone could watch me," she'd said, dramatically wringing her hands. "Just imagine if someone was watching me day and night, and then turned into a stalker! I'm so afraid, Daddy."

She could always make his heart melt when she told him she was scared. It worked every time. It made him turn from a stern, glacial Norse Viking into an affectionate and understanding father. Except where her future and his business were involved. That had been laid out for her—a straight, narrow track—and there was no exit.

She'd tried the fear number, saying Seth was too old, too grown up, and she too scared to marry him, but that had been waved away impatiently. After all, they'd grown up together. End of story.

This was in her own best interest, and in time she'd come to understand that.

"Here we are." There was relief in Lucia's voice. "I can't wait to get in the shower. Traveling in summer is such a grimy business." She got out of the car, her cream silk blouse and pants flawless, her hair in a perfect knot, her makeup still fresh.

Naomi felt sweaty and grimy herself, but then she'd insisted on wearing yoga pants and a sweatshirt for the long flight from Toronto to Geneva. Even in her family's private jet the space seemed cramped, the coffee stale after a few hours.

This was one thing she admired about her parents: they traveled as if they were going out for dinner, her father in a suit and tie, her mother meticulous. Beside them she looked like a stray cat, a homeless child they'd picked up along the way and taken along in the hope of domesticating her.

"I wish we could live at home all the time." Olaf sighed, glancing up at the ornate façade of the building. "I feel so displaced here. The things one does for the family business."

It always came down to this, every single time: People were just marionettes, figures who had to play their parts in the bigger picture. They all, each and every one of them, belonged to the Carlsson empire. Their lives belonged to those hotels and properties all over the world, and she, Naomi, would be sacrificed at its altar without a second's hesitation.

"I don't see why we can't," Lucia was saying, following him into the foyer, where a liveried doorman was waiting to open the elevator doors for them.

Naomi loved those doors. Wrought iron, made to look like branches with leaves and flowers; and if she looked closely she could see a nymph hiding among the foliage, a sprite playing hide-and-seek with the passengers of the elevator.

"Why do we have to live in Switzerland, Olaf? You could manage the finances just as well from Carlsson House."

Uncomfortably, he shook his shoulders. "It would mean a lot of traveling for me, darling. I'd have to go back and forth at least twice a month. And, well, the money is here."

"Yes. Yes."

They both threw glances at Naomi, but she didn't react.

She'd asked her father once why the company's finances had to be dealt with in Geneva, and he hadn't given her a straight reply, had mumbled something about taxes and privacy, and then fished a couple of banknotes out of his money clip and pushed them across the table at her. "Don't worry about it," he'd said, "you won't have to worry about the finances; your husband will do that. You have other jobs waiting for you, and they'll be more fun, I promise."

"I like Geneva," Naomi said into the silence, "and I can't wait to see Fleur and Manon. I'm sure there'll be lots of fun things to do this summer. Oh, please let there be a ball at the yacht club!"

"Oh yes!" The tense line of Lucia's lips curled into a smile. "I'm sure there will be! We need new gowns, Naomi! Too bad you didn't bring your birthday dress!"

"Yes, a pity." She'd never wear that dress again, she was certain of that. She was even certain that she'd never again wear pink chiffon, or anything pink, for that matter. It would always remind her of that awkward moment on the terrace when Seth had put that ring on her finger without even trying to kiss her.

A kiss, a real kiss. A tight embrace, a man's body close to her, warm breath on her skin, arms that would hold her, never let her go…

"Do you have the keys, Olaf?" Her mother's voice tore her from the delicious reverie when the elevator stopped with its usual small jerk and a sound as if a mouse had been caught.

"Yes, yes."

Her head lowered to hide her blush, Naomi followed her parents into the spacious apartment.

JET-LAGGED, tired from sitting for hours aboard the Gulfstream, Naomi sank onto her bed. The windows were open; the sounds of the street below and the promenade along the lakeshore on its other side drifted in on fat streaks of sunlight, and the scent of the trees.

She lay there, her hair wet from the shower, wrapped in nothing but the cool touch of a linen sheet, her eyes closed drowsily as she listened to the melody of French voices, the tinkle of an ice cream cart, the shouts of children from the playground on the promenade, and sighed.

Freedom, those sounds spelled freedom. No one would stop her if she wanted to go out, if she said she was going to meet her friends. All it took was two steps. Two steps away from the glass doors of the house, and across the street, and she was free.

They would be waiting for her by the kiosk, drinking coffee, smoking, their eyes following the boys strolling past: her friends Manon, Giselle, Fleur, and Marion, and sometimes, when she didn't have anything better to do, Fleur's older sister, Pauline.

They'd hang out on the promenade until the sun went down, sometimes renting a boat to paddle toward the high plume of the fountain; sometimes sitting on the quay, dangling their legs in the cool water, gossiping, laughing, sharing secrets, making up outrageous stories about how their future lives would be—young women, enjoying summer, enjoying their lives.

At some point they'd dry off their feet, slip on their sandals, put on fresh lipstick, and saunter down the narrow streets of the old part of Geneva for something to eat, some shopping, a bit of flirting, and then hurry home for dinner with their families before they met again like a flock of doves to spend the evening dancing, promenading, teasing the young men who'd gravitate around them, ready to do almost anything the girls demanded.

"Don't fall in love," her father would always tell her before giving her money to spend. "You know Seth is waiting for you. Don't go and break his heart."

But he never kept her from going out, as if he knew that she needed this freedom, needed to pretend to be free to fly and be a bit wild before she got married.

He'd look at her, up and down, his glance hovering for a second on her bare legs and short skirt; but she always managed to throw him off by rising on her toes and planting a kiss on his well-shaved, cologne-scented cheek and promising to be back soon or, if not, call and tell him where she was, and to please send the car to pick her up later.

With a sigh, Naomi turned away from the window and pulled the sheet over her face.

Just one hour. She'd rest for one hour and then get dressed. She'd wear a linen dress and the flat sandals she'd bought in Toronto. And then she'd call Fleur and ask her to tell the others that she was back in town.

She wanted to go out for dinner with them, sit on the deck of the yacht club with the water under the planks giving the wood hasty little kisses when a boat passed by. They'd drink champagne and eat oysters and French bread with garlic butter, and she'd have chocolate cake for dessert.

Her eyes refused to open. She knew they were tightly shut, and yet she was certain she could see everything around her: the rose silk wallpaper with the tiny rosebuds, the painting of her as a little girl playing tea party with her dolls, the framed photos of Apollo, and the keepsakes on her vanity table—concert tickets; a rose she'd gotten from Fleur's brother, Pierre, together with a first, chaste kiss on pursed lips, now a brownish, dried husk with faded leaves; birthday cards; and a sprig of mistletoe nicked from the big wreath at Fleur's family house.

It was May, and she was back in Geneva for the summer. Nothing could possibly go wrong.

Chapter Eight

IT WAS THE insistent rhythm of the drums that first caught her attention.

For a moment Naomi stood in the middle of her room, the handle of the vacuum cleaner in her slack hand, and listened. The angrily humming motor vibrated up to her shoulder, telling her to get on with her work, but she couldn't.

Kicking a chair out of the way, she lunged toward the radio to turn up the volume before she realized that pulling the plug on the vacuum would be more effective.

In the sudden silence, the music filled the room like a warm blast. It was all around her: the humid heat, the blue darkness under the dense foliage; and hidden among them, a sleek, dangerous beast with a seductive voice calling out to her.

She could almost see it: striped fur rippling over taut muscles, amber eyes watching her attentively, the great paws digging into the wet, fragrant earth in expectation, and she, its willing prey.

He wasn't even singing about the jungle but about some river and its sound, and how it drew him down to the water; and even though those drums and the bass were like the thundering heartbeat of a dark, rainy forest, that voice dominated the song, shaped it, and willed it to follow its lead.

That voice. She'd never heard that voice before. It wrapped around her like a veil, like a merciless mist, and cut off her breath.

Holding on to the edge of the table, she listened. There was something in the way he sang, something that caressed her skin and made her heart stop and nearly forced her to her knees.

"All my life I've been waiting for this moment..."

He was talking to her. That stranger, that strange singer, he was talking to her, and about her; she knew it. Angrily, Naomi shook herself to get away from the grip of the music, but it only clung tighter.

"River's heartbeat, river calling; that is all I came to hear..."

And again those drums and their relentless, pulsing rhythm.

"Leave me alone," she whispered. Her hand wandered to the radio's controls, ready to turn it off, but she didn't. She couldn't. Instead, she turned up the volume some more, until those jungle drums throbbed in the air and shook the window panes.

The song ended with an almost insulting chord, sucking the music back into itself, leaving an embarrassing silence behind.

"A new kid on the block," the announcer said. "I'm sure we'll hear a lot about him in the future. The tour dates have just been announced. Stay tuned; we're going to read them out to you over the next hour. You should hurry and secure your tickets; this act will soon be sold out!"

"Tell me the name, you idiot!" Naomi yelled.

"Hailing from Brooklyn, New York, he's one songwriter who will blaze to international stardom…"

The door flew open. Her father stood there, his tie hanging loose around his upturned shirt collar, his brow in deep furrows.

"Turn that down right now," he shouted. "You're waking up the neighborhood with that insane noise!"

She hadn't caught the name, and she was ready to cry over that. She wanted to grab the radio and throw it out the window, throw it at her father, shake it until its insides came loose and jingled the singer's name with their dying breath.

Instead she turned it off and sat down on the edge of her bed. "Sorry, Father," she said. "That was a pretty cool song. I wanted to hear who…"

"I don't care," Olaf interrupted her. "I don't care who sang, or who wrote the music, if it can even be called that at all. Just turn the volume down, if you please."

"It's turned off." It came out sullenly, but Olaf ignored it.

"Thank you very much, young lady. Now come and have breakfast with us. Your mother is waiting." Turning away, as an afterthought, he asked, "And why are you vacuuming your room? Won't Mathilde be doing it later?"

"I dropped my powder box, and I didn't want it rubbed into the carpet." She didn't add that it had been nearly full or how angry she was at herself.

"Right. Right. Well, it's clean now. Put away the vacuum." On the way back to the dining room, Olaf turned and added, "Go buy a new box of powder and stop moping. You're as pale as chalk, for goodness sake. It's just some stupid scented powder! Get a grip!"

SHE couldn't eat. She could hardly hold her coffee cup. Both hands wrapped around it, she let her parents' conversation drift around her, barely listening. There was the mention of Bregenz and the festival again, about going there to see the *Abduction From The Seraglio*. Lucia was shaking her head, saying she hated that opera and how it was too long and too wordy, and she couldn't muster the patience to watch it ever again, not even in a spectacular setting.

"Instead of running after finding the girl and getting away, they stand around and sing and sing and sing about how they have to go now, let's go now, we really need to leave, and now, and then get caught. It's just too stupid. Mozart makes me impatient with his music."

Olaf laughed at her. "I know. You want the drama of Verdi."

"Yes. Verdi. Give me Verdi over Mozart any day." Lucia reached for another croissant. "These alone make me glad to be back in Europe. We should really think of adding a bakery to the resort, Olaf, so we can have fresh bread when we're at home."

"Now here's a thought…"

And they were off on one of their interminable discussions about how to improve the hotels, how to make even more money with them, how to be more outstanding and exclusive.

Naomi drifted away. Her parents didn't even notice she had left. For a moment she stood in the doorway watching them, watching how her mother pulled apart her croissant to sniff at the inside, wondering if maybe they should add a hint of cinnamon, and how her father offered her the salty, French butter they preferred and told her to try it with the bread.

"I'M going out," Naomi said. There was no response, so she left.

Fleur and Manon were waiting for her when she crossed the

street; big cups of café au lait sat on the table in front of them. Manon was sporting one of those cigarettes with colored paper, her favorite brand, and today it was a light-green one.

"There you are!" she called when she saw Naomi. "Good to have you back. It's been utterly boring here without you. How was Canada?"

"Boring." Sinking into a chair, Naomi raised her hand to signal the waiter. "I counted the days. Canada is for old people. I hate it there."

"So how is your boyfriend? What did he give you for your birthday?" Fleur looked like a hippie. There were flowers woven into her golden braids, and she wore a long skirt with flounces and a bikini top. Naomi imagined trying to go out like that, and what Olaf would say to her. She'd probably end up locked in her room.

"A horse. An Arabian thoroughbred. A filly."

"Ohhhh, very nice! I'm jealous!" Manon threw her a smile, hands clasped to her chest. "He must love you so much!"

"Yeah…" The waiter had brought her coffee, and she used the cup as an excuse to hide her face. "I don't know if he loves me. I think he's pleased with marrying into the Carlsson family. I don't matter a lot."

"Come on, Naomi!" Fleur handed her the sugar. "He must be in love with you to go out and buy you a horse. What a glorious birthday gift!"

"Yes." She wasn't going to complain. She wasn't going to tell them that she really didn't care for the filly and would have preferred some affection instead, some show of love, even the tiniest bit, like a hand holding hers, a kiss, an embrace, a word of love whispered during a dance. "I don't really want to marry him though. I'd like to pick my husband myself." There. She'd said it.

"I know what you mean, sweetie," Fleur said, and rose from her chair to give Naomi a hug. "It's hard to have that kind of duty. I'm so glad I'm not an only child, and I'm glad my parents don't own a hotel or any kind of empire. I can marry who I want!" Her silver laughter bubbled up and made her blue eyes shine. "Of course, I'll never marry a poor man. I'm too spoiled for that. Also, we French are a bit less romantic about arranged marriages." She shrugged. "We can always have lovers, *non*?"

"Exactly," Manon added. "We don't marry for love. Maybe you need to be more like us, Naomi. Less Canadian and more French." Which was a funny statement since they weren't really French but Swiss.

Naomi needed to change the subject, and fast, before she started to cry or became sick.

"I heard a song on the radio this morning," she said, "and I didn't catch the singer's name. It was something about a river in a jungle, and there were those drums…" She broke off. "Actually, he wasn't singing about a jungle at all. It only made me think of a jungle, and…"

"You mean Jon Stone." Manon threw a grin at Fleur. "You must be talking about his song "The River," Naomi. That does sound like a hot night in a jungle. Those drums, yes? They make me think of naughty things, hot and steamy things." A faint blush crept into her cheeks. "And of course, he looks divine too. Made my heart go wild when I first saw a photo of him in *Geneva Glam.*"

"He's in *Geneva Glam*?" Naomi's palms felt clammy. "Which one?"

"This month's. Oh, and his album is all over the place! They play his songs on the radio all the time! Where have you been, the North Pole? What kind of music do they listen to in Canada? Seriously?" Throwing some money on the table, Fleur got up and grabbed her purse. "Come on, finish your coffee! We're leaving!"

Naomi did as she was told. "Where are we going?"

"To the record store of course, silly. We need to get that album for you. And then we'll buy a *Geneva Glam* and introduce you to Jon Stone. But I'm warning you; you can't have him. I'm going to marry him." Abruptly, Fleur stopped walking. "Oh, and he's coming here! We have tickets for his concert! I have one for you too!" Again she wrapped Naomi in an embrace. "Can't leave you out of the fun, can I? We're all going! Papa promised to let us have the limo; we'll go in style! It will be so grand! And we have really good seats: third row, right in the center. You're coming, aren't you?"

"Yes." Her heart was hammering so hard that Naomi was sure

they could see it, could see her shake from the rapid pulse under her skin. “Yes, of course! I’ll come!”

“Good, good! And now, to the record store we go!”

“There’s this new designer store quite close to it,” Manon said, hurrying to catch up with them. “I want to go there too. I need a couple of dresses, desperately.”

“You always need new dresses.” Fleur offered her arm, and that was how they walked along the promenade: three girls, sylphs enjoying the summer, butterflies meandering toward a very bright, very inviting flower.

Chapter Nine

IT was almost as if she didn't want to go into the record store, as if something in her didn't want to know more about the singer and his music.

Standing in the open shop doorway, watching her friends browse through the shelves, Naomi hesitated, but it was too late to run.

Fleur was coming her way, an album in her hand. "Here he is! Naomi, meet Jon Stone."

Her hand nearly refused to rise, as if it was scared that something weird would happen, something it couldn't deal with.

"Isn't he a dream? Look at those eyes, and, ohhhh, his mouth! Don't you just want to kiss those lips? I know I want to!" Fleur ran her fingers over the cover, over the image of the young man standing on a street corner, a guitar case by his side, his black hair windblown, his gaze moody and distant. It looked as if it was raining, as if he was in New York City, somewhere on the streets in the dusk of a fall day.

Naomi was almost sure she could hear the noise of the city, could feel the pulse of the big city; and there he stood, a fixed point in a tumultuous universe, creating his own small space of silence and music.

"He's from New York," Fleur was saying, but Naomi already knew.

She knew it as if he'd told her himself, as if she'd been there that day when the photo was taken.

There was a woman in the background, a blurred image of a young woman walking into what looked like a bookstore, and somehow that seemed to have some kind of impact on him, on Jon, as if he had to force himself not to turn toward her, as if it was a conscious leave-taking.

"Here, I'll buy it for you. It will be a late birthday present." Fleur pressed the album into her shaky hands to search for money in her purse. "And you're welcome; you need some sexy in your life, my dear."

"Thank you." It was all Naomi could say.

There it was, listed on the back, the first track on the A side of the record: "The River." Written and performed by Jon Stone.

"Have you listened to the other songs yet?" Her voice had trouble getting past the raspy knot in her throat.

"Yeah, sure. Up and down, backward and forward. And I have the pics of him from *Geneva Glam* on my walls. Had to buy the stupid thing twice to rip out all of them." Her wallet in her hand, Fleur looked up. "Some were on the back side of others, you know. Stupid. They really shouldn't do that with pics you want to rip out. I've heard that there's going to be a centerfold in another magazine in a few days. We need to watch for that and get it before it sells out." She took the album from Naomi and went to pay for it.

THEY went on to buy the magazine for her, and then to the new clothes store, where Naomi watched Manon try on one dress after the other, nodding gamely, smiling when one of them made a joke; but in her hands was the album, and her attention was on the cover photo and not on her friends.

She couldn't even say what she felt. It was a mix of excitement, curiosity, and something that felt like fear, like apprehension, and yes, anger.

"Look at this, Naomi." Fleur was holding up a white top: a flimsy, lacy thing without sleeves and a nice neckline, just right, not too bold and not too stuffy either. "I think this would look great on you. Why not try it on? Let go of that record, for crying out loud. It's not as if it's going to run away. We can sigh and moon over him later, in my room."

Naomi wasn't so sure that she wanted to share the music with anyone, but she tried on the top.

It was lovely, and very light, and just the right thing for a hot Geneva summer.

"And here!" This time it was Manon, and she was holding up a cherry-red linen dress with a lovely full skirt and a square neckline. "This has your name on it, Naomi."

"My father will give me hell," Naomi muttered. "Not even a week back in Geneva, and already I'm spending money on new clothes."

"Oh come on!" Manon laughed at her. "Your father has more money than the Rothschild family. He won't even notice."

And that, Naomi realized, was a sad truth. He'd not notice, and if he did, he wouldn't care. Or he'd tell her how he loved when she looked nice and how it made him proud.

"Money isn't everything," she said softly. "There are a few things more important than money."

"Look who's talking. As if you'd know how to survive without your generous allowance." Fleur patted her shoulder in a show of indulgence. "It's okay. Go on, buy that dress, and the blouse too. And then we'll go to my place for a swim."

Naomi began to protest that she hadn't brought her bathing suit, that she'd have to drop by at home and get one, but she didn't. With a shrug, she replied that she'd have to buy one, and yes, she was entitled to that; after all, she hadn't done that this summer yet.

"Impossible." Manon gasped. "Of course you need a new one!"

They took a cab to Fleur's house outside Geneva on the eastern shore of Lac Leman.

Naomi loved that house. It reminded her of the grand old villas on Lake Como, where she's spent a few weeks with her parents a couple of years ago as guests of some Italian family that was related to her mother somehow. There had been stone stairs leading down to the water where a yacht swayed dreamily on the gentle blue waves. The air had been heavy with the scent of flowers, and it had seemed to her that the only two beverages served had been coffee or champagne, with the odd martini thrown in. She'd loved how the dark, tall cypress trees had held their own against the bougainvillea, which had tried, in a rampant splash of pink, to take over the entire countryside, and how everything seemed weathered, mellowed into a softer hue of itself.

There were no cypress trees on the grounds that belonged to Fleur's family, but pines, shady sycamores, and roses…so many roses that the yard was drenched in their perfume. There were no stone steps leading to the water either, but they had a large swimming pool, and a great selection of fruit juices and pastry.

Sitting in the back of the cab, Fleur leaning on her shoulder, Naomi opened the glossy magazine.

"There, there!" Excited, Fleur pointed, nearly ripping the pages in her excitement when Naomi stopped leafing to inspect a picture of a new Chanel winter coat.

"The Golden Boy from Brooklyn," the heading read. Naomi stuck out her tongue in a show of distaste. Trite, that's what that line was, trite, and totally unimaginative. She was sure she'd have done better. He certainly deserved it. There he was, Jon Stone, in a beautiful head shot; and his lovely dark-brown eyes were looking directly at her. It was true; he had a wonderful mouth, and the way a smile lurked in its curve was almost too much, almost like a challenge. His hair was a bit too long, a bit too unruly, but thick and black; and it curled around his shirt collar in a totally enticing manner.

There were more photographs: Jon, alone on a beach, gazing away over the water; leaning against a black Porsche; sitting in a studio, a gorgeous guitar on his knees and another man leaning over him, pointing at something on the music sheets on the table in front of them.

The article that went with the photos wasn't very long. All she could glean from it was: he was born in Brooklyn but now lived in Los Angeles, that his first album had made gold, and that he'd toured the United States with great success.

"How old is he?" Naomi asked, but Fleur shrugged. "Maybe twenty-five? Twenty-eight? It's hard to tell with all the makeup they plastered on him for the photos."

She'd know, of course. Her father was a designer for one of the great Italian labels. He'd given them a special treat two summers ago when he'd taken all three of them to Milan and used them as models for his latest collection. Fleur and Manon had looked wonderful in the elaborate evening gowns and cocktail dresses, but they'd all been too long for Naomi. Fleur's father had given her an apologetic smile and said he couldn't make them any shorter for her; the real models were all as tall as beanstalks and needed this length.

"It says here that he's on a big tour through Europe this summer. And there's something about his guitars."

"Two concerts here in Geneva, Naomi! And we have tickets for both nights. They sold out in two days, and the concert is still two months away."

"We should go early and try to catch them when they arrive for the soundcheck. Maybe we can get him to autograph the *Geneva Glam* photo for us." Fleur held up the open magazine right next to her face, and it looked as if Jon was smiling at her.

Naomi's heart ached seeing her friend so close to his lips.

"Why would I want an autograph," she scoffed, turning her head away. "I'm sure he knows how to write his own name. He doesn't have to show me he can."

Pauline, Fleur's older sister, was crossing the lawn to the pool, a portable record player under her arm.

"Why not listen to the divine boy while we laze around in the sun?" she called. "That's his job, after all, isn't it? To entertain the girls."

Her eyes closed, sun hat drawn over them, Naomi lay in the sun, the music flowing through the hot afternoon light, the voice, that voice, wrapping around her bare limbs, touching her skin like kisses.

There were other songs, quieter songs, where he was really singing, soft and slow, modulating his voice, using it to express hurt, and pain, and lost love.

"And when you look again, I will be gone
The door will close, you'll be alone.
Your wilted love's too much to take
Your silences, your smile's a fake
You drowned my love in bitter words
And cut my heartstrings with your swords
Of fear and doubt and misery ..."

Her eyes flew open at the harsh sadness of the song, and she sat up. The others hadn't noticed, or chose to ignore it. They were mixing fruit cocktails, debating where to go for the evening, laughing when Pauline dropped an ice cube into her glass and splashed juice on her dress.

They weren't listening.

Naomi, though, she felt the pain deep in her heart. It nearly made her weep, and it wasn't the song, or the music, but the raw feeling in the way he sang.

She looked around.

There was the lake, glittering in the generous Mediterranean sun, the snow-tipped mountains all around; and here she was, stretched out on a chaise, while her friends made drinks.

But Jon was singing about broken hearts, and loneliness, and loss, about living without love; and it felt as if he was singing about her, about her own longing for someone who wouldn't see her as a business deal but as a girl, just a girl, nothing special.

"I'm not going to the soundcheck," she said. "I wouldn't feel right making him stand there selling his soul for an autograph."

The others stared at her, suddenly silent.

"I don't think it's that bad," Pauline replied. "After all is said and done, it's his job."

"Maybe." Naomi got up and took off her hat. "But I don't want it. I'm not going to be a breathless fangirl for him." She walked back to the house, her album and her magazine clamped under her arm.

She wanted to be alone, alone in her room, with Jon.

Chapter Ten

HE SANG HER to sleep.

His voice followed her into her dreams. She kept looking back over her shoulder, trying to see him, but there was only the sound of his voice, and the music of his guitar.

In her dream she was standing on a beach, and it was a lovely, warm morning. The sun had just risen; the water looked like a pale opal in the gentle light. There were some palm trees, black, slender silhouettes against the translucent sky, and at her feet, in the lacy curl of the surf, shells and stones, and the odd piece of sea glass.

"I want to find amber," she could hear herself say, and someone laughed; someone laid his hands on her shoulders.

She was walking, following the curve of the shore until she came to a headland, and boulders blocked her way.

Her hands full of the pebbles she'd collected, she turned and walked back, matching her stride to her own footsteps in the sand. They'd been nearly washed away, but their shallow imprints were still visible. There were no other traces except her own, and she wondered why that was; she could feel the presence of someone else, right by her side, right behind her.

The funny thing was she wasn't afraid of that unseen companion. Instead he made her feel safe, loved, desired.

There was a path up the beach into a green wilderness, through a gate in a fence, and for some reason it beckoned, but she hesitated. The stones and shells had disappeared from her hands; she stood there on the sand alone—no voice, no presence whispering to her anymore—and she felt lost.

"Where do I go now?" she asked into the sudden silence, but there was nothing. Nothing but the sound of the wind rustling, spinning the grains of sand in a whirling dance accompanied by the heartbeat of the surf.

"Where do I have to go?" she called again, but the beach was already retreating into the darkness of the Geneva night and the familiar sound of early-morning traffic down on the street.

Confused, Naomi sat up in her bed.

Dawn had just begun to stretch its first tendrils over the mountains, long, thin fingers of lighter blue on dark. The street-cleaning vans were ambling along the promenade.

"You are a fiend, Jon Stone," she mumbled. "You have no right to come into my dreams. Leave me alone, you silly man."

She threw back the covers and climbed out of bed to start the record again—for the sixth time since she'd come home—careful to keep the volume down.

She knew all the words by heart, and now, listening to "The River" again, she hummed along with Jon, sang under her breath:

"*River's heartbeat, river calling, that is all I came to hear. River song and river roiling in the darkness of the night…*" and she felt, again, the dense jungle around her, the heat and humidity, the hot breath of the predator waiting in the shade of the dripping foliage, and down there between the trees, down in the glade where blue moonlight glinted, the river itself, murmuring jungle secrets.

Naomi plucked the journal from the drawer of her bedside table. She hadn't written anything in it since her birthday; there hadn't been enough time. But now she sat on her bed, the heavy book open on her knees, pen in hand.

There were words in her head; they were lining up, dancing, waiting for her to let them pour onto the paper.

She didn't even have to think; the rhymes flowed out of her as if they'd been waiting for this moment since she'd been born.

Come to my secret garden, in the middle of the night
Come to me, I will be your guiding light
Like fairies we will be in our secret garden
Dancing in the stardust, the moon our only warden
I am your lover, my heart wants only you
You are my keeper, you know me through and through.
Come to me my love, the night is calling
Come to me, just come, while dusk is gently falling.

It was that easy.

At the back of her mind, there was even the trace of a melody, a gentle, slow tune, nothing at all like the humid throb of “The River,” nothing like it’s driving rhythm, just a sweet invitation.

She could see it: a beach, a path, and it led into a shady garden, into a wilderness of jasmine and bougainvillea, of nodding roses and fragrant cedars. Hidden among those bushes stood a stone bench in an arbor, a secret nook in a silent corner.

The song drifted on the rustling of the leaves, on the scent of the flowers, and followed the trail into the shady glade, where it poured its secrets into the thick, dew-covered grass.

“Forever and ever,” she heard a voice whisper, but it was so low that she couldn’t make out who it was, talking to her through her rhymes.

Her parents were stirring; she could hear her father humming as he walked past her door to the dining room, and her mother as she called to the maid to hurry up, she was late.

When she tried to move she realized she was stiff and cramped from sitting still for so long. Stretching her limbs, she got up to climb back into her bed where she leaned into her pillows and pulled the journal toward her.

THREE sets of lyrics. She had written three complete song lyrics, and there were more bubbling away somewhere inside her, she could feel it.

“You’re robbed me of my sleep, you fiend,” she said, nudging the magazine by her side. But she didn’t close it, didn’t push it away. “What are you doing to me? What is going on here?”

Writing lyrics had never crossed her mind before, at least not like this. Again Naomi wondered who might have given her the journal, how they had known it would come in handy so soon.

“Okay,” she said, the journal on her knees again. “Okay. So this is why you’re here, right? This is what you were meant for?”

She’d put on the record again, and this time she closed her eyes and listened, listened without letting her own words distract her.

It wasn’t really rock, the music Jon was playing. It wasn’t what they called pop either. It wavered somewhere in between, and then again, it was totally something all its own. He sang too well for a real rock performer, and he wasn't smooth enough for mainstream pop. There were no folk elements, so that didn't work either, and he certainly wasn't country Western.

His songs has a touch of grandeur, something of the big band sound of Sinatra or Matt Monro, and yet, despite the big orchestration, they had a sparse, almost naked feeling to them.

And of course, there was that voice. It was a deep voice, a wonderful baritone, well modulated and definitely trained; and yet when he sang "The River," when he let those drums take over, it sounded as wild and raw as a call from the jungle, as passionate as rapids foaming over rocks.

The sun had risen over the mountains; it was throwing bright beams onto the carpet. Birds were singing outside her window; life had begun to pick up on the promenade.

"I need my sleep," she said to Jon, and closed the magazine. "You may be far away, in a different time zone, but I'm tired and need to sleep. So please shut up for a while and leave me alone."

The last notes of music dwindled away as the last song ended.

The journal under her cheek, Naomi closed her eyes.

SHE wondered where he lived, and how.

There was this one shot of Jon leaning against that car, and in the background she could see a wall, a high cast-iron gate, and somewhere behind it, hidden among greenery, a white house. It was a very big house, more like a mansion, with palm trees framing it.

"Is this where you live?" Naomi asked. "This doesn't look like New York City. You're in Los Angeles, right?"

Her parents had left; her father, as always, had gone to his office where he managed the Carlsson finances, and her mother to the university to teach her English class.

Naomi had asked her once why she taught English when she was Italian and English was her second language, but Lucia had only given her a blank stare and shrugged.

"I like it" had been her response. "I never thought about it. I've always wanted to teach English."

Alone at the breakfast table, Naomi stared at the photos of Jon.

"My family is weird," she told him. "They're all over the place, and they put money before people. I'm not like that. I don't care about the money and the business."

She looked around guiltily. The maid was somewhere in the apartment, busy cleaning or doing laundry. She'd served Naomi coffee and then vanished.

"I'd much rather play the piano all day long, or write lyrics..."

The journal lay open beside her plate, right next to the magazine. In the shower she'd had another idea for a song text, and she'd rushed out, her hair dripping, to write it down before it blew away.

"You realize I'm writing those lyrics for you, right?" Naomi tapped on the image, right on Jon's nose. "I'm not a writer, and you make me write song lyrics. Something is not right here." She took another sip of coffee. "And what am I supposed to do with these now? I'm not a stupid songwriter!"

Coffee cup in hand, the journal and magazine clamped under her arm, she drifted through the living room, peeked into her father's study, greeted the maid, Mathilde, who was dusting the library, and ended up in the music room, where the Steinway grand was beckoning.

Naomi never practiced in the morning. Her fingers felt stiff, and her head wasn't awake enough. Mornings were the time when her parents were out at work, and the apartment belonged to her. In truth, she preferred playing when they were around and could hear her.

She had the vague hope that one day her father, while working at his desk or sitting in the library reading, would raise his head and hear her playing Brahms or Rachmaninoff, and come in to listen and tell her that he'd been wrong, that her talent would be wasted running the family business, that she should instead train to be a concert pianist.

Naomi knew it was just a dream. She was good, but nowhere near good enough for the stage.

Suddenly morose, unhappy, she put the cup on the closed top of the piano.

She wasn't good enough for anything. She hated numbers, and contracts, and everything connected with the hotels; but she wasn't outstanding at anything else either. Useless.

The journal propped open on the music desk before her, she rested her hands on the keys. She was useless. Nothing more than something pretty and decorative, just like Seth's silly little horse.

Useless, with no real reason to be alive. Useless, except as a pawn in her father's schemes.

Her fingers gliding over the keys, she found the melody of Satie's "Gymnopedie No. 1." Slowly, in very measured steps, it unfolded and drifted through the room, up to the stuccoed ceiling and out the window, mingling with the street sounds below.

Naomi closed her eyes. Paris in fall, Paris in the rain. Walking through Paris, alone with the fall rain painting bizarre shadows on the pavement. She had been carrying a red umbrella, her music in a folder stuffed inside her coat to keep it dry. Olaf had told her to wait for the car to pick her up after her lessons, but she hadn't. She'd wanted to walk all the way from St. Germain across the Isle St. Louis and along the Seine to their hotel near the Louvre.

Olaf had been livid when she got there cold, wet, and bedraggled.

"I wanted to walk through Paris," she'd replied when he shouted at her, asking where she'd been and what she'd been thinking. "I wanted to walk and feel the city."

Lucia had looked away, her lips pressed into a narrow line, and shook her head.

"What if you'd been kidnapped?" Olaf had grabbed her arm, furious. "What if you'd run into trouble?"

"At least it would have happened while I was doing what I want," she'd thrown back at him with all the outrage of a fifteen-year-old girl. "At least that would have been my own decision."

Her gaze fell on Jon's photo.

"Or maybe not," Naomi said in a soft voice. "Maybe I am a songwriter! Maybe I can do this! Let's find out, shall we?"

Chapter Eleven

IT WAS AS if she'd opened an entrance to a secret realm, as if she'd found a small, hidden door somewhere in a dark corner of her closet and, like Alice in Wonderland, had slipped through it before she knew what was happening.

There she was, a confused, overwhelmed child, while all around her the words danced, spilling down mossy hills, tumbling over stones like a frothy brook, coiled around the wind and dancing among the flowers in a meadow.

As soon as her pen touched the paper the sentences and phrases flowed out of her as if she'd never done anything else in her whole life.

Songs, there were songs, so many of them, as if every moment had one of its own, each one held secretly and she alone possessed the key to set them free. Everything was a song: the tinkling of the ice cream van, the spill of the great fountain in the lake, the drone of the planes swooping in to land at the airport. The birds in the trees, the voice of a child, her mother calling her for dinner—everything went into the red journal.

They were stories: she could see them everywhere. Open-mouthed, astonished, she watched life pass by below her window, and it seemed to her that everyone carried their own bubble of stories on their shoulders, visible only to her.

Some were bright and shiny, some colorful as a rainbow, and some gray and heavy, bowing their wearers down with their load.

Lucia caught her staring at a woman in an expensive convertible driving past as they left the house one day and asked Naomi if she was all right. Was she running a fever, or had she eaten something that hadn't agreed with her?

No, Naomi said, shaking her head. She was still staring at that woman, at the way she had coiled her golden hair at the back of her head to look like an intricate knot of braids, and how her neck seemed so fragile and elegant under that mass of hair. There'd been a big, white poodle on the seat beside her, a well-groomed and exalted dog staring back at the people on the sidewalk, his tongue lolling in laughter, his collar sparkling with what seemed suspiciously like real diamonds.

"I'm fine," Naomi said, "really, fine."

She could hardly wait to get back to her book and pen, and to share her thoughts and impressions with the creamy paper.

HER father threw her an irritated glance when she asked if she could use his office.

"Only for an hour," Naomi added. "I just need the typewriter."

"And what do you need it for?" Olaf was on the way out. She'd picked the perfect time.

"Oh, nothing. Just something I have to do for school. They want it typed, not hand-written."

She was delighted. He would be late if he stopped and gave her another harangue about how she was wasting her time with those stupid piano lessons, and how he was wasting a lot of money on something she'd never need once she was married to Seth.

Naomi had won that argument a couple of times, pointing out that as Seth's wife she'd have a lot of cultural obligations, and she'd cut a much better figure if she knew something about music, theater, ballet, and literature.

Olaf had raised his eyebrows for a moment but then nodded thoughtfully and replied that yes, it was actually good thinking, and he'd gladly pay for the conservatory if that gave her additional poise and education.

His patience was running out though. Two semesters, that should be enough of that, and it was time she settled down and tried business school, or get married. Or both.

THE door fell shut behind Olaf and Lucia, and Naomi, journal in hand, sat down at her father's desk.

It was a huge desk, made from some expensive tropical wood, antique; and the chair that went with it had red leather upholstery, much like her journal.

"Here we go." She knew her lyrics by heart. She could almost sing them, they had that kind of feel, a natural rhythm.

"Before I lose my nerve," Naomi told Jon's photo, "And before I watch you sing here in person. Because, you know, everything might change then. Maybe you're not as interesting on a stage. Maybe I'll walk out in disgust, seeing you."

It wasn't true of course. Naomi was quite certain that such a thing would never happen.

She sat there, her fingers on the typewriter keys, staring at nothing, wondering what life was like as a music star.

In the photo, Jon didn't look like someone who partied hard. He looked like a healthy, tanned young man, physically fit, someone who'd cut a good figure on a surfboard, who'd catch the attention of girls on the beach.

She tried to visualize it: sunset, and the water like molten gold. The sand still held the day's heat, and the wind rustled in the palm trees.

And there they were: young gods, carrying their boards, running toward the water, hair blowing, their silhouettes cut sharply against the mellow light. She could hear their laughter, hear them calling to one another, and off they went, tossing their boards and themselves into the waves with the abandon of dolphins playing in the surf.

She'd never been to California; for that matter she'd never been to New York. Olaf refused to have too much property in America, saying they had enough hotels already and he preferred Europe and Canada. He even refused to take her to the Met. Opera, he insisted, should be watched where it was first created. Milano. Venice. Paris. And maybe Hamburg, but only because the productions were so outstanding.

"But the Met!" she'd complained at some point after reading that Placido Domingo would be singing in *La Boheme*. He'd shrugged and said that once she was married she could talk her husband into taking her, if that was what she wanted.

WITH the lyrics in hand, Naomi returned to her room.

There was an address on the back of the album, a postbox somewhere in Los Angeles, which she had typed on an envelope.

She'd written a note to go with the lyrics. There was just one sentence: "Sing this."

A challenge, a dare, and nothing more. She was not a silly fan. She refused to be one of those screaming girls fainting at his feet.

The envelope sealed, she took it to the kitchen, where Mathilde was getting ready to go shopping.

"Would you please take this to the post office for me?" Naomi asked, and Mathilde nodded and promised that she would.

Back in her room, hearing the girl leave the apartment, Naomi sank down on her bed. Her heart was racing, her face hot with excitement.

"What have I done?" she whispered. "What made me do that?" She lay down on the pillows and closed her eyes.

She was a fan, no doubt about it, and she'd done the unthinkable: She'd sent a singer, a rock star, her version of fan mail. The only thing missing was a pink, heart-shaped sticker on the envelope and maybe a card with a scented kiss inside.

Disgusted, Naomi rolled onto her stomach and hid her face in the quilt.

She hadn't even thought about it first but had blindly followed a silly instinct, some drive she couldn't name. For nearly a week she'd done nothing else but work on those verses. Manon had called, Fleur had dropped by and asked what she was doing, holed up like that when outside the sun was shining and summer was in full swing, and they should be hanging out at the yacht club and flirting with boys.

Naomi had stared at her, but her mind had been following a new song idea that was taking her on a walk through winter in London, and loss, and promise, and a rainy shade of hope. The words had danced on her tongue, had knocked against her teeth as if they wanted out; and she had let them, had allowed them to slip outside.

Fleur had stopped talking about the summer ball and her new dress to listen, to gaze at Naomi in mystified wonder.

"It's nothing," Naomi had assured her hastily. "Nothing. Rehearsing for school, and I'm having trouble with this new Mozart piece I'm supposed to play. Mozart is such a nitwit."

"Nitwit," Fleur repeated thoughtfully. "I've never heard that word before."

"It means idiot."

That had made Fleur laugh. They'd gone out together, had strolled all the way along the promenade to the Lac Leman Hotel near the old part of town and to its beauty salon for a manicure, and then sat on the terrace with coffee and ice cream and watched the expensive cars roll past.

THERE was nothing she could do. The letter was on its way to California, to Hollywood and that post office box, and there was no way now to change that.

Naomi sat up, brushing her hair from her face.

No one would answer anyway. No one would look at her silly rhymes; they would land in the trash like all other fan mail, and her life would go on as always. Seth would come visit, they'd go out together, he'd be nice and patient, and in time she'd come to love him enough to live with him and lead a boring, slow life at Carlsson House.

Or not.

Maybe someone would indeed look at her verses, would read and speak them and hear the flow, and show them to Jon. He'd be sitting in the studio, working, composing, recording; and someone from his staff would put those sheets down in front of him, and everything would stop. His singing, his guitar playing, everything would stop while he gazed at her words and listened to their melody.

And then…and then he'd drop everything he'd been doing and jump on a plane to come find her. Just like that.

Laughter foamed in her chest at that thought. That was how it was going to be: Jon Stone would come to find her.

She picked up the phone. It was time to do something, to find some kind of distraction, and get out of the house.

SHE couldn't tell anyone.

Something sat on her shoulder like a huge, black rock, like the invisible presence of a grinning demon ready to blast her secret into the world at the first available chance.

Fleur kept throwing her worried glances as they sat on the jetty at her parents' house, dangling their legs in the cool water of the lake.

"You're acting so strange lately," she remarked. "Has something happened?"

"No, nothing. I'm thinking about what I should wear to the ball. I'll look like a child in anything but black satin, and no one will dance with me," she replied. "And I do want to dance, and not only with my father or yours. I want to have some fun!"

"No worries, we'll have fun. The ball is a week after the concert, so that will be glorious! First we get to see the lovely Jon Stone live and up close, and then we'll wear our new gowns to the ball. I'm thinking chiffon this year. Why not chiffon for you too, Naomi? Chiffon always makes me feel like a princess."

"Not chiffon." Definitely not chiffon. That much she knew for certain. Not so soon after her birthday and the memory of standing on the terrace with Seth. Even now, just a few weeks later, the memory pinched her throat.

"I want black satin," Naomi repeated, closing her eyes, her face toward the hot sun. "Black satin, and a narrow, slit skirt. And a bare back."

Fleur's gasp was quite audible. "But you can't wear something like that, Naomi! We're too young for that; it would be scandalous!"

"Yeah." And it would make her stand out, show the world that she was different, special, and not contained by their rules. She drew a breath to speak, and realized that she was on the point of telling Fleur about the lyrics and what she had done with them. But there was no way she could. It would forever and for all time be her secret, that shameful thing she'd done. She'd thrown her feelings at some stranger, some glossy centerfold superstar, without knowing anything at all about him.

That voice though.

That voice, and the way he sang, as if his rawest emotions were floating on the melody, as if every tone, every phrase, every chord of his guitar told his life story.

"Maybe we should go to the soundcheck after all," she said, opening her eyes to watch a speedboat zipping by, the people in it waving to them, shouting. "We may get a chance to see Jon up close and chat with him. I think we should have a chat with him."

There was no reply for the longest time, so Naomi turned toward Fleur to see her friend staring at her, her mouth open in a perfect circle.

"You really think about him day and night, don't you?" Fleur asked, and there was more than just a twinge of envy in it. "You sound as if you're best buddies with him, as if you played in the sandbox together as children. You're talking about him as if it's him you're in love with, and not your stupid Seth."

"Ha. If only." Her eyes closed again, she imagined Jon standing next to Seth, dark, tall, and handsome, and her personal red-headed dwarf; and she was coming down the stairs again for her birthday ball. They were both looking toward her, Seth and Jon, and she knew for whom her heart was beating.

It was a very clear song, a loud one too. She'd never have danced with Seth that night if Jon had been there.

Never.

Chapter Twelve

"I'VE BEEN THINKING," Olaf said over dinner a few days later. "We should buy half a dozen horse sleighs. Or even better, have them made. I really like that idea of offering guests sleigh rides across the estate in winter. We could even have races on the frozen lake. You had the right idea, Naomi, with that Christmas wedding. I'm really happy with that." He offered her the platter of roast beef. "Now what about that white fur cape? What kind of fur were you thinking? Ermine? Mink? We will need to order that soon."

The last bite of meat got stuck in her throat. "I don't really want fur. That was just…an idea. But I can't wear fur. All those animals killed, just so I can look pretty! No. I'll settle on white velvet, I think. That should do. And a silk lining."

"But you don't mind killing all those silk caterpillars in their cocoons, do you." Her father smiled at her. "All those butterflies, killed and boiled for your wedding cape."

"Fine, then it'll have to be just velvet and wool." Her mind wasn't on the subject. Two weeks had passed since she'd sent Mathilde off with that envelope, and slowly, very slowly, her mind was calming. No one would react. With every day that passed, she was more certain that her impulsive act had gone unnoticed, and nothing bad would happen.

Jon wouldn't show up at her door, out of the blue, and drag her away into his life, demanding that she write more lyrics for him.

She'd lain awake for so many hours the past two weeks thinking up one scenario after another. The worst one by far was Jon showing up asking for her, and her father opening the door to him.

Oh, how to explain, how to tell Olaf what she'd done—and yes, it had been a crazy impulse, nothing more; and no, she didn't want anything to do with that stranger in the doorway, even though he was a dream of a man. Her heart had hurt, seeing Jon retreat, seeing him leave in that vision. The door had closed, and he was gone. And she, in miserable cowardice, had slunk back to her room, a prisoner again. She'd torn open her window and watched him walk away…in the rain. Yes, it had rained in her fantasy; and there he was, the collar of his jacket turned up, walking away, and then, just then, when she thought everything was lost, he'd turn and see her, and everything would be clear. He'd know, and he'd come back, rapping on the door, telling Olaf that he didn't care about promises to other men; she was his, and he was taking her away now.

And then he'd storm into her room and pick her up, and away they would go…

"White horses," Olaf was saying, and for a moment Naomi stared at her plate, confused, still caught up in her daydream.

"We'll need white horses. We'll have to go horse shopping. How many do you think we need, Lucia? How many sleighs?"

And her mother, smiling brightly at him, her chin propped on her fist, replied, "I wish we could have troika sleighs. Do you remember that scene from *War and Peace* where they race across the open plain or lake or whatever it is? I love that scene. It's so carefree, before the war begins."

"You're such a romantic." Olaf held out his hand for the bread basket. "I have no idea if any special training is needed for that. We'll have to try and find out." He laughed. "I really like this. We'll have to have paths cleared through the forest for the sleighs. I love it! Just imagine all those tiny bells ringing out their merry tunes!"

"I'm in the mood for Christmas now." Lucia waved at the closed windows. "It's so hot outside, we've had the air-conditioning running day and night, and you talk about snow and frozen lakes."

The phone rang, but they didn't react; they were that deep in their discussion.

With a sigh, Naomi put down her napkin and went out into the hallway to pick it up.

"Hello?" she said, sure it was one or the other of her father's business associates. They often called at night, and mostly during dinner.

"Is this the Carlsson residence?" A strange voice.

"Yes?" Naomi replied carefully.

"My name is Sal Rosenberg," the voice said. "I'm calling on behalf of Jon Stone."

"What?" It was a meager croak, the sound of a frog being strangled.

"I'd like to talk to Naomi Carlsson, please?" he went on patiently, and with a trace of humor.

"I'm…that's me." Beads of sweat were forming on her brow. Her eyes darted toward the dining room where her parents were still amusing themselves with snow and sleigh rides, and how many stablehands they'd have to hire.

"Oh good. You sent us those lyrics? Well, Mr. Stone would like to talk to you about them. You're in Geneva, it says in on your return address. We'll be there in a few weeks, during the European tour. Would you be able to meet with us?" And he added a date, and a time, and a place.

Her lower body had turned to liquid. That was it. She was a marble statue propped on a pile of jelly, and speechless to boot.

"Yes." There. She'd pressed out that one word successfully.

"Oh good. If something should interfere and we have to change the time or date, I'll give you a call. All right? Thank you for submitting those lyrics! Jon sends his regards."

"Yes." This time she couldn't speak because her jaw had dropped so far, it felt as if it had hit the sideboard.

Jon sends his regards. Jon Stone was sending her his regards.

Her hand was shaking so hard she had a hard time putting down the phone. Leaning against the wall, Naomi took a deep breath, trying to calm her thundering heart.

Jon sends his regards.

"Who was that?" Olaf called from the dining room. "Something important?"

"No. Nothing." She had to sound normal, her normal, boring, collected self. They'd know right away if something was amiss. "Just Fleur, about her new ball gown." There. That they would believe right away.

"Oh dear, yes!" Lucia was pushing back her chair and on her way to the hall. "Good thing you reminded me, sweetheart. We'll go shopping for gowns tomorrow, shall we?"

"You can take the jet and go to Milan if you want." Olaf, walking past them on his way to his office for a cigar and a brandy, breezed a kiss on his wife's cheek. "Take the kid to Valentino and let her shop her heart out. Give her anything she wants. My lovely, clever daughter, with the brilliant ideas for the resort!"

Lucia raised her eyebrows at Naomi. "Did you hear that? Do you fancy a day trip to Milan?" And added, to Olaf, "Please remind me to get our passports out of the safe, dear. We'll need them!"

"I'll go get them now." He rose and vanished toward his study.

Naomi wondered if there was a way to make them let her keep hers now that she was eighteen. It would feel like a door to freedom, as if she held the token to her own life, having her passport in her care. That, and the money she'd received for her birthday, well hidden behind her books.

"Sure," Naomi said. "That would be lovely. Milan would be really lovely."

Chapter Thirteen

HER GAZE LOCKED on the mountains, and then the landscape of Italy, as their jet hurtled from Geneva toward Milan.

At the very last moment, when they had been ready to leave for the airport, Fleur had called and begged to go with them, couldn't she please go with them, she was bored out of her wits and would love a day in Milan.

"Sure," Lucia had said, "but not the others too. I'd be frazzled to my bones with all of you on one plane. Herding a flock of geese would be less stressful than hearing your friends chatter during the flight."

But she had smiled while saying that, and added that she loved the girls, and that she was glad Naomi had so many lovely friends.

She even let them have some champagne with their breakfast on board, saying if they were old enough to go to Italy for shopping, then they were definitely old enough for a glass of bubbly.

Fleur, between mouthfuls of omelet and French bread liberally slathered with butter, informed them that her father was expecting them at his studio, and he'd be pleased to present his new haute couture collection.

"I love this fall's gowns," she said. "Lots of red, and cream, and black!" Her finger flew out to point at Naomi. "Hey, maybe you'll even find your black satin thing there!"

Lucia laid her hand on her brow. "Not again, Naomi? Are you still going on about that black dress? Good heavens, it would make you look like…like…"

"A tart?" Fleur added helpfully. "And you're not tall enough to carry it off anyway."

"It wouldn't! If Valentino designs it, it can hardly be trashy, can it?" Naomi felt like pouting.

"Did you know that Valentino is Jackie Kennedy's favorite designer? He designed her wedding dress when she married that Greek tycoon, what was his name again?" Tapping her finger against her chin, Fleur broke off to think. "Onassis. That's the name. So when Mrs. Kennedy decided to marry him, she had Valentino create her wedding dress! How cool is that? I'll do the same. When I get married, I'll go to Florence and have them design a wedding dress, just for me." She pursed her lips at Naomi. "Have you thought about yours yet?"

"About what?" She didn't want to hear, let alone talk about it, so Naomi turned her head away and gazed out of the window. All she saw were white mountains and some tiny clouds.

"About your wedding dress, when you marry Seth! You must be thinking about it! I know I would, day and night. And the cake, of course!"

"Oh, Naomi has long since made up her mind about that," Lucia answered, relieving her of responding. "She wants a Christmas wedding with a white fur cape."

There was a small stab of pain behind her eyes, and Naomi rubbed them. "Velvet," she said, "not fur. With a hood. And no veil."

"Oh…" Fleur's blue eyes sparkled at her. "I love that! I'll be your maid of honor, yes? And Manon, Marion, and Giselle your bridesmaids?"

"Yes!" As if a suffocating black cloak had been lifted off her shoulders for a moment. "Of course you will! We'll have to pick out colors, and dresses, and…" Naomi's voice trailed away. She picked up a piece of cheese from her plate and tossed it into her mouth. "But there's still lots of time. I don't want to think about it until after the engagement party."

Seeing the smile on Lucia's face, Naomi added, "Of course, you'll all have to be there for that! Right, Mama? The girls all need to be there!"

"Of course!" Lucia took her hand and squeezed it. "Of course they'll be there! I'm so proud of you!"

"We could try on wedding dresses!" Fleur clapped her hands. "And imagine we're brides!"

"Well, Naomi is a bride." Again Lucia gripped Naomi's hand. "And she's all excited about it! Her wedding will be gorgeous!"

Naomi closed her eyes and leaned her head against the plane window.

THEY were greeted by Fleur's father, George, and a small army of models, ready to present the label's newest designs. Like butterflies in brilliant shades, the girls stalked up and down in the showroom while Naomi, Fleur, and Lucia were served coffee and tiny petits fours.

Naomi wondered how he expected his customers to fit into his creations if he fed them cake, but she ate one after the other until her mother moved the plate from her reach.

"You're ruining your appetite for lunch," Lucia said. "And you won't fit into one single gown if you finish those off."

"I don't like any of them anyway," Naomi whispered back. "I want to go to Valentino's!"

With a sigh, Lucia patted her arm and promised that yes, they would go to Valentino's but they had to pay their respects first.

"And I want a Gucci purse." Leaning back on the velvet couch, Naomi watched another girl march in, her head held high, hands on her hips, eyes staring into the distance. Her legs seemed endless, like matchsticks tacked onto her thin body, clearly visible in the short skirt she was wearing, and her knees stood out in brutal boniness,

"I'm too fat for those dresses anyway. And too short."

"Naomi!" Lucia shot her a venomous glare. "You're acting like a teenager! What's gotten into you?"

"Well, I am a teenager. And I hate these models. They look thin even in fifty yards of tulle. I'll never look like that."

"And a good thing too! You have a lovely figure! Now stop moaning and fidgeting and pay attention, will you? They're going to show us the wedding dresses in a moment."

Yes, and those were what she really didn't want to see. Fleur was sitting on the edge of the couch, nearly wringing her hands in anticipation, while Naomi wished she was miles away, in another country, maybe on another continent. The last thing she wanted to be reminded of was anything to do with weddings.

"I wonder if there are special dresses for engagement parties?" Fleur said, and George nodded.

"We do that often," he replied. "Many girls want themed gowns for their engagement balls." And added, to Naomi: "When is your engagement, Naomi?"

"New Year's Eve," she mumbled, trying to sink even deeper into the cushions.

"How about red? What do you think of the same color, and different cuts for you and your bridesmaids?"

Lucia was watching her intently, her dark eyes narrowed in worry.

She had to make an effort. She needed to pull herself together and be nice, sweet, and friendly, or she'd have to answer to Olaf for it later.

"Not red." Naomi propelled herself from the couch. "Manon can't wear red; it makes her look like she's been sick. We need to find something that will work for all of us. Right, Mama? I've been thinking about that since we came here."

"Yes! Yes, you're right!" Lucia sat up, smiling again. "I never thought of that, but you're perfectly right! We do need to consider this carefully!"

"Every girl can wear rose," George offered, picking up a huge catalog of fabric samples. "Rose is perfect for girls your age, with your clear skins and shining eyes. What do you think of rose?"

"I just had that for my birthday." Naomi wondered if choosy and petulant would work. "I can't possibly wear rose again for my engagement. I can't decide right now. Really, Mama." And popped another of the tiny cakes into her mouth. This time Lucia let her, her mind on other things.

"She's right, George," Lucia said. "We need to think about this. For now I'd like to see that blue suit again, please. I think it has my name on it."

IN the car, going from George's studio to the Via Montenapoleone, where all the other big labels had their stores, Naomi wondered if it would give her some space if she did try on a wedding dress after all. It wouldn't be such a chore; and maybe she could get Fleur to play along and do it too, and then it would be like playing princess, like make-belief, and not like some huge black gate in a huge black wall that meant her future.

"Sometimes I think you're not really looking forward to your own wedding," Lucia said out of the blue. "Aren't you happy about how everything is falling into place? I remember you telling me over and over how you'd marry Seth when you were grown up, and that he'd better not fall in love with anyone else until then. We thought it was your dream, marrying him."

"I said that when I was six, Mama."

"But does that mean you don't like Seth? Your father and I think it's such a wonderful match, and since you're going to take over the business in a few years..." Lucia had pulled off her kid gloves and was folding them between her fingers, folding them until they resembled an exquisite leather origami piece. They matched her caramel-colored suit and her Hermès purse.

"No, I like him." She felt her face flood with hot blood, seeing Fleur staring out the window as if she was trying to not be there, not listening to this exchange. "I like him, Mama. It's just that I feel too young to get married." Naomi took Lucia's hand in hers. "And you know, it's fine now; it's still one and a half years until then. It's okay!"

"But do you love him?"

Naomi wanted the bottom of the car to fall out, and herself with it. "Can we talk about something else now? I'm really hungry, and I'd love lunch before we try on more dresses. Can we? I'd really love some pasta."

Lucia sighed. "All right then. Lunch it is. God, to be eighteen and have the appetite of a horse and the figure of a young goddess."

They sat in the shade of the arcades with a fine view of the cathedral, and Lucia allowed them to order a glass of wine with their lunch, saying that if she was old enough to be engaged, she was certainly old enough for that. And they were in Italy, her home country, where wine wasn't considered the devil's own drink but something natural, and healthy.

"At home in Positano," she said, "we always have wine with lunch and dinner. My family has their own vineyard and make their own wine." With a wistful gaze at the church, she added, "I miss being there so much. Life is so much gentler in Positano than it is in Canada."

Naomi opened her mouth to ask why she didn't return more often, why she didn't follow her heart if she was so homesick, and wasn't life was so much more than getting married and settling down, especially when you were only eighteen years old.

But just then, just as she was ready to spill out all her anger and unhappiness, the Italian music from the restaurant's speakers ended, and she heard the first chords of "The River," and Jon's voice. Jon, and he was calling to her, reminding her that it wouldn't be long now, only a few weeks, and to sit tight and not get herself into trouble.

Naomi looked down at the menu.

"I'd like scampi," she said, and her voice nearly tripped with the sudden joy. "Lots and lots of grilled scampi. And when we're at Valentino's, I want to try on wedding dresses!"

Chapter Fourteen

THERE IT WAS: a brand-new ball gown, a lovely rose creation with a tight bodice and a wide, swinging skirt that ended at her ankles. It had many layers of black tulle under the pale satin, and there was some black lace peeking from the low neckline.

Naomi adored it. She adored it more than any dress she'd ever owned, and for a second, trying it on in the showroom, she'd even forgotten about Seth and the pressure of getting married. For a moment she'd just been herself: a girl looking forward to the night she'd be wearing this, and how the young men would be watching her enter the ballroom. All chatter would stop as they stared at her, and it would feel so good.

Lucia had insisted on buying her a shawl and a small evening bag to go with it, saying you never knew; the evenings could be cool on the lake, and she needed something to put her tissue and lipstick in. Naomi had no problems with that.

So here was her new dress, and lying on her bed, her chin propped on her hands, she wondered if Seth would really come over for the summer ball.

He'd called and said that he wanted to visit, and when did she think would be a good time; but before she could open her mouth to reply, Olaf had taken the phone from her and told Seth to come over for the summer ball. It would be lovely to go together, and Naomi could introduce him to her friends.

Standing beside her father, hearing Seth's enthusiastic response, she'd turned away and locked herself in her room for the rest of the night, listening to Jon sing.

"I'm so tired of having to pretend all the time," she said to his picture. "I wonder why my father can't just love me and be proud of me the way I am. I'm not a bad person! I'm not a hippie or anything, I go to school, I try to be nice to everyone, and I take care of myself. I read books! And I love music, and writing, and…and…"

Angry tears made her vision blurry. She sat up so they wouldn't spill onto Jon's face. "And I should run away. I really should. I don't need their money, and the stupid estate; all I want is a quiet little place, time to play the piano and write, and my own, small family. That's not asking too much, is it?"

She imagined herself getting up from the bed and walking over to the library, where her parents would be sitting, talking and enjoying their brandies.

She saw herself standing in the doorway, her hands knotted behind her back, and Olaf looking up, noticing her. She'd open her mouth to tell them that she didn't want to be their heiress, and she didn't want to marry Seth either.

"I don't love him," she'd say. "I can't bear the thought of sharing a bed with him, let alone…" Yes, she'd choke on that sentence, and wish with all her heart that Olaf would understand what she was trying to say.

But he'd only raise his eyebrows at her, like he always did when she tried to speak up, and stare her into silence. And then she'd drift away, the chastised child, the one who had no say in her own life.

Her father hadn't let her keep her passport.

"Nonsense," he'd said, taking it from her hand. "It goes where ours are. They won't get lost in the safe. And anyway, all our documents are in there; why change now? You can have it whenever you need it."

The summer ball wouldn't be until after Jon's concert, so at least that wouldn't be ruined for her. She wouldn't have to go and watch him sing with the fresh memory of Seth on her mind.

"I'm a timid, sorry thing," Naomi whispered. "That's what I am. If I had any guts at all I'll rage and storm, and fight with them until they're tired of hearing me scream and rant and whine, and they let me do as I please." The tears were dribbling down her nose, and she wiped them off with the back of her hand. "But that's just not me. I'm not that strong. And to be honest, I'm afraid of my father." She sniffled once more, then tried a shaky smile. "And I love my parents. I want to do what's right! Only I don't know what's right."

And there it was, her dilemma, the big bad thing that was breaking her heart.

She didn't know.

DANCING, she dreamed she was dancing in her new dress, and she was wearing ballerina slippers with it to appear shorter that she was, so she could look up at Seth.

Only when she did look up, it wasn't Seth she was dancing with. It was someone a lot taller; her head was below his chin, and she had to tilt it to see him properly. Her mystery man was in a finely pleated linen shirt and a very nice tux, and he danced well. The music seemed familiar, and then again not, as if it was only the ghost of music, a forgotten memory, a wisp of a melody.

"I'm wearing the wrong shoes," she said in her dream, and looked down at her feet.

"No, you're not," her dancer said, and now it was Seth talking to her, and when her gaze traveled back to his face it was his, level with hers. His breath hit her, heavy with wine and a hint of garlic. She tried to pull away, but he wouldn't let her, gripping her around the waist, pressing her body against his.

"You're my wife," Seth said. "Dance with me."

Naomi woke up with a scream on her lips and tears on her face. Dawn was near; the first touches of light were brushing over the mountaintops. She couldn't remember falling asleep, but she was still in her clothes, and her face had been resting on the open magazine, and Jon's photo. It was ruined. Moving in her sleep, she'd crinkled it, and her tears had soaked through the glossy paper and left splotches.

"What have I done?" She wiped her hand over the paper, but it only made it worse. "You're all messed up!"

That made her cry even harder. "You're just a stupid photo in a useless, stupid magazine, and I'm crying over you. Good grief!" Angry at herself, angry at her sorrow, and her dream, she got up to toss the magazine into her wastebasket. "There. That's where you belong, and everything that makes me think of you. What a crazy idea that was, sending you a letter, writing lyrics for you! Good-bye, Jon Stone. You're nothing more than a dream, and I have to grow up and…and…"

She couldn't say it. There was no way those words would pass her lips.

"And think of wedding gowns. There. I should have accepted Seth's proposal right away. Then I'd be wearing his ring right now, and the thought of you wouldn't be such a temptation. As if you could do anything to make me happy."

Still sobbing, Naomi went to open her window. A fresh morning breeze floated inside, bringing the scent of the lake and the mountains with it.

"I'm not sleeping properly," she said to the trees and the sky. "And I'm talking to a photo in a stupid magazine. I'm talking more to that stupid photo than I am to my parents and friends, and put like that, it sounds sick! It sounds as if I've taken leave of my mind! My life is here." A drop was hanging from her nose, a tear that had gone astray, and she brushed it off. "I have everything a girl could dream of. A nice home, kind parents, friends, lovely dresses, and the promise of a good and caring husband; and still I want to get away. I really need to grow up."

Chin held high, lips clamped tightly, she closed the window and opened her closet. She'd dress properly, get the maid to do her hair, and ask her father to take her out for lunch. And she'd demand that his car and driver pick her up. If they wanted her to be the heiress, she should start acting the role and stop playing around with her friends.

She could even ask him to let her work as an intern at the bank until university started in October. Olaf would be over the moon if she did that, and it would certainly be followed by expensive gifts, and more freedom.

The cherry-red dress in her hands, Naomi sniffled one last time.

Maybe that was really the right path, and her parents had known all along. Maybe they did know what she needed better than she did herself, and maybe it was a good thing for her to listen to them.

"I'm meeting you next week." Dress still in hand, she sank down on her bed. "You aren't just a dream, right? You're more than a picture in a magazine. And I'm going to meet you."

It sounded preposterous, unreal.

She hadn't told anyone about her lyrics, or about the ominous phone call. It was locked away deep inside her heart—her secret, her treasure, the tiny crack in the door to freedom.

"I can do this." Putting the dress aside, she retrieved the magazine. It fell open to Jon's face all on its own, as if it knew she didn't care for anything else on those pages. "I can do this. You aren't unreal. And I'll meet you and that Sal person in a few days."

The dress went back into the closet. Naomi got out of her jeans and shirt and put on her nightgown, went into her bathroom to clean her teeth and wash her face, then slipped into bed. The covers drawn up to her ears, she closed her eyes.

No more dreams of dancing and no more dreams of men, strange or well known.

She'd dream of horses. Of Apollo, and racing him across the big lawn behind the house. And she'd dream of beaches and walking along the surf at dawn, collecting shells and pebbles, while a big, orange sun rose behind a range of hills. There would be dolphins, and surfers, and a boy with a dog. There would be a jogging couple, a ship far out at sea, and beside her someone whose love and and tenderness flowed around her like a silk shawl, like the softest touch, the sweetest song.

And everything would be well.

Chapter Fifteen

"I SPILLED COFFEE all over it."

Fleur blanched. "Are you out of your mind? What were you doing, oozing all over him during breakfast? What did your parents say? Did they go ballistic, seeing you drool over someone other than your future hubby?"

"I wasn't…" The breeze blew Naomi's hair onto her face, hiding her blush. "I wasn't ogling. It just happened. And it wasn't at breakfast. I was sitting on my bed."

"Uh-huh." Fleur tapped her shoulder. "Ogling is ogling, regardless of the time or place. What is it with you and that singer? I admit he's cute, and he has a killer voice; but Naomi, really? We have the ball to think about, right? Have you found the right shoes for that lovely dress yet?"

They were sitting on the café terrace of the Lac Leman Hotel, the same hotel where she would be meeting Jon. The weeks had melted away, and now it was just one more day. One more day, one night, and she'd be sitting here with Jon talking about lyrics, and songs, and music.

"Flats. Mother wants me to wear flats when Seth is present. She says it doesn't look good if I tower over my fiancé."

"Wow, is he that short?"

"Rub it in, Fleur. Rub it in." Naomi was ready to throw her coffee at her friend. "But yes, he is. Seth is…he's sort of squarish. Stocky."

"Like a dwarf?" Intrigued, Fleur leaned forward. "Really? Like one of the hobbits in that book about a ring? The Tolkien one? You make him sound like he stepped from its pages!"

"Sort of. I don't know. I think it's unfair to call him that, but yes, I think he'd make a great hobbit."

They giggled, a bit ashamed, a bit excited, and happy to share a forbidden joke.

"And it's not as if you're tall."

"Yes, thank you, Fleur. You're really being a great friend today."

Her sore spot, and she didn't want to be reminded of it.

"Oh come on, Naomi." Fleur poked her shoulder. "You know you're beautiful. Dainty, pretty, and that lovely curly hair…I wish I looked like you! I'd trade my straight blond mane for yours in a second."

Slightly mollified, Naomi took another sip of coffee and unwrapped the tiny piece of chocolate that had come with it.

"But still," Fleur went on, "if you have to wear flats so you don't…"

"Oh, stop it! I need a new *Geneva Glam*, and I have no idea if that issue is still available, and I need it, because…" Naomi clamped her lips shut. So close, she'd been so close to spilling her secret by saying she wanted Jon to autograph the photos for her.

Of course she wouldn't ask. There was no way she could ask for that, not during a meeting where they'd discuss her lyrics and what he thought of them.

"My dad has a couple of them lying around." Fleur waved to the waiter and ordered chocolate ice cream when he came by. "I'll get one for you." She narrowed her eyes at Naomi. "But you need it? What do you need it for?"

"Nothing! I just…*want* it. That's all."

"You know what my dad said after we were at his studio? He said he would love to do a photo shoot with you. He adores you, Naomi. He says you're the loveliest girl he's ever seen, and that's saying something, with all those models he has around him all the time. He'd love to design a complete collection for you, and for dainty women like you."

"I'm not dainty! How I wish everyone would just stop saying that!" It made her uncomfortable, and it scared her a bit. "I'm going to tell you something, Fleur. Being 'dainty', as you call it, has some huge disadvantages. Everyone thinks they have to protect me, keep me from getting hurt, from being harmed. No one ever thinks I can do anything on my own. My father believes the only right thing for me is to be handed from his care to my husband's, and my husband-to-be thinks the only thing standing between me and certain disaster is his incessant vigilance." It hurt. Somewhere deep down in her throat it hurt, spelling out these truths. "They're always telling me what to do and what not, and how they think my life should be. I hate pretty and dainty! I wish…" Naomi waved at the sidewalk below the terrace, where a tall, stately woman in her midfifties was walking her dog. "I wish I was her. Tall, not young, not pretty. Someone who can make her own decisions." She balled the napkin in her fist. "Our exterior doesn't define who we are. That's what we have brains for."

Fleur raised her hand. "Hey, it's okay. I never said you were a dumb blond. You aren't even blond. And you're certainly not stupid!" Leaning forward, she gripped Naomi's wrist. "Hey. I don't know what's eating you right now. But I think that wedding thing is getting to you. I wish they wouldn't push you into that so soon, give you more time to grow up and be yourself. Wouldn't it be lovely if you could go to Paris with me to study art or music for a few years? We'd have such a great time! We could share an apartment in St. Germain and throw avant-garde parties, where young socialist men would read their poems to us or play Debussy on our piano. And we could go to the opera every weekend or see the ballet!"

Naomi could see it. She could see that vision so clearly, it almost made her weep. She'd wear narrow, black pants every day, the kind that made Audrey Hepburn look so cute and sexy; and she'd wear heels all the time, even at home in their apartment. There'd be posters of Gauguin paintings on her wall, all those strong, dusky women who ruled their own lives and lived on fish, and coconut, and pineapple.

She'd learn to cook. They'd experiment in their tiny kitchen, they'd learn to cook and then invite friends for dinner parties by candlelight. They'd spend Sunday afternoons at the Louvre, sitting on one of the benches and marveling at the art, watching the many, many tourists, and then drift around the corner to the Galerie de Jeu de Paume and wander among the brilliant flowers of van Gogh, the translucent light of Turner, and Gauguin's tropical lushness.

"I wonder where they'll stay while they're in Geneva?" Fleur said.

Naomi, torn from her reverie of freedom in Paris, blinked.

"You know. Jon, his band, and all the others who are on tour with him. I wonder where they're staying. Which hotel."

"But..." Here. The word had been sitting on the tip of her tongue, ready to jump out. Here, and it made her look around, made her realize that she was only hours away from being right here again, maybe even at this table; but it wouldn't be Fleur smiling at her, eyes as round as glass marbles and blue as the Caribbean Sea. No, it would be someone else altogether.

Maybe he wouldn't even smile at her. He might be completely bored by the whole meeting, only present because his manager had insisted. He'd be sitting there, gazing into the distance, glancing at his watch, hoping it would be over soon, and then walking away, returning to his room and things more interesting than a silly teenager with some lyrics.

The thought was so sad she hid her face behind her cup, and pinched her eyes closed against the sting of new tears.

"I have no idea," Naomi said, setting down her cooling coffee. "And I don't think they'll announce it either. I wouldn't, I know that much. Just imagine, all those fans hanging around in the lobby."

"I so would!" Blue fire lit up Fleur's eyes. "Oh, Naomi, just imagine! What if they'll be staying here? What if we come here tomorrow morning for coffee, and he's sitting right here, right here on this terrace enjoying the view and the sunshine! Can you imagine how cool that would be?"

The secret was right there, waiting on her lips, waiting for her to take a breath.

"So what do you think? Should we meet here tomorrow, bring the other girls, and hang around waiting for Jon Stone to show up? Like real groupies? Fangirls? Wouldn't that be fun? We should dress properly for that." Tapping her finger against her chin, Fleur thought for a moment. "There's this new dress my dad brought home yesterday. I'll talk him out of it. He said it would look best on me anyway. It's real short, and..."

"I don't think we should do that."

Deflated, Fleur pulled down the corners of her mouth. "Oh come on, Naomi. It will be fun! And then we'll all go to the soundcheck together! I'll ask my dad for the big limo, and we can drive out to the stadium and have some champagne and wait for the band and Jon to show up."

It was so crazy. She'd never done anything even remotely close to this, and it felt like a wonderful adventure, like a day of freedom she'd never even dreamed about.

"I can't…" Naomi started, but Fleur waved her away.

"Of course you can! Who's going to stop you? Just tell your parents that Pauline and Walter will be there too, and they'll let you go, I know it. Hey, I can get Pauline to call your father and promise to look after you, you precious 'dainty' princess!"

"I can't, really. I promised not to…not to…" What to say? She had to find some good excuse quickly, or the truth would spill out and everything would be lost.

"You know, you really make it easy for your father to sit on you." Angling for her purse, Fleur fished out a couple of bills and tossed them on the table. "You don't have any backbone at all. Why don't you just stand up to him from time to time? Throw a tantrum? Throw a plate or something? Don't you know how scared they are of that? Men will do anything to avoid a temper tantrum. Anything."

"That's not how it works," Naomi whispered, "My father isn't like yours. He would just send me back to Canada, and I'd never be allowed to leave the house again without his consent."

"Nonsense! You have your own trust fund, you're of age, you're a grown woman, you can damn well do as you please."

The waiter came over and collected the money, giving Fleur a wink and a grin, which she rejected with a flick of her wrist.

"No one can make you marry someone you don't love, and no one can make you lead a life you don't want. No one, not even your old man. All you have to do is to say no."

She couldn't imagine it. There was no way she'd confront her father like that and let his wrath roll over her like a tempest at sea.

"I couldn't." The weight of that wrath, the crest of that wave, were ready to inundate her even here in the friendly, dry climate of Switzerland. "I'm not like you, Fleur. I can't stand up to my father and…and…I'm not like that."

"Yeah, I know." It came out in a strange mix of tenderness, impatience, and a hint of protectiveness. Fleur patted her hand. "I know, darling. You're the gentle rose, the timid fairy, and my dad's dream of a designer's muse. It's okay. I understand." She sighed again. "We'll just have to find a different way for you, a stealthy path to freedom. And we will!"

Naomi stared at the empty tables of the café, wondering where she would sit with Jon tomorrow. Tomorrow…

Chapter Sixteen

HER MOTHER WALKED in to find Naomi in her bra and panties amid a mountain of clothes,.

"What in God's name is going on?" Lucia asked from the door, "What are you doing?"

"Nothing!" Naomi picked up a pair of jeans. "I can't make up my mind. I don't know what to wear today."

Lucia bent down to retrieve a dress from the carpet and put it on the bed. "This is so not you! What is going on?" Her gaze fell on the journal, lying open on the quilt. "What's this?" She'd picked it up before Naomi even had the chance to take a breath.

"When did you start keeping a journal? I've never seen this before."

"It's nothing! A birthday gift, and I've been fooling around with it a bit." Naomi stretched out her hand, but Lucia turned away, leafing through the pages.

"You're writing poetry," she said. "Lovely poetry too! I never knew you had such an artistic streak, Naomi! Listen to this!" Sinking down on the corner of the bed, Lucia read aloud the words of "The Secret Garden." "How lovely this is, my dear! So gentle, like the touch of a summer breeze!" She was in one of her silk business suits, this time a mesmerizing ocean blue that set off her black hair and made her skin look even more translucent.

"I'm... Mama." Carefully, weighing her thoughts before they had even formed into words, Naomi sank down next to her mother, the top she wanted to wear in her hands. "Mama, can I tell you something? Something really, really secret? And would you promise not to tell Daddy, at least not yet?"

Slowly, Lucia closed the journal. "You know I don't like keeping secrets from your father, sweetheart."

"I know, I know." There was a lose thread at the seam of the white blouse, and her fingers were picking at it without her permission. "It's just...I'm sure he'd not allow it, if he knew. But it's really something small, nothing to get in a fuss about, and Fleur, and Manon are in on it, so…" A lie, a quick lie, and Naomi had to swallow against the fear of being caught. "So I won't be alone."

Silently, the journal on her knees, Lucia waited.

"There was a contest…" Another lie, but at least something that would make the whole thing plausible. If that was even possible. "There was a song-writing contest, and I participated. And I won!" Naomi's finger flew out, pointing at the journal. "That song you just read? The one you like? It won! And the artist who…" That was not the way to go; she could see it in Lucia's wrinkled brow. "The record company who did the contest, they want to meet me today. I think I get a prize or something."

"There's no way you're going to meet strange people from record companies on your own, Naomi!" Lucia took a deep breath to go on, but Naomi held up her hand.

"I know. And I agree. That's why the girls are coming, and we're meeting them at the Lac Leman Hotel, out on the café terrace. It will be totally in public! There will be a thousand people there for lunch when we go. Only…" She held up the white top. "I don't know what to wear. This one?"

"I'm not happy about this, Naomi." Rising, Lucia dropped the journal on the pillow. "How did they inform you that you won? How did you submit? Where are they from, these people, and who are they? I don't think I can let you go there without your father's knowledge. You know how dangerous this can be, dear. You're the Carlsson heir; you can't go traipsing around with strangers—it might be a plan to abduct you!"

"But Mama! Not from the terrace of the hotel, and not with my friends there! I don't think there's a safer, more public place in all of Geneva. Please, you must let me do this!" She could feel her throat tightening, feel the burning in her eyes. "You expect me to get married next year; you and Daddy tell me I'm grown up, so you must trust me enough to let me do something, just once, something on my own! Please let me feel like an adult just this once, before Seth takes over from Father and has control over me! I really want to feel free, even if it's only this one day of my life."

"You know that's utterly ridiculous, Naomi. You have your freedom! You run around with the girls all summer long, and we trust you to be careful, don't we? No one is watching you when you go shopping with Fleur, and no one is telling you how much you can spend. Your father finds it endlessly fascinating how you can go out and buy just one dress, one lipstick, one book, when he gives you such a generous allowance." She glanced at her watch. "I have to go."

They stood facing each other, mother and daughter, both of them silent.

Finally, Lucia said, "Fine. I'll call school and tell them that I won't be going in today. And I'll escort you to that ominous meeting."

"No! Mama, no. I must do this on my own. It was like this: I sent them a couple of those lyrics, and then a few weeks ago they called here. Said since they were on a concert tour in Europe anyway, they'd like to meet and discuss the terms for using my lyrics."

The *Geneva Glam*, it was still there, in her wastebasket. "Here, look." The magazine fell open on it's own, and right to the smudged photo of Jon. Blushing, Naomi added, "I spilled coffee on it."

"This is the guy you're meeting?" Lucia took the paper from her. "But I've seen his face all over town: on posters, and in newspapers! It seems he's a real star! You're meeting him, Naomi?"

"I'm not sure." That was the saddest part of this whole thing. She didn't even know if she'd really get to meet Jon or just his agents and lawyers. "Sal Rosenberg called. He's Jon's manager. He said Jon wanted to talk about the lyrics. Which means Jon wants to meet me, but it may also have been a phrase of courtesy, or..."

"Okay."

"What?" Naomi was sure she had misheard.

"I said, okay." Lucia's slender hand wandered over her hair. "I don't even know why I'm saying this, and I hope I won't regret it. But yes, okay, you can go. I know Fleur has her head screwed on straight; she wouldn't let anyone mess with you. Also, they know us at the hotel. They'll watch out for you. I'll call the manager and ask him to place security close to you. Is that okay?"

"If they don't stand behind my chair the whole time..." In fact, and she'd never admit it to her mother, the thought made her feel better about the whole thing.

"I really hope I'm not being bamboozled into doing something stupid, Naomi. Oh well." A faint smile swept over her face. "Are you a fan of this Jon Stone? Was that the music we've had to endure ever since we returned? No wonder you're all excited and confused. Ah well, I think I can decide this without your father, just this once." The smile deepened into dimples. "I remember being flustered and excited over…over rock stars. And how I dreamed that something just like this would happen to me. I'm amazed, Naomi! You really managed to win this contest thing? I'm proud of you!"

"Yes, well…"

"I'll call the hotel now." Lucia raised a well-manicured finger. "Mind you, Naomi. No going to hotel rooms with those people, and nowhere private at all. You stay outside and in sight of security all the time, is that clear? Don't let them talk you into going somewhere private, no matter what."

"Yes, Mama." That was a promise she could easily make.

"And I want you to call me immediately afterward. I'll be at school; you can reach me through my secretary."

Naomi looked after her as Lucia returned to the hall and picked up the phone. She could hardly believe her good luck, and how easily it had been. She'd be free, just as soon as she finished dressing and Lucia had left for university.

She was free! All by herself, she'd walk along the promenade and to the hotel, and Jon would be there waiting.

Of course, there was the fact that she'd lied to her mother and that she would soon be adding more lies to that as yet small pile of untruth.

"I won't be back for lunch," she called when Lucia put down the phone. "I'll be going back to Fleur's place, and then we'll all go to the concert tonight. You know; I told you about it."

"Yes, yes, you did." But Lucia seemed uncertain and was about to ask when Naomi added, "I did ask when we were on the plane, back from Milan. Remember? Fleur said her father would provide the limo. We're all going together, and Pauline, and Pierre, and

Walter will be there too. You said I could go!"

"Well, if that's what I said..." Again, Lucia glanced at her watch. "All right then. Go. But come back straight away, you hear me? I don't want to get into trouble with your father over this. Good Lord, I have to go!"

"I may be sleeping over at Fleur's house," Naomi shouted after her mother, but the apartment door was already falling shut, and she was alone.

She was alone, with no one to stop her, and no one asking awkward questions.

Flat shoes. She would wear flat shoes, just to be sure, just to stay away from awkward moments. Maybe he wasn't tall at all. Maybe Jon was just as short as Seth, and they had just been very clever with those photos. Maybe he wasn't even half as good-looking in real life, and she'd be disappointed into silence, seeing him stand before her.

So flat sandals it was, and an unassuming white top with her jeans, and her hair down her back in its usual braid. No fuss for Jon Stone, and maybe that would get her through the meeting all right.

MEASURING her steps, taking care to walk slowly, and not run and break out in a sweat, she walked up the promenade.

Five hundred and thirteen steps, that was how far she had to go. She and Fleur had counted the stretch a million times, strolling along, arm in arm, ready for some shopping or just some ice cream in the sun.

Halfway to the hotel, Naomi stopped to turn and look at the lake, at the shades the trees were casting on the road, at the snow glimmering on the mountaintops. The air smelled of lavender from the big flowerpots lining the sidewalk, and from the kiosk an aroma of coffee drifted over to her.

Sometimes, in the quiet of the night, lying awake with her window wide-open, she imagined that she could hear selkies singing in the moonlight. She pictured them playing in the spray of the fountain, or saw them come onto the shore to explore the playground, to sit in the swings and marvel at the humans' ingenuity.

Selkies, and their slow, sweet music, and another song of secrets and deep waters, of hidden waterways that connected lakes, and rivers, and oceans, highways for the merfolk; and some of them had found this lake, this enchanted place, and settled here. They sang to her; they called to humans who didn't feel at home in their lives and dreamed of other places.

And when they got lucky, when those humans got really lucky, they were invited to come along, to start a new life in the water.

Whispering the words to that new song, hearing the whisper of the selkies, Naomi entered the hotel.

Chapter Seventeen

SHE COULDN'T SEE a thing.

The sun streaming through the door and windows bathed her in light, hiding everything inside in shadow. There was no movement, no one talking loudly or acting important enough to command her attention.

There was no one who looked like a rock star with an entourage, waiting to intimidate her. Sunglasses in hand, she took another step, leaving the light behind, and that was when she saw him.

It was he, Jon, there was no doubt about it. He looked just like his photo: well-groomed, nicely dressed, like a pool of quiet in the shadowy depths of the big hotel lobby.

He'd seen her too and was rising from the couch he'd been sitting on, and for an instant it seemed as if he was reaching out toward her, but then his hands wandered into his jeans pockets.

He was staring at her; there was no other way to put it. Jon Stone was staring at her as if she was something special, something he'd never seen before; and he was alone. There was no entourage, no group of people nervously hovering around him; it was just him, a young man of Seth's age, tall, with black hair that curled around his shirt collar; and he was trying to smile but somehow it didn't work.

Carefully, slowly, Naomi walked toward him, wondering if it was a trap after all and he the bait to lure her away to more sinister places. From the corner of her eye she could see hotel security moving. They did it casually, without looking her way, but it made her feel better to know someone was watching out for her.

It was funny: as much as she said that she hated being protected all the time, right now it felt good.

"I'm Naomi." That would have to do as an introduction.

"I'm Jon," he replied, and it made her bite her lip.

"Yes." As if he needed to say that. As if it wasn't clear to the entire world who he was.

They stood, gazing at each other, speechless; and Naomi realized that he was indeed all that the magazine photos had promised: tall, beautiful, tan; and his eyes held that same promise she knew from his pictures.

"Aha. And here she is, the elusive poet." She'd heard that voice before. "I'm Sal Rosenberg."

He didn't look at all like she'd imagined. Sal was young, not much older than Jon, a lanky, tall young man with bobbing black locks and a lean, spare face.

"We talked on the phone," Sal said, holding out his hand to her. "Remember? I was the one who called you."

"Yes. You called." She couldn't help herself; her gaze strayed back to Jon, and to the way he was watching her.

"Maybe we should go and sit outside." Sal pointed toward the terrace. "The sun is lovely. We could have some coffee? Cake? Ice cream?" When there was no response from either of them he added, "I know I want coffee."

They wandered outside and sat in the shade of a big, red umbrella. Again Naomi could see security taking their places near the door back into the building and beside the stairs leading down to the sidewalk. There were enough men to be noticed, and it was only now, only when she was seeing Jon by daylight, that it occurred to her that maybe they weren't watching out just for her but for him as well.

There had been something about a fan committing suicide on the sidewalk right outside his record company; Fleur had told her about it.

She wondered how it would be to deal with something like that, how the guilt and shame could ever abate. How would you be able to move on and still enjoy life.

Coffee was served, a tray with cake, and at Sal's request, ice cream.

Naomi hid her mouth behind her hand. Fleur, how she'd enjoy being here right now, with Jon Stone sitting across the table asking her if she wanted coffee or would she prefer something cold, or–grinning–hot chocolate?

But Naomi didn't want anything. She wanted to sit and stare, and take in the fact that she was really facing Jon Stone.

He seemed so nice. There was a gentleness about him that she hadn't expected, as if he had tuned into her thoughts and was waiting, giving her time to get used to the situation and the strangeness of it all.

Sal was talking. He was telling her how the envelope with the lyrics had landed on his desk, how he'd opened it and known right away that Jon would want to see them, and how he'd called him, made him come down to the studio.

"He went all crazy over them," he said, "as if he'd never seen real lyrics before. Snatched them out of my hands and ran off with them. We didn't see him for two days." Clearing his throat, Sal added, "As you can see, we're being very up front with you. Jon said he doesn't want you to think we're trying to cheat you or anything. So. What's the deal with those lyrics? What do you want for them?"

She hadn't really been listening. Across the street, on the promenade, Naomi could see the familiar shape of Fleur's favorite straw hat and beside her, Manon and Giselle. They were climbing out of a cab and sorting themselves, debating where to go first, what to do.

Naomi leaned back in her chair, trying to hide behind Sal as well as she could, and held her cup in front of her face. It didn't work very well this time though, because it was a small espresso cup and not one of the big café au lait ones.

"We need to talk about contracts and money," Sal was saying. He sounded slightly confused, as if her maneuvers puzzled him. "Have you thought about what you want out of this?"

"I really want those lyrics," Jon said. That voice made her forget everything else, even Fleur, who was directing the others across the street and toward the terrace. He was smiling, giving her a smile that belonged to her alone, as if she was the only girl in the world.

"You can have them. I don't want any money." There. Anything, anything at all to get away.

Jon pushed back his chair. "Will you take a walk along the water with me? Just you and me?" He was holding out his hand to her. It was a very nice hand, well shaped, with long, strong fingers. It wasn't hard at all, laying hers in it.

There was no way she could avoid the girls. Fleur was as always, leading the way, pointing at the hotel, holding her hat with her other hand. They looked like a small flock of hens, getting ready to storm the barn, and it made Naomi want to giggle.

Sal was still talking to Jon; they were standing close to the steps leading down to the sidewalk, and here she was, her hand in the rock star's, waiting by his side to go on a walk with him.

"All right," Jon was saying, moving away from Sal, "we'll be back in time. No worries. We'll just take a short stroll."

Naomi tried to hide behind him, tried to keep her head down and become invisible, but it didn't work. Of course it didn't work.

Fleur stopped in the middle of the street, right in front of a bus, and stared. She was the only one who'd noticed, the only one of them who wasn't craning her neck to get a view of the limousine that had just pulled up at the hotel entrance and the photographers flocking around it.

"That must be him," Manon called, pointing, rushing; and for a second it was only Jon and her, and Fleur, insects caught in a tiny bubble of time, seeing one another.

The bus honked its horn, and the moment was over. Jon pulled her forward, toward the promenade, but Naomi was looking backward, at Fleur and her flight to the other side of the street. Safely on the sidewalk, she turned, standing on the curb, her hand still on her hat, her mouth open in a silent shout, her eyes blue lakes of wonder.

"This is such a lovely place," Jon said. "I think I could spend some time here."

She turned her back on Fleur and the hotel, and wandered away with him, her hand in his and her attention on his voice.

LIKE a dream, it was like one of her dreams. Here she was, strolling along the lakeside, and Jon was with her, looking at her, smiling, talking, touching her hand as if it was the most precious thing in the world.

Reality was better than any of her reveries where he'd come to their apartment door and demand to see her, push Olaf aside and come inside to find her, and off they would go, into the sunset, into a new life in a place far, far away.

Jon was talking, he was speaking to her, telling her how stunned he was to have found her and had she felt it too, had she felt the world shift and change the moment they'd met?

He stopped walking when they reached the kiosk, the same one she could see from her bedroom window.

Naomi looked up, trying to imagine herself behind that curtain, watching Jon Stone and a strange girl standing under the trees, talking. She wondered if she'd recognize him from there, if she'd know right away that it was Jon.

She wondered what she'd be seeing: a young man and a girl standing close together, talking softly, hands touching, drifting away from each other then returning to the touch like dancers in an elaborate, slow rhythm.

She'd watch them move, watch how their bodies were moving toward each other while pretending to be strangers, and she'd see the kiss.

Yes, she'd see that kiss, and the way the young man laid his arms around the girl, how his embrace seemed to engulf her and carry her away.

And she'd feel how the world tilted for that girl, how in that instant when their lips touched she understood that no amount of dreaming, or wishing, or hoping was like the real thing, the real touch of love.

HE was talking to her, telling her that he could never let her go, that she'd have to come with him to the soundcheck so he could be sure she didn't run off and disappear in the strange city, and Naomi found herself nodding, agreeing to go with him, stay with him, at least until after the show.

There was no way she could refuse him. This. This was what she had wanted, always.

Jon was looking at her, only at her, as if the world had fallen away and there was only the small spot they were standing on left, as if the rest of the universe didn't matter.

"Yes," she replied, still breathless from the kiss, her lips still tingling, "yes, I'll come."

The concert ticket was burning its way through the leather of her purse. So useless now. Everything was different; she had stepped through the magical mirror, and everything was different. She was on the inside, and the rest of her life happened somewhere else.

They returned to the hotel, where Sal was pacing the lobby, throwing dark glances at his watch. "You're late," he called when he saw them. "We really need to go, Jon."

There she was, Fleur, sitting on one of the couches, as quietly as a pillow, her gaze steadily on Naomi. The others were nowhere in sight, and that made Naomi let go of Jon's hand.

He stopped, giving her a questioning look.

"I'll be back in a second," she said. "I've seen a friend, and I really should let someone know where I'm going. My parents…I should let them know where I'll be."

"Yes, of course!" It was Sal who understood first. "Please, do tell your friend that you're coming with us?"

"Yes, Naomi is coming with us." Jon, and he sounded as if he were laying down a new law.

She called home from the hotel desk, but only the maid, Mathilde, was there. Naomi told her to tell Lucia that she was hanging out with Fleur and Manon, and everything was fine.

Fleur rose when she came over, waiting for her to speak.

"I'm going to the soundcheck with Jon and the band," Naomi said, and Fleur nodded. "It's a long story, Fleur. I promise to tell you. I'll meet you at the concert?"

"Yeah. Sure." Rising on her toes, Fleur was watching Jon and Sal. "I'm really curious to hear how this came about. Did I just see you holding hands with Jon Stone? How…"

"Don't ask. And please, Fleur. Please don't tell my parents. If you are my friend, please keep my secret."

Fleur popped some gum into her mouth. "Hey, this is the biggest thing since the Beatles broke up. I'm not telling anyone. But you have to promise to tell me everything about it later. Everything."

"I promise."

They were moving toward the exit, toward the bus, all of them except for Jon, who came over to her.

"Can we go?" he asked, with a friendly nod toward Fleur. "The bus is waiting."

"Sure." As if she'd never done anything else. As if this moment had been waiting for her all her life.

Chapter Eighteen

SHE SAT BESIDE him on the bus, her hand in his. Jon was talking to her softly, telling her how he knew that he would have to hold on to her forever and ever, how she was like a miracle, a fairy princess who'd left her magic realm to be with him, to share his life.

"What am I supposed to do with you now?" he asked, his eyes on their hands. "I can't risk you leaving. You might vanish back into the mist, like the dream you are. And I don't think I could bear that. There would be no concert tonight, or tomorrow, or ever again."

So strange, so unreal. Here he was, the young star, the dream of all her friends, and he was holding onto her as if she was the last girl in the world. He was smiling at her, giving her a puzzled, gentle smile.

"My good fortune, my great luck," Jon said, "to be the one, to be the songwriter you picked. I don't know what I've done to deserve it, but I sure love it. Everything changes now. I've been waiting for you for so long."

Everything was upside down: She wasn't with the other fans hanging out at the fenced gate to the venue compound, wasn't one of the screaming and waving girls. She was on the inside, staring at them from the bus as if from an aquarium as they passed inside.

"Wanna go give out some autographs?" Sal came up to Jon, holding out a pen and postcards.

For a moment it looked as if Jon would decline, but then he nodded and took the cards from Sal. "Sure." He sighed. He sounded less than enthusiastic.

Naomi stood with Sal and watched him walk away to where security was keeping the fans at bay. There was a blond young woman at his side, and the man he called Russ, another manager, producer, or something along that line. He'd greeted her with a nice, British accent and blushed, shaking her hand.

That blond girl though, Sally, hadn't even glanced her way, as if she wanted to make Naomi disappear by ignoring her.

"So tell me about yourself." Sal lit a cigarette, then offered the box to her and when she declined, wrinkled his brow at her. "How old are you anyway? You look a bit young, to be honest. Please be honest with me, Naomi. You know it could hurt Jon enormously."

"I'm eighteen."

"That's..." He cleared his throat. "That's really young. You're just a schoolgirl!"

"I'm not." Naomi tried to stand up straighter, as if that would make her seem older. "I'm at university, and..."

One breath more, and it would have slipped from her lips like a traitorous ribbon of truth. Engaged.

She wasn't engaged, not yet; and there was no need to tell anyone here about Seth, no one at all. In fact, looking back at the tall gate and the high-mesh fence, she felt free.

"Really? University? You must tell me more about yourself. But for now..." Gently taking her elbow, he steered her toward the back entrance of the venue. "We should go inside and get out of range of the cameras. Don't worry, Jon will be with us in a few minutes."

She'd never been inside a stadium, let alone in the catacombs where the locker rooms were. The place smelled like old sweat, unwashed clothes, and toilets, mixed in with freshly mown grass. Their steps echoed through the unadorned, dimly lit hallways and got lost somewhere in the depths of the huge building.

There was a lot of noise too: the clanking of metal, the rumble of big trucks, shouting, hammering.

The stage, Sal pointed at an exit that shimmered like a square of light in the distance. They were just now finishing with the stage. They brought their own stage, he added, in containers, by truck.

Giving her a small smile he said, "Jon is like the sun, and everyone and everything that travels with him are his planets, his meteor belt, his galaxy. I like to think of myself as Jupiter. Big, important, reliable. And you..." The smile widened into a grin. "You're probably some other important element. Maybe Earth? I don't know."

"Not Earth. Earth is old, has always been there. I can't be Earth. I'm something new."

"That's true." He gazed at her with new respect, with something like curiosity. "You're indeed something new. Like a comet blazing through our small system of well-regulated heavenly bodies. How interesting!" He dropped the cigarette butt and ground it into the tile floor. "You are an interesting little thing. What in the world made you send us those lyrics?"

"I didn't send them to you. I sent them to Jon." Someone would ask eventually. "I heard him on the radio, and that made me write them. And since they were written, I thought I might as well send them. That's all."

Never. She'd never tell this man Sal about her daydreams, how she had conjured up one fantasy after another, and how it had kept her sane, with the day of Seth's arrival drawing close.

There had been a debate over breakfast, one that didn't include her, as always, about where to put up Seth.

He couldn't stay at their apartment, Lucia had argued; that was improper—the thought alone made her want to blush. Olaf, though, had told her to forget her Catholic schoolgirl inhibitions and get real. This was the eighties, and her Italian prudery was totally uncalled for. There was a guest suite, after all; and if she felt uneasy about Seth and Naomi sharing an apartment, well, there were always earplugs to be had at the pharmacy.

Of course neither of them had thought to ask what she thought about it. They'd been talking about her and Seth as if it was the most normal thing in the world that he'd stay at their place and that at night when her parents had retired, Seth would sneak through the apartment and into her room. The thought alone was enough to make her shudder, and there was no way to make the vision appetizing. None at all.

"WELL, yes. You know what I mean. You sent them to his office at the record company. Which means me. More or less. You didn't really think Jon opens the mail himself, did you?"

They'd entered a big room where a buffet had been set up along one wall. It smelled delicious. The aromas of coffee, and warm bread, and cooked food danced in the air. A few people were sitting at the tables, eating, chatting, waiting.

"As soon as Jon is ready, we'll go up for the soundcheck and rehearsal," Sal said. "Is there anything you want right now? We'll all have dinner here after the soundcheck."

"Coffee, please." She followed him to the coffee urn and took a paper cup. "Is this how it always goes?"

"Yeah, pretty much. Not very glamorous, is it?" Again he threw her his sharp grin, but this time the mirth danced in his eyes too. "It's more like a freaking circus. We are like a wandering circus, and Jon is our most prized act." He tilted his head. "I think he's the lion, yes? Or maybe the tiger. The one beast everyone comes to see."

"Well, yes…" Something didn't seem right about this comparison, but Naomi couldn't quite put her finger on it. It seemed too cynical, too jaded for people who were only a few years older than she was herself.

"Don't get me wrong." Sal handed her a cupcake. "Jon is a star. A real star. He deserves every good thing that comes his way. He's brilliant, very nice, and a good friend."

From the stage, the first sounds of music could be heard. It seemed to drift through the maze of corridors like an echo searching for a song: haunted, distorted, mournful.

"They are starting." Sal put down his cup. "Let's go."

In the hallway they met Jon, coming in from the sunlight, the blond girl right behind him. His face lit up when he saw Naomi.

"There you are! I was afraid Sal might have spirited you away, and I'd never see you again. Come on, time to sing!"

HE sat her down next to the keyboard player, on the piano bench, telling him to watch out for her, then picked up one of the guitars waiting in a line for him. It was a moody, dark instrument with the voice of a baritone, much like Jon's. It growled when he touched the strings, growled and stretched, a big beast waking from sleep.

"The River," and here it was, live, played by real people and sung by Jon, and even now, in the sun-drenched bowl of the stadium, it sounded steamy, and darkly inviting.

"You're the poet, aren't you?" Sean, he'd been introduced to her, and he was talking to her without missing a note on his keyboard.

Naomi liked his smile. His eyes were afloat with gentle humor and a quiet love that seemed directed at everyone around them.

She nodded. "Yes, I am. I have no idea what I'm doing here…"

"Oh, I'm sure he does though. Jon has been talking of nothing else but your lyrics for weeks. I think if he'd been able to get away with it, he would have ditched the entire tour and come straight here to meet you." He winked at her. "I'm sure you're a huge surprise to him too. Young and lovely, and a poet. I wonder where this will lead."

That made her giggle and blush like a stupid high school girl, and just then, just when she was raising her hand to hide that giggle, Jon turned.

"Don't touch, Sean," he called, and there was a trace of fear in his voice. "Don't touch what's mine!"

Sean laughed. "Okay, okay, don't get all worked up! Jeez, man." And added, to Naomi, "See? What did I tell you? You better go and join Sal down in the front row or he'll never work properly."

Naomi scrambled down over the edge of the stage, feeling like a pro doing it, as if she'd grown up around rock stars and stages in stadiums. The music was flooding around her: loud, insistent, as powerful as a stormy wave. Jon drove it; he drove his song into a passionate statement, into a call for love. The guitar he was playing wove around his voice like a second singer, with the same timbre, the same depth.

Sal handed her a can of Coke when she dropped into the seat beside him.

"Tell me about yourself!" He had to shout to be heard over the rhythm of the jungle river.

"I'm nobody," Naomi said, "just a girl living in boring Geneva." She shrugged. "I've just entered university, I like to dance, and I like writing lyrics. That's it, basically."

"Really." Again that shrewd grin.

Carefully, weighing her words, she told him about the summer ball, and how she loved to go skiing in winter and hang out with her friends at the lake.

She'd not known she was a writer, Naomi told Sal, until the moment she'd heard Jon's voice on the radio. It had been as if a door had opened for her, and the words had just spilled out. There was nothing special about her lyrics. They had simply happened.

Again she shrugged. There was no other way to explain it, she said, and she didn't even know if there would be more.

The red journal was in her bag. She'd picked a large purse so she could bring it, in case anyone wanted to see the originals. Only no one seemed to doubt her story. Least of all Jon.

It was as if someone had built the world she wanted from her lyrics, as if someone had built her dreamworld and then invited her inside, into the perfect escape, the only path that made any sense at all.

Jon, and there he was, right in front of her, putting down his guitar and announcing that the soundcheck was over; he had more important things to do just now. He was looking at her as he said it, and then at Sal, with a frown, and jumped from the stage much like she had done.

"Uh-oh, here comes trouble." With a sigh, Sal rose. "I'll see you later." And walked off, whistling "The River" melody.

Chapter Nineteen

IN THE DIMNESS of a lonely hallway, Jon kissed her again.

This time she put her arms around him, dared to return the embrace, and the kiss.

From far away came the sound of voices, of engines rumbling and plates clinking, but she was alone with Jon, in a forgotten nook of time and space.

"You're mine," he whispered to her. "Oh yeah, I know it. This feels so right. I'm falling in love with you, Naomi, and I can't bear the thought of ever being without you. You must be mine!"

"That's not how it works," she mumbled, helpless against his touch and the sweet words, "I'm nobody's own. I'm not." Lip service, nothing more, a show of spirit in a hopeless struggle.

"Yeah, we'll see about that." He kissed her again, harder this time, deeper, his body tight against hers.

Naomi wanted that embrace to last forever. She wanted to get lost in it, never to let go, never be somewhere else but in his arms. This, this was what she had dreamed a kiss was supposed to be, how it was described in songs and poems; and it lasted nowhere near long enough for her taste before Jon let her go.

"I have to get ready," he said, his mouth still close to hers, close enough to feel the electric tingling. "Come with me to my dressing room. We can talk while I change and they plaster makeup on me. Please come?"

Her lips were ready to agree, but she shook her head. "No. I don't want us ending up on the couch." There, she'd said it, mentioned the unspeakable thing. "I'm not a quick number in some random dressing room."

Surprised, Jon drew back. "Of course you aren't! I never meant it to sound like that at all! I'm sorry, Naomi." He ran his fingers through his hair. "Of course not."

They parted at the door to the dressing room, where Russ, a makeup artist, and the blond girl were waiting for him. Jon briefly introduced her, saying her name was Sally, and she ran his office.

Sally had given her a brief nod without looking at Naomi directly, as if she didn't want to acknowledge her presence. She was a pretty girl, with astounding, white-blond hair that she wore gathered into a sassy ponytail. Naomi admired her short, polka-dot skirt and the red patent leather purse slung over her shoulder, and the ease with which she moved through this alien world.

"I'll go find Sal," Naomi said, "and some coffee."

Jon nodded, and it felt as if he was moving away from her, as if, entering the dressing room, he'd crossed an invisible border into another realm, one in which her place was still undecided.

"I'll see you later," she added, and he swiveled to look at her, his brow wrinkled in concentration, his eyes fixed on something only he could see.

"Don't get lost," Jon replied, "and don't run off. Please."

"I won't. I promise." Everything. All these people around him were doing everything to smooth the path for him until he stood on the stage and poured his songs and his love out to his audience. He'd turned into the star, into the man who'd harnessed the beast of his creation. Even though there were others in the room with him–Sally, the makeup artist, and Russ–he seemed to be alone, distanced, lonely in a place only he could see.

It was hard. She didn't want to go; she wanted to stay close to him, take away that sense of isolation and make him smile. But the door closed, and she was in the hallway, and the magic was gone.

SHE found Sal in the hospitality area, where he'd offered her coffee earlier. He was sitting with Sean and other members of the band, nursing another cup, but he got up and came toward her when she walked in.

"There you are." It sounded a little startled, and relieved.

"Jon is getting ready," Naomi said, and then clamped her lips shut, blushing, when he raised his eyebrows at her.

"Of course he is." Sal took her elbow. "Come, let me introduce you to the band. Seems like you're going to be stuck with us for a while."

She sat with them, a glass of orange juice in her hand, and listened to them talk about acoustics, the weather, and how they'd slept in their hotel beds. Sean was telling the others of his foray into the city and how he'd bought enough Swiss chocolate to last him for the rest of the tour and still have some to take back home to California. His gaze drifted to Naomi.

"I'm sure you eat chocolate all the time, right? If I lived here, I sure would. It's so much better than anything I've had in the States. I wonder why that is."

"It's the milk," Naomi replied without thinking. "The Swiss cows lead a happy meadow life."

They laughed, but it was a friendly, kind sort of laughter, and Sean patted her shoulder.

"Of course. Only now I have this image of cows wandering into chocolate stores to be milked. Really crazy. You Europeans are really crazy."

"I'm not European." Again the words had popped out of her without taking a detour through her brain.

Interested, Sal leaned forward. "Really? Where are you from then? You live here though?"

"Yes, we do live here. Because of my father's work." She was telling them more than she'd meant to. Everything she said would lead to more questions, and ultimately to spilling her secret. "He's a banker. He works at a bank."

There. That was close enough to the truth but still far enough away.

"Aha." Sal was still gazing at her, curiosity making his dark eyes dance. "That makes sense. Being a banker in Switzerland. I understand."

"Jon needs new picks. I should go and get them, and put them in his little bowl." The guitar player, Jones, stretched and rose from his chair. "Man, that guy loses more of those things in one show than I do in an entire year." He walked off, a piece of cake in one hand.

"I wonder what made you write those lovely lyrics?" Sean was smiling at her. He had the gentlest smile she'd ever seen on a man;

it hovered between his mouth and his eyes like the dim glow of a candle on a stormy night.

"Just the music. I heard Jon on the radio and wanted to write for him." Naomi stuck her hands between her knees. "It seemed as if he was calling to me, and I had to answer." The memory of that moment made her face feel hot, and she hung her head to hide it. "I was angry at him. The song made me angry. But in a good way."

Toying with his coffee spoon, Sean waited for her to go on.

"It felt like a challenge. I don't know how else to say it. He was singing, and what he said needed an answer. So…I sat down and replied. Sort of."

"Aha. I think I know what you mean." There was no sarcasm in Sean's voice, no hint of making fun of her at all. "He has that power; he makes you want to listen, and respond." Putting down the spoon, Sean poured more coffee for himself. "When I first met him he was a young, starving songwriter in New York City. He walked up to the stage in that bar and began to sing, just like that, as if no one was listening. And the interesting thing was, they were all listening. That place was packed, noisy, when he started; but one verse into the first song, it was as quiet as a church. He has that talent, Jon does. He makes people notice him. He was made to be a star."

Naomi, watching him turn the cup between his hands, didn't reply for a while. Around her, around their table, the stage crew were moving toward the buffet, their part of the job done. There was a strange mix of tension and relaxation in the air of the room, as if flood and ebb tides were meeting and hovering on the cusp of a wave, uncertain about which way to go next.

She could feel that tension in the members of the band, and Sal, in the way they kept glancing at their watches, and how they started a sentence and then broke off and let it dwindle away, their minds racing ahead, counting down the minutes.

"It's not hard to see," Naomi said, her eyes on her hands. "He shines like a star."

Sal leaned his elbows on the table. "You know what totally knocks me out? The way you're taking all this." He nodded toward the door that led into the hallway. "You're a fan, aren't you? One of Jon's fangirls. And yet here you sit, totally relaxed, looking as if it doesn't matter. As if meeting a rock star is something you do every day. You were sitting on the stage next to Sean as if you'd been doing that all your life, and you, a young little thing…" He stopped, cleared his throat, and took a sip of coffee. "Anyway. I take it you and Jon have discussed how he'll use your lyrics and we can start negotiating a contract?"

He sounded like her father, and for an instant all the joy went out of her, thinking of her parents.

"I don't know," she said. "I told Jon he could use them. I wrote them for him, and if he likes them, they're his. I didn't really think about money and contracts."

"Bless you, darling." Sean, and he was laughing at her, shaking his head. "Don't let Sal walk all over you! You wrote those words. They'll always and forever be yours. You are entitled to your share."

There was movement in the doorway, a flash of silver, and they turned.

"Ah," Sal mumbled, glancing at his watch again. "He's fast today. I wonder why."

Naomi had to look twice.

It was Jon, and yet it was someone totally different. He was in his stage clothes, black pants and a flashy shirt embroidered with sequins or something similar, and it glittered with every movement, even with his breath. His hair was plastered into obedient waves, his face powdered, and he was wearing eyeliner. He stood tall, straight, like an effigy of himself, a glossy version of the real man, and it almost scared her.

"Fifteen minutes," Sally called, coming up behind him. "You want something, Jon?"

He shook his head. "Just a moment with Naomi, and then the band."

She followed him out into the hallway.

"I want you on the stage tonight," Jon said, touching her shoulder gently, wrapping his hand around it. "Will you be there? Will you watch me from the side of the stage? Sal and Russ will be there and watch out for you. I'd love for you to be there. It would make me feel as if I'm singing only for you."

"Yes, of course." As if he needed to ask.

"You don't have to be afraid. No one will see you. You'll be hidden by the curtains. No one will see that you're up there."

His hand fit perfectly around her shoulder.

"I'm not afraid." It was true; she'd never felt less afraid in her whole life. Everything around her—the flow of people, the sounds and smells, even Jon's made-up face, the tight timing—it all felt as if it was ordered by the beating of her heart, by the natural flow of her blood. She could surf on it as if it was her own special tide.

"You're amazing. You're so special, so very special." His lips brushed her brow, but he didn't kiss her. "I wish we could be alone somewhere, just you and me, and discover each other." He sighed. "I have a wonderful house in Malibu. It has a huge, incredibly wild garden. And there's a secret nook, a hidden arbor, with a bench. I love to sit there at dusk and watch the stars come out."

"The Secret Garden." She didn't dare touch him for fear of disturbing his perfection.

"Yes." Jon's fingers traveled down her bare arms until he caught her hands in his. "My secret garden, and you, my lovely, mysterious girl, you with me, there. And I'd sing to you while you lie in my arms. Under the stars, surrounded by jasmine and roses, just you and me, and the world far away."

Sally appeared in the door, looking their way, and Jon took a step to block her view.

"I wish I could make you come back to California with me. Don't you feel it, Naomi? Can't you feel how the universe has shifted, how the stars have aligned, how they're at last in the formation they were meant to be? I can feel it." He laid his arms around her. "I can feel that my feet are finally on the ground, I've touched earth. I'm home. I have the piece of my heart that was missing."

Carefully, very carefully, trying not to mess up his makeup, Naomi rose on her toes and planted the breeze of a kiss on his lips.

"I know what you mean," she replied, "I know exactly what you mean. It's such a surprise. Here you are, the great star, and you pick me. Of all the girls in the world, you pick me."

The words had spilled from her lips before she'd even thought them, and now she blushed and drew back, but Jon didn't let her. They stood, gazing into each other's eyes, lost in the moment.

The band filed out of the hospitality area and into their dressing room. Sean was last, and he touched Jon's arm in passing.

"Five minutes," he gently said, smiling at Naomi.

Jon, with another sigh, let her go. "I have to go. I have to go be a star. But remember, I'll be singing just for you." He turned to leave, but Naomi held on to him.

"Jon," she said, and he stopped. "I can still see you." Puzzled, he took a breath to ask, but she went on: "You're still you, you know. No amount of hair spray and makeup can change that. I'm still seeing you."

Chapter Twenty

FROM WHERE SHE stood she could catch glimpses of Fleur, Manon, and the others. All she had to do was take a tiny step forward and peek around the heavy black curtains, and she could watch them dance in their seats, crazy young women ready to storm the stage and devour their idol.

Jon, live onstage, was not what Naomi had expected. He didn't act like a rock star; there were no crazy antics, no outrageous demolishing of guitars or setting pianos on fire; there wasn't even any dancing or jumping around. Most of the time he just stood at the microphone and sang, playing one of his guitars, or when he took a break to talk to the audience, sitting on a bar stool that he dragged across the stage himself. There was a small table near Sean's keyboard that held a glass of water, a small towel, and the bowl of guitar picks, and that was it. The band was well dressed, all of them in jeans and shirts, nothing eccentric, nothing extravagant. The emphasis was on the music, and on Jon's voice.

He kept looking her way, every time he switched instruments, every time he ended a song and the applause flooded the hollow of the stadium; and when he had introduced the band and every member played a brief solo, he came over, grabbed her around the waist, and kissed her.

"I know what I missed," Jon whispered to her. "Now I know what I missed. There was this empty spot, and now it's filled. I was missing you!" And moved away before she could respond, before she could even catch the breath to do it.

And there he was, Jon Stone, singing "The River," bathed in blue and green light, whipping the song into a steamy beat, the guitar slung on his back, his hands around the microphone. Sean was standing at the keyboard hitting the keys, his shoulders moving with the rhythm, a bright smile on his face.

Fast, hard, the melody nearly drowned out by the drums, the song washed over the audience and all the way up the slopes of the mountains and into the starry night sky.

Jon let the last notes dwindle away on his guitar, the wide, foaming river now no more than a gentle trickle, a softly bubbling spring in some hidden forest nook.

His hand around the microphone again, he waited until the crowd had calmed down.

"I'm singing for a special person today," he said, "someone I've only just met and who has impacted my life like no one else before. Sometimes magic happens. I know, because it has just happened to me."

A sigh rose from the audience. It sounded like a gust of wind, like a breeze sweeping over the trees surrounding the stadium.

"So I'm sharing this special gift with you. I'm singing from the heart: from mine to yours, and to my magic."

The first chords of "Forever" came from the violins, a sweet ribbon of song that carried the words of promise and hope.

Sally, just behind Naomi, mumbled something about him going maudlin and how she hoped he'd collect himself before he started on "Wilted Love" or he'd go to pieces out there onstage. She didn't say it in a kind voice either.

Naomi pulled her shoulder blades together. It felt as if someone was standing there with a dagger, ready to push it into her spine.

"He'll do just fine," Sal replied, sounding impatient. "Let him do his thing. You know he'll be fine." And added, to Naomi, "Are you okay? Would you like me to get you a chair? It's a long time, standing through the entire show."

She laughed at him. "I'm fine! I couldn't sit if I tried, not with Jon rocking the place."

Sal's mouth twitched. "Right. I forgot how young you are." His hand came to rest on her shoulder in a brief squeeze before he pulled it back and sank it into his jeans pocket, grinning sheepishly.

THE concert was over much too soon.

Twenty-two songs they'd done, and three encores, before the audience let them leave the stage.

Sal gestured for Naomi to follow him back into the catacombs, where they waited for Jon to come down.

Sally was holding a bathrobe and a bottle of water, which she handed to Jon the moment he appeared. While he drank, she wrapped the bathrobe around him, rubbing his back.

"That was a great performance," she said, giving him a blinding smile. "Really great! Maybe your best in Europe so far."

"Yeah." His voice sounded gravely, tired. "I know." His eyes sought out Naomi. "It was easy tonight. I knew why I was singing." Reaching out to her, he caught Naomi's hand. "Give me ten minutes to get showered and changed, and then we can be off. There will be a party at the hotel, and I hope you'll join us."

"For a little while." It was so close to home. Any time she wanted to leave she could just walk out the door and get into a cab, or even walk.

"For a little while?" Jon's brow crinkled in dismay. "Only a little while?"

"Today, yes." She didn't want to discuss it, with Sally and Sal listening. "I have to go home soon. I'll be missed."

"If you're as grown up as you say you are, a short phone call should take care of that, right?" Sally quipped, her hair shining like a silver halo under the harsh glare of the neon overhead lights.

Naomi was still wondering how to respond when Jon said, "You are absolutely right. If you said you'd be home right after the show, then you should be. I'll take you; let me get cleaned up and then I'll take you."

"And the party?" She wanted to go. She wanted to be there when the band and Jon partied after a concert. "I'll go to the hotel with you and stay a bit, and then take a cab home. It's not..." Very far, she'd been on the verge of saying. "If it's okay with you," she said instead, and that sounded even worse, as if she was asking his permission.

"Of course!" Jon looked a mess. His hair, so beautifully coiffed before the show, hung in sticky, straggly strands around his face. Sweat had ruined the stage makeup, and his eyes were tired, exhausted. All the glamour was gone. All the vibrancy, the glory of being a star, melted away by the limelight. With another crooked smile he left them to enter the dressing room.

"Hurry, Jon," Sally called, turning away from them and toward the hospitality area, "the kid needs to go to school tomorrow."

Naomi felt her face turn hot. She raised her chin and looked after Sally, taking a deep breath, but Sal shook his head. He took her elbow and led her away.

The dressing room door was closed, and she didn't really feel like intruding.

"You can go inside if you want," Sal said. " He'll be sitting in front of the mirror now, taking off the makeup. He hates the stuff. But the stage lights make you look like a ghost without it. And we can't have that, can we?" A grin tugged at his mouth. "The girls need to see him at his best. Here, I'll knock for you." And did it, before she could respond.

The makeup artist opened the door to them, and Sal pushed her inside.

"Jon, I'll leave Naomi with you, if it's okay. Sally is showing her claws."

The door closed behind her. There she was: inside the sanctum, in the star's most private space.

And now, with his face wiped, he didn't look like a star at all.

Jon smiled at her through the mirror. He was still wrapped in the bathrobe, still holding the water bottle.

"So did you like it? Was it what you expected it to be?"

That made her smile. "No, it wasn't really how I expected it to be. I never thought that I'd be standing behind the curtain watching you perform. I thought I'd be down there with my friends, jumping and screaming just like them."

His eyes sparkled at her, and that took some of the tiredness out of his face. "You could have jumped and screamed where you were; I'd not have minded! I think though"—and he smirked at her, saying it—"if you had done that you'd never have heard the end of it from Sally. She can be catty, that one. She's very protective."

"Yes." It didn't feel right. It didn't feel right to be here, inside his dressing room, when in a moment he'd go into the shower and change, and he'd probably not care very much, or mind, if she saw him in a state of undress.

Naomi wondered how it was to live like that, always in public, always with people around to look after him and his needs. She sat on the edge of the couch, her hands clamped around her knees, and it seemed to her as if their lives weren't that different after all. In his own way Jon was as confined as she was, had to follow the same rigid protocol of security that she wanted to escape.

"That house I was telling you about," he said into her thoughts, "it's right on the beach. I often go for a walk at dawn, when no one is around and I have it all to myself, and watch the sun rise over the mountains. It's lovely, very serene. It has a roof garden, a decked space between the wings of the building, and from there you can see the ocean and the hills. I love that spot. I love to watch the sunset from there. It's a big house."

"And you live there all by yourself?" Displaced. For a moment her vision seemed to shift, and all she was seeing was a strange man, a tall, smiling, strange man, and it scared her. They were alone in the room, the door was tightly shut, and there was Jon, giving her a small, secret smile.

Naomi swallowed and moved her shoulders against the sudden prickle of unease.

"All by myself, yes. I have a housekeeper though." He shrugged. "And a couple of security people. They live in the driver's apartment over the garages. It's a sad necessity."

She'd read about it. There had been two sentences about the incident in the *Geneva Glam* article, just a brief mention. Suicides of fans were not the right subject for the glossy pages of a fashion magazine. She'd tried to picture it: a girl, a young woman much like her or Fleur, and she'd been so obsessed with the star that she'd chosen to die at his feet, cutting her own throat.

Naomi's hand wandered to her chest, feeling for the beat of her heart and the gentle pulsing in her carotid artery. There it was, the rhythm of life, just under her skin, warm and regular, reassuring.

"Yeah." Jon's gaze had followed her movement, and his eyes dulled with the memory. "Yeah, because of that."

Out on the street, on a public sidewalk too. She'd not only killed herself for unfulfilled love but had done it in public, with people around her to witness it. The disgrace, the shame was almost more than Naomi could imagine. Strangers, and they'd seen the life pump out of her, and watched her die on the pavement.

"Hey." Gentle, he said it so gently that she looked up, startled. "I'll jump in the shower now. Give me five minutes, okay? And then we can leave and return to the hotel. God, I'm so ready for a cold beer!"

And, picking up his street clothes, he vanished into the bathroom, closing the door firmly behind him.

Chapter Twenty-one

SEAN OPENED THE piano in the hotel bar without even asking. The keys came to life beneath his fingers, and before they'd even ordered drinks, Jones had his guitar out and was playing along.

They flocked around them, glasses in their hands, and sang or hummed along with the songs they'd just performed onstage, in front of thousands of listeners. There were a few other guests in the bar, but they watched from afar, never intruding, applauding when one song ended, before they began a new one.

Jon didn't take part in it. He was sitting beside her on one of the couches, watching his band, smiling at their antics, holding her hand in his.

"I can't sing now," he said. "I'm all used up for today. With you there I gave it my all tonight. Had to impress you, so you'd come back tomorrow."

Naomi looked at their entwined fingers: his, long, strong; hers small and thin compared to them. "You don't have to impress me. That's not how it works."

That made him smile. "How does it work then? You said you could still see me, when I was ready to go onstage and was all dolled up. Which part of me do you prefer?"

The question was so silly and needy, Naomi had to bite her lips.

"You're you," she replied. "I can't chop you up into parts. You're Jon, all of you. All that makeup and the terrible shirt, they don't hide who you really are." She had to catch her breath. The situation was too strange. "I'll have to leave in a minute. It's almost midnight."

"My Cinderella. Will you leave me a shoe then, so I can find you tomorrow?"

It was funny, but even a line that was beyond ridiculous sounded nice when Jon Stone said it.

"You won't need my shoe. I'll meet you. Promise."

HE took her home in the limo, and when they had arrived, Jon glanced up at the imposing façade.

"This is just across from where we stood this morning, on the promenade."

"Yes." It was hard to believe that it had only been hours ago.

"I'll wait for you over there." Jon pointed at the kiosk. "Tomorrow morning. You'll come? You'll have breakfast with me and the guys? And then you can show me Geneva. We'll spend the day, and then..."

"Yes." Her heart was beating fast and hard. "Yes, I'll meet you."

But when he tried to kiss her, take her hand, she shied away, suddenly afraid, suddenly awkward. "Someone might see. Not here."

"Oh, okay." Pushing his hands into his pockets, he took a step away from her, smiling. "I understand."

The car was waiting, the driver patiently behind the wheel, looking away from them.

"Naomi." Coming from Jon, spoken with Jon's voice, her name sounded like the wind stroking flowers, even to her. It was a sound she wanted to hear forever and ever. "I'll be there. I'll wait for you."

She didn't want to go; she didn't want to return to her old, rigid life, to the company of her parents, who'd certainly still be up waiting for her, waiting to question her on where she'd been, with whom, and how it had been. They'd do it lovingly, even try to show some interest, but she knew the only thing that mattered to them was her safety.

"Do you really have a centerfold of me in your room? Sally said you do."

That made her stop, her hand on the door. "No. I don't." The thought made her want to giggle. "I did have the *Geneva Glam* article, but..." She hesitated. "I fell asleep on the page with your picture. And now it's all rumpled."

"You don't need it anymore. You have the real thing now." He said it so softly, so gently, that she wanted to turn and go back with him, run away with just her purse and leave everything else behind.

"I know. Good night." It was so hard; it was the hardest thing she'd ever done, walking through that entrance and away from him.

HER parents were in the library, as always, for a last sip of brandy, a last quiet half hour before they went to bed.

Naomi stopped in the door.

"I'm back," she said, and Olaf looked up from his book.

"Did you have a good time? I heard a limousine pulling away just now. Was that Fleur's? I'm glad they brought you safely back home."

"Yes, and we loved it! We're going again tomorrow. There's a second show." It wasn't really a lie; she would be at the show, and she hadn't said with whom. Technically, it wasn't a lie.

Lucia pursed her lips. "Really? You do know that Seth will be here next weekend. There's a lot to talk about, and a lot to get ready."

"No worries, Mama. We'll get everything ready. But tomorrow… we have plans for tomorrow! We want to go shopping in the morning, and have lunch, and then we'll hang out at Fleur's place until we go to the show. Please? I promise to be here all next week and do whatever you want me to." Pleading, like a kid. Bargaining, the way she'd learned to do growing up as an only child, and the heir.

"Well, I guess that will be good enough. I always feel so much better when I know you're with Fleur. Her father is a very careful man, and he watches his daughter closely. No nonsense happening there." Olaf returned to his book, but Lucia was gazing at her with a wrinkled brow, and her lips hadn't relaxed yet.

"I won't be here all day. And there's a good chance I'll sleep over at Fleur's. We want to party after the show." There. She'd laid down her plan, and so far there was no opposition.

"All right, miss." Strangely, it was Lucia who seemed more interested than her father, and that was very unusual. "I expect you to call tomorrow night, when you're at Fleur's, after the show. And I expect you back for breakfast on Monday morning. I'll take you up on that nothing else for the entire week in exchange for this romp. Are we clear?"

"Yes, Mama." It was difficult to talk past the hard, sharp-edged lump in her throat. Eighteen. Not a child, not a grown-up; she was stuck somewhere in between, where everyone else treated her as an adult, and at home, with her own family, she was a schoolgirl. "I'm off to bed. It was a long day."

But Lucia followed Naomi into her room, closing the door behind her and leaning against it.

"So tell me. I want to hear about that meeting, and leave nothing out."

Naomi sat down on the corner of her bed. "Nothing. We had coffee on the hotel terrace, and Fleur was there, and they said they wanted to use the lyrics and we should be talking about contracts." She pulled up her shoulders. "Nothing has been decided yet. There wasn't a lot of time. Mr. Stone had to go to the rehearsal, and everyone had to go with him. We went to the show. It was great! We liked it, and we want to go again."

Even at this time of day, close to midnight, her mother was impeccable in a dark-blue silk dress and matching sapphire earrings. Not a hair was out of place, the makeup perfect. It made Naomi think of Jon and his glossy stage version, and that made her wonder if this would be expected of her too as Seth's wife.

"So are you meeting those people again? Did you really get to meet Jon Stone himself? That star? Did you get an autograph?" A very faint blush crept onto Lucia's face, but it was a blush nevertheless.

"Mama…" It was hard not to giggle. "You like him!"

"He's a good-looking young man, and some of his songs are very nice. Not that river one, mind you. That's way too wild for me." Lucia came over and sat down beside Naomi. "So did you get to talk to him?"

"Yes." What to say? It hadn't really been talking. "We talked, and we'll talk again tomorrow. I'm meeting him for lunch. Only…I didn't want to say earlier…"

"I see."

They sat, mother and daughter, thinking, listening to the silence.

"I envy you a bit." The diamonds on Lucia's finger threw radiant rainbows when she moved her hands to fold them in her lap. "I had nearly forgotten how it is to be young and charmed by a singer. I used to dream of meeting my idol, of running into him; I even made up a scenario where he'd be in Positano on vacation, incognito of course, and I'd recognize him. We'd spend a few glorious days together, wandering on the beach or in the orchards, and I'd show him the olive groves and the chapel on the mountain." She smiled, taking Naomi's hand. "And then he'd leave, return to his life, and all I'd have would be sweet memories."

"Who was it?"

"What?" Lucia let go of her to smooth her skirt.

"Your idol, who was he?" It was strange, sharing these dreams with her mother; and Naomi wished they had hot chocolate and cookies, and that they could snuggle up on her bed and exchange fantasies. But Lucia rose, once again herself.

"Nobody you know," she replied, "an Italian opera singer. And it was a long time ago. I think he's still around, but retired. Anyway. If you have a date with Fleur and your Jon Stone tomorrow, you better get some sleep. It's late. I have to be at university early too. Good night, sweetheart."

It didn't feel right. It didn't feel right to lie to her mother, to keep things from her that seemed so good, so exciting, like being on the stage, getting a kiss from Jon, and knowing she'd meet him again the next day.

But all Naomi said was "Good night, Mama. Thank you for trusting me."

Her hand on the doorknob, Lucia gave her a small smile. "Well, you did have a really good argument, my dear. It's true; if we think you're old enough to marry, you should also be old enough to know right from wrong, bad from good." The smile widened into something suspiciously like a grin. "But I think I prefer not to discuss this with your father. I'm not sure he'd understand."

FLEUR was still up.

"What?" she said, breathless. "What was that all about today? I want to hear every little detail, and don't you think you'll get away with leaving anything out, missy. I saw you up there, on the stage.

When Jon took that break and went over to you and kissed you, I saw that! And now I want to know why Jon Stone would go and do that and onstage, too!"

Naomi sighed. It was such a long, convoluted story, and she was so tired. "I promise I'll tell you everything. But Fleur, first I need your help. Will you help me?" She went on to tell her about the lyrics, her promise to Jon to meet him the next day and how she needed a cover, and how she had told her parents she'd be with Fleur.

"But you aren't going to be with me, right? You're going to hang out with Jon." Fleur, cutting to the heart of the matter, as always.

"Yes. And during the show. And…maybe after. Maybe for the night. And breakfast." There, she'd said it, and the hand holding the phone felt sweaty.

"Okay…" Fleur hesitated, and that was saying something. Fleur was never out of words. "I get it. You're having a steamy affair with a rock star. You're a groupie! You're rocking the boat before you get engaged to your staid, boring Seth! Good for you, Naomi!" Her laughter dripped through the phone like tiny beads of honey. "I can do that for you! I'll lie until my tongue falls off if it's for a reason as good as this one!"

"I love you. You're a wonderful friend, Fleur." Naomi wanted to hug her for understanding and accepting so easily.

"Hey, Naomi. Do you think you can get him to autograph my album for me?" Breathless, she sounded breathless with excitement.

"Sure. I think that will be easy. He's very, very nice, you know."

"Man. You and Jon Stone. You, the quiet one, and Jon Stone! My dad will be tickled to death! He's always saying to watch you, that you'd surprise us all yet. And here you go! This is way crazy! Of all the girls in the world, Jon Stone picks you. Go figure."

"Yes."

And said like that, it was indeed the greatest miracle in the universe.

Chapter Twenty-two

THE RED DRESS.

She hadn't worn it before, but this seemed like the right day for it. Standing in front of her mirror, Naomi inspected her image: a young girl with long, black hair neatly tied into a ponytail, wearing a sleeveless red dress and flat sandals, with a purse that was a little too big, but she didn't want to leave her journal behind.

There was nothing out of the ordinary: She was just another girl. No one in Geneva would even notice her. No one would look twice.

Her heart light, her feet twitching to be gone, she ran down the stairs to the lobby, disregarding the elevator and the doorman's shout of warning when she shot out of the building and right across the road to the promenade.

For an instant, her heart beating like a crazy machine, it occurred to her that Jon might have changed his mind, that he might not even show up; and what then, what would she then do with her freedom and the day?

But he was there.

He stood near the kiosk, looking her way, and when he saw her he opened his arms.

This time she flew into them.

THEY walked through the old part of town. She took him to her favorite chocolatier when Jon confessed that he loved Swiss chocolate. Naomi made him taste the marzipan and the chocolate truffles, and laughed when he started to buy boxes of them.

"I want you to come to LA with me," Jon said after she'd made him try the marzipan. "I want you to come and stay with me."

She nearly choked on her bite of chocolate, but he was looking at her, and there was no trace of anything but sincerity.

"I really want that, Naomi. I want to have you in my life forever and ever."

"But you don't even know me! We've only just met!" It was the best she could come up with.

"I don't think so. I feel like I've known you all my life, as if you've always somehow been there, but I couldn't see you because I didn't turn, or wake up, or speak fast enough. It feels as if you are there in every melody I ever wrote, in every song I ever sung. It's always been about you!"

Naomi didn't know what to say. It was so unreal: Here was this hot, young rock star in jeans and a shirt, the sleeves rolled up to show nicely shaped, tan arms; and he was pouring his attention on her as if she was the only girl in the world.

"But Jon."

"No, it's true." He didn't seem to mind that the store owner was listening. "I know what I feel. It's like this: I've always had this feeling that there should be more, something deeper, something that just felt right. And the moment you walked into that hotel lobby, that moment when I first saw you, I knew it was you. Even before I knew you were the girl with the lyrics."

"But, Jon," she repeated, and he shook his head.

"I know, you have doubts, you're afraid, you don't know me yet. But look at me, Naomi, and tell me you don't feel the same."

There they were: strangers, and yet she had to admit that it indeed felt that way; that yes, she was ready to run away with him.

"Jon." Naomi was holding a truffle, ready to pop it into her mouth. "I can't just run off with you! You're leaving Geneva tomorrow, and…"

"So come with me! Come with me on the rest of the tour, and then we'll be off to LA, and my house in Malibu. We'll walk on the beach, you and I, and explore the garden." He stopped to think for a moment. "Are you afraid? I'm quite wealthy; I can give you anything you desire, I can provide for a…"

She could hear the word as if it had escaped on the wings of the breath he'd just exhaled, as if it had been there, hovering, ready to be spoken; and no degree of silence could keep it unsaid.

Wife…he'd been ready to say it, she was sure of it. How different it felt, how amazingly, stunningly different it felt. The prospect of

being Jon's wife! Her heart agreed; it was beating in a rapid rhythm.
"No more marzipan for you," Naomi said, and he laughed.

THIS time when they reached the venue and Sal asked if Jon wanted to give autographs, she pointed out Fleur to him and asked him to make sure and sign her album.

"Your friend?" Jon held out his hand to Sally, who put a tour book in it without even asking. "I have something better then." With a wink and a grin he sauntered over to the waiting group and picked out Fleur.

From where she was standing with Sal and Sally, Naomi couldn't hear what he was saying to her, but she could hear Fleur laugh, surprised, delighted, and it made her happy.

"Nice," Sally muttered, "really nice. Now he's got them all worked up because he's being extra attentive to that girl. A friend of yours, I take it?"

"Yes, a friend of mine. And she's a very nice girl." It had come out rather catty, and it made Sal cough on his cigarette. "She's kind to everyone, even people she doesn't know."

Sally's eyebrows shot up and vanished under her bangs. "Hey, it's my job to protect Jon."

"Funny," Naomi shot back, "I thought he had security people for that."

The sad part was that she actually liked Sally. Naomi liked that she was so fiercely loyal, that she really cared about Jon. She could see herself and Sally being friends, going out for lunch, shopping, singing along side by side during a concert, and going for walks along the beach. But here she was, marching away into the venue without glancing back at either Jon or Sal.

"Let it go." Sal lit another cigarette. "She cares for Jon. She cares a bit more than is good for her. There was a time when they were nearly an item, but it never happened. When Jon was after her she gave him the cold shoulder, and when she relented he'd already turned away. It wasn't meant to be. Those two, they were not meant to be." He shrugged. "For many reasons it might have been an ideal match. Her father owns the record company, and she's one clever cookie. Those two as a couple would have been a great thing. I think Sally regrets it a lot."

Breathing was hard. Something was squeezing her heart.

"I know how that feels." It took some effort to get those words spoken. "I know how it is when everyone thinks you should marry someone because it would make everything so much easier for them all, except they never stop to ask how you feel about it. They never ask if you're in love, or if you even want to get married, or if you have other plans, plans of your own. They just assume you think the same way, and you want the same thing. Only you don't."

The cigarette forgotten, Sal was staring at her.

"I'm sorry." She could feel blood rising to her face. "I didn't mean…I was trying to say…"

"Yeah." Sal tossed away his cigarette. "I get what you're saying. You're having a little fling with Jon before you get married and settle down."

"No! That's not what I meant," Naomi said, but Sal waved her away.

"It's okay, kiddo. Whatever works for you. I'm glad you and Jon get along so well; it will make working together in the future so much easier. He wants more songs from you; you do realize that?"

"Oh yes." And they were all there, those songs, patiently floating just below the surface, wisps of rhyme, fragrances of words. It seemed to her that they were multiplying, as if since the first meeting with Jon they were calling to other lyrics, to those hidden deeper inside, to come, come; they could see the light, and their purpose.

Jon was coming back. There was an easy swing in his steps, and his face was lit up with a smile.

"That friend of yours, she's such an imp! She told me to say hello to you, and could you bring her backstage? Quite clever! So do you want to? Bring her in?"

She didn't know what to say. The star, and he was asking her permission to bring someone into his own private space.

"Come on, let the chick in." It was Sally, standing in the backstage entrance. "Be good, Jon. Give her something to remember for the rest of her life."

Naomi, gazing at Sally, had the feeling that there had been some tears. Her dark eye makeup wasn't quite as immaculate as it had been earlier.

"Okay then." Jon was watching her too; his tone was very thoughtful. "Sally, will you go and bring her in? Take security with you though. I'll be in my dressing room until the band is ready. Someone call me." He took Naomi's hand as if it was the most normal thing in the world and pulled her inside with him.

"I'LL wait for Fleur," Naomi said, and Jon nodded.

He would be in his dressing room if she needed him, he told her. Everything was different now. She was his responsibility; he cared about her safety, no harm could come to her, ever. Hesitating in the doorway, he laid his arms around her and pulled her into an embrace.

"Tonight I'll go onstage and sing my heart out for you. I can't wait for the show to be over; and you and me, my sweet Naomi, we'll have the whole night to discover each other. I'm the luckiest man in the world. The loveliest girl in the world wants me."

That was how Fleur found them, their arms wrapped around each other, smiling, whispering, secret lovers in a forlorn underground hallway.

Jon, letting go of Naomi, threw Fleur a wink and closed the door, leaving Naomi alone with her.

"So," Naomi said. Her hands felt shaky. "Here we are. Would you like some coffee? Cake?"

"Uh-huh." Fleur stood there, the tour book and her purse in front of her body like a shield, chewing on her gum with verve. "You know, I thought you were kidding, and that my eyes had lied. I was really ready to believe that. And then there's Jon Stone, coming right up to me, freaking picking me out in that group of crazies and writes this on the tour book he's brought along, for me!" She held it out to Naomi. "Seriously? And what did I see just now? Have you moved on from holding hands to public groping? In one day? Kill me now, Naomi Carlsson, you sly little rat!"

Jon had signed the tour book and added, "For Fleur, with love, it's a pleasure to meet you!"

From the other end of the hallway, from the hospitality area, Sally was coming toward them. A backstage pass on a lanyard was dangling from her hand.

"Here." She held it out to Fleur. "You'll need this. Have fun!" And gave Naomi a twinkle of a smile. "If you want anything, you know where to find me. I'll go take care of the promoters and the press now. See ya!" Her silver-blond ponytail bobbed merrily as she walked away, and the short polka-dot skirt she was wearing swung with her steps. Sally had a love for red, and for polka dots; that much was clear.

"Who's she?" Fleur asked, pointing at Sally's retreating back with her chin. "The girlfriend?" And then laughed at her own question. "Stupid. Of course not! You've slipped into that role, and within one day, it seems. Wow, do you really think he fell in love with those lyrics you sent him and then, seeing you, with the entire package? Not that it's hard to imagine. You always were the prettiest of us all."

"I'm not..." His girlfriend. She had meant to say that, but it seemed like a lie. "Come on," Naomi said instead, "let's get some coffee. The band will be hanging out in hospitality now, just before the show. I'll introduce you to Sean and the others. It will take a while until Jon is ready." She took the lanyard from Fleur's unresisting hand and slipped it over her head. "And wear this. Security can get very strict if they see you without it backstage."

Listening to her own words, listening to how calmly she spoke them, she had to smile: It was almost as if she'd become part of Jon's life overnight, as if everything he'd said had become true, because it had been his wish.

Chapter Twenty-three

FLEUR DIDN'T WANT to watch the concert from behind the curtain.

"Are you crazy?" she asked. "I don't want to hide here, and not be able to scream and cheer. And after the show, what? You and your lover will be off to a romantic dinner and then…Well, yes. And I'll be all alone with these people. No, I'm bowing out, and I'll spend the evening as a mere fan."

They were sitting at a table in hospitality, cradling coffee mugs, watching people come and go, absorbing the special, unique atmosphere.

"I could get used to this," Fleur said, and sighed. "It's a lot like backstage at a fashion show, only without all those super nervous girls and the stench of hair spray. And of course there aren't any fabulous gowns."

Sally appeared in the open doorway, a clipboard in her hand, glancing at her watch. "Fifteen minutes," she called, and Sean got up from his chair. He stretched, yawned, and flexed his fingers.

"Time to rock the house! Are you coming, Naomi?"

As if she'd always been there, as if she was part of it all.

"Just a minute, Sean," she replied. It felt so good. It made her feel safe, free, happy, all of those at once.

"Do you believe this? Do you really think you can fall in love in one day?" Fleur was leaning back in her chair, looking like a model herself with her long, slim legs and her golden mane.

"I don't know." Naomi pushed away her mug. "I thought it was… you know, a girl crush, rock star adoration, the normal stuff. But the moment I met Jon for real, something happened. He sat there in his dark corner of the lobby, and all I could see was the most wonderful man in the world. It had nothing to do with him being a star." She tried a smile, but she knew it came out more like a crooked grin. "He stood, and the way he was looking at me, the way he almost opened his arms to me…" Babbling, she was babbling, and it was the most embarrassing thing ever. "I don't know, Fleur. I can't explain it! It just felt as if suddenly everything was clear and easy."

"You're not supposed to feel like that at our age, you know." Fleur unwrapped another stick of gum and popped it into her mouth. "You should be like, oh my God, Jon Stone kissed me, and now I'm never going to wash my face again! And then faint a bit, or whatever. But no, not you. You go straight from one kiss to eternal love, and you're as cool as a cucumber about the whole thing when you should have called me so we could have talked about it all night."

"I never said that! I never said anything about eternal love." Naomi poked her arm. "And I did call you, and we did talk for quite a while. And you said you'd cover for me, for tonight!"

"Yeah, sure I will! Stop fretting! Jeez, you make me think he's your first affair ever! Get a grip!" There was no response, which made Fleur look up.

"Your first affair," she repeated, as if she wanted to make sure of the reaction, but none came. "Seriously, Naomi? Come on. Tell me I'm imagining things! You can't really be telling me that if Jon hadn't walked into your life, that you would have gone into marriage as a… well…a virgin bride? Seriously? Come on!"

"I'm not like you!" Naomi's face was burning. "My father isn't a generous, liberal, modern fashion designer! My father would drag me back to Canada and lock me up if he knew about this, and I'm not even talking about…you know. He'd rip into me for just being here right now."

Fleur put her hand on Naomi's. "Hon, I know. Stop worrying. I was just so surprised! I mean, we all know you're the good kid, the one who never gets into trouble, who wouldn't even touch a cigarette let alone some weed. You deserve this! And I'll help."

There was a movement in the doorway, and they both looked up. Fleur gasped, then choked on her gum.

"Holy shit," she hissed, and that made Naomi laugh. It blew away the tension of the moment.

Jon was once again the glittery effigy of himself, this time in blue.

"Are you ready?" he called, "Can we start?"

"Is he asking you if he can start the show?" Fleur pinched Naomi's arm, whispering. "Jon Stone is asking you if you're ready?"

"Sounds like it, yes." Excitement bubbled in her stomach. Last night had been dreamlike; she'd waded through it like a puppet, but this felt as real as anything she knew.

"I'll be in the band's dressing room." Jon came over, still fiddling with his cuff links, and bent down to plant a kiss on her hair. "Five minutes, and we're off." His hand touched her shoulder in a brief caress.

"I'll take Fleur to her seat." Naomi rose.

AT home. Her heart was singing a new song, one of homecoming and peace among all the turmoil, one of feeling like herself, like a whole human being.

"Take security and Sally, babe." Jon threw her a kiss on his way out,.

"Boy." Fleur gathered up her purse and the tour book. "Wow. Look at him! Isn't he just the most perfect being ever? The way he looks, and how nice and considerate he is, and that voice, and his music..."

Naomi, laughing, shook her head. "Now who's the fangirl, Fleur?"

"Yeah, me. Count me in. I'm a fangirl."

Naomi took her as far as the security line that separated the backstage area from the auditorium. Sally was with them. She smiled and seemed happier than before. She even waved Fleur away and told her she could keep the backstage pass if she wanted, it was okay, and yes, it would make a lovely souvenir.

Together, she and Sally watched how Fleur was escorted to her seat by a security guard and how she proudly showed Manon and Giselle her autograph. For a moment Naomi felt fear constrict her breath, thinking of how one of them might spill her secret. She didn't doubt for a moment that Olaf would have her shipped back to Canada, tightly observed and escorted by bodyguards, unable to run or communicate. He'd do it lovingly, explaining to her that she was just a child, one that needed to be watched day and night, and she didn't know what was good for her.

"Come on." Sally was tapping her shoulder. "Let's go. I'm sure Jon is waiting for you, and he'll flip if you aren't there before he goes onstage."

IT was different this time. It felt as if she'd done it a million times before, as if this was where she belonged, and the people around her were old friends.

She was there when the band filed past on their way to the stage, and every one of them gave her a smile, a wink, or touched her arm, much like touching a mascot.

Jon was last. He stood beside her, his arm around her, waiting until the band had played the intro and it was time for him to go. Russ was there, holding the guitar and a pick, ready to hand them over to Jon.

"Not too many encores tonight," Jon said to Sal. "We have plans, and I want to be gone right after the concert."

"There's a party." Sal's brow crinkled. "There will be some of the promoters. They'll want to meet you."

"Okay then, ten minutes." His grip on Naomi's waist tightened. "But then we're off. Tomorrow morning we leave, and there are a few things that need to be put in order before that."

"Put in order?" The crease on Sal's brow deepened. "What are you talking about?"

"Not now."

He was drifting away; Naomi could feel it in the tension building in his stance, in the way his body was moving when the rhythm picked up and the music got louder.

Jon nodded, and Russ held out the guitar.

Naomi stepped away from him. His attention was moving away from her, from everything around them. It was running up those steps ahead of him, taking him to where the music was. Formidable, that's how he looked, formidable and eternal, a demigod come to walk among the mortals, someone who lived in other spheres.

That image lasted only for heartbeat, then he was Jon again, and she was in his arms.

"Two hours," he said softly so only she could hear. "And we'll be alone, and you'll be mine."

"Yes."

His eyes sparkled at her. "Come on then, my sweet fangirl; let's bring down the house."

HE sang with verve, with abandon, throwing his songs into the starlit sky, breathing in the applause, giving his music to the audience as if it was a blanket of love on a frosty winter night. With love, he sang, with the utter certainty that he was giving them the best part of his soul. His eyes kept straying to Naomi. She was once again at the side of the stage, hidden by the curtain, with Sally and Russ and Sal, a part of their family now. A couple of times she peeked down at her friends, dancing and singing just like the night before, and had to smile: Now she really was on the other side, on the inside; and with Fleur having been there and seen it all, she had the verification.

Jon was singing "Wilted Love" again, and just like the night before, the sad bitterness of the lyrics made her want to weep.

She remembered hearing it for the first time when they had been hanging out at Fleur's swimming pool, and how she'd hid her face from the others. Not now though; there was no need to hide. There was nothing left of the sadness and regret. She wondered what had made him write it, wondered why he thought he needed her lyrics; his were perfect. She could never have written anything like the disappointment and loneliness in the simple, stark lines he had chosen.

The song taunted her: it made her want to respond, just like "The River" had made her sit down and write "The Secret Garden."

Here he was, singing about a love that was as dead as leaves in late November. There was no way to revive it, no way to rescue it. The door was closed, the sound of it falling shut, final.

Words were forming in her head; they were dancing, falling into place, bringing the trace of a melody with them, as always.

Naomi whispered them under her breath, whispered them toward Jon and his song of a million good-byes, and they fluttered like little rainbows of hope and love.

Almost as if he could hear her, as if he could see those words surround him, Jon turned to her and smiled. His dirge turned into a swift and cheerful wave, a last farewell to what had hurt and abandoned him, and he swung into the next song, "Statue of Liberty," the ode to his hometown. The band followed, giving the noises of New York City a melody.

Naomi sang along, dreaming of going to New York someday, of walking along the avenues and down Broadway, and by her side, walking with her, showing her the town, would be Jon.

And she would be free.

Chapter Twenty-four

HE TOOK HER hand and led her away from the party, and she came willingly.

When they'd reached the elevators, Jon stopped and asked, "Will you come to my room?"

Swallowing against her fear, Naomi nodded.

In the elevator, alone, she whispered, "It's only…I've never done this before. So if I'm clumsy or anything…"

Jon kissed her into silence. "Don't be afraid. There's nothing to be afraid of. You do want to though?"

"Yes!"

He smiled at her vehemence and repeated, "Don't be afraid. I promise, there's nothing to be afraid of."

And there wasn't. It wasn't scary or awkward for a moment.

Lying in his arms, much later, Naomi recalled Giselle talking about her latest affair, how she had made fun of it and described how she and her lover had started fighting and how she'd stalked out of the room, leaving him there on the bed, naked, unsatisfied, shouting names after her.

Jon, though, was singing "The Secret Garden" to her. Very softly, his lips close to her ear, he sang the words she'd written, but with his melody. Dawn was stretching its fingers into the night sky; they'd made love and talked all night.

Drowsy, she listened to him telling her he loved her, that he wanted her to come away with him, come to California, and live with him in his house on the beach. She would be his, forever and ever, and they'd lead a life of bliss and joy.

She could imagine it: a large bedroom, the doors to the roof garden open to let in the sea breeze and the rustle of the palm trees. And he'd be there, Jon, lying close to her, his breath stroking her face, his arms holding her tight; and together they'd watch the dawn, just like now. They'd get up and have coffee, and then walk through the garden and out onto the beach as the sun rose over the hills. She'd search for amber and pretty stones, and there would be no one else: only Jon and Naomi, together, forever.

"I love you," Jon said again, kissing her shoulder. "I want you in my life. I can't imagine life without you anymore. Come with me."

She knew she couldn't, and she didn't know how to tell him.

"Life without you would be meaningless." Jon sat up when she left the bed, the sheet wrapped around her. "I can't imagine how I'd go on alone. You're so lovely, so dazzling. Please come with me, Naomi. I promise, you'll not want for anything. I'll take care of you; you'll live like a princess."

"I can't." There, at least she'd managed to say it.

"Why not? Tell me why not. I'm sure there's nothing that I can't take care of. Come with me."

He was so beautiful, sitting there in bed, against the headboard.

"And please come back to bed. Please?"

"You can't help me, Jon." The idea alone made her knees shake with terror.

Jon, he'd show up at their door, and her father would be there to open it.

Jon, impetuous, stormy, would ask for her, no, would demand her; and Olaf would tear into her room, shouting that he wanted an explanation, and right now. A fight between Olaf and Jon was the worst possible image ever. The house would explode, she knew it; the building would explode into dust and debris if those two clashed. It would be like a battle between gods, an earthquake of tempers.

He held up the blanket for her when she crept back into bed, and into his arms.

Safe; she felt so safe in his embrace. She could close her eyes and know no harm would ever come to her as long as Jon was there.

"I can't go away with you now, Jon." There, and that was as close to the truth as she could get. "I need a few days. I need to get a few things sorted out before I can go."

"What is it? Can I help? I'm willing to help, Naomi. Don't lock me out."

Mirth bubbled up in her at that thought. "No, you can't help.

I need to get my passport, and it's locked up in the safe…" again talking too much. "I'll think of something. Don't worry, Jon."

"In the safe…" he began, and she knew he'd ask and ask until she told him everything.

Kissing him, blowing soft kisses on his lips, Naomi said, "I want to go away with you. I love you, Jon. But it can't be tomorrow. You'll have to trust me."

"Meet me in Amsterdam then. I'll have Sal get you a ticket, money, whatever you need. Come to Amsterdam!" His embrace tightened. "Promise to meet me in Amsterdam!"

"I promise to try and meet you there. But if I can't make it, if it takes longer…" She was on her back, and he was looming over her, ready to kiss her again. "I'll follow you anywhere, my beloved. If it's not Amsterdam, it will be California. I love you, Jon."

The words had left her lips on a breezy ribbon of truth. Naomi was quite sure that nothing ever before had felt that easy to say.

"I love you," she repeated, just to hear them again. "I love you."

And she let him take her away from herself.

IN the bright light of morning, in the hotel lobby, everything they'd said and done during the silence of the night seemed blown away.

Standing among the suitcases, the reality of loss crashed over her head like a huge wave of salty water, it hurt that badly in her eyes and chest. Jon was there, holding her hands as if he never wanted to let go, looking at her as if he knew this was the end.

Promise, he kept repeating, promise, promise; and she did, even though she had no idea how she was going to do it, how she was going to get Olaf to hand over her passport. It was all she needed to run away. She had money, and she had a place to run to, a safe haven at last, to run and hide, and escape her fate.

Something in Jon's eyes told her that he could see her sadness, could see that there was a good chance that she wouldn't be able to make it, and it broke her heart.

"I promise, Jon," Naomi said. "I really, really promise to try." Her mind, racing ahead, saw her hiring someone to break into the safe, saw her running from the police, ridiculous, wild portraits of desperation that would never work. She would have to be wily, and a very good liar, to get her passport without Olaf becoming suspicious.

Anger at her father, at her family, rose in her chest like acid; and she leaned her head against Jon's chest to hide it.

"Baby." A sigh, a dollop of sadness, and it added to her desperation.

Sal was coming toward them holding a big envelope that he handed to Jon.

"Here." Gently, he disentangled himself from her embrace. "Naomi, look. Money. A plane ticket. The name and address of our Amsterdam hotel. My phone number. My Malibu address. Please come. Please come."

"Jon." It was Sal, glancing at his watch.

The plane was waiting, she knew it, and she couldn't bear to see him leave.

"I have to go." Out on the curb, right next to the bus, Jon took her face between his hands and kissed her again. "I hate to leave you like this. You can't begin to imagine how much. I wish I could stay with you, stay until you're ready to leave with me. Or stay forever, if this is where you want to live. I love you. I need you in my life, forever and ever." A small laugh escaped him. "To think, two days with you and my whole life is upside down. I'd give up everything for you: the music, the success, even my life. Please. Come."

All the blood had left her head, had dropped to her feet, making them heavy, unable to move, and her lips unable to speak. Clasping the envelope to her chest, she managed a faded "Good-bye," but that was all. The sorrow was too deep, too overwhelming.

"Jon, the plane." Sal, his voice sounding pained, regretful.

Jon let go of her hands. It was as if she was drifting away from him, as if an ocean was ripping them apart; and all she could do was watch as he sailed away to distant shores, to faraway places, and she was left behind, a captive of the mountains and her father's plans.

From the front steps of the hotel, she watched the bus pull away, and it seemed as if it was dragging away her will to live in its wake.

She was alone again, lonely. The heavy cape of sorrow sank onto her shoulders as she slowly made her way back home, and into her golden cage.

LUCIA was there when Naomi unlocked the door to the apartment, standing in the hall, next to the phone, a cup of coffee in her hand, the saucer in the other. She'd never drink from a mug, her mother. It was always fine bone china, and part of a set for at least twenty-four.

"Well," she greeted Naomi, "and here you are. A bit late for breakfast though."

"I'm sorry. It was late last night. We slept in. But here I am now!" It sounded like fake cheerfulness even to her own ears.

Lucia didn't respond but returned to the dining room to get a refill of coffee. "I heard the show last night was amazing. Sold out too!" She held out the coffeepot to Naomi, who shook her head. "So what became of that contest, and your lyrics? Did you talk to Jon again?"

"Yes." Naomi rubbed her eyes. It was too hard. "He wants them. His lawyers will be in touch with the contracts. I guess Daddy should take care of that for me."

A smile appeared on Lucia's face. "Or Seth! You're marrying a lawyer, after all!"

"Right." She wanted to be alone in a dark, small nook where she could cry her heart out and no one would bother her.

"He's coming early, Seth. He called last night and said he'd be here on Thursday instead of Friday. He wants a day to get over the jet lag before the ball."

"Cool." She couldn't even think of Seth, or the ball, or her old, normal life. Everything was different now, and she wanted it that way. "I'm so tired. I think I'll take a shower and then take a nap. Will you be back for lunch, Mama?"

"What's that in that envelope?" Lucia pointed, and that made Naomi realize that she was still holding it, still pressing it to her chest.

"Oh, nothing. Some music sheets Jon gave me, with tunes he

hasn't found lyrics for yet. He wants me to try and see if I can come up with something. And the address of his music company so I can call if I can do it." Breaking. Something deep inside her was breaking, and she was sure it couldn't be her heart, because she'd left that on the steps of the hotel.

"Just as long as they're not taking advantage of you, sweetheart. I really wish you'd involve Seth or your father." Lucia put down the cup. "I have to run. Why don't we meet for lunch? I'd love to take you out. We haven't done anything together since we got here. Maybe ask your father too?"

"Sure. I'll go lie down now. Call me when you're ready to get together?" Naomi didn't wait for an answer but drifted away to her room.

"One o'clock, at Luciano's!" Lucia called after her.

Shutting the door behind her, Naomi allowed the tears to flow at last.

Chapter Twenty-five

SITTING BETWEEN HER parents Naomi let their conversation drift past her, their laughter rising like a wall of bricks around her bleeding heart.

It was still there; her heart, it hadn't really gone with Jon and vanished. It was there and hurt in a way she never imagined it could.

She wished she'd stolen the pillowcase from the hotel room to hide in her bed, to have Jon's scent to cling to. He was gone, and maybe forever. She tried to hang on to her memories of their night together, but at the restaurant with a plate of steaming pasta on the table in front of her, they seemed to retreat into the shadows, tired dancers with bleeding feet.

Lucia was talking about Seth and the upcoming weekend, and what to wear to the ball.

"You, of course," she said to Naomi, touching the back of her hand with a well-manicured finger, "are the lucky one. That dress is lovely, Naomi! Seth will be delighted seeing you in it. But I need something for my old, aging body, something that won't make me look like a sack of potatoes."

Lucia was joking of course. It was visible in the way the light danced in her eyes and in the smile Olaf gave her.

"Sophia Loren in her best years can't compare to you, my dear," He told his wife and, reaching across the table, took her hand in his. "You could go in a nightgown and outshine every woman there."

"Please!"

Naomi's groan made them laugh and ask for the dessert menu.

"Though I really shouldn't," Lucia moaned, "or I'll end up looking like the tubby Italian I am. Coffee and a tiny sip of Amaretto for me, please."

Naomi wanted buttercream, sugar, whipped cream. She wanted to fill up the emptiness inside her with something creamy and sweet, and lots of it. Tiramisu, and coffee, and a sweet liquor sounded about right to her. She glanced at her mother's watch. Almost two in the afternoon. Jon would be in Paris by now, getting settled in his hotel room, thinking of the soundcheck and the show tonight. In a few hours he'd be onstage, singing to a new audience. She wondered if he'd miss her, if he'd even think of her or if he'd forgotten about her the moment he got on the plane.

And if she really managed to get away, if she got on that plane to Amsterdam, how would he greet her? Would all the passion and love be gone; would he even care?

The thought was more than she could bear. Hastily, she took a sip of her espresso and coughed, hiding the sudden tears by complaining that it was too hot and choking on it.

"Here." Lucia was holding up her glass of Amaretto to Naomi. "Drink this."

The alcohol burned her throat, warming her and incongruously making her feel better. The sad image of Jon turning away from the window, turning back toward his friends and letting go of her memory, faded a little, felt less painful.

Lucia was talking about Seth again and what they would do once he was here: Would he like to see Chamonix, or Mont Blanc? Did he like to sail?

"You should know," she said to Naomi. "He's your lover, after all."

It hurt like a stab. Never. Never in her life would she imagine Seth making her feel what she'd felt last night in Jon's arms. She couldn't imagine wanting to see him without his clothes, let alone Seth undressing her, kissing every inch of skin he exposed, caressing her…

"Maybe not sailing." Olaf lit his after-lunch cigar. "I don't think Seth has ever spoken of sailing. I know he's really into horses though. And I think he'd love to see the offices and meet some of the people there. He'll be working with them soon enough."

"Yes, darling." Lucia signaled to the waiter for more coffee. "But please remember that he's coming here for Naomi, not for business. Don't keep him busy all the time. The lovebirds want to be together. Right, honey?"

"Right." She needed Fleur; she needed to spill her tears, needed someone who knew and who'd let her cry. Instead she had to hear Lucia suggest a shopping spree, a mother-and-daughter afternoon at the designer stores of Geneva, and didn't she feel like something new.

Naomi held her head. "I can't. I'm wasted after partying all weekend with the girls. I really need to go home, soak in the tub, and hide in bed. I'll never drink champagne again, I swear."

Both of them laughed at that; Olaf even clapped her shoulder in friendly commiseration.

"Somehow I don't believe you," he said. "Girls love champagne, especially if it's pink and expensive. But you do look a bit done in. Maybe getting some rest before your fiancé gets here is a good idea. And there's the ball next Saturday to think of too."

SHE barely made it home.

Alone in her room, she sat on her bed, *Geneva Glam* in her hands. An old, obliging accomplice by now, it fell open to Jon's image on its own. There he was, and now the man in the photo seemed like a stranger. He wasn't her Jon anymore; he was the star, the public person, the man who'd forgotten about a fling in a hotel room somewhere on his European tour, and had moved on to new adventures.

The envelope. She'd pushed it under her pillow to hide it from prying eyes. Now she took it out and opened it.

There was some money, two thousand American dollars, and that made her smile. They were useless here unless she took them to a bank and exchanged them for Swiss francs.

In a travel agency folder she found a first-class ticket to Amsterdam, undated. All she had to do was call the airline and book it. And there was a smaller envelope, with Jon's handwriting on it, addressed to her. Inside was a note, on hotel stationery, and she wondered when he'd found the time to write it.

My love,

I know you'll read this after I'm gone. And I know you'll wonder if this really happened, if I'm serious, or if it was just a game for me. Let me say this: I love you. It's not supposed to happen like this, I know. But fate made it happen, and I believe in fate. I also believe in love at first sight. Please come to me, please come to Amsterdam. If you're doubtful, or afraid, or for some reason you can't make it, call me. If I don't hear from you at all, I'll return to Geneva after the tour and find you. We belong together. I can't imagine going on the stage in Paris tomorrow without you there. My heart was silent, and now, with you, it sings.

I love you,
Jon

Under those words he'd written an address in Los Angeles, an American phone number, and the name of the hotel in Amsterdam.

Crying again, Naomi put the letter back in its envelope and then hid everything in her journal.

She tried to picture it: There wouldn't be a lot of luggage. She wouldn't take anything with her, just her journal, her money, and her passport. She'd make a clean break, leave everything else behind.

The thought of leaving her parents like that made her cry even harder; and, pulling her quilt over her head, she curled up on her bed and drifted off to sleep and into wild, disordered dreams.

WHEN Lucia woke her, it was almost dark. Feeling disoriented, she sat up, rubbing her eyes. It felt as if the world had tilted, and she was in the wrong place, in the wrong time.

"Fleur is on the phone," Lucia said. "She sounds as if she's going to implode any second. You better go and talk to her." And added, on her way out, "And dinner is ready. Your father is home; we'll eat in a moment. Tell Fleur you'll call back later."

Her dream was still in her ears and in her mind, but the song was rapidly drifting away from her to be replaced by Olaf's voice in the hallway, demanding to know why the phone wasn't hung up and where was Naomi? She could hardly be gallivanting through town with her friends again, could she?

"Stop yelling," Naomi heard her mother reply, and rather crossly, "the child is napping. She's all done in after her wild weekend, but at least she's clever enough to sleep it off. Go on inside; the table is set. I'm sure she'll be there in a few minutes!"

"That child is getting out of hand. All this partying and staying away overnight," Olaf grumbled. "We really should watch her more closely."

"Olaf, seriously." Something that sounded suspiciously like a slap on an arm could be heard. "If you believe she's old enough to get married, then she's old enough to stay overnight with her friends."

"That's totally different. Who knows what kind of mischief they cook up, those girls…"

The voices drifted away as they moved toward the dining room.

The quilt wrapped around her shoulders, Naomi traipsed out into the hall and to the phone.

"Hi," she said, and yawned. "I'm sorry; I fell asleep."

"You're going to meet me for dinner, my girl! You owe me big time!" Fleur said, and she was doing her best sergeant drill voice.

"Nah, can't. Table is already set, and I'm dead tired. Tomorrow? At the café?" She was cold despite the quilt. The lack of sleep was catching up with her.

"Seriously? You're going to make we wait until tomorrow? Just tell me this then. Where did you spend last night?"

Naomi glanced over her shoulder to see if she was alone. "Not at home."

"Are you sure?" Fleur's squeal was so loud that she had to hold the phone away from her ear.

"Of course I'm sure, you silly git. Don't shout! My parents will hear you!"

Breathlessly, Fleur went on, "And how was it? I mean, did you spend the whole night? What was it like?"

Naomi squeezed her eyes shut. "Fleur, really. I'm not in a mood to talk right now. My parents dragged me out to lunch, and I haven't even had time to think about it. Please can we talk tomorrow?"

"Yes, and now what? He's gone, isn't he? I know there's a concert in Paris tomorrow. Was that it? Naomi, really?"

"I don't know."

Lucia was calling for her, saying her dinner was getting cold and did she want some wine?

"I have to think about it. I have no idea what to do." Tears were welling up in her chest again, painful, bitter. "He wants me to meet him in Amsterdam, and then…and then…"

Fleur squealed again, and this time it sounded as if someone was strangling a cat. "Oh my God, he wants you to come after him? You really, honestly caught Jon Stone! He's crazy for you, I know it. I saw it in his face, in the way he treats you. You must go! You totally must go, Naomi! You really can't want to marry that old stick Seth when glorious, wonderful, perfect Jon Stone wants you!"

"Yeah." Fleur had a very neat way of sorting her thoughts for her. "Yes, I agree. I can't… I couldn't…" The thought alone made her shudder again.

"You need an escape plan! I'll help you! I'll help you get out of there, and help you meet your lover. Oh dear Lord, this is the best thing that has ever happened! I'm so proud of you!"

Giggling. Fleur, despite her sadness, made Naomi giggle with her bright, lucid words.

"Okay. Coffee, tomorrow morning. Be there! Ten o'clock sharp, on the hotel terrace." Only Fleur would pick that place so soon after she'd been there with Jon.

It was the best place ever.

Chapter Twenty-six

SHE WALKED TO the hotel slowly, retracing every step she'd taken with Jon, remembering every word they'd spoken. It seemed like a lifetime ago now in the light of a new day.

Naomi wondered where Jon was right now, and what he was doing. It was summer in Paris, and he'd be strolling under the arcades along the Rue de Rivoli, where his hotel was, and he'd look across the street at the Louvre and the Tuileries. He hadn't said if he'd been to Paris before or if it was a new, exciting experience for him. They hadn't had a chance to talk about it.

They hadn't talked about a lot, Naomi realized. She didn't know much more about Jon than what she'd read in that magazine article, and he knew nothing about her.

And that was the great miracle: He hadn't asked. He hadn't cared; all he'd wanted was what he saw, just the girl, just her.

She stopped near the spot where he'd first kissed her, and touched her lips with one finger. The memory made her smile, and threatened to bring back the tears.

Paris. How she wished she was there with him now, having breakfast on one of the balconies; fresh French bread, salty butter, and strawberry jam. Down below them, the noisy life of a summer morning. She'd show him the town, take him to the Rodin museum and to the modern art exhibits in Les Halles, eat lunch with him on a bench among the Niki de Saint Phalle Nana sculptures and then later, at night, discover the lights of Montmartre.

They'd take a long walk along the Seine and wander across the Ile Saint-Louis, and return via the Île de la Cité and the flower market near Notre Dame.

It occurred to her that she didn't even know where the venue was, or if it was open air like here in Geneva or an auditorium.

The sun was shining through the trees, throwing a mosaic of shadows on the gravel of the promenade, spelling out mysteries of life. There weren't too many people around; it was too early for lunch, too late for breakfast. On the playground, a kindergarden class was playing a noisy game with a ball, carefully watched by three adults. A few yachts danced on the water, crossing through the fountain's spray, making it shimmer in iridescent colors.

The world was moving on, nothing had changed; it didn't care about her aching heart or how her life was going. She was too small, too unimportant, to merit attention.

When Naomi arrived, Fleur was already on her second cup of café au lait; the waiter was busy removing the empty one with a few flirty words and a wink at his pretty customer. When she saw Naomi she jumped up, nearly knocking the man and her new cup of coffee over.

"At last!" she called across the street. "I thought you'd left already, and I'd never get to know what happened!"

Naomi dropped into a chair. "Sometimes, Fleur, you're exhausting. Sit down, for crying out loud! Everyone is watching us!"

It wasn't true, of course. No one was looking; no one cared.

"Tell me, tell me, tell me," Fleur sang, waving to the waiter to bring coffee for Naomi.

"Good grief. You're giving me a headache! Will you let me sit for a moment?" Stealing the tiny bar of chocolate that had come with Fleur's cup, she slowly unwrapped it before popping it into her mouth. "There's nothing to tell! Jon is gone; he's in Paris now. And then they'll go on to Amsterdam, then Ireland, I think, and then back home. That's it."

And said like that, summed up into a few tour stops, it sounded drearier than ever.

"But you're going to Amsterdam, right? You'll go after him?" Fleur pushed the plate of croissants toward Naomi, who took one, but only to shred it into tiny pieces while she talked.

"I don't know. I don't even know if I should go. What if it was only a one-night thing for him? What if he laughs his butt off when I show up in Amsterdam? I just don't know, Fleur. And then, I need my passport. It's in my father's safe, and I have no idea how to get to it. Not even Jon Stone can smuggle me into other countries without my passport."

"But do you want to go? How do you feel about it?"

"Yes." There was no sense in lying. "Yes, I want to go."

She'd have to hide, that much was clear. If she really went away with Jon, if she went to Los Angeles with him, she'd have to hide from her father. It would be a difficult life. And she could never tell Jon about it.

"Well then, it's settled. You're going! Now all we need is to trick your father into giving you that passport." Her brow in busy wrinkles, Fleur stirred sugar into her coffee. "Can't you say we're going to Milano to see my father's new collection? I know he wanted to create something just for you. Would that work?"

"Not this week. Seth..." She could hardly say the name. "Seth will be here on Thursday; and anyway, if I want to meet Jon in Amsterdam, I have to go on Wednesday."

"And today is Monday, so it's really tight, time-wise. What to do?"

Naomi had no idea. Miserably, she watched a fly circling Fleur's baguette, ready to plunge into the jam on it.

"I know!" Fleur's sudden squeal made Naomi jump in her chair. "Is there anything else in the safe that you could want without raising suspicion?"

"My jewelry. Why?"

A wide, impish grin spread on Fleur's face. "Listen. This is how you do it. You tell your father you want your jewelry, or at least some of it. You'll have to play this really well though, or he won't believe you!" Happy with herself, Fleur took a big bite of croissant and jam.

"Why would I want my jewelry?" For a second, for less than a heartbeat, there had been the blink of hope, but it was fading rapidly.

"Oh man, Naomi, you can be so dense! Your fiancé is coming over, isn't he? Seriously? Won't you be going out for dinners, to concerts and stuff? You need new dresses, and a lot of them! And shoes, and purses, and all kinds of stuff..." She grinned brightly. "New, sexy underwear! Lacy bras and tiny panties! And of course you need your jewelry to make sure it will go with new dresses!" Leaning forward, she whispered, "You need to get him to let you in that safe. And then when you get out your jewelry boxes, you slip the passport between them! Easy as pie!"

It sounded easy, the way Fleur put it. Her hands around the big cup, Naomi pondered Fleur's plan.

"I'd have to time it well. If I tell him just before he's ready to leave for office…"

"Then he'd have no other choice but to open it for you and leave!" Fleur finished the sentence for her. "Brilliant! That should work! And then you're off with your prince, off into the sunset of Los Angeles!" That made her pause. "All right, and now tell me how this all came about anyway. You came back from Canada, and you hadn't even heard of Jon Stone; and a couple of months later you're making out with him in his dressing room. I want to know what happened, missy."

So Naomi told her about the lyrics, how she'd sent them off to Jon, about Sal's call out of the blue, and how they'd wanted to meet her, in exactly the same spot where they were now, even the same table. Only this time it was Fleur sitting in the chair where Jon had been.

"I saw him in the lobby, waiting for me," she said, "and I fell in love. I don't know what else to tell you."

"Yes, but obviously it was mutual," Fleur interrupted. "I don't think Jon Stone gives a crap about girls being infatuated; there must be so many of them wherever he goes." She shrugged. "Including me. But you… I mean, Jeez, Naomi! He gives you a plane ticket, and his private address! Yes, he's serious about this."

Suspicious now, she glared at Naomi through narrowed eyes. "I never knew you were a writer! You never said! So do you write other stuff too? Stories? Novels?"

Naomi shrugged her shoulders. "I didn't know myself. It was a spur-of-the-moment thing. I typed them up on my father's typewriter, shoved them in an envelope, and gave it to the maid to mail before I lost my nerve. I never expected a response, let alone a phone call! I'm so confused."

"But you love him?"

"I do." It was so easy to say to Fleur. "I'm heartbroken now. And I've been wondering, what if he's already forgotten me? What if it was a game for him, and he's found someone else? Another girl, for Paris?"

Fleur slapped her bare arm, and hard. "Listen to you, you cry-baby! Stop whining, and get a grip! Do I have to repeat it? Private phone number! Private address! And I'm sure he didn't even ask you to keep them secret, right?"

Naomi, rubbing her smarting arm, shook her head.

"That's what I thought. He wants you to come! He wants you to follow him!"

"Well, he did say he'd come back here if I didn't show up," Naomi admitted, pulling her arm back just in time to avoid a second slap. "Stop doing that! You'll give me a bruise, and then I'll have to explain!"

That made Fleur sit back and fold her hands in her lap. "Your father is downright crazy, do you know that? Why is he like that? It's not as if you're on the verge of running away..." She huffed. "Okay, bad example. But what I'm trying to say is, you're such a good girl! You never do anything without his consent; he knows where you are all the time, and with whom..." Again she broke off, laughing. "Damn, you really are a deep one. When you decide to stray, you go all in. No harmless flirting for Naomi Carlsson; it's all or nothing for you." Gently, Fleur reached out to lay her hand on Naomi's. "You're the quiet one, the careful one among us. I bet if I told Manon and Giselle about your fling with Jon, they'd never believe me. They think you'll be Daddy's good little girl and marry the man he's picked for you. They feel sorry for you, did you know that?" She giggled. "And here you are, plotting your dramatic escape, two days after meeting the man. What a thrill that will give them!"

"But you can't tell, Fleur!" Panic, and it felt hot and prickly. "You can't ever tell anyone! I'm sure my father would send an army after me if he knew where I was!"

Fleur retrieved her hand and slumped back into her chair. "He will know, sooner or later. You're a grown-up. You can pretty much do as you damn well please, even if Olaf thinks otherwise. And we do live in a culture where women can pick their own lovers or husbands. Your father has no hold over you whatsoever." She pushed away her cold coffee. "And that passport thing! You need to get at that thing pronto. It's yours, and you have a right to it."

"He says it's safer in the safe."

"'He says it's safer in the safe,'" Fleur repeated her words, mimicking Naomi's unsteady voice. "Of course it's safer in a safe. That doesn't mean he can keep it from you when you want it. You're not his property."

But that was it. That was just it. She was, at least in Olaf's eyes.

Chapter Twenty-seven

"THERE WAS A call for you, Mademoiselle," the maid said when she opened the door for Naomi, "From a man. He didn't give his name, but he said to thank you for the marzipan."

"Oh!" She had to think, and fast. "He's just a friend from university. I told him where to go for the best chocolate and marzipan here in Geneva. That's rather sweet of him to call!"

"He said he was in Paris, and he was enjoying it very much; and if you ever go to Amsterdam to be sure and call him there." Mathilde pinched her mouth, trying to remember the words. "That was all he said."

"Thanks! He's from there, you know, Amsterdam." Naomi's heart was racing. She wondered if that was enough to satisfy the girl's curiosity. "He's going back home now. Too bad, he's a really great composer. I liked working with him."

Half-truths, as always. Not really lies, not really truths, but something of both, and it had kept her afloat all her life.

"Madame also called. She and Monsieur are going out for dinner tonight, and she wanted to know if you're coming too. They're meeting some business friend of Monsieur?"

One sentence and her blood had turned to slush. "Which business friend? Did they say?"

"*Non*, Mademoiselle. They will be home early to change. I'm to have tea ready by three." With a small curtsy, Mathilde vanished into the kitchen, and Naomi fled into her room.

He'd called! Jon, and he'd called. He had taken time out of his busy life to call her from Paris, and he hadn't given her away! As if he knew, as if he'd sensed that she needed the secrecy as much as she did.

Her heart burned thinking of it; he'd called, and she hadn't been there to talk to him. She wondered what he'd be thinking of her; one day later and she was already going out, while he sat in his Paris hotel room, calling her.

Jon. Her pulse was beating rapidly. Jon, and she would go.

There was a travel bag in her closet that she used when she stayed overnight at Fleur's or when she went away for the weekend with her parents, and that's what she'd take. It was roomy enough for a couple pairs of jeans, some summer dresses, shoes, and her toiletries.

Her eyes fell on the rose dress, still hanging on the closet door where she could see it all the time.

"I want to take you," Naomi said, "only it doesn't feel right. You were meant for the ball, and Seth, and it feels like betraying someone if I take you along. But you're so pretty."

She didn't even know if she'd ever need it in Los Angeles, if there would ever be an occasion to wear it. It would mean going out in public, at Jon's side. Somebody would be sure to take a photo of them together, and her cover would be blown.

"I don't care. You're coming with me." She retrieved the bag in which it had originally been stored and zipped it around the dress. It would have to go separately; there was no way the many layers of tulle would fit in any travel bag.

Packing. She was packing, and she hadn't even realized it. One more day and she'd leave this room, this apartment, this city; and as far as she was concerned, it would be forever. The journal and her money were in her handbag, a book for the flight, and Sal's envelope. The only thing missing was her passport.

Sitting on her bed, Naomi looked around. She'd grown up in this room. A few years ago it had been redone, turned from a kid's space into a bedroom for a young lady: the frolicking pink of a little princess had been driven out by powdery colors—rose, cream, gray—and the cot replaced by a wide, comfortable bed with a chiffon canopy. She loved this room; she loved the view and the sounds. It made her feel at home, and safe. And she was giving it up willingly, for a view of the Pacific.

THERE was noise in the hallway; her parents were home, her mother calling for the maid, asking if tea was ready, and did she get some of those apple tarts, and to please serve it in the library.

"Naomi? Are you coming?" Olaf was tapping on her door.

Her heart thundering in her throat, Naomi kicked the packed bag under her bed. "In a second," she yelled, her voice snapping with fear. "I'm not dressed!"

"Hurry up, child! We're going out tonight!"

Child. Again, child, and it made her recall how Seth had said that to her, much in the same tone Olaf was using now. As if she belonged to them, as if they could do with her what they wanted. Any kind of remorse, any second thoughts, died. She would do it. She'd leave.

Putting on one of her nicest afternoon dresses, she decided to go out with them. She had to plan her escape and not make anyone suspicious by staying behind. She pulled her hair into a tight bun at the back of her neck, put on some makeup and her pearl necklace.

OLAF and Lucia looked up when she walked into the library in her heels, dressed to kill.

"Very pretty, Naomi," her father said. He sounded pleased. "This is how I like to see you, not in jeans and one of your flimsy blouses. You look like a lady!"

"I need new clothes." She flounced over to the couch and dropped into it. "I really need new clothes."

Lucia raised her eyebrows.

"Seth is coming, and I can't possibly wear the same dresses I wore last summer or when we were home this year for my birthday. What will he think? That I don't care how I look? I can't do it!"

Carefully, Olaf put down his cup. "Well, I don't know what to say. You're the one who needs to be literally dragged into a shop. I've been telling your mother for years to dress you properly! So you want money? There isn't a lot of time; when do you want to go shopping?"

"Tomorrow morning, first thing. I'll take Fleur along; she has a better eye than I do. I'm not sure I'll be home for lunch either. And maybe on Wednesday too."

"But I can't go with you, Naomi! I have important appointments tomorrow, and I'm completely booked on Wednesday." Lucia held out the plate of apple tarts, but Naomi shook her head.

"You don't have to come with me, Mama. I know exactly what I want. I need cocktail dresses, maybe another evening gown, and some light afternoon dresses. And shoes. And purses."

"Yes, yes." Naomi had never seen her father this flummoxed before. "Of course you do! I wonder why your mother didn't think of that!"

"I did!" Lucia shot him a glare. "I tried and tried to make her buy dresses when we were in Milano; but with Naomi, it's 'just throw on something so I won't be naked', and that's hard to change!"

"Well, I've changed now. Seth coming here made me realize that I can't run around like a schoolgirl anymore." Taking a dainty sip of tea, Naomi batted her eyelashes at Olaf. It was now or never, before her courage drained away. "Daddy, could you please open the safe for me? I want to go through my jewelry, and maybe take some with me to see if they go with what I want to buy."

"Yes, of course!" He rose to go into his office, Naomi following him.

She couldn't believe that it was going to be this easy. All her agonizing, all her dark plans, and here he was, her father, happy to oblige her whims.

"How long do you need?" he asked, turning the safe lock. "I need to go take a shower and change for dinner soon, and before that I need to make some phone calls."

"Oh, I don't know. But I'll be fine, Daddy. I can just close the door, and it will be locked, yes?" As if she knew anything about safes.

"Yes. You shut it, and then turn the knob any which way. That will lock it. And remember to put the picture back over it."

There was some kind of irony, Naomi thought, that the safe was hidden behind a portrait of her in a ball gown, standing on the terrace, the trellis with the climbing roses in the background. Her dress had been picked to harmonize with the roses, not because she'd liked it. Lavender-colored velvet had never been her favorite. In the painting, she looked as if she'd just climbed out of a Jane Austen novel, and she despised it for it's old-fashioned style. Olaf had commissioned it for her sixteenth birthday, to commemorate that special day. She'd asked him why it was special to turn sixteen, and he's given her one of his perplexed looks that made her want to wilt.

It was important, he'd said, because it meant she wasn't a child anymore but a young lady.

"Which pieces do you want to take? I'm not delighted with the idea of you traipsing around town with valuable jewelry in your purse."

"I don't know yet. That's why I want to take them out and look."

There it was: her passport, wedged between her parents', peeking at her, waiting to be removed.

"Oh all right then." Olaf reached into the safe and brought out a fat wad of cash. "Do you need cash where you're going?"

She blanched before she realized he was talking about shops and not Amsterdam. "No. Yes. I don't know?"

"Well, here. Better make sure." He didn't even count it, he just pressed the money into her hand. "Consider it an early engagement present." He got out another bundle of Swiss francs. "Here, in case you decide you want new jewelry too. Though I'm sure you'll be fine with your credit card. I've just filled up your account." His glacier eyes softened. "Not that a lot was missing. You really don't spend much money. I like that a lot, Naomi. You're very careful with your allowance, and quite frugal. A very good trait in a girl born to wealth." He pressed her shoulder briefly. "But this is not the time for you to be frugal, my dear. You're getting engaged, you're going to go out with your future husband, and I commend you for wanting to looking like a Carlsson lady. Have fun shopping!" Glancing at his watch, Olaf sighed. "Okay then, I'll leave you to it."

On his way out, in the doorway to the hall, he turned and added, smiling, "I'm very proud of you, my darling."

So easy.

All she had to do was reach out and take it, and they would never notice it in her hand. She could easily hide it between the money and take it to her room, and no one would see.

She stood, gazing at the velvet boxes with her mother's and her own jewelry.

There was her ruby necklace, and the circlet her father had given her for her birthday. In the red box, the largest one, was Lucia's set of pearls, the one with the lovely diamond clasp that made her look like a queen. Naomi touched it, brushed her fingers over the velvet, thinking of her mother wearing it when they'd been in Hamburg to see Placido Domingo sing in *Tosca*. Olaf had taken them to an oyster restaurant right in the middle of town where they could see the lake and the fountain, much like here in Geneva, only smaller, cozier. There had been no mountains either, and it had been cold and rainy. It had been a lovely lunch, with her father gently making fun of her mother for not finding a restaurant on her own; and to make it up to her he'd ordered a bottle of champagne for them, and Naomi had been allowed a sip too.

Lucia had looked magnificent in her dark-red silk dress, with those pearls on her white skin, when they went to the opera house that evening. She had been so proud of her mother and her beauty, so proud to be her daughter.

"Good-bye, Mama," she whispered, taking out one of the boxes, the one with the rubies. The passport vanished under it, between her palm and the velvet. "I love you."

The safe door fell into its lock, and Naomi replaced the painting.

Chapter Twenty-eight

"SO WHERE ARE your new dresses?" Olaf asked when she returned home the next night. "I thought we'd get to see something pretty!"

Naomi pouted. She was a good pouter; she'd been practicing it in front of the mirror for years. A cute pout often worked wonders with her father, especially if she remembered to pull up one shoulder and give him a big-eyed flutter over it.

"I didn't find a lot today. Just one dress, and it needs to be shortened. Of course. We'll be out again tomorrow. Fleur's father brought some pieces from the new collection from Milan, and he says he made them thinking of me. So I'll be over at their house tomorrow, trying them on. And then they probably need to be altered too." She sighed. "It's a curse, being short and stumpy."

"What nonsense!" Olaf put down his cigar. "You are neither short nor stumpy. You're just right! A lovely girl with porcelain skin and beautiful hair. And a pretty face. You're perfect, my dear. You remind me a lot of Audrey Hepburn and how she looked when she stood outside that Tiffany window in that movie. Only I wouldn't want to see you in black."

Naomi knew which movie he meant. She'd never cared for it. It had made no sense to her, and she'd hated that the girl had tossed out her cat. That was the one part of the movie she'd really, really hated; and it didn't even help that she went looking for it at the end of the movie, or that the cat was still there, in the filthy alley where she'd kicked it out.

Coming home, she'd found her parents in the library, like every evening when they dined at home, her father with brandy, her mother with Amaretto; and they were listening to some music. This day, it was Gluck's *Orfeo ed Euridice*, one of her favorites.

"I didn't buy anything black, no fear," she said. "I'm not going to a funeral, after all."

"But that black satin dress you keep going on about, Naomi." Lucia patted the couch beside her, and Naomi sat obediently. "When you're thirty it will look stunning on you." She winked. "If you can keep your figure after having babies. It's not easy, you know. A pregnancy changes your body. And I'm sure you'll have more than one baby before you're thirty."

Nausea. Yes, that was it, at the thought of being in bed with Seth, of opening herself to him, and…

"I have to get out of these clothes," she said, swallowing hard. "I'm sweaty and grimy from shopping all day."

Orfeo and Euridice, and how apt that was. He'd been told to go ahead, and not to turn around to see if his love was following him. Singing, he'd walked through the depths of hell to find her; and then because he couldn't bear the uncertainty, he'd looked back, and lost her forever.

And she was Euridice in this sad tale; she was the one following, trailing after the music and the song, trying to evade the dangers and snares on her difficult path to her beloved.

Closing the door to her room, she leaned against it and looked around.

One more night. Her last night ever in this room. She'd walk out of the house after her parents had gone to work, hail a cab, and vanish; and no one would know where she'd gone.

Fleur had told her to leave a note for her parents. "It's safer, trust me," she'd said. "You want them to know you ran away. If you don't, they'll call the police, Interpol, the FBI, the CIA, whatever. Knowing your father, probably the KGB, the Vatican, and the United Nations too. You don't want that, Naomi. You want to be left alone, right? So tell them."

"And do you think that will stop him?" Scary, that thought had been so scary: Olaf, descending on Jon's house, the record company, his management office with the wrath of an angry, wronged Viking, brandishing an imaginary sword.

But Fleur had only shrugged. "It doesn't matter, Naomi. You're of age. You're free to go where you please. If there's a note, your parents can't do a thing. You left of your own free will. No one will come after you. They can't."

"If my father doesn't burn the note and tell the world that I was abducted."

"Well, that's easy then." Fleur had jumped up from her bed, where they'd both been lounging, and brought out a sheet of stationery. "Here, write one to me, as well. If your father flips, I'll have the evidence that you decided to leave and that no one dragged you away."

So clever, Fleur was so clever. But here she was now, and she had to sit down at her desk and write that letter to her parents, had to tell them that she preferred running away with a stranger to their loving, caring, suffocating plans for her.

HER passport was in her purse.

She'd not returned the rubies to her father yet, and he hadn't asked.

She would take them with her, just like the money he'd handed her. And the rose dress. Her credit card, and that had been a harder decision. There was no way she could take it and use it. They'd find her, trace her through it; and it didn't feel right to go on using her account after she'd run away from this life.

It was on her desk already, next to the empty jewelry box, and now she'd add her good-bye note to the sad little collection.

"Dear Mama, Dear Daddy," she wrote, " When you read this, I'll be far away. Please don't be angry at me. But I can't stay and marry Seth. I've tried so often to tell you that I don't love him, but you wouldn't listen. I don't want that kind of life. Please don't worry about me. I'll be fine. But I really need to lead my life the way I want to and not how you planned it for me. I love you. Naomi."

It sounded clumsy, selfish, and even ominous; but she folded the note up and stuffed it in an envelope. Finding the right words for her parents wasn't at the top of her to-do list.

Showered, in her bathrobe, she returned to the library where her parents were still enjoying the evening.

She sat on the couch beside Lucia, her head on her mother's shoulder, the tiny glass of Amaretto her father gave her on her knee. They'd moved on from Gluck and were now listening to Handel's *Xerxes*; and, closing her eyes, Naomi let the music wash over her. She'd played the "Ombra Mai Fu" aria a million times on her piano, sometimes even singing along, the beautiful Italian words rolling over her tongue like little orbs of meringue.

Lucia was humming; Naomi could feel the music vibrating in her mother's body, could feel her breathing concentrate on the difficult notes. She'd heard Lucia sing that aria once, in Italy, in her hometown of Positano, during a recital at the local church. How proud she'd been, seeing her stand in front of the altar in a long, cream dress, her thick black hair in a braid much like her own. Clear and strong, her lovely alto voice had filled the space, and it had seemed as if it hadn't taken any effort at all to master the coloratura passages.

"Well," Olaf said when the music ended, "I'm off to bed. Early start tomorrow. I did tell you that I'm going to London, right? Have to be at the airport by seven. There's this lovely inn in Oxford that we want to acquire."

Lucia sighed. "I wish I could go with you! We haven't been to London in months. But I'm all tied up with the exam preparation."

"How about you?" Olaf nodded at Naomi. "Want to come? Keep your old dad company? We could go to Harrods afterward, if you want. You love Harrods, don't you? And maybe you can find one or the other piece of clothing there."

So tempting, and so nice, but Naomi had to shake her head. "I can't, though I'd love to! But I promised Fleur's dad." Her heart was breaking a little.

"Next time then." Olaf pecked a kiss on her hair. "Sleep well, and have fun tomorrow!"

At the door, he stopped. "You don't need your passport, do you? You did say he was here in Geneva, right?"

Her pulse stopped. "No, he's here. I don't need anything, thank you."

"Well, if you need more money, ask your mother, or ask Fleur's father to wait a day until I'm back, and I'll write a check." He took another step and halted again. "Or I can give you a signed check, and you put in the amount when you know what you want?"

Her chin dropped. It literally dropped, and it took some effort to close her mouth again. He'd never, ever offered to do that before. Never. "No. No, thank you, Daddy; I don't think that will be necessary. I mean, it's not as if I'd grab the dresses and run. No worries."

With a grin, he left the room.

"You're so nice and friendly tonight," Lucia said, refilling her glass. "How come? That's not the normal you. Is it because Seth will be here in two days?"

Naomi took a deep breath. "Mama, what if I told you that I don't really love Seth? That I really don't want to get married just yet?"

Lucia laughed. "You imp! For a minute I almost believed you! You're not good at subterfuge, let me tell you! I can read your face like a book, and there's nothing but happiness there. And maybe a bit of exhaustion, but that's understandable, with the life you're leading just now."

Her lips moved, but Naomi couldn't say a word. They were stuck somewhere between her throat and her eyes, stuck like a frozen waterfall of tears.

"Good night, Mama," she managed after a few heartbeats. "I'm off to bed. Won't be home for lunch tomorrow, and maybe not dinner."

"Have fun, my sweet." Lucia kissed her forehead and, rising, smoothed Naomi's hair. "I'm so glad that everything's going so well for you."

ALONE in bed, alone in the dark, Naomi cried into her pillows. Jon's letter beside her, she read it over and over again. She cried, full of remorse for something she hadn't even done yet, and for the love of her parents.

She'd crumpled up the note to them and written a new one, one that seemed more loving, more apologetic; but in the end she'd smoothed out the old one and copied it out. There was nothing else to say.

"I tried," she said to Jon's image, sobbing. "I really tried, didn't I? What else can I do?"

She imagined a world where she was free, where she could tell her parents she loved someone else—a singer, an American rock star, a songwriter—and they wouldn't throw her into the Carlsson jail but ask her to introduce her boyfriend to them, to invite him for dinner, and yes, if that was her choice, then they would accept it and welcome Jon Stone, future son-in-law. And they'd see her off at the airport when she went away with Jon, off into the sunshine and freedom. They'd be there for Jon's concert, cheering him on, proud of him and his success; and they'd visit them at the Malibu house, go with her to the beach, watch the tide roll in and the sun set.

Jon would show them Los Angeles, take them to his studio, take them to dinner on the beach, where they'd eat heaps of shrimp and drink cocktails with little umbrellas stuck into chunks of pineapple.

At last she fell asleep, her hand on Jon's photo; and in her dreams she could hear the surf, and seagulls, and Jon calling her name.

Chapter Twenty-nine

SHE HEARD THE door close behind her parents, and the stillness that followed.

Her bag was packed, her dress ready to be carried away.

In her red dress, her hair pulled back in a ponytail, Naomi stepped into the hall, listening for the maid, but the apartment was silent. The doorknob in her hand, she took a deep breath and looked back.

This was her home, the place where she'd hung out with her friends, where she'd tried to battle her father, and where she'd learned to play the piano. Her room was exactly the way she had wanted it, how she wanted her private space to look. Her lovely dresses, her purses, her jewelry—everything, everything would be left behind.

The note to her parents was on her desk propped against the empty velvet box, where they would be sure to find it.

In the elevator rattling down to the lobby, she tried to imagine them reading it: late at night when they'd gotten worried, after they'd called Fleur and learned that she'd never been there, that she had vanished. They would go to her room, find it unchanged, as if she'd only gone out for the day. Then they'd find her letter.

She could see it: her mother, sinking down on her bed, the sheet of paper in her lifeless hands, pale with shock and panic; and her father, storming out to call the police, call the airport, but no one would be willing to help him, because there was a letter, because she'd taken her leave.

The doorman held the entrance door for her, asking if she needed a taxi, and she nodded. Yes, please, a taxi.

She'd called the airline and booked her flight, had confirmed it too. By ten she'd be in the air, and soon after she'd be leaving the city in the mountains on her way north. Never. She'd never done this on her own. There had always been the family jet, and when they got out, a limousine would be waiting to take them wherever they wanted to go. In all her life, traveling with her parents, Naomi had never navigated an airport terminal, much less alone.

When the cabdriver asked her where she wanted to go and she said to the airport, please, he glanced at her through the mirror. "Which terminal, miss?"

She had no answer, so she plucked out her ticket. "KLM?"

"International, then."

As if she knew.

Fleur had given her a few tips: She should go to the counter, the one with her airline name on it, and they'd want to see her passport and ticket. She didn't have enough luggage to check it in, so she could take it with her on the plane.

Naomi had listened, bemused, confused, and nodded.

"And the duty-free shopping, Naomi!" Fleur had laughed at herself. "I know you don't really need it, but it's so fun, shopping at the airport. Take some chocolates for your lover! And your dress—if there's a free seat, put it on that. Or give it to the stewardess to take care of."

Again she'd nodded, wondering if they'd have coffee on board, or food.

Fleur threw her a very strange look and hadn't said anything for a while.

Then, slowly, she'd asked: "You've really never been on a commercial flight, have you? I know your family has a jet, but really? Never ever?"

"No." Naomi hadn't known why, but she'd felt ashamed, as if she'd missed out on a part of life. "My father sometimes takes a regular plane when he travels alone, but if my mother and I are there, never."

"Maybe I should take you then," Fleur had suggested. "I'm not comfortable letting you do this on your own. I could at least take you to the gate."

"No." She knew she had to do this by herself.

Here she was, the airport looming ahead, her heart beating a fearful staccato in her chest. The cab stopped; she paid and got out, her dress on one arm, her purse and travel bag on the other. No one looked her way, no one noticed her: everyone was intent on his or her own flight.

Inside, she looked up at the huge board announcing the departures, and the counter and gate numbers.

"You're early," the lady at the counter said, processing her ticket. "There's a lovely day spa near the VIP lounge, if you want a manicure or something."

"No, thank you." Naomi stuffed her passport and the boarding pass into her purse. "I'll go and take a look at the duty-free stores." The way it had come out made her feel independent, adult, and quite proud of herself.

She was free: No one told her where to go or what to do, and it made her wonder why she hadn't claimed more of her life, why she hadn't insisted on being more independent, more her own person.

Naomi knew she wasn't a fighter. She'd told Fleur over and over again.

"I'll always avoid a confrontation, if I can, no matter with whom," she said. "I'm not like you, Fleur. I don't argue well enough, and I never learned how to throw tantrums."

"It's never too late to learn," Fleur had offered. "I can teach you!"

They'd laughed about it, eaten another piece of chocolate from the big box Fleur had opened. Someone had given it to her father and he to her.

"The thing is, you can't be afraid of throwing something," Fleur had said, weighing a coffee mug in her hand. "But first, make sure that it's empty, and not too valuable. And it can't have any special meaning to you. Because then the joy of destroying it would quickly turn into remorse, and we don't want remorse. Remorse is the worst enemy of tantrums. It seriously stinks."

Thinking of Fleur and their last conversation, Naomi wandered through the terminal and into its depths to the gates. She had to follow the signs, stop and read them, to figure out where she should go.

Once she was through passport control and inside the transit area she peeked into the duty-free shops, astounded at the eclectic mix of wares they offered.

A phone booth, that was what she needed. She had to ask at a newspaper stand for directions. With the number of the hotel in hand, she made her call. Two hours, she told the concierge, please to tell Jon Stone or his manager, Sal Rosenberg, that she would be arriving at Schiphol airport in about two hours. He promised to relay her message, and, relieved, she hung up.

There was a café that offered a view of the tarmac and the planes standing ready to be boarded. She sat down at a table close to the windows where she could watch the flights take off and land.

She sat nursing her coffee, observing the people coming and going; all of them seemed to be turned inward in a weird sort of way, as if they had to collect themselves, had to find out who they were before they could get on a plane.

She was just about to call the waitress and pay for her coffee when two businessmen came in and sat in a booth at the other end of the restaurant.

"Of course," she could hear her father say, "we'll have to turn it into a B&B if we expect an improvement in the UK numbers. I'm not particularly pleased about them right now."

"Not nearly," the other agreed. "We'll have to have a closer look into acquiring a London house, I think." He looked at his watch. "What a nuisance. Why in the world did they cancel that flight? Now we're stuck here, and we'll be late."

"Yes." Olaf shook his head. "And of course it happens the one time when the jet isn't here. My brother needed it, so I sent it back to Canada. Damn."

He hadn't seen her. His briefcase was open on the table, and he was rummaging in it.

Naomi glanced at the cup in front of her. It was empty, and it wasn't particularly pretty. She pushed it around on the saucer, wondering if throwing it here, in a restaurant, would still qualify as a tantrum; but she was pretty sure it wouldn't. It was far more likely to bring airport security, and she'd be detained long enough to miss her plane.

Putting a ten-franc note down under her cup, she waited until the group of people at the table behind her rose and got ready to leave, and in their shadow, she fled.

Her heart was racing, sweat beading on her back as she rushed to the gate and hid in a corner.

The flight for Amsterdam wasn't called for another hour, but she didn't dare move away from her nook behind the newspaper stand in the waiting area, and then when the gate was opened, she hurried through boarding pass control as fast as she could.

Only when the flight attendant had helped her stow her dress in one of the overhead compartments and promised not to let anyone put anything on it and she was in her seat did she breathe easier. Her hands clamped around the armrests, she watched every person entering the plane, still expecting her father or the police to come after her and drag her off the plane and into custody.

A rumble went through the plane. Two flight attendants were closing the doors, laughing, joking, talking about the weather in Amsterdam.

They were moving.

She was on a plane, all on her own, and there was no turning back. They were taxiing toward the runway, the pilots running through all the tests, ready for takeoff.

Amsterdam. She was really doing it. She was really on the plane. If only Fleur could see her, see how she coolly put on her seat belt, nodded politely to the man sitting next to her, and smiled as he opened his *Wall Street Journal*, just like her father would. She smiled when the purser walked past to check their seat belts and seat positions.

"There'll be champagne as soon as we're in the air," he whispered to her, "and I'll make sure you get yours right away." With a friendly wink he moved on, and at last Naomi could lean back and breathe.

The engines began to roar, the metal body of the plane vibrating with the power, and they were off.

The land rapidly fell away, the mountains shrunk, and the lake turned into a blue puddle deep below. It shone in the morning sunlight, a bright mirror, a beautiful sight among the snow-covered peaks. Soon even those became invisible as they hurtled northward, and across unseen borders, away.

The purser kept his promise and brought her pink champagne, together with a snack of fresh strawberries, crackers, and cheese. He winked at her again and said, "Just ring if you want more, darling."

Beside her, the businessman folded his newspaper and tucked it away, asking for coffee. Someone would be right with him, the purser said, and left.

"There you have it," the stranger said, smiling at her. "A lovely young lady like you gets the champagne, but he wouldn't get me a coffee himself. I have to admit though, I'd have done the same."

He was flirting, Naomi realized; he was flirting, and the purser too. She wasn't Olaf Carlsson's daughter anymore.

She was a pretty young woman traveling across Europe on her own. A grown-up who didn't have to explain where she was going, or why.

At last she was free.

Chapter Thirty

SAL WAS THERE to meet her.

Her heart sank as she walked toward him, and fear crept up her limbs.

Jon hadn't come. He'd changed his mind and sent Sal to tell her, to turn her around and send her back to Geneva. More money would be shoved her way, a few words of regret, and she'd be on her way home before she even knew it.

Sal smiled though and took the garment and travel bags from her.

"Well, now I've seen everything," he said instead of a greeting. "I was ready to bet a king's ransom that you'd never show up. But here you are, and even in Amsterdam's unfriendly light you're as pretty as an angel!"

She couldn't ask. Her throat was so dry, all her words were stuck.

"Sorry for the inconvenience," Sal went on, directing her to the waiting van, "but there's no time to go to the hotel first. They're at the soundcheck already. There were some technical problems. I'll take you with me straight to the venue." Again he grinned, and this time it was the kind of smile shared between friends. "Jon was ready to throw a fit when I said I'd take you to the hotel first."

"He wants to see me?" The question popped out before she'd had a chance to think about it.

Sal barked a laugh. "You're not seriously asking that? Really?"

SHE'D been to Amsterdam with her parents to visit museums and go for a boat ride on the canals in the city. It hadn't been overwhelmingly pretty like Strasbourg or Paris, nor as sophisticated as London or as ancient as Prague. Driving to the venue, they didn't even go through the center of old town but drove around it on highways that were as boring and neutral as anywhere else in the world. It was raining, and the low, dark skies made the landscape look like a drawing on a chalkboard—one that had been wiped with a wet sponge.

Not that Naomi cared. Her mind was racing ahead, to the moment when she'd see Jon again, and she wondered how it would go, how he'd react.

"The concert is completely sold out," Sal was saying. "He's doing very well. I'm really happy with Jon's success. I'm sure it makes you happy too?"

It seemed like a weird question. "Sure. I'm happy for him too," she replied, wondering if that was what Sal wanted to hear.

"He's making a lot of money." He was looking at her expectantly. "He'll be very wealthy soon. Well—he's quite wealthy now."

"Nice!" Of course he would be wealthy. Nothing else made sense.

"Being who he is, there are people who'll try to take advantage of him."

Slowly, very slowly, the pieces fell into place. "Are you suggesting that I came here to… I don't know. Because Jon is a star, and there's something in it for me?"

"I don't know." Sal showed his teeth in a feral grin. "Did you?"

It was so funny, in a twisted way. She was sure she had more money in her trust fund than Jon Stone had made in his entire career. A lot more.

"Not really. I came here because Jon wanted me to. You were the one who handed me the ticket, remember?" There, that had come out spunky enough to make even Fleur proud of her.

"Oh, yes, yes. I'm sorry, I didn't mean to insult you! I know Jon wants you here; he's throwing one tantrum after the other, and I'm certain it will stop once he sees you." The mirth fell from Sal's face to be replaced by real worry. "I care. You must know that I care a lot for Jon, and not just about his career. He's a very good person, and a dear friend. I don't want any heartbreak for him."

Heartbreak, how well she understood that.

"You see, I can imagine a girl being enticed by living the Hollywood life in a mansion on the beach, driving around LA in Jon Stone's Porsche, and shopping her heart out on Rodeo Drive. But that's not what his life is about. He's a serious musician under all the glamour and the shows. Writing music is hard work. Jon needs someone who's willing to share that quiet life too. The working life. Not someone who'll take him away from it."

Naomi looked at the raindrops running down the window. It seemed as if they were writing sad love songs on the glass, a mix of tears and words, one melting into the other.

"I don't need a Hollywood life," she softly replied. "Trust me, Sal. That's the last thing I want."

He poked at the travel sack with the dress in it. "Valentino, very nice. I wonder why you're bringing a Valentino gown if you're not hoping for movie premieres and Academy Award parties."

Sadness. Sadness and more lies, when she wanted nothing more than to get away from them.

"It was a gift. And it was meant for a special occasion that I'll never attend now. It's very pretty, and I just couldn't leave it behind. Don't worry. I'll probably never wear it. But I want to be able to look at it now and then."

That made him sit up straighter so he could look into her eyes. "You're really doing this, aren't you? It's not just a fling with a rock star while he's touring Europe. You're really thinking of going back to LA with Jon!"

"If he wants me, yes." This was a lot easier to answer, and something that didn't require lying. "If he wants me to, I'll go with him."

"And what are you leaving behind, Naomi Carlsson? What are you leaving behind in Geneva?" Sal's voice sounded gentler now, and friendlier.

"Nothing." The raindrops looked like torrents of tears now. "Nothing that I need. I've brought everything that I want in my life with me."

A crease of worry grew on Sal's brow. "But surely you have family, friends, and you said you were attending a university. Was it that easy, leaving it all?"

"I never said that." She tried to smile, but it didn't come out very well. "But it seems like Jon is more important than anything back in Geneva."

"Except for that dress."

"Yes. Except for the dress."

The van left the highway.

"We'll be there in a minute," Sal said.

SHE could hear the music the moment Sal pulled the backstage door open.

There it was: Jon's voice, Sean ripping into "The River" on his keyboard; and it sounded as if they were performing for an audience.

Sal was muttering something about letting off steam, but she ignored him. That voice, it reeled her in, had its hooks deep in her heart. No matter how she twisted and turned, no matter how much she willed it, she couldn't resist its pull.

The auditorium was dark, drenched in blues, dark purple, and jungle greens—a huge bowl of night colors—and streaming through it a wide, mysterious river: the song.

Naomi stood, feeling the music vibrating in her bones. Jon was holding the rosewood guitar, the strings giving up their chords under his fingers, his eyes closed. He was belting out the words, throwing them into the darkness like a challenge, like a call to the mysteries of a forbidden forest.

She knew she'd be able to stand in that spot for all eternity, watching him, listening to his songs, and never feel the years passing. She could grow old and die in that exact spot—a mummy, a statue, a memory to Jon's music.

He hadn't noticed her yet; he was singing with an abandon and intensity she'd not seen before, almost as if he wanted to rip into the fabric of time and reality with his voice.

Sal came up behind her. "I've put your stuff in Jon's dressing room," he shouted into her ear. "I have a feeling he won't mind." Patting her arm lightly, he went away to join Russ and the technicians at the mixing table at the back of the auditorium.

Jon opened his eyes, and the song stopped as if a knife had been driven into it. He handed the instrument to the guitarist, Jones, and jumped from the stage to run to her, run into her arms.

"You really came!" It flowed out in a breathless sigh, the relief of a million years in it.

"I promised, didn't I?" She could hardly say it through the kisses he was raining on her lips, on her face. "I said I would!"

"You're here!" Jon kept repeating it over and over until Naomi pushed him away, laughing.

"Yes, I am! Stop saying it, Jon!" She hadn't known her heart could be this light. She hadn't known there was this kind of joy in her soul.

"Let's go," he said. "Let's go and be alone for a moment."

Before she could reply, they were on their way to his dressing room, a young couple, laughing, playing, breathless in their excitement.

"I didn't think you'd come." The door closed behind them, and she was in his arms again. "I was so afraid you wouldn't come, that you'd changed your mind, that there wasn't enough love, and you wouldn't want to leave your life in Geneva."

Again he kissed her. Naomi wrapped her arms around his neck, holding on.

"It was a lot to ask, I know." Jon lifted her up and sat her down on the edge of the dressing table. "When I left you, when the bus pulled away and I saw you standing there at the curb, Naomi, my heart broke. You looked so lost, so lonely; and me, I had to move on, had to go away. And my heart broke. I wanted to turn around, let the tour go to hell, whatever, give up everything, just to be with you again. And now here you are!"

"But I love you!" There, she'd said it. "Of course I came! I promised!" She'd never tell him how hard it had been in the end, how suddenly, in the moment when she'd least expected it, her parents had shown her real love; even her father had started treating her as a real person.

"Yes, yes, you did."

How she loved to be kissed like this, just like this; how she loved his embrace.

"But words are only that, words, and we say a lot in a day. It doesn't mean we always follow through." His arms tightened around her. "I'm sorry I had to send Sal. This venue is a beast, and they can't get the sound right. But you're here now! Have you eaten? Would you like some coffee? I think they're done setting up the buffet in the hospitality suite. Want to go and check?"

"Not quite yet." Nothing was awkward. She had wondered how it would be seeing him again, if they'd feel like strangers, if the magic would be gone; but it wasn't. It felt just the same: magical, wonderful, eternal.

"Not quite yet?" His dark eyes smiled at her.

"Not quite yet. I think I'm not quite done kissing you."

Jon laughed. It was a happy laugh. "All right, I can do that. I'll kiss you for the rest of my life and never get tired of it. Come here then, baby, and let me kiss you!"

Chapter Thirty-one

THEY TRAVELED TO London together, where they stayed at a hotel not far from Harrods.

He'd always wanted to go there, Jon said; he'd heard so much about it, and now he wanted to go there and shop, and would she come?

It wasn't a long walk; they had to cross the street, and she pulled him back just as a red bus rumbled past and he was looking the wrong way. Muttering that he'd never get used to traffic coming from the wrong side, Jon hooked her arm through his and said, "You'll have to watch out for me then. You've been here before, I take it?"

"Yes, often." It had slipped out before she could stop herself. So she shrugged and added, "My father comes here on business. Sometimes I would come with him."

"And then you'd visit Harrods? So you've been there?"

They were walking down Brompton Road, and he was looking at her as if London and its many sights meant nothing at all.

"I've been inside, yes." Naomi wanted to stop right there and kiss him again. "I love buying tea at Harrods. They have the nicest tea tins."

"But you never drink tea! You're as coffee crazy as they come!" Jon nodded at the doorman as they entered the huge store.

"Yes. But I like the tins. I collect them. And sometimes I even make tea." Naomi took a deep breath of the perfumed air of the cosmetics department on the ground floor. "I really like the grocery floor. Although I've never bought anything there. Yet."

"Well, we could! We could buy containers of food and take them back to the hotel and eat them sitting on the bed, watching TV. Or we could take them to the venue and have whatever we bought for dinner, when everyone else has to eat the hospitality service stuff."

He made her laugh. He made her laugh, and he made her heart

sing. With him it seemed as if there wasn't a worry in the world.

"We could!" Her imagination refused to wrap around that image: the two of them camping out on their bed, watching cartoons, and eating samosas from Harrods when one of the best restaurants in London was right there at their hotel.

"So what do we want to look at?" They stopped at one of the information boards near the escalator. "A pet shop? Really?" Jon shook his head. "And I thought I'd seen it all."

"I don't think they sell pets." She was laughing again, and every time she did it seemed as if another piece of ice crumbled from her heart. "But they have the weirdest stuff ever, like designer shoes for poodles, and little coats for dogs, and diamond collars for cats."

He gazed at her, amazement in his eyes, and Naomi shrugged. "It's true! This is the place where you can get anything. It's the craziest store in the whole world."

"So what do you want? Come on, tell me. I promised to take care of you, and it starts here and now." Slinging his arm around her neck, he pointed at the board. "I'm sure we can find something pretty for you here."

"I don't need anything, Jon. Really. I'm happy."

That brought out another of his lovely smiles and earned her a kiss. "That's not what I asked."

"Jon." How to tell him that she'd had her share of pretty things, that her life had been dictated by being a lady, by looking correct, by wearing the proper clothes for the time of day and the occasion. "I want to live with you in California, and write songs with you, and walk on the beach. That's all I want. I don't need anything. I want to lead the hippie life."

"That's all you want? Really? Nothing else?" His lips brushed her hair.

"Yes, well, maybe something else." Again she had to laugh. "But that's not something you can buy here."

"It isn't." Serious again, Jon held her hands in his. "I can't believe you're really here, with me. I laid awake that night in Paris and wondered if I'd ever see you again. I knew I'd return to Geneva if you didn't show up, and walk right up to your door and demand to be let in. Would I have been let in? Would you have opened the door to me?"

That one was easy since it would never happen now. "Of course, Jon. I told you I'd come, so only something dire would have kept me back."

"And your parents?" There was this one crease that appeared between his eyes when he was confused or worried, and it made him even more beautiful.

"It wasn't easy." She pulled up her shoulder. "But I really don't want to talk about it. I'm here, with you, and that's really all that matters, isn't it?"

"Yes. Yes, it is. I just don't want anybody to be hurt or alienated. I know how important family is." He nodded toward the escalator. "Care to go to the men's department with me? I think I need to buy something, even if it's only a shirt, just to prove to myself that I was really here."

"The men's department is over there." She pointed, and again he gave her that curious glance.

"So who was the man who took you shopping here before me? A secret lover you haven't told me about? Do I need to be jealous?"

Another piece of ice fell. "You're so silly! It was my father. He hates Harrods; he says it's for show-offs and tourists, but we used to come here anyway because I love its quirkiness. Now stop quizzing me, or I'll make you go to the Hermès department and buy me a Birkin handbag."

"Yes, let's do that! If that's something you want, let's do it!" He was ready to turn around, but Naomi pulled him back.

"Jon! Stop being so silly! Come on, let's get your shirt and then we can walk around a bit, and you can comment on the weirdness all you like."

HIS mother, he told her as he tried on shirts, had only come to California once to visit him, and she'd not been thrilled by the way he lived. She'd left soon, but not before he'd seen the way she'd avoided his eyes and pinched her lips. It all meant so little to her, his big house, the German sports car, the studio, and the people in it.

"Music isn't a real job to her," Jon explained, sticking his head through the curtain of the changing cubicle. "She can't grasp it, measure it."

"Sure she can." Naomi held up a cream silk shirt for him to inspect, and he shook his head. "You should have showed her your bank statements; maybe that would have impressed her."

"It's not about the money. She knows I make a lot of money." He took a red shirt from her. "It's about…oh heck, I don't know what it's about. My brother is a surgeon, my sister a teacher. My father was a surgeon. That kind of thing. A profession."

Naomi tried to imagine his family, but in her fantasy they all looked like Jon: tall, dark-haired, handsome.

"I think she'd have loved for me to go to medical school too. That would have made her proud: her sons, and both doctors. I really tried to get used to that idea, but it just didn't work for me. I'm different, the odd one out, the idiot savant. No one else sings or writes songs in my family." Buttoning the shirt, he looked at her. "My sister teaches music though. And you? Any siblings? What do your parents do? Does your mother work?"

"She's an English teacher." Again, half-truths. "My dad is a banker. They're boring, nothing special. And no, no siblings. I'm the only child."

"And what was your subject at college? You did say you were at college, right?" He handed the shirt back to her. "I think I'll take that one. And the blue one too. Not the cream, though."

"Why not? It looks great on you, with your dark hair and your nice tan!"

"Oh okay then." A slow, tender smile pulled at his mouth. "If you want it, then I'll buy it."

Naomi sat on the sofa outside the cubicles, the shirt in her lap, and she had to pinch her eyes shut.

A different world. She was in a different world, one that overlapped with hers, happened in the same places, and yet it was so different, like a parallel universe, like something going on at the same time yet separated from her old life by a thin, invisible membrane; and she'd pushed through it without even really realizing it.

"You only brought that small bag," Jon said. He was back, pushing his fingers through his hair, gazing at her quizzically. "I'm thinking you can't possibly have brought all the stuff you need. Let's go and get what you need, okay? We'll be on the road for a few more days, and you're not really thinking of washing your clothes in the shower, are you?"

"That hotel has a very good laundry service." Again she hadn't thought about what she was saying. "But yes, you're right. I really do need underwear and…and maybe some light clothes." Anything to steer him away from asking more questions. "It's hot in LA now, isn't it? What do girls wear in California in the summer?"

He took the shirt from her and moved toward the checkout. "Shorts. And cute little tops that leave their midriff naked." Grinning, he waited for her to follow. "And Rollerblades. Or surfboards. Have you ever surfed?"

She shook her head, promising herself to think before she talked again. "No, never. I've also never been to the US and never to California. But I think I've read somewhere that it never gets cold, and that it's always sunny."

"Well, not always. It does rain sometimes, and it gets cool at night. The nights are almost never hot. Sometimes when I go out on the beach in the early morning there are dolphins playing in the surf." He took the bag with his shirts from the lady behind the counter. "I still can't believe you're really here, and that you're really going with me. It's like a dream." Lost in thought, he gazed at her. "Maybe I should ask you to marry me right here and now, just to make sure you won't change your mind and run off. I'm sure they have a jewelry department! Come on, let's go find it, and I'll buy you a ring!"

Naomi laughed. It was a good kind of laugh too, one that made the last pieces of ice burst away from her heart in tiny, rainbow-colored shards, and they fell around her like glitter, like magic dust.

"I'll not marry you here and now, Jon Stone! Let's see how it goes once we're in LA, when we wake up side by side every morning and…" The sentence died on its way from her tongue to her lips.

"Yeah," Jon said softy. "Yeah, and I can hardly wait for that new life to begin. I can't wait to show you the garden, and walk with you under the cedars. And the beach, and the house. Now it all makes sense." He laid his arm around her. "I thought Sal had lost his mind when he urged me to buy that huge house with all that land too. I've spent hours wandering through the house, and back and forth across the property, and all the way along the wall around it, wondering how my life would look ten years from now and if I'd still be the only person living there, a lonely man with a huge, silent house. But now I know it was meant for you, for you and me, for us to live there, together."

They entered the food court, and Jon stopped walking, overwhelmed by the splendor and opulence.

"I think I've changed my mind," he said. "As much as I like the idea of having a picnic with you, I'd never be able to make up my mind about what to buy here. Come on, let's go back to the hotel. I'll buy you lunch there. But first we're going to get you some summer clothes for California."

Chapter Thirty-two

IT FELT STRANGE to be in a hotel that didn't belong to her family. It felt even stranger to be on a floor that had been completely reserved for them, with security next to the elevator so no one could enter who didn't belong to their troupe.

Sal had given her a pass and told her to carry it with her at all times, because no one would be admitted without it, absolutely no one.

Naomi had glanced at Jon, but he'd shrugged and nodded, and got his own pass out of his jeans pocket and held it up.

"All of us. Even me. Which is funny, isn't it? As if there were two Jon Stones running around in this world."

"You don't really look that unique, you know," Sal had mumbled sourly. "You never know if there's an impostor hiding somewhere, ready to jump out and slit your throat." He blanched and shut his mouth so fast that his teeth clicked.

"I'm sorry," he went on after a moment of icy silence. "Sorry, Jon. That was a bad example."

"Yeah." Jon, his eyes closed, took a very deep breath. "It's okay, Sal. Won't go away by not talking about it. Forget it."

Turning the small plastic card over and over in her hands, Naomi followed him into his suite. Their suite, she had to remind herself, theirs. She stayed here now too.

And there were her shopping bags, obligingly delivered by the hotel bellboy who'd taken them from her when they'd entered the lobby, right after he'd offered them a refreshment, and could he lead them to the restaurant.

"Sure," Jon had replied, and that's where they'd sat, on the terrace at the back of the building overlooking the garden.

She'd sat in the same spot with her parents many times after a shopping spree on Bond Street or Harrods, and they'd had lunch and talked about where to go that night for some music or to see a play.

Fear crept up her back every time the door opened and someone stepped through it, expecting it to be her father, by now knowing where she was, and with whom. Come to bring her back home. He'd surely take her straight to the mansion in Kleinburg, and she'd be locked up until her wedding day.

Seth—she wondered if he knew yet, and if he even cared.

She was quite sure he was not too happy; after all, the Carlsson fortune had just slipped from his grasp.

"I'll have to leave soon."

Jon's words ripped her out of her thoughts. "Go? Where?" Panic turned her brain to ice.

"To the soundcheck, of course! Are you coming? Or would you rather do something else now and come over later for the concert?" He glanced at his watch. "Maybe you'd rather get some rest?" His eyes twinkled. "Or do some more shopping? I'll make sure you get a limousine and a driver."

"No!" Naomi threw her arms around him. "No, I want to go! I don't want to be where you're not! Of course I'll go with you!"

"Ah, Naomi." He kissed her, holding her in a tight embrace. "You must be a fairy, a dream come true. I know it's so because I saw it happen when you walked into that hotel lobby in Geneva. There was all that sunlight pooling in the entrance, and you, you stepped out of it as if you'd just descended from a different reality. Or you were made in that moment. That's it! You were created for me, out of sunlight and mist. Only for me, my love, my mystery maiden!"

"Jon." Again she saw Seth, the way he'd been standing there on the terrace holding out the ring, and how his eyes had slid away from her and back to the ballroom, as if he regretted asking her to come outside even though it was a lovely summer night. He'd asked her to marry him and hadn't even looked at her. Only when the ring had been on her finger had he smiled.

"Yeah, babe. I'm right here. And I'll never let you go; don't be afraid." Jon kissed her again. "You'll never have to be sad, or lonely, or unloved again. I promise. And as soon as you let me buy you a ring, we'll get married. I want to. Very much."

That made her laugh. "You're such a romantic, Jon! Let's give it a bit of time, okay? I'm not going anywhere, I promise. A ring won't change that. But I'm not ready to marry just yet. Will it be enough if I promise to love you forever and ever, and to never leave you?"

"It will have to do, I guess." But he smiled. "I understand, my love. And you deserve something better than a hasty wedding on the road. You deserve a big reception, and a real wedding dress, and flowers, and a church." His brow creased. "A church? Do you want to get married in a church?"

"Yes, Jon. I do. And it will be to you or no one. That I can promise." And she knew it was the truth, because it was her heart speaking.

SHE sat with Sally while Jon got ready for the show, saying that she'd seen enough of murky dressing rooms to last her a lifetime; and Jon, throwing a crumpled tissue in her direction, called that she'd not seen nearly enough of them to have an educated opinion, but if she preferred Sally and coffee to him and face powder, he could take it easily. He laughed too, shouting after her, and the tissue landed somewhere on the floor, in an undecided spot, neither close to the wastebasket nor near her. Sal, sighing, picked it up and shook his head at them, but he too was smiling.

"There's a lot of fun these days," Naomi could hear him say just before the door closed, and it made her smile.

Sally waved at her when she entered hospitality. "They're serving us some lovely cake and shortbread and stuff!" She pointed at the buffet. "We made Harrods do the catering, and I'm overwhelmed." And gave Naomi a puzzled look when she laughed.

There were the samosas she'd been thinking of, and the meat pies, and curries, and the petits fours she always had to stay away from because they were just too tempting to ignore. And now, popping one into her mouth, Naomi had to swallow against the sweet icing and the bitter taste of sorrow.

Lucia had always bought some of them anyway, even though Naomi asked her not to, commenting that she was a young girl, and teenagers could eat whatever they wanted without gaining weight. She knew only too well how Naomi would howl later, regretting her decision. And she'd been so right; once they were on their jet, as soon as it taxied to the runway, she'd ask her mother if she could have the tiny cakes. Lucia would hand them over and watch in bemusement as they vanished before the plane even took off.

"I love these," Naomi said, bringing a plate of petits fours over to Sally's table with her mug of coffee. "I'm crazy for icing. Give me iced cake over chocolates any day."

She was wearing one of the summer dresses Jon had bought for her that morning, and she felt great in it.

"You're running away from home, aren't you."

Naomi choked on the cake.

Sally didn't look at her; she was holding a bottle of Coke, picking at the label with her bright-red fingernails that matched the top she was wearing. "How do I know? You didn't bring any luggage worth mentioning. You go out and buy new stuff first thing after getting here. And you're hiding. No calls home, no "I have to tell my mom!", no mention of your family, nothing. You ran away from home, and you're hiding." She took a gulp of her Coke. "And I'm wondering if that could be harmful to Jon or if it's okay."

"I'm not harming Jon!" It came out much too fast and panicky to convince Sally.

"Look," she said, putting down her Coke. "I like you. You're a bright, pretty kid, and Jon is obviously head over heels about you. Those lyrics of yours are killers, and you seem to be well educated. If I tried I couldn't find anyone better for Jon. But there's this aura of mystery and secrecy about you, and that makes me wary." She grinned mirthlessly. "I'm a woman. Trust me, I can see it." Sally brought out a pack of menthol cigarettes and offered it to Naomi, who shook her head. "That travel bag you brought, it's from an expensive designer. I know the brand. Not really trendy but a classic. Something parents would buy you for Christmas. And that garment bag…The name of that designer is printed on it like a scream! And you travel well. You've been on planes and in hotels often; you know your way around. You don't wait for Jon to show you everything." She tilted her head and pinched her eyes into skeptical slits. "In fact, you are showing him how Europe works. He told me you saved his life today when you pulled him back when he was almost run over by a bus. You're educated, your manners are impeccable, and you sure know how to dress."

The cakes didn't look so luscious anymore. In fact, they seemed like little poisonous toads stuck in sugar and cream.

"When I was in Canada a couple of years ago," Sally went on, "I went skiing with some friends, and we stayed at a very nice hotel, a really nice hotel. And it was part of a chain, the Carlsson Hotels. I wonder if you've ever heard of them? They are family owned, and there's a pretty young heiress, I've been told."

Naomi raised her chin. "No, I've never heard of them."

"Uh-huh." Sally picked out one of the petits fours, a pink one with a tiny silver pearl on it, and bit into it. "I'm thinking that if I was that girl, and I knew all that responsibility was coming my way, and I'd just fallen in love with a handsome, talented, and very charming rock star…" Her face relaxed into a smile. "I'd run away too. And I'd want to keep my secret at all costs."

"Not at all costs." This was a battle she could fight. All she had to do was think of Fleur and look at the plain, white coffee mug on the table. "There's a limit to what I'd do to get away from that, if I was that heiress. I'd not want to harm anyone, ever. I'd not purchase my freedom at the cost of broken hearts. Life as an heiress can't be that bad, can it? But yes, you're right. I'd not want my secret to be known. I'd rather be me, just any girl, and be loved for what I am and not for my family's wealth. I'd want that more than anything at all."

Sally got up and went over to the buffet and returned with a bottle of champagne and two glasses. The cork popped nicely, and they watched it fly across the room and drop next to the door.

"Now that's something I can understand. I'll drink to that!" The champagne bubbled in the glasses. "Here." She pushed one of the glasses toward Naomi. "Isn't it great that some people can keep secrets so well?"

"Some better than others." Naomi raised her glass and clinked it against Sally's.

"You said it. Some better than others. I'm not sure men can keep secrets at all though. And some men shouldn't be burdened with secrets, ever, because it would worry them into distraction."

They grinned at each other, and Sally poured some more champagne.

Chapter Thirty-three

THEY ARRIVED IN Los Angeles late in the afternoon.

The sea shone like silver in the lazy sun, like a rippled mirror reflecting the sky.

Sally, from the back of the plane, was singing "I'm home, I'm home!" and dancing in her seat until Sean and Jones joined her and changed the song to "99 Miles to LA."

Naomi, her head on Jon's shoulder, remembered when she'd heard that song for the first time. Five years ago it had been; she'd been thirteen, and a mutinous teenager. In London, they'd been in London to see a musical, and her father had taken them to dinner at a Japanese restaurant. She'd stared at the sushi rolls with the outraged disgust of a child waiting for reasons to throw a tantrum, and that song had played on the radio. It had made her want to cry; the sad melody and the yearning words had pulled at her heart that badly.

"Oh shut up, you!" Jon shouted at them, half laughing. "You're so off tune, my ears are screaming!"

"So sing along with us," Sally cried. "Come on, Jon!"

He waved her away, saying that he was all sung out, as dry as the desert in Arizona, and no, he wouldn't open his mouth to sing for a while, not for the rest of the year, and maybe even longer, thank you very much.

The way they traveled had been a surprise to her. Like a group of school kids on a field trip, they'd scrambled onto the bus that took them to the airport, and they'd piled aboard the private plane as if it belonged to them, bickering over seats, insisting that this one or that particular one belonged to them, and no, they sat there all the time, every time they flew.

Naomi saw them start a pillow fight with the small pillows supplied by the airline.

"Yes," Sally'd said, coming up behind her, "you're traveling with a bunch of kids. Let no one say you weren't warned."

It was so different. Living with these people, musicians, was so different. No one talked about money, or business meetings, or anything related to business at all. Instead, they talked about going home, being at home with their loved ones again, and how they couldn't sleep in hotel beds, and that they'd bring their own pillows next time. And they talked about music. They talked about music all the time: during meals, on the bus, before soundcheck and after, and then again after the concert. They rehashed last night's show over breakfast and on the way to the next airport. They wrote songs during their bus rides, and they brought their instruments into the cabin of the plane so they could have an impromptu session whenever they felt like it.

It was on their flight from London to Dublin that Naomi first heard her "Secret Garden" played by the band, sung by Jon. Embarrassment prickled on her skin, hearing her own words, but she was the only one feeling awkward. No one was looking her way or trying to involve her. The lyrics belonged to them now; they were interwoven with Jon's music, no longer strangers.

Sal kept repeating how he missed a good burger, and Sean sighed and told her how he couldn't wait to get to the beach and on his surfboard.

"Dolphins," he'd said, his eyes shining, "Sometimes the dolphins come out to play. There's no place like California, and no city like Los Angeles. You'll love it, Naomi. Music everywhere, and laughter."

She'd had a strange dream the last night on their tour, in Dublin.

She'd dreamed she was on her way to Los Angeles, alone, and the airport was somewhere in the mountains. She had to make her way down to the shore on her own. There were no cars, no highways; she had to walk down the mountainside and into a village made of tents and banners, a hippie place where naked children ran in a meadow and the grown-ups wore colorful, flowing clothes. They came out to greet her, those forest fairies, and welcomed her, fed her, and let her rest for a while until one of them offered to take her down to the shore and into the city.

In an open carriage they descended into LA, only it wasn't anything like a modern city. Transparent, pastel towers rose into a lavender sky, gossamer bridges connecting them to each other. There was music in the air: ethereal, breezy melodies that seemed to hold the city together, seemed to make those towers grow from the white sand.

Her driver took her all the way to the beach, where she got out near a row of huts, each one painted in a different color. She knew Jon lived in one of them and so she walked along the row of buildings, reading the names of the owners on the doors, until she reached his. She knocked and entered, and there was the band, sitting around a table, and they welcomed her like a long lost child who had returned at last.

When she'd told them her dream over breakfast they'd laughed, all of them. They'd wondered what she'd had for dinner, or if someone had mixed magic mushrooms into the omelet that she'd had for breakfast.

"I'm so sorry, Naomi," Sal had crowed, patting her shoulder. "But LA looks nothing like that. Nothing. Really."

She knew that, of course. But it still had been a lovely dream, a happy dream, and it had made her wake up full of anticipation and longing for a place she'd never seen.

So here she was. As the plane descended, she looked out the window at the sea below. She could see big waves rolling toward the beach, white-crested ocean hands grasping for the land, wearing capes of blues and greens, brilliant hues kissing the generous shore.

"This is home," Jon said softly, taking her hand. "I hope you'll like it. I hope you'll be happy here."

"It doesn't matter where we live," Naomi replied. "I'll always be happy as long as you're there."

His eyes shone even brighter than the sun.

THE van took them along the highway and through the city, and then along the shore, until it stopped at last outside tall wrought-iron gates set into a high wall that marched away, hiding the estate from prying eyes.

"Here we are. Home" Jon said, a tinge of nervousness in his voice.

Gravel crunched under the van's wheels as it slowly approached the house. In the dusk, Naomi could see palm trees and dark bushes, and then, after following the gentle curve of the driveway, the house.

It wasn't a small house; it wasn't really a house at all. It was a mansion. Not as huge and sprawling as the Carlsson manor, but large, really large, and a lot more inviting than the strict, gray walls of her family home. The white façade was joyfully interrupted by balconies and big bay windows; a porch led onto a tiled terrace, and there was even a turret jutting from the roof like a jaunty finger pointing at the sky. The entrance was lit, and so were many of the windows, to welcome the master home.

"This is where I live." Jon, getting out of the car, held out his hand to her. "Let me show you the house."

They wandered through the rooms together: the large living and dining areas on the ground floor, the kitchen, his studio, the porch, and then up the wide stairs to many unused rooms, until they entered his bedroom with its roof garden.

Returning downstairs, Jon led her through the garden wilderness, following the meandering path among jasmine and bougainvillea bushes, and unlocked a mesh wire gate leading out onto the beach. The sun was setting, pouring copper light on the water, bathing it in shades of gold and red.

At the water's edge, Naomi stopped, her feet in the warm surf, her hair blowing in the gentle breeze.

"The tide sounds like the heartbeat of the planet," she said. "Isn't it lovely? Like calm breathing, the steady pulse of a huge, slumbering creature, like the creature that carries us through the galaxy."

"I knew it." Jon gathered her into a tight embrace. "I knew my heart was right when it decided to fall in love with you the moment I saw you. You are magical! The magic is in you; you bring it with you wherever you go, Naomi. You can't be just a girl. Surely you forgot, but you must be a star that dropped from the sky and lost her memory, or a selkie come from the depths of the ocean and turned into a lovely human, and just for me. You're surely a miracle."

"I'm nothing of the kind." She had to close her eyes, and still it didn't feel real yet. It was so hard to believe that she was truly here, in Los Angeles, and with Jon. "I really am just a regular girl. Nothing fancy about me!"

"Well, maybe you can't see it yourself, my lovely fairy maiden, but for me you're all that: miraculous, wonderful, my forever love."

THEY were all alone in the house. The housekeeper had left food in the fridge, with a note on how to heat it up if they wanted it and not to worry about the dishes; she'd take care of them in the morning.

Naomi had never eaten Mexican food. Jon lifted her up and sat her on the kitchen counter like a child, and handed her a glass of red wine.

"I'll get you dinner," he said, and from her perch she watched him handle plates and bowls, and the frying pan.

"Have you always lived alone?" she asked.

The many things they didn't know about the other. The many things she'd never, ever share with him.

"Not very long, no. Since I came to LA, more or less. A couple of months before that, in New York, but I wasn't really alone. I shared an apartment with Sean. And before that..." He glanced at her over his shoulder. "I lived with a girl. We broke up when I signed my first record deal and decided to come to California. She wanted me to lead a 'real' life, whatever that is. My life doesn't seem unreal to me. In fact, it seems pretty real right now."

"What was she like, your old girlfriend?"

Jon shrugged. "She was nice. Pretty, that strawberry-blond kind of pretty. But she put all these limits on herself. Her goals were so narrow, so dismally narrow. If it had been up to her, life would have been a straight road to marriage, kids, retirement, and death. And I couldn't walk that road. Not with her, not with anyone. Life is more than that. A lot more than that. And I want to see where those roads lead."

"Yes." He was voicing her own feelings, her own needs.

"So what about you? What were you doing before we met?"

The food was beginning to smell delicious. Naomi hadn't realized how hungry she was. “Nothing. Lazing away the summer, hanging out with friends. And then you happened. That’s all, really.” She could see that he wasn’t quite satisfied with her reply, so she added, “University would have started in fall. I’d have returned to that if you hadn’t happened.”

“So what was your major; you never said?” The pan in hand, Jon ladled chili onto a plate and held it out to her.

“Arts.” That was as close to the truth as she dared to go and yet not a straight out lie either.

“That must have been nice.” He handed her a piece of French bread. “I can see you doing that, in a town like Geneva. A cultured, sophisticated life. Very nice.” A boyish grin flitted across his face. “I’m afraid I can’t offer sophisticated to you. I’m just a regular guy, with a staunchly middle-class upbringing. I hope I’ll meet your expectations, Naomi.”

“Oh, you already have.” She slid off the counter to sit at the dining table with him. “All I want is you, and the music, and you.”

“You said that twice, you know. The *you*. Does that mean I count double, against the music?”

“Oh, at least twice, Jon.” She wondered how he could even ask. “The music would be nothing without you. You shape the music; you pluck it from the spheres! Without you the music would be as silent as a house with no people, a shore without the surf, a…”

There was a new song there; she could feel it. She could feel the words falling into place, ready to be fixed on paper.

“And…and…” she said, food forgotten, and even Jon. “And can I have a piece of paper, please, and a pencil or something?”

Chapter Thirty-four

HE WATCHED HER, bemused, as she scribbled down one line after the other, sometimes using her fingers to count off syllables, sometimes murmuring the words to herself, testing them for rhythm and rhyme.

Her dinner, long forgotten, had turned cold, and he'd returned it to the pan to reheat it; but she had pushed it away again and asked for more paper, or better, a pad. Yes, did he have that, legal pads, or stationery, or something similar?

"Come," Jon said, and took her hand. He led her to his studio, and to a cabinet, which he opened.

"Here. Whatever you need to write, it should be in here. And if it isn't, we'll go out tomorrow and get it for you. In fact, we should turn one of those unused rooms into an office for you. Would you like that?"

She didn't respond right away but looked around the studio.

"Or would you rather have your own niche here, with me, so we can be together?" It came out a bit breathless, a bit shaky, but he knew he'd said the right thing when she beamed and nodded.

"Yes, I'd like that very much, Jon! I'd love to be here, with you, and not somewhere else, by myself." She hesitated. "But only if it's okay with you. I don't want to be a burden, or a nuisance."

"You could never be a nuisance, let alone a burden! Let's go out and get you a desk or couch or whatever you want first thing in the morning!"

THEY went to bed with the door to the roof garden wide-open to let in the breeze from the ocean and to listen to the surf's slow song.

It seemed to Naomi as if the night was alive with sounds: the waves dancing on the beach, the palm trees rubbing their dry leaf fingers in glee, and the crickets tuning their instruments for a concert under the bushes. From far away she could hear the city: a police siren now and then, the steady hum of traffic, even after midnight.

She lay, safe in the cradle of Jon's arms, her eyes half closed, and marveled at the change in her life.

She wondered what her parents were doing now, if they had accepted her decision, if they'd returned to Canada to inform Seth that there would be no wedding, not now and not later.

So many good-byes, and so many words left unsaid.

Fleur. Naomi wondered if she'd ever see her again. Maybe someday, when she was older and more secure in her own skin, she'd go back and visit. She'd return to all the places she'd loved in Geneva, and maybe even Toronto.

She could see it: From the airport, they'd take the detour through the city, and she'd show Jon the CN Tower, and they'd drive up Yonge Street until the city dwindled away and all that would be left would be rural Ontario, and dark trees, and wilderness. All the way up to Lake Simcoe they'd go, and then turn around and toward Kleinburg, where she'd show him the family house so he could see where she grew up.

And later he'd take her to New York and to the club where he'd started his career. Maybe he'd even introduce her to his family, proudly, presenting her as his love, his future wife, his one and only.

New York. She'd never been there.

Olaf hated New York as much as he hated the rest of America. In his best moments he'd called it infantile, a country of teenagers, the playground of the world; and no, he'd not go there, let alone own property there.

"What's wrong with Europe?" he'd ask, and dramatically throw out his arms as if he wanted to embrace the old continent. "What's wrong with being civilized and cultured?"

And every time, Lucia would gently raise her eyes to him and remind him that he wasn't European either; he was Canadian. After all, his family had left the Norwegian home turf generations ago, and his Norwegian was shaky at best.

Olaf, always fond of arguing with his wife over irrational matters, would draw his brow into a very good imitation of a Norwegian blizzard and respond in a sepulchral voice that no one whose ancestry was Scandinavian ever forgot their home. It was woven into their blood, the old Viking songs still ran in their veins, and would she like to hear him sing one of them for her?

Those moments had always made her laugh so hard that she'd ended up stuffing something into her mouth, sometimes a napkin, sometimes one of the sofa cushion, and sometimes her fist.

A lonely tear dropped from her face onto the pillow.

Naomi could feel its path from the corner of her eye down her cheek, leaving a wet trail behind like a snail after a rainfall. She imagined crawling out of bed and down to the kitchen, where she'd pick up the phone and call her parents to tell them that she was okay, everything was well, and not to worry about her: she'd found love and happiness.

Only she couldn't imagine her father caring to hear that from her at all, or even listening to her.

He'd never listened to her, unless she'd said something he wanted to hear.

Jon moved, mumbling in his sleep, and she crept out of bed.

Wrapped in the quilt, she wandered through the big house, opening every door, stepping into each room. There were so many of them, all unused, empty shells of their former beauty.

It seemed alive, that big house, and sometimes it seemed to hold its breath when she turned on the lights in a particular spot, as if awaiting her verdict.

"Don't worry so much," Naomi said into the silence when she entered a room on the ground floor that had obviously been a library once but now was only a deserted hull. "You're lovely, and you know it."

She could see it brought back to life: the rooms furnished and decorated, lived in; and the roof garden transformed into an island for repose, with flowers and comfortable chairs, and maybe even a daybed.

There would be dinners with their friends and barbecues out on the terrace; and there'd always be music, and love.

The dried tear path on her cheek itched, and she rubbed at it. There was no reason for tears.

PULLING the quilt tighter around herself, she turned on the lights in the studio.

There was a Steinway grand in the middle of the room and along the wall, within easy reach of the piano bench, the guitar stands. She counted four. They were still empty; Jon hadn't taken the time to remove the guitars from their cases yet.

On the top of the grand lay music sheets, some with notes scribbled on them, others with lyrics or part of lyrics; and among them, as if they belonged here, as if they'd always been a part of Jon, were her own.

Her fingers shaking, Naomi picked them out and sat down on the bench.

Here they were, the threads that had woven her life into Jon's. He'd added his own comments to her typed-out words, and they were directed at her; he'd been talking to her through her rhymes, asking her how she'd come up with that particular line, or what she'd thought when she'd written that verse; and under one text, in bold letters, "Who do you think you are? You're driving me nuts with these!"

Giggling, shocked, Naomi slapped her hand over her mouth.

That, and it had been the same for him! He'd felt as annoyed, as restless with her words as she'd been with his music; and he'd returned the feeling to her with that sentence.

Willfully, he'd drawn staff lines on the same sheet and thrown down the notes, much in the same untidy way she'd seen on Beethoven originals, as if he'd been battling a melody he didn't even want to hear, as if someone else had been leading his hand.

Softly, as softly as she could, Naomi lifted the keyboard lid and played the short tune with one finger, like a first grader, like someone who'd never touched a piano before.

"What are you doing?"

She nearly jumped off the seat.

Jon, in his shorts, barefoot, and rubbing his eyes, yawning. "I woke up and you were gone; and for a moment I thought I'd only dreamed you, and that was the worst moment ever. And then I heard the piano? What are you doing here in the middle of the night?"

"Nothing." Hastily, she closed the piano and put the sheets back. "I couldn't sleep, and wandered through the house, and ended up here. And..." Her hand came down on her lyrics. "And then I saw these. And, Jon..."

"Yeah." A soft smile shone on his face. "Oh yeah, those." He came over to her. "How everything changed when I saw those! I wanted to get on a plane and find you right away, and shake you until you spilled all your secrets. I wanted to know who you were, and slap those sheets down, and demand to know what you thought you were doing, sending me those lyrics."

"But..."

"No, no excuses! You rattled me badly with those words of yours. How did you do it? How do you do it?" He tugged at the quilt, and she opened it to let him in. "I watched you last night when you wrote that new song; it's more like a poem, like a ribbon of words, and they just tumble out of you!"

His arms were warm around her; and, leaning into him, Naomi again had that overwhelming feeling of being secure, of having arrived in the place where she belonged.

"I don't do anything," she said, her cheek on his chest. "It's just that, words."

"I think we should go back to sleep." He yawned again. "I'm dead tired. Aren't you tired?"

She was, but every time she closed her eyes she felt as if she was awake again, and back home facing her father's wrath.

"Yes, I'm tired too. Let's go back to bed."

"We don't have to go back to sleep right away," Jon suggested halfway up the stairs. "We could talk a bit, or if you don't feel like talking we could do other things, more interesting things, than just talk."

That made her laugh. And it made her stop at the top of the stairs and turn to him.

"I can't believe I'm really here," she said. "I can't believe all this has really happened! Look at you, the most beautiful man in the world, and you fall in love with me! And you want me here! It's really a bit much to take in."

"Says the girl wrapped up in my quilt, fooling around on my Steinway. Says the same girl who sat on my kitchen counter a couple of hours ago and then proceeded, before dinner, to write me another killer song. I think if anyone in the whole wide world has the right to be here, it is you." Jon picked her up and carried her back to the bed. "You're as light as a child, Naomi Carlsson, and as lovely as a flower. I hope my life won't crush you. I hope you'll not want to run from me, or my weird life, ever. I promise to do everything I can to make you want to stay."

"You're the only one talking about leaving, Jon." She curled up into him. "I'm not thinking of leaving. I'm still trying to understand that I've arrived."

"Tomorrow we'll go and get you a couch or whatever, for the studio. And then we'll take a vacation. I want to get away from the business for a few weeks and do something fun. We could drive up the coast to San Francisco and stop wherever we like staying for a couple of days. Try the wines, wander under the giant redwoods in Sequoia National Park. Or we could go down to Mexico and lie around on the beach in Acapulco. Whatever tickles our fancy." His voice sounded tired, gravelly, like after the concerts.

"Or we could stay here," Naomi whispered, "and do nothing. Walk on the beach. Discover the garden. And hide, and let no one else inside."

But she got no response. He'd fallen back asleep.

Chapter Thirty-five

"THERE'S NO OTHER way to tell you. I'm happier than I've ever been."

Naomi opened her eyes to bright sunshine. From the bed, she could see the tops of the palm trees and a deep-blue sky. The surf was thundering; and, closing her eyes again, she imagined huge rollers throwing themselves on the wide beach in a tantrum, the sea angry, tossing white foam much the way Fleur told her to toss mugs.

Again the yearning for her friend tugged at her heart.

"No!" Shouting. Jon was shouting at someone, and it made her heart beat faster in fear. "We're not even going to debate this. She's a grown woman and has made up her mind! I'm not her keeper, and I won't make her do anything she doesn't want to do!"

The fear blossomed into panic. Sitting up, Naomi pulled the quilt up to her chin, listening, but nothing more was said. She hadn't heard who he was yelling at, if there was another person in the house or if he was on the phone. She could hear that he was on the terrace below the bedroom window, but whoever he was yelling at was either inside the house or not there at all.

"No," Jon was saying again, and this time there was real anger in his voice. "That is not going to happen. Not without her say, and certainly not over her head."

Her heart was beating hard. She pulled up her knees and wrapped her arms around them, trying to make herself as small and invisible as she could.

"But why not, for crying out loud?" It was Sal, and he was shouting back at Jon.

"I don't even know what you want, Sal. We got home last night, and you're here already, checking on me? What am I, your kid? Get the hell out of my house and give me a break!"

"Jon."

There was a pause. Naomi imagined them standing, facing each other like two tigers, slowly circling their shadows.

"Jon, listen to me. All I want is to make sure she didn't run away from home, that she isn't a minor so you don't ruin your career over a love affair. Please?"

Blood rushed into Naomi's cheeks. Mortified, embarrassed beyond reason, she threw back her covers and jumped out of bed.

"So where is she?" Sal, and she'd never heard him talk to Jon like that before. There was nothing of the kind, nearly gentle tone he'd used toward her during the tour.

"In my bed!" Jon replied, throwing the words at Sal, "In my bed, and she's still asleep, after we made love all night long, if you must know! Is that what's bugging you, Sal?"

"My God, Jon."

"Don't do that, Sal. Don't go all patronizing on me."

His voice, the voice he was using to talk to Sal, the tone, were nothing she ever wanted to hear directed at her. Listening to them made her think of her father and how he'd use that very same tone to order her around.

Her hands shaking, she grabbed Jon's discarded shirt from the day before and threw it on. Her purse was on the table. She got out her passport.

Like that, her hair wildly flowing, her legs naked, Naomi stepped out onto the balcony.

"Good morning, Sal," she called down, leaning on the balustrade. "You don't have to shout. I really don't care to be woken up by shouting men. Here." Holding our her arm in a graceful arch, thinking of Fleur and her lesson on tantrums, she dropped the passport. It landed at Jon's feet, who picked it up and grinned at her.

"If you don't believe what I tell you, check my age yourself. And no, I wasn't lying. And as for running away from home, I can't see how that is your business since I'm legally an adult."

Jon handed her passport to Sal. "Go on," he offered, "go on and check for yourself. She's right."

Her knees shaking, her hands quivering, Naomi returned inside and sank down on the edge of the bed.

She wondered how Olaf would have reacted to an act of defiance like this. She tried to picture it: her shouting back, throwing things, speaking up for herself; and maybe she should have done that. Maybe she should have stood up to him and not tried to evade the loving oppression.

She saw herself at her birthday ball, and how she'd allowed them to treat her like a piece of furniture, how she'd let Olaf and Seth decide her fate.

"No more," she muttered,. "No more. And no one."

With a deep sigh, Naomi looked around. Her new home. She'd chosen to be here. It had been her own, willful decision, and she'd left everything behind for it. Her sanctuary, the place where she could at last be herself.

"THAT was quite an entrance," Jon said, handing her a cup of coffee. "I'm impressed by your sense of drama!"

Her passport was lying on the kitchen counter, right next to the package of bread.

"You're such a surprise, over and over again. So quiet, so gentle, and there you go, shouting at Sal from the balcony like a liberated Juliet. Very lovely!"

"You woke me up with all that yelling." The coffee was excellent; she held her cup with both hands and inhaled the aroma.

"Yeah, I'm sorry, babe. Wasn't my idea. I could've kicked Sal's ass, I was that annoyed." Jon wiped his hands on a kitchen towel. "Now. What do you want for breakfast? The housekeeper won't be here for another couple of hours, and we'll have to fend for ourselves. Do you want me to cook eggs for you? Toast? I know you have a penchant for fried mushrooms, but there aren't any in the house." He tilted his head, smiling with a new idea. "Or we can go out for breakfast, if you want! Explore the town a little, drive along the shore! What would you like to do?"

Nothing; she wanted to do nothing. She wanted to sit on the kitchen counter all day long and look at him, hear him talk to her, and take in the marvel of what had happened.

"I don't know." The ocean was calling to her. "Take a walk on the beach? Not go anywhere? You must be exhausted after all those weeks on the road and in hotel beds."

He was, Jon admitted, ladling scrambled eggs onto a plate for her and if she was fine with it, he didn't mind a few lazy days.

They had breakfast together, sitting out on the terrace in the mild morning sunshine.

"This is what I do," Jon told her. "This is how I write my songs. I hide here in my house, turn off the phone, and don't answer the door." That made him grin. "Well, I never answer the door, to be honest. That's what the housekeeper and security are here for. Can't have fans walking in on my privacy, right? Privacy has become something I need to protect at all costs." A shadow flew across his face. "It's a weird thing, fame. You do everything to get it, and once you're there you realize you've maneuvered yourself into a prison of your own making. It's lonely sometimes." He waved away the melancholy moment. "But not anymore! Now I have you, and everything will be so much better!"

She'd never thought about it that way. She'd never wondered about fame, or how it could have a dark side.

"Tell me about your old life," she said, and immediately regretted it, full of fear that he'd ask the same of her.

But Jon shrugged, and poured more coffee. There wasn't much to tell, he told her, and talked about his family again, how his mother still ruled the household with an iron fist, and how his sister had just gotten married and was expecting her first child. They were a regular family, he said, shrugging, and there was nothing interesting about them.

"But you," he added, "you're a mystery girl! Canadian passport, and you live in Switzerland. You dress well; you have great taste and manners. I think there's something you're not telling me."

Naomi hid her face behind her cup. "Not really. There's nothing to tell. I was born in Toronto. My father is a banker. His company sent him to Geneva. So that's where he works and where we live. That's all."

She didn't tell him about the private schools, about being driven to school and college by her father's driver, or about the Carlsson hotel empire.

"And you play the piano!"

Dangerous ground, and she needed to divert his attention. "A little. My mother taught me a bit. But I'm nowhere near as good as you are, or Sean. I can read music, yes. But I think all European kids can. It's taught in school." She laughed. "We even had to learn the scales by heart! Our music teacher would make us recite them. I never knew why."

"You're kidding! Why would someone want to do that?" Leaning forward, intrigued, Jon asked, "And do you speak French? Yes, you do; I heard you talking to that man in the chocolate store!"

They smiled at each other, lost in that memory, and it seemed as if it had happened years ago, in another lifetime.

"You made me eat that marzipan, and then you said I couldn't have more of it. So cruel, Naomi!"

"Only because you went all maudlin and soppy on me! We'd only just met, and you were talking about forever!" She tossed a toast crumb at him. "And I stood there, totally dumbstruck, and that was the first thing that popped into my head."

She was talking to him like she talked to Fleur: The words came easily; they slipped from her heart directly onto her tongue. There was no need to think and wonder if she'd say something that she would be punished for in some way.

"Yeah, well, so was I, dumbstruck. The most beautiful girl in the world was feeding me sweets, and her fingers were touching my mouth; what did you expect me to say? You siren, you knew exactly what you were doing! How is a man supposed to keep his head in such a situation?"

"Sheesh, you're easy to impress. That was just chocolate!"

He was gazing at her mouth, gazing at it with softly intense eyes. "Yeah, easy to impress, when the right thing comes along. You didn't have to do much to impress me, my sweet selkie. All that was needed was to see you stand there in the light in that hotel lobby. My heart fell, and me with it. I'm totally enthralled by you. You're everything I could dream up, everything. A flawless being, the perfect maiden, an eternal mystery."

"Jon."

"No, you are. Let me say this, and let it stand, my version of the truth. This is how I want my life to be: you, here, sharing it forever and ever. We'll share our days and nights, and music; and we'll walk on the beach and count the sunsets until we've grown old together. Every new day will be a new miracle. We've found each other, and the secret of love."

The sun was shining on his hair, giving it red highlights, casting a halo around him.

"I like that," Naomi said. "I like that vision. It's the best version of life I can imagine. Yes, Jon. Let's live like that." She got up and went around the table to kiss him. "Because, you know, you're my dream version of a man. I couldn't have made up a better one."

Jon pulled her down onto his lap. "Then we have a deal. It's you and me, baby, forever and ever."

Chapter Thirty-six

IN THE MORNINGS, just after dawn, she'd creep out of bed and walk down to the beach while it was all hers.

Jon had showed her where the key to the gate was kept, muttering it was high time to have another one made and to please always lock it after herself when she left or returned.

"Can't have strangers traipsing around on the grounds," he added. "And trust me, there are some paparazzi out there just waiting for a chance like that."

He'd also told her never to go alone, always to take one of the security guards with her. He didn't want her harmed or abducted; she was his life and his love.

But Naomi couldn't bring herself to wake someone up just because she wanted to take an early-morning walk.

Jon had introduced her to the guards, and they'd greeted her with the same solemn stiffness as every security person she'd ever met. On the way back to the house, she'd wondered aloud if perhaps they were all related: one huge, ancient family of warriors, pledged to protect the wealthy, famous, and powerful.

Jon had laughed at her, had marveled at her limitless fantasy, and asked if she'd ever thought of writing stories or a book. He was curious to see what she'd come up with.

"I'm not a writer," she'd replied softly, hanging her head, all her bravado used up. She'd told him how Fleur had asked her almost the same question, and that made Jon pause on the doorstep, gazing at her thoughtfully.

"Have you called your friend or your parents since we got here?" he'd asked, and she'd looked away.

Not yet, she'd told him, there was still time, she wanted to get settled in first, and anyway, her parents would be on vacation in Italy now, and she had no idea how to reach them.

Fleur, on the other hand, that bothered her. She missed her

friend, and she really wished she could just pick up the phone and call her; but she'd create an awkward situation for Fleur. As it was, she could honestly tell anyone who asked that she had no idea where Naomi was. But all that would change the moment Naomi called her.

SHE loved those early-morning walks.

Alone on the beach, she felt free in a way she'd never felt before, not even when she'd been flying over the golf course with Apollo, leaving outraged shouts from the golfers as they fled from her and her horse.

But that was just the point: It had always felt like a flight, one that ended at the estate gates. A tolerated, measured flight, a vision of freedom inside well-defined boundaries.

Here in Malibu, she was truly free at last. The sky and the sea were her limits, and the wind carried her songs across the water until they mingled with the ocean and came to rest in the sigh of the waves.

Walking along the beach in the lacy curl of the surf, she looked for unusual small stones, shells, and amber. Every day she'd bring something back and show it to Jon: a pearly shell, a black stone with a turquoise vein, a pebble as round and shiny as a marble.

She placed them on the tiles next to the bench in the secret arbor where they rested, offerings to the unseen god of the garden.

Jon regarded them with puzzled amusement; but he never made fun of her, and he never reduced her finds to what they were: ocean debris, scattered remnants from distant shores.

Often, returning home from one of her forays, Jon would still be in bed, half asleep, and she'd crawl back under the covers. He'd complain about her being cold and wrap her in his arms and the quilt, and they'd fall back into the light slumber of early morning.

They lived in this quiet and undisturbed bubble of new love and solitude for nearly three weeks, following the slow, sweet rhythm of their love and the tides, and no one broke into the cocoon they'd spun around themselves.

The words flowed out of Naomi, falling into rhymes without any effort at all; and there would be Jon, ready to snatch them out of her hands, hungry for them, and she'd watch how he moved to the piano and brought them to life with his music.

It seemed almost too easy, to much like play, to be real.

Bemused, astonished, she watched him work with her lyrics, speaking, humming her words, his brow pulled together in concentration; and that made her wonder all the more: Jon Stone took her writing seriously, valued it, and loved her.

One morning, finding her standing in the middle of the bedroom, her arms crossed, he asked her if anything was wrong.

"Nothing," Naomi said without thinking. "Nothing at all. Only I wish we had a carpet here. And curtains. I love lace curtains blowing in the breeze." She waved at the bare walls. "And some art. This room is so bare, Jon; it's almost as if no one lives here. It's so transitory and stark." She added, after a moment's thought, "The entire house is. There are so many empty, unused rooms! Why are they empty?"

Perplexed, he shrugged. "I have no idea! I didn't need them, I guess. It's a lot of wasted space. I'd be happy in a small beach house. Just, you know, a bedroom, a living room, and a kitchen."

"And a bathroom, hopefully," Naomi added, laughing. "But you have this house."

"It's not really my house, you know." Jon laid his hands on her shoulders, standing behind her. "It's ours now, yours and mine. You're the mistress here. So if you want to change anything, do it! I want you to feel at home here, Naomi. I want you to own this place, make it yours. You're the reason I bought it in the first place." His cheek came to rest on the top of her head. "It's strange, but I kept seeing you. You seemed to be around all the time, like a fairy. I saw you dancing in the garden at dusk, and I saw you on a winter day in New York City, wearing a blue coat; and your silver laughter went through me like a knife."

"I've never been to New York, Jon," Naomi reminded him, but he went on, undeterred. "It wasn't really you, I know that. But it was as if I was always seeing you, in every girl that walked past me, in every turn of a head that caught my eyes. It was always you. And all my songs, they were written for you too. I know I was searching for you without even knowing it. There was this big, empty space in my soul that's filled now."

"And here I was just talking about carpets."

"Yes, darling, carpets." He let go of her to step back and spread his arms in a grand gesture. "And curtains, and art, and furniture for the other rooms. We'll have to make up uses for them, you know. Or we can decide to sleep in a different one every night; that should keep us on our toes."

"Or we could have a couple of guest rooms, Jon." He made her laugh; her heart was light, living with Jon. She felt both free and ensnared, at the same time.

"Guest rooms," Jon repeated thoughtfully.

"Yes, Jon. Guest rooms. For when your mother or family want to visit. Or Fleur."

"Or your family! I like that idea!" With a nod, he caught her in another embrace. "I like that a lot! I'd love to meet your parents sometime."

"Yes, sometime. Maybe." She didn't want the conversation going that way. "But first we need to furnish the rooms."

ON the way back downstairs, Jon said, "You know you never talk about your family, Naomi? And I'm sure you haven't called them yet either. Did you run away from home after all?"

"You can't run away from home if you're legally an adult, Jon."

He stopped on the last step and turned back to her. They were eye to eye for once. "I know that. But there's something…I don't know. Something of a mystery about you that makes me think you didn't part on the friendliest of terms with them. Am I right?"

"If you must know, yes. You're right. And I don't want to talk about it. Everything is fine, Jon. Or…" she laid her hands around his face. "Or are you looking for a reason to get rid of me? Because if that's the case, just say so."

"Good grief, no! That's the most dismal prospect ever!" A new idea seemed to occur to him, and he took her hand. "Come on. It's time we left this love nest and explored LA. Come, I want you to meet some people!"

She protested that she needed to change, needed to put on something other than the jeans and t-shirt she was wearing, but Jon didn't listen.

"You're the prettiest girl in town, and you'd be even if you were running around in a potato sack. Come on; you don't need anything!"

They were out of the house and in Jon's Porsche before she could reply. The huge gate swung open, and they were off, the top down, music roaring from the speakers.

Jon drove her along the shore, telling her it was the Pacific Coast Highway, part of State Route 1, which runs along the ocean for more than six hundred miles, from Medicino County north of San Francisco, ending in Dana Point, just outside San Juan Capistrano.

"Someday," he shouted over the music, "we'll drive up and down that road, shall we?"

Naomi nodded. She loved it. She loved the sunny road, the music, the view of the sea, and she loved Jon.

Once, lounging with her friends by Fleur's swimming pool reading some fashion magazine, Manon had asked how one could be sure they were in love, if there was a some sort of test?

Fleur had given her a cool stare over her sunglasses and replied that, of course, the sex had to be great. You couldn't be in love with anyone if the sex wasn't extraordinary. Nothing else mattered.

But Naomi, sitting beside Jon in his car, watching him drive, watching how the wind messed with his hair, knew that it wasn't enough. This, she decided, this was love: making plans for the future, deciding on how to decorate a house, trusting the other enough to go out without even a purse, without a single penny, and knowing him so well that she didn't have to worry. This was surely love: waking up to a new morning, and being happy to have another day with Jon, and wishing for many, many more.

"I'm taking you to meet the two people who were my first friends when I got to LA. They are both astounding people. I think you'll love them."

They parked the car near the Venice Beach pier and strolled along the beach, stopping often to give Naomi time to take in the views and the curiously unique ambiance.

"You were right," she gasped, pointing at the girls with flowing hair and scanty clothes whipping past them on Rollerblades, "and I thought you were making fun of me!"

He led her to a dusty, slightly neglected store, nearly invisible among all the gaudy and lively tourist shops.

"Here." Jon opened the door for her.

Stepping into the gloom, Naomi was met by music. It was loud, and the sound was excellent.

"Handel," she said, "*Xerxes*." Instantly she was thrown back to the night she'd last heard that opera. A knot of sorrow blossomed in her chest.

"Well, if it isn't the world-famous Jon Stone! I'm glad you remembered us!"

An elderly woman came into the light from the murky nook behind the counter. She had long, very curly hair with a color that hovered somewhere between silver and ash gray.

"Rose!" Jon hugged her, kissed her cheek, and let her ruffle his hair as if he was a small boy. "I've brought someone I want you to meet, Naomi."

Rose looked around him. A slow, sweet smile transformed her face into radiant beauty.

"There she is," Rose said. "You've found her! Your muse, the girl all your songs were about. And yes, she looks just like I thought she would."

Chapter Thirty-seven

"SHE'S THE ORIGINAL fairy," Rose said, opening the door to the courtyard behind her shop. "I think I'll have to entice you to come and live with us, here in my little garden. You would fit in so well!"

Sunlight streamed in through the open door, dust motes dancing on its beams, and with it, the sound of wind chimes and a guitar, masterfully played. The melody seemed to dance on the strings and wrap around the tinkle of the chimes. It was coming from a building at the other end of the narrow yard, and Rose was leading them toward it, along a path made of white gravel. On either side, roses nodded in the warm midday air, bees hovered over lavender bushes among sweetly scented jasmine. It was a true fairy garden, a nook of quiet and peace amid the noise and energy of the pier and the promenade.

"This," Jon whispered to Naomi, "this is my secret place. Whenever I feel sad or lonely, or when the music won't come, I drive down here to visit Rose and her husband, Roy. They're like my parents, only better, different. They understand music; they know what it means to be me."

"Shush," Rose interrupted, and threw him a stern glance. "Don't tell that girl nonsense stories. You know very well that it's all about your talent, about your music. You've been given a great gift, Jon Stone. Don't you ever treat it as a joke!"

"Oh, I wasn't..." Jon began, but she held up her hand.

"I know you weren't, and I'll make sure you never start. The moment you don't take yourself seriously as a musician, you'll become a useless Hollywood stud, my boy, and I'll slap you about the head and neck until you turn back into a human."

Naomi hid a giggle behind her hand as Jon gave her a silent, helpless shrug.

They entered the workshop at the back of the garden. The comforting, warm scent of wood and coffee greeted them.

On a stool in the middle of the room sat an elderly man in a leather apron, a guitar on his knee. A thin, gray braid hung down his back, and clasped between his lips was a wooden guitar pick. When he saw Jon, he took it out.

"Oh hello! Back from the tour? You're still yourself, I see," he said. "Good to see you!"

Rising from his seat, he handed Jon the guitar he'd been holding. "Here. While you were gone, I made you a new instrument. Have a look."

It was a beautiful guitar, made from a reddish wood with a fine grain that looked like golden threads running through it. It reminded Naomi of blond strands of hair blowing in a sunset wind.

Jon ran his fingertips along the generous curve of the body and up over the twelve strings. "A beauty," he said softly. "You know how to melt my heart, Roy."

"Well, go ahead and play it then." Gruffly, Roy waved at Jon. "Make her sing."

"I'll get us some tea," Rose suggested, and vanished into the sunlight that hung in the door like a thick, gleaming curtain.

"Did you bring back any new songs?" Roy brought out a piece of chamois and wiped the guitar. "There. You're leaving fingerprints, Jon. A little respect, if you please."

"I didn't bring back new music." Picking at the strings, Jon tuned a couple of them before he began to play. "Instead I brought back the essence of my music." He smiled at Naomi. "Everything makes sense now."

Roy took off his glasses and blinked at her as if he'd only just now noticed her, after Jon had mentioned her.

"Oh yes," he said, "the fairy. I thought she'd wandered in from the garden and only I could see her, so I wasn't going to say anything."

"Naomi's no fairy." Jon laughed. "But she might be a selkie. I think she might be a selkie. Or a star, fallen from the skies."

Roy stepped closer to Naomi, peering at her with narrowed eyes. "Nope. Definitely a fairy. Can't you see the fairy dust sparkling all around her? Maybe you can't see it, Jon. Maybe you need glasses?"

"My eyes are fine, thank you very much!"

"The Secret Garden" dripped from the strings of the guitar like rose petals in a mellow wind.

"Ah," Roy sighed, "Yes, you did bring back new music! Somehow I had a feeling that would happen! And listen to you, so fragile, so sophisticated! You've grown, my friend! Your music has grown." His eyes drifted back to Naomi. "But what's the deal with this fairy, Jon?"

Shaking his head, putting down the guitar on the worktable, Jon said, "I found her in Switzerland, in Geneva. She walked into my life from a puddle of sunlight; she just appeared. And now that I'm thinking about it, you might be right about the fairy thing. Yes, she could very well be a fairy."

"Did she tell you her name? You know that's how you make them stay with you, right? Either by kissing them or by speaking their real name." Sticking out his finger, Roy poked Naomi on the arm, but gently. "She seems to have a physical body now. So I guess you did kiss her. Or you know her name."

"Well, she did say her name was Naomi. That was the first thing she said to me. I'm guessing she wanted to be caught. And yeah, I kissed her too. So she's mine doubly now, yes?"

"Yes, I think so. Good thinking, Jon." He winked at Naomi. "I can see why you wanted to be sure about her. Good thing you have that huge, wild garden. It must seem like a paradise to any fairy creature. Chances are she'll stay for a while."

Naomi was quite sure she'd never heard a crazier conversation, or a more entertaining one.

"I've offered her the house too," Jon said thoughtfully, "and she likes it. Says it needs some decoration, and more furniture though. I think fairies are afraid of empty rooms."

"Ah! Yes!" Roy nodded vigorously. "Didn't you know that empty rooms are fairy traps? You'll have to change that, and quickly, or she'll get suspicious. And then you'll wake up one morning and she'll be gone, vanished without a trace, and you'll never see her again. Better take care of those fairy traps fast, my friend."

"I want her to stay forever." Jon held out his hand to her, and Naomi moved into his embrace. "What do I have to do to make her stay forever?"

Roy tapped the side of his nose. "There's an old legend. If I remember correctly, fairies that get attached to a human need a lot of love, and gentle attention. They need to be treated well, and never be neglected or taken for granted. That's about all. But if you fail in any of those, they'll silently, gracefully step back into the light and their hidden realm. And they'll never return, no matter how much you plead."

Rose returned with a tray holding a teapot, cups, and a plate of cookies in her hands.

"What are you talking about?" she asked, setting the tray on the table, right next to the guitar, which made Roy snatch it up and cradle it like a child.

"About fairies, and what you have to do to keep them." Again the chamois came out and did its slow dance across the guitar's face.

"Ah." Teapot in hand, Rose nodded slowly. "There's an old tale about where the fairies live. It's a place in Norway, a mountain called Glitter-something. It's very high and forbidding, and there's snow on its slopes all year round. It's a very high mountain that looks out over the land."

"Glittertind," Naomi softly said, "It's part of Jotunheimen, the highest mountain range in Norway. It's very lonely and rough up there."

They stared at her.

"In Norway. The mountain?" she added, waving her hand in the direction she supposed east, and north, should be.

"The fairy speaks," Roy cried, pointing at Naomi. "Did you hear that? The fairy speaks!"

"Oh, stop scaring the girl, you silly old man." Rose, shaking her head, held out a cup of tea to her husband. "I'm not seeing any fairy here. All I see is our Jon, and the love for this girl shining in his eyes."

"But you must admit that she does look like a fairy," Roy grumbled, winking at Naomi. "Girl, tell us about that mountain! How do you know anything about mountain ranges in Norway?"

They were staring at her, all three of them, curious, fascinated.

"School." She breathed in the fragrant aroma of the tea. It smelled of summer, and meadows, and sunshine. "We learned that at school. I remembered, because the name of the place was so pretty." Another lie, another careful half-truth.

"In Canada?" Jon held out his cup for more tea, and Rose refilled it. "Wow, your schools must be so much better than ours then. I can't recall learning anything about Norwegian mountains."

Giving him a vague smile, she shrugged.

THEY told her how Jon had shown up in the store one cool and sunny winter day, and demanded music paper and a pencil, and how he had sat down at Rose's piano right there and then and written a song about the beach, and the sunset, and loneliness.

She'd seen his enormous talent right away, Rose said, her eyes shining at Jon. He'd been new to California, a lost boy, stranded on the Santa Monica promenade; and around him had been that aura of music, as if the melodies were floating around him like an invisible crown.

There was this guitar, Roy joined in, that he'd been working on for years, in small steps, never quite clear about its purpose. He'd whittled and polished and fretted over it, and then Jon had walked in and everything became clear.

"He bought it," Roy said, glaring accusingly at Jon. "And he paid a lot of money for it, and then he went and threw it through a window."

Bending down, Roy pulled a battered carton out from under the table. "Here, I've kept it. What a sorry dead thing it is, the rosewood guitar. He killed it. I guess it had to be or the thing with that poor girl would have killed Jon instead. But…"

He brought out the battered body of the guitar and laid it on the table.

It lay there, a dead, broken instrument, mute in its twisted agony.

Naomi reached out to touch it, to run her fingers over the satiny gloss of its front and the shards of broken wood. It seemed like an offering, a sacrifice to the cruel gods of fame.

"I built him another one, of course, and it may even be a better instrument." Roy picked up the neck of the instrument, now dead. "But this one was special. It was a piece of my heart."

"I'm sorry, Roy; I'm so sorry," Jon mumbled, but Roy shook his head.

"No, Jon, don't apologize," he replied. "I'm glad you did it. I'm glad it was there to soak up your burden of sorrow, and take the guilt and sadness with it when you threw it through that window."

"So, fairy princess," Rose said, after taking a deep breath to shake off the gloomy memories, "tell us about yourself, darling? How did you meet our Jon?"

Naomi blushed, the timid teenager once again, and told her story, told these strangers how she'd heard Jon sing on the radio, and how she'd felt the compulsion to write lyrics for him. She left out the part about Fleur and the magazine photos though, and she didn't tell them about her panic after she'd sent the lyrics to the record company.

"And me," Jon added, taking her hand, "she walked out of the light and into my life. I'll never, ever forget the moment I first saw her. She walked right up to me, unafraid, so calm, so lovely, and suddenly I knew what I'd longed for all my life. This girl, and her shape fits into my arms as if she'd been cut out of my embrace and now returned. Since I've met Naomi, I know what love really means, and what peace feels like. I have both. I feel complete."

They smiled at him, Rose and Roy. Their hands crept toward each other across the table and met in a puddle of sunlight, where they rested, the fingers entwined, the rings on them glinting the Morse code of love.

Chapter Thirty-eight

THE CASE WITH the new guitar carefully stowed on the backseat of the Porsche, they drove home.

Remorsefully, Jon promised he'd take her downtown someday soon, but he just couldn't leave the instrument behind or wait another day for it.

"I can hear the new melodies," he told her, swerving around a huge, red truck. "I can't wait to write them down. The tips of my fingers are tingling."

She didn't need the town, Naomi assured him over and over again; she was happy where she was.

"I've seen enough towns; in the end they're all alike," she said, and snapped her mouth shut. Jon didn't reply, so she added, picking her words carefully, "If you live in Europe you get to see a lot of places. It's so small, and everything is close together."

"Yeah. That's true. You cough once, and you're in a different county. Amazing. And the landscape varies so much!"

He stopped the car to wait until the gate swung open. "There is something about you that makes me think you really are a fairy. Maybe Roy wasn't that far off. It always seems as if only part of yourself is here in this world and the rest is in some other realm."

The gravel crunched under the weight of the wheels, the wings of the gate locked with the sound of a sour bell. Naomi breathed easier. She was back in the safety of the house.

Like a fortress, it was like a fortress for her: no one could enter without Jon's permission; no one could come and claim her.

It smelled delicious inside, of garlic and herbs. The housekeeper, Amparo, was there, preparing dinner for them.

"Mister Sal called," she shouted from the kitchen when Jon entered. "Said he'll be here for dinner. He wants to discuss a new project."

"Ah," Jon muttered, and then sighed. "Yeah well, guess our grace time has run out. Was to be expected."

He went into the studio with the new instrument, where he removed it from the case.

"I'll just want to play for a moment," he muttered. "Just give me ten minutes."

Naomi wandered away to give him some space. She got the key to the beach gate from the kitchen, told Amparo that she'd be outside, and left the house.

It was hot on the terrace; the sun was as relentless as a brass hammer fresh from the forge despite the breeze coming from the ocean, but it got better once she was in the shade of the tall bushes. Walking silently, she could hear the susurration of insects and of leaves touching each other, the whisper of blossoms as they unfolded and spilled their fragrance into the air.

Barefoot, her hair freed from the braid, Naomi unlocked the gate and stepped out onto the hot sand.

Her toes curled into it, leaving little dents. She had to rush to get to the cooler, wet part of the beach, where she stood in the surf to cool off her soles and look out toward the endless horizon.

It had felt wrong at first to see the sun wander toward a horizon in the ocean. There'd been an odd sense of being on a different planet, of being cut off from everything she knew. The time was different too: She was many hours away from Fleur or her parents, and that made California feel like the perfect sanctuary.

She wondered what time it was in Geneva now, in the early afternoon. Ten hours, Jon had told her; he thought it was either nine or ten hours, but most certainly a lot. And had added that he felt sort of lost himself, from one coast to the other, with the entire continent between his old and his new home.

"In New York," he'd said, "I felt like I knew the rules, the limitations, and how to break them. Here, no rules apply. Or if there are any, I haven't figured them out yet." He'd taken the stone she'd just picked up. "Sometimes I think luck is the only rule for Hollywood. You either have it or you don't, and it doesn't matter at all if you're talented."

“Then you must have the luck of the devil,” she replied, and Jon had smiled.

Yeah, the luck of the devil, he'd repeated her words, and he sure hoped he wouldn't have to pay for it someday.

THERE were people on the beach at this time of the day: a young couple with two small babies, a runner in an orange sweat suit, some kite flyers, someone sitting in the shade of the palm trees from Jon's estate, and, out on the water, surfers on their boards,and some dolphins. A cool wind was driving big rollers toward the shore, where they crashed on the sand with operatic drama.

Naomi followed the line of new debris just out of reach of the waves, the key dangling from her wrist. The dress she was wearing didn't have any pockets, so she collected shells and pebbles in her skirt, which she held together like a pouch.

She had a ritual for the beach by now; she'd walk as far as the point where it curved out into the sea and a rocky cliff cut off her path. There, she'd turn around and return home.

Home, and how that sounded. She had a new home, one where she could move freely, do whatever she wanted, whenever it seemed right to her. It had taken her a while to realize that, and to break old habits and well-learned rhythms. There was no fixed time for dinner unless she decreed it. There was no huge breakfast buffet like the one at the Carlsson house; she could choose to eat, or not, if she felt like it.

And most importantly, no one pressed her to dress properly, to be well-groomed and to please wear lipstick.

That was a rule she'd never understood. Lucia never explained why it was so important to wear makeup, as important as wearing clean, matching underwear.

Naomi hadn't touched her lipstick since she'd run away with Jon, and no makeup; and no one seemed to miss it, or even notice.

She wore jeans or the light, flimsy summer dresses she'd bought in London; her hair was either in a braid or loose. And that, she knew, was something Jon loved.

He loved her hair, loved to knit his hands into it when they were in bed making love.

Even thinking about that made her blush and hang her head to hide her face. She'd never even imagined it being like this, the sex thing. Fleur's and Manon's tales of their lovers had not prepared her for the all-consuming, intense passion, for someone being so focused on her that the rest of the world simply vanished.

Jon's soul wrapped around her like a soft, warm coat; it kept her safe and happy, and she couldn't get enough of it.

SOMEONE was taking pictures.

It was the solitary man sitting with his back to the mesh fence that was the border to Jon's property. He was using a camera with a zoom, and it seemed as if he was taking photos of the ocean, the gulls and pelicans; but when she looked away she saw from the corner of her eye how he moved and directed the camera at her.

Naomi stopped in her tracks, but nothing happened. The stranger pulled his baseball cap down, shading his face, and sat back. He pulled a box of cigarettes from his pocket and lit one. That's how he sat there, his eyes closed, legs crossed, listening to the surf.

Carefully, very carefully, she walked up to the gate and unlocked it, her eyes still on the man. He was fiddling with his camera again, holding it against the light, peering through the lens with one eye. Naomi could hear it clicking as he took one shot after the other, and it was again aimed in her direction.

As fast as she could, she slammed the gate and locked it behind her. Only when she was halfway to the house did she allow herself to breathe.

Sweat was beading between her shoulder blades, and her hands trembled when she put down her loot on the terrace table.

Paparazzi. Jon had said to watch out for them; they were always hanging out somewhere. He had warned her and told her to take one of the security guards with her, and she'd blown it off into the wind. In her deep yearning to be free, she'd taken the risk, and now here she was. Her photo would probably show up in one tabloid or the other, and her secret would be blown. Cursing herself, cursing her carelessness, she sat in the sun to rub the sand off her feet.

Jon stepped out of the house. “Babe, were you on the beach again?” His hand came to rest on her bare neck, cool and firm against her hot skin. “What did you find today?”

He bent down to inspect the pebbles and shells as if they were jewels she had procured at great danger.

“This one is lovely,” Jon said, holding up a piece of sea glass in a translucent blue, “like a piece of the ocean itself.”

“I think it’s part of a mermaid’s crown,” Naomi replied, taking it from his fingers to polish it on the hem of her skirt. “Can’t you just see it? She’d wear a circlet made of gold, and set in it would be pearls and rubies, and…”

She’d worn that circlet only once, at the ball on her birthday, and now it was languishing in the safe in Geneva. She’d never wear it again.

“And the mermaid princess wears it every day, from morning to night. Her father, the king of the ocean, has warned her often with his dire words to be careful with it and not lose it.” She dropped the bauble back into his hand. “But she doesn’t listen, of course. She’s just too proud of it. So one day when she’s frolicking with her friends among the long fronds of seaweed, she gets too close to the house of old man octopus, and he lashes out at her for being disturbed during his afternoon nap, and he plucks her crown from her. The princess begs and begs for him to return it to her, but he says no, she can’t have it back, she needs to grow up first and learn how to be respectful to her elders.”

“You’re so miraculous!” Jon stood, brushing off his jeans, and lifted her up from her chair. “You’re like that mermaid princess, you know, only you don’t have a crown. I think I’ll have to get you one, and then you can wear it all the time. No one will tell you when and where you can wear it; it will be all yours. Yes, I should do that!”

Kissing her, carrying her in his arms, he danced a slow waltz back into the house, and all the way through the living area into the hallway.

Naomi, her arms tightly around his neck, her skirt swirling, laughed, her heart light, her blood singing.

"Someday I want to see you in a tux," she said, swinging her legs, "I'm sure you look to die for in a tux."

"Hey, I do have one, you know." He kissed her again. "If you want we can go upstairs and I'll put it on for you, and then take it off again. Only I'm not sure I'll put on anything else soon after."

"I think that's a very good plan." Willing. She let him kiss her again and move toward the stairs. "But what about Sal? Aren't you expecting him at any moment?"

"Dammit." Jon sat on the stairs, holding her in his lap. "I'd rather do something else now."

"And me."

Which made him kiss her deeply, his arms around her.

That was how Sal found them when he walked in through the open terrace door.

Chapter Thirty-nine

"WELL," HE SAID, "seems as if I've shown up at the wrong time."

It wasn't so much that he didn't look their way. It was more as if his eyes slipped over them, as if they were invisible to him, as if he could only see a shimmering where they were supposed to be but nothing more.

"You're here now," Jon sighed, "so I guess everything else will have to wait. Amparo made her famous mole with tenderloin strips just for you. You can't make her unhappy by not staying for dinner."

Reluctantly he opened his arms and let Naomi get up. His eyes smiling, he watched her gather her long hair and braid it, her fingers moving among the long curls like fragile shuttles on a loom of midnight-black silk.

"Yes, Sal," Naomi said, "I'll go change; don't mind me. Then we can have dinner, or would you care for a drink first? I'm sure Jon has something you'll fancy."

She left and, walking up the stairs, she could hear Sal mumble an apology for being such an idiot the other day, and he hoped Naomi hadn't been too annoyed, or Jon. He'd meant well; after all, it was his job to look after Jon.

"Well, not exactly." Jon's voice sounded dry and amused. "That's not exactly how I see your job, Sal, but it's okay. I think you could trust me a bit more to do the right thing, and Naomi too. She's no fool, that girl. She does have her secrets, I'll give you that. But don't we all."

They moved away, gravitating toward the studio, and Naomi closed the bedroom door behind her. Standing in front of the open closet, she gazed at the neat lines of clothing: Jon's side of the space ordered, neat, and hers a jumble of flimsy dresses, summer tops, and a couple pairs of jeans, two pairs of sandals.

The closet didn't look as if she lived here. Her clothes looked as transient as the entire bedroom, as if this wasn't a permanent place for her. The thought scared her more than she could grasp.

She'd shoved her travel bag into a corner on the lowest shelf. Her money was hidden in it. So far she hadn't spent much; everything she needed was either in the house already, or she'd ask Amparo to get it for her when she went shopping.

Her worldly goods were minimal, and she liked it that way; it made her feel free and unencumbered.

She'd done it.

Naomi, thinking back at the past few weeks of her life, gazing into the tall mirror of the big walk-in closet, pinched her eyes shut and looked again: She was seeing the same girl as always—the same long, black hair; the same dark eyes; the same shape and skin—and yet someone else lived inside that body now.

Someone who'd tasted freedom, who'd dared to take that leap and found herself suddenly mistress of a mansion on the beach in Malibu, and the lover of a rock star.

No one told her what to wear, what to say, or what to like; and if she was ever uncertain, ever unsure, Jon was there to tell her not to worry, she didn't need to make up her mind just then, they had all the time in the world. And if she wanted a swimming pool in the garden instead of a cedar copse, well, that was one of the easiest things ever, and what color tiles did she fancy?

Jon. She still couldn't believe what had happened.

Sitting on the edge of the bed, her hand reached out for the phone. She knew Fleur's number by heart; it slipped through her fingers eagerly.

Pauline answered.

"Oh my God, Naomi!" she cried. "Where are you? Do you realize half of Switzerland is in mayhem because no one knows where you are? Your parents are frantic!"

Her heart beating fast, her chest tight, Naomi tried to take a deep breath and failed.

"I left a note," she replied, and her voice sounded as thin as a blade of grass. "They know I wasn't abducted or anything. I just left. Where's Fleur?"

"You just left? Good grief, girl, you can't just leave! Don't you know how much heartbreak you've caused?" Pauline sounded like a parent, like a humorless, rigid parent, like Naomi's father. "You better call your parents," she went on as if she'd been reading Naomi's mind through the line, across the distance, "Your mother hasn't stopped crying since you left, and your father is beside himself! Your fiancé was here for the ball, and after learning that you'd run away, he returned to Canada that same evening. What a disaster!"

"I'm fine. I'm fine, and exactly where I want to be." This was not how she'd imagined it. She hadn't even considered the possibility that someone other than Fleur would pick up the phone. "Please tell Fleur that I'm fine. I'll try and call again."

Naomi threw down the phone as if it was a dead rat. Betrayed, she felt betrayed by the thing, and ripped back into a reality she thought had died the moment she got on that plane with Jon.

She wondered if someone would corner Fleur and make her share everything she knew—now that she'd called—and tell them where she was. The thought was enough to make her want to crawl into the bed and hide beneath the covers.

From downstairs, through the open balcony door, she could hear Sal and Jon talking. This time it sounded a lot friendlier.

"...a lot of music," Sal was saying. "Maybe we should consider an album, using only those songs. I can see that happening!"

"Yeah, me too." How happy Jon sounded, delighted, carefree. "It should be something special, a lovely color, a gentle image."

She had no idea what they were talking about. Both seemed enthusiastic, excited.

"I was wrong, Jon," Sal said, speaking around his cigarette. "I was wrong, and you were right. I'll have to learn to trust your gut instincts. But to be honest, the whole thing scared me. Well, it scared me a lot. I never thought there would be more songs, more music, with her around. But together you two seem like an endless well of creativity. I'm glad Naomi is here. I'm glad you insisted."

There was a small pause. She could hear the click of a lighter, Jon's mumble of thanks. Then he said, "She's like a muse. I only have to watch her return from the beach, to see her like that, and my heart is ready to burst into melody. I've captured that fairy, and I'll make sure she never wants to leave. Having Naomi here is like living an enchanted life. It's as if only these two things matter: the music and her."

"Yes, well."

Their voices drifted away, back into the house, and the terrace door closed behind them.

Naomi again gazed at herself in the large mirror from where she was sitting. Her reflection stared back at her: a young girl in a light-blue dress, wild hair caught in a messy braid, hands folded in her lap, her bare feet crossed.

She looked like a waif, a piece of the debris she had collected on the beach, just as translucent and undecided.

Her mother—if her mother could see her now, she'd probably faint, or pull her away by her untidy braid and to a salon to give her a good makeover, and then put her on the next plane home to Canada.

She'd come so far since her birthday, when her greatest worry had been how she could escape Seth and his fish-like hands, his insipid promises of an endless future, and that stupid horse he'd bought.

"Child," she muttered, pulling the rubber band from her braid, "no one calls me child. I'm not his child."

Her dress, sandy and crumpled from carrying her loot back from the shore, floated into the hamper.

Under the shower, washing her sandy hair, Naomi vowed to take better care of herself. Jon had fallen in love with a well-groomed, elegant young lady, not with a tramp. She could do at least that much.

She owed her parents that much.

THEY both looked up from what they were doing, almost like boys caught doing something forbidden.

"Uhm," Sal said, and he was actually blushing.

Jon, though, held out his hand to her. "Come here, have a look at this! I think I love it."

They'd been working on something, on some sheets spread out on the closed top of the grand.

"You look lovely." Again Sal's eyes slipped over her as if she was no more than a shimmering in the air. "Lovely dress."

"Yes." A soft, gentle smile spread across Jon's face. "You wore that in Geneva, when we went out to buy marzipan. I think it's my favorite dress on you." His hand was warm and firm around hers. "Look, baby, what do you think?"

They'd been writing playlists. They'd been writing playlists of her songs, of the songs she'd written with Jon.

"Are you planning a new tour?" Her heart sank a little at that prospect. The quiet summer life was just what she wanted.

"A tour? Good Lord, no!" A bark of panicked laughter escaped Sal. "No, sweetheart, we're thinking of releasing an album with those songs. An entire album with your songs." He waved at Jon. "And his music, of course."

"But..." She wasn't sure she liked that idea. "But you don't have to put my name on it, do you?"

"Why not?" Sal's eyebrows nearly vanished under the curls bobbing on his forehead. "Why don't you want your name on the album? I can't imagine why you wouldn't want that. You should be happy and excited!"

"No..." She leaned into Jon. "I'm fine with the way things are. I don't want anything out of it, and I don't want my name on any album cover. The songs are Jon's. The credit goes to him."

"But Naomi, really. It could be the start of a great career for you!" Sal held up the sheet with the list of songs. "Look how much you two have done in just a few weeks! You and Jon are an amazing team! You two write songs the way others eat potato chips. You should claim what's yours." He glared at her, his eyes squinched. "Or are you trying to hide something? Are you hiding?"

It wasn't easy to talk through a dry throat, but she managed. "Hardly, Sal. If I wanted to hide I wouldn't hang out with someone like Jon Stone, would I? And what would I be hiding from?"

"I don't know." Putting down the sheet, Sal turned his back on her. "But if I wanted to hide, I'd certainly pick a famous person's house, with the high walls and the security. I'd try and live with someone who lives as protected as Jon Stone. And you'd never have to leave the house, right? Everything you need would be provided, and no one could get at you."

"And I'd never go out to any grand Hollywood affairs, and I'd not keep nagging my lover to take me to the Academy Awards. Or the Grammys. I wouldn't ask him to take me to Rodeo Drive to buy gowns for those occasions either."

It had come out with the proper panache to make him turn back to her, his eyebrows raised again, but this time in amusement.

"Oh right," Sal crowed, "now you sound like a real girl. Well then, I'll have to make sure you get invitations to those, right? And tell Sally that you want to go shopping. And make Jon understand that he can't wear that same tux year after year."

"Whatever."

She'd talked herself into a neat, tight corner, and they were smiling at her, Jon and Sal, happy.

"Now let's talk about that new album," Jon said. "I'm thinking a rose cover."

Chapter Forty

HE'D BEEN PLAYING the same melody over and over again, all morning long, sometimes the way he wanted it to sound, sometimes painfully slow, hitting each key as if an entire orchestra was hidden beneath it, and all he had to do was wake it up.

It grated, that melody, and it refused to come to life.

Naomi, sitting on the couch by the window, tried to concentrate on her lyrics, but those notes made it impossible.

Closing her eyes, she saw Jon hammering away at a stubborn block of marble, trying to reveal the statue hidden in the stone; only the marble didn't budge, and all he managed to do was make tiny chips of stone fly across the room instead of create a piece of art.

It was so obvious; the problem was so obvious. She knew exactly what he needed to change to make it work.

She could just walk over to the piano, take the pencil, and, with a few strokes on the staff lines, show him where he was stuck.

Only that would bring more questions, more doubtful glances, and there were enough of those already. Her disguise wasn't working as well as she'd thought.

She couldn't hide who she was, couldn't hide her upbringing.

It had never occurred to her that she'd give herself away through small, day-to-day things such as the way she asked for linen napkins when they were having dinner, or how she had decorated their bedroom.

Jon, curious, had come upstairs while the decorators were there and stood in the door, bemused.

The carpet, he'd said later over tea, he really liked the new carpet; and, without thinking, she'd replied, "Yes, it's lovely, isn't it? I've always had a soft spot for Aubusson carpets."

Jon had given her a slow, wondering look, patiently waiting for her to explain.

"They're made in France," Naomi at last had said, "near Geneva."

That had seemed satisfactory; there were no more questions. It had been a lie, of course. Aubusson was smack in the middle of France, a long drive away from Geneva.

"JON."

He looked up from the keyboard at her.

Naomi couldn't help herself. She put down the journal and went over to him. "Jon, why don't you try a minor key for those three bars, here." Putting her finger on the paper, she pointed out the segment that hurt her ears so much. "And then, in the reprise, you might use B major to make it poignant, take away the sadness."

He didn't react, so she took the pencil and drew new staff lines, and in quick, neat strokes, the modulated version of the song.

"There." Pleased with the result, she returned the pencil to Jon and, with a kiss on the top of his head, went back to her couch.

"How did you do that?" Bemused, Jon stared at her changes. "How did you know what to do?"

Caught again, but this time she knew what she'd done.

"School, Jon. Every child in Europe learns that at school." And it was true; she'd learned it at school, but it had been an expensive and exclusive private school for the children of diplomats or those with very wealthy parents.

"I told you before that we had to know the scales by heart and how to transpose them." She shrugged. "It was fun." Naomi breathed in the sense of quietness and peace this room gave her. "It was just regular school stuff. We even took tests on it. And we had to sing." That memory made her smile. "I'm not the best singer in the world."

"You're a pretty good singer!" Jon put down the pencil and came over. Dropping onto the couch beside her, he pulled Naomi onto his knees. "I've heard you sing, you know. You walk through the garden sometimes and sing. I can hear you. Your voice is sweet and gentle, and it makes me think there's truly a fairy living among the jasmine bushes. And then I'm glad I'd never let any gardener change anything, because then surely the fairy would leave me. No, everything has to be the way it is just now."

"You're avoiding writing that song," Naomi reminded him. "You're lazy, do you know that? You've been fiddling with that piece for days now. I'm sure the melody is etched into my brain forever and ever."

"Yeah, and then you come along, and with a few strokes you change everything." His hand dug into her hair, tugging slightly. "And now, here I am totally confused, muddled, and helpless, and you laugh at me."

"Not laughing!"

His lips were warm and gentle against hers; his arms held her tightly.

"You siren," Jon whispered, "first you mess with my music, and then you claim me, here on your couch of seduction. We need to finish that album, you and I."

"I'll leave you to it then and go out on the beach. It's a lovely day, and I need a walk." She tried to climb off his lap, but he didn't let her.

"Why don't we go out," Jon suggested. "We've been holed up here for weeks, and while it's nice and cozy, and just the thing I needed after the long tour, I'd love to take you to the studio and have you meet some people; and I'd like to go for lunch somewhere nice. What do you say?"

There was no way to talk him out of it. She knew she couldn't hide in the house forever.

"Okay then. I'll go change, and then we can leave."

Her feet dragged all the way up the stairs. But she changed from the shorts and top she'd been wearing into a dress, piled her hair into a knot, and slipped on sandals. The purse dangling on her arm, Naomi hesitated. Then she put her passport into it, and some money. She didn't know why it seemed so important to be independent, but it made her feel better.

Her credit card, she hadn't brought that. There was her huge trust fund, but she'd never touch it, never give in. She'd vowed to herself that if it didn't work out here with Jon, if they couldn't stay together for whatever reason, she'd find a job, work as a waitress;

but never, never would she return to her parents and the prison they'd built for her.

There was no scenario that she could imagine, no excuse, to go back to Toronto, and her family home.

JON drove her into town, again with the top of the car down, the sun shining on them.

Naomi loved these drives along the ocean; the vast expanse of the Pacific, the sun setting into its waves; she loved LA. People were friendly, relaxed, as if they were on an eternal vacation.

"We need to talk about Christmas soon," Jon said when they stopped at a red light. "What do you want to do for Christmas, baby?"

"Christmas?" Naomi hadn't even thought about it.

"Yes, Christmas. Two months and it will be Christmas. How do you want to spend it? Would you like to go back to your family for a visit? Do you want me to come? Would you like to go to New York with me and meet mine? What would you like to do? We could also kiss them all good-bye and go somewhere on our own, take a vacation, something like a honeymoon, if you want. Have you ever been to Hawaii? Would you like to go to Hawaii for the holidays?"

Christmas. How wonderful that had always been at the Carlsson mansion, with the huge tree in the library, and the many, many lights strung throughout the house and the winter garden. There'd be fruit cake so lavishly doused with rum that you could get drunk on it, and hot chocolate, and a huge roast goose for dinner. There had always been houseguests, and many, many presents for her.

Music, there'd been music, and dancing, and singing. And romping in the snow.

"I'm not going home to see my family," Naomi said, her face turned away from him. "And it doesn't feel right to meet yours just yet. I don't know. I guess I'll just stay here. But you can go, Jon! If you want to see your family, do go! I'll use the time to start writing a novel. I'm totally fine on my own."

Jon threw her a long, thoughtful glance but didn't respond for quite a while.

"Of course I won't leave you alone here, and certainly not for Christmas," he finally responded when they'd reached the building's garage. "We belong together. I thought this was forever and ever. I mean for it to be that way, Naomi. I want you to be honest with me, and say what you really want." The deep rumble of the Porsche's engine died when he turned the ignition key. "This is no summer affair for me, baby. I'd never have brought you back to California if I wasn't dead serious about you." His hands clamped around the steering wheel. "I've always believed in true love, in love at first sight. I knew it would be this way, that falling in love the moment I saw the right girl would be the only way to make sure she's the right one. There are too many who love me for what I am and not very many for who I am. You…" His hands left the wheel and gripped hers instead. "You, Naomi. You're the one. You're the girl who understands me in and out, who doesn't give a whit about fame and all that crazy stuff. I'm still me, underneath all the glamour, and I need someone who sees that me." A crooked smile made its way to his lips. "And I hope I'm the same for you. I want to be that someone in your life, Naomi. I want it a lot. I feel at peace with you, and yet every day is a new adventure. I need you a lot. I need you at night, in my bed; and I need your bright mind and your beauty during the day, like this morning, when you…" He shook his head. "When you set that beast of a song straight for me with the stroke of a pencil. You're my miracle, my wonderful miracle. Whatever you want, it will be done."

A door closed somewhere, and the sound echoed through the garage like a clap of thunder.

"Jon." That name, and how it sounded, coming from her heart, the eternal promise, the truth of love, safety of an embrace. "Jon, I came away with you. I left everything behind and came away with you. I can't imagine being without you. Not for a day, not for a moment." There, she'd spelled it out, and it hadn't been as hard or as maudlin as she'd expected. "And I know I've made the right choice. I know this is where I belong." Tears were creeping up her throat.

She could feel their tiny claws. "I love you, Jon Stone. I love you when you're all made up and turned into your own effigy, ready to go onstage and make love to thousands with your voice; and I love you when you're unshaven and in a foul morning mood, yammering for your coffee."

Jon's lips softened into the smile she knew so well by now, the one that made her want to kiss him over, and over, and over again. "You're very good at yammering for coffee, Jon."

"Look who's talking." The tone had changed; they were playing again. Jon jumped out of the car to hold the door for her. "You and coffee. You're a monster of caffeine need until I get you your first cup. Don't tell me how grumpy I am in the morning!"

"But Jon, can't you see?" Naomi wrapped her arms around him. "Can't you see that I love you? Can't you see it?"

"Heck, baby, I can indeed. I can see it in your eyes, and in the way you're looking at me, and in your sweet embrace. Yeah, I can see it."

They kissed, right there in the gloom and gasoline odor of the garage.

Chapter Forty-one

SHE'D NEVER BEEN inside a recording studio.

Walking close beside Jon, holding on to his hand, she followed him across the marble floor toward the elevators.

"Where, Jon?" she asked. They'd come up the stairs from the garage, and she turned to look at the big glass doors of the entrance. "Where did it happen?"

He nodded toward the street. "Right there. Right outside, on the sidewalk."

It was so hard to imagine. He'd said it had been evening, so it had been dark; and there, waiting, would have been the fans, and one of them was that girl.

"Come." Jon put his arm around her shoulders. "Don't think about it. It happened, and it's over. Trust me, I've spent enough time mourning and being angry." The elevator chimed, and the door hissed open. "I was even angry at that poor girl for a while. I hated her for making me feel guilty when all I'd done was do my job. She had no right to kill herself over that. She had no right to lay that burden on me. That's how I felt."

"And you were right, Jon. It wasn't your fault at all. You don't have to carry that burden."

He was gazing down at her, his eyes smiling, his arms around her. "Yeah, it's my burden, love. It happened because of me, because of who I am, and what I do. I'll have to carry it around forever and ever. I'll never forget how her blood sprayed all over me. The smell of it,and how it felt so sticky, as if it wanted to permeate my skin. It was terrible. I never use that entrance anymore now. Although I'm sure the stains are no longer visible, I can still see it in my mind."

"Oh, Jon."

"Don't worry, baby." He kissed her briefly. "It's my burden, mine alone. And hey." A small smile lit his face. "I like your approach to fandom a lot better!"

"You were easy to catch," she replied, her heart a bit lighter. "You're so easily swayed by a few words."

"It's the way they're put. You couldn't win me over with just any words. Yours now, they come with their own music, clamoring to be put to song. How could I not be enticed? And then you come along, the loveliest girl in the world…"

"Are you at it again?"

They turned to see Sally standing in the hallway, a pack of documents clasped to her chest, shaking her head.

"Really," she said, "one would think you have time enough for that at home. But no, smooching everywhere, and all the time. Aren't you afraid of being caught by paparazzi? You know they're out to catch you like that, Jon, don't you?" She was looking at Naomi though and not at Jon. "If you want your image on the front page of every tabloid between here and London, just keep it up."

"Hey, I don't care," Jon replied, his arms still tight around Naomi. "Maybe then I'll have my peace, and girls will stop chasing me."

"In your dreams," Sally muttered, and vanished into her office.

"She's turned into such a sourpuss lately. I don't know what's wrong with that girl." Jon sighed, steering Naomi toward a door at the end of the hallway. "Sally used to be all fun and laughter before we left on the tour. Now, she hardly speaks to me."

"She has a crush on you, Jon." Naomi wondered how he could be so dense. "Can't you see it? She's struggling hard to hide it."

"Yeah, well." Uncomfortable, Jon shook his shoulders. "That too is not my fault."

"No, it isn't."

That made him laugh. "You think so? It almost seems that in your eyes I'm totally blameless."

"Well, you are, Jon." She shrugged. "I don't know about totally, but for this, yes." Her eyes sparkled at him. "You're doing what you do best, and it's not your fault when people fall in love with you."

"You know," Jon stopped just outside a door with a blinking DO NOT ENTER sign on it. "We've never talked about the men who were in love with you. We never talk about you. How many broken-hearts have you left behind, running away with me?"

"None." And that she could say with absolute conviction. "Not one, Jon. There was no one who loved me the way you do, or who wanted me in his life. I was waiting for you to happen."

TO see them all again, the band, Russ, Sally, and Sal, and in the studio was more fun than Naomi had expected.

Sal brought her coffee and asked her to stay in the control room with them, while Jon joined the band in the studio. She could see them through a big window, the same one Jon had thrown his guitar through.

Sitting on a table, her legs dangling, Naomi watched them try out her "Secret Garden," and then record a demo tape.

Jon, his guitar on his knee, introduced them to the new songs they'd been working on, playing them, singing, and Sean, sitting beside him, listening, nodding, smiling.

She loved that voice. Someone had obviously taught him to sing the vowels and be short on the consonants, to breathe right and use his chest not his throat for singing. He was a good baritone, a velvety timbre, and he knew how to modulate it well.

Watching them, she wished Fleur could be here to enjoy the session with her. She'd love it, she'd love this glimpse of real life with Jon Stone, when he wasn't on the stage or passing through a hotel lobby.

She'd also enjoy seeing him at home, in his studio, and she'd be tickled pink to learn that this American guy couldn't light a barbecue grill.

Thinking of Fleur made her think of her parents, and Naomi wondered where they were now and how they were doing. A couple of times during the past week she'd been close to picking up the phone and calling them; but then she'd pulled back, certain there would only be fury, sorrow, and accusations.

Seth, how could she do that to Seth, and hadn't everything been perfect, just the way she'd wanted it?

She knew there was no way she could hold her own against Olaf's anger, and so she didn't call, and wouldn't.

THEY went out to dinner together—the band, everyone—to a place on the beach.

Naomi had the feeling that they knew the place well, that they came here often, and liked it. There was a long table waiting for them on the patio, only a few steps away from the sand. The Malibu pier was not too far away, and in the setting sun it looked like a beast ready to stalk away into the ocean, a stiff-backed, glittering monster that had come to realize that it no longer wanted to be tethered to land. Walking away, it would shake all the humans off its narrow back, tossing them down into the waves.

"Like an enchanted whale," she whispered, and Sal, sitting next to her, leaned over.

"What did you say?" he asked. "I didn't understand." And as if to underline his words, he briefly touched the back of her hand lying on the table next to her napkin.

"Oh, nothing." Embarrassed, blushing, Naomi pulled her hand away. "Just thinking about the pier."

Jon and Russ stopped to listen.

"I was just wondering…you know. The pier, it looks like a big beast that's been tied to the shore, maybe by some bad sorcerer or something, and it's really a deep-sea creature, an enchanted whale or something, bound and punished, and forced to amuse the puny humans." Her embarrassment fell away as she spun the tale, and her heart beat faster as she sank deeper into it. "He did something and was punished, that whale. And here he is, anchored to the land, with his belly in the waves but his back forever in the sun, until someone comes along to break that spell and set him free. I think he must have done something really bad to deserve this captivity. Maybe he overturned a ship, and people were harmed? Or…or he fell in love with the wrong whale maiden, and her father chased them down and asked the king of the sea to…to…"

Too close to her own truth, too close to secrets she never wanted to spill.

"Well, the pier looks that way. To me." She raised her glass to hide her hot cheeks. "Don't mind me."

No one said anything for a while. Waiters brought their dinner, huge platters of seafood, lobsters, shrimp, fried fish fillets, salads, and fresh French bread. There were pitchers of beer, and for Naomi, wine. Her heart clenched a bit at seeing that bread, it reminded her so much of breakfasts in Geneva.

"I think you have a wonderful imagination," Sal said gently. "You have a real gift, Naomi. You see the world with different eyes. Everything seems to come alive when you talk about it."

A crease appeared between Jon's eyes but vanished the moment he saw her gazing at him, smiling.

"Yeah," he added, and picked up a grilled shrimp from the mound of food. "You do, darling. Sal is right; you have a wonderful imagination. I'm so lucky to be the one guy in your life, the one you love."

Sally rolled her eyes, and Russ coughed into his napkin.

"You should really think about writing a novel," Sal went on, offering Naomi the bread basket. "It seems like a waste just to write lyrics. Have you ever thought about that?"

"That's exactly what I said to her yesterday." Jon snatched the basked from Sal's hand. "Didn't I say that yesterday, babe?"

"Yes, you did." She picked out a piece of bread. "And maybe I will. But I don't feel ready for it just yet. I think I need a bit more experience for that. Lyrics, however, are easy."

"I'm going shopping for some winter clothes tomorrow," Sally said. "Should we go together, Naomi? We could have lunch and do some celebrity hunting. That's always fun!"

"Winter clothes? I thought it was always warm in LA." The lobster was excellent: tender, succulent, and doused in butter, just the way Naomi liked it.

"It will get cooler. Not cold and nasty, but cooler, and there will be some rainy days. I'm thinking of getting a red coat. With polka dots, of course." Sally tilted her head, regarding Naomi critically. "Not your style though. You're not a polka-dot girl."

"No, never have been. Although my birthday ball gown…" She clamped her mouth shut just in time.

No one else had heard, or even listened, except for Sally; and she was nodding, biting her lips, as if she wanted to remind Naomi to shut up, and fast.

"I don't need much," Naomi said. "Maybe a cardigan or two? I have no plans to go out a lot. I'm fine staying at home, living a quiet life."

This time though, Sal had heard her.

"What?" he asked. "And what was that about the Grammys and the Oscars? I've requested the tickets for you! You need evening gowns galore, my pretty maiden; there will be parties to attend! Make Jon hand over that credit card, and let Sally advise you on what to get. And shoes and whatever else a girl needs to be glamourous and beautiful. You're going with Jon Stone, Naomi. You have to sparkle like a diamond when you walk the red carpet with him!"

"Don't worry your pretty little head, Sal," Sally replied for her. "Leave the important things to us. And by the way, I think you were a bit hasty with those tickets. I have a feeling Jon will be nominated for the Grammy. It's just a feeling. But a strong one."

The others fell silent, all their attention directed at Sally.

"Damn," Jon said at last, "and here I thought I'd get away with wearing the old tux."

"You can dream, Jon Stone. So not happening." Sally popped a shrimp into her mouth.

Chapter Forty-two

"YOU'RE JEALOUS OF Sal!"

"Nah."

The Porsche was whipping up the coast, toward home. There was a last trace of defiant red hovering over the horizon, casting an ominous sheen on the ocean.

"You are so! And you were competing with him at dinner. Seriously, Jon!"

He stared straight ahead, at the dark road and the traffic around them. "Not. I'm not jealous. I just don't want him looking at you that way and flirting with you."

"Jon!"

"Don't 'Jon me!'" He stomped on the brake to avoid a truck that had just entered the highway. "My mother does that too when she's annoyed at me. I know what that tone means!"

He sounded like an obstinate kid, like a chastised teenager, and it was too funny for words.

"I'd never fall in love with Sal! Is that what you're afraid of? Really? You can't be! Jon, how could you even think that!" She had to fight hard to keep her laughter hidden. "Look at yourself, and then look at Sal! No girl in her right mind, with that kind of choice, would settle for Sal. No one. And me, not ever."

"Well, you say that now." But he sounded mollified, as if he was ready to believe her. "Only he's trying hard. I don't want him to try."

"He's doing nothing of the kind! You're so silly, Jon! I'd not give Sal a second glance, just like I never..." Again. She'd nearly done it again. "Like I'd never fall in love with anyone else as long as you're around."

"Because I need you, babe." He turned off the highway and onto the road that led to the mansion. "I need you so badly, you're so deep inside my heart, if you walked away, I think I'd die."

"But Jon." As if she would. As if she could, or wanted to. "I'm here! I ran away from home to be with you! I'll never leave you!"

The gate swung open when they pulled up to it.

"You say that now. But what about when I get old and wrinkly, and can't sing anymore? What then?"

This time she did laugh. The car stopped outside the house, the deep roar of the motor ending with one last gentle sigh.

"When you're old and wrinkly I'll be an old hag with gray hair, and probably walking with a cane. I think we can safely assume that we'll be a lovely old couple, just like Roy and Rose. Only we won't have to drink our tea in a workshop that smells of glue and wood."

"Can you imagine that?" Jon stopped at the bottom of the stairs to the door. "Can you see us together, aging, growing old, raising children, having grandchildren? I can. I do." He spread out his arms. "And they'll talk us into building a pool so they can come visit in the summer and romp in the water. And we'll still be here, still go out on the beach every morning and sit in the arbor during hot August nights."

"Yes. Yes, I can see that." The image was so vivid; they'd have a daughter, a lovely little girl with Jon's musical talent, and she'd be raised to think and say what she wanted; she'd be raised to be free. Or a son. A son with Jon's looks, his dark hair and the same mouth, the same shape to his lips, and those intense, black eyes. It would hurt and hurt to look at him, so much like his father, so beloved, so wonderful.

"Yes, Jon. I want that." And she did.

"But first, my love." He caught her in his arms. "First, before we have children and grow old, we'll have to get married; we'll have to make that promise to each other. I want to put that ring on your finger more than anything else. I want to make sure you'll never disappear the same way you stepped into my life. I need that security, badly."

"Can I please be nineteen first? Or even twenty?"

Jon laughed. It was an easy, happy sound. "Of course you can. I keep forgetting how young you are. We have all the time in the world. I promise not to bring it up again until you feel ready for it. Okay?"

"Okay." Naomi started up the stairs but stopped on the second step, laying her hands on his shoulder. "All I want right now is what we have: a peaceful spot in the universe, a small oasis that's all our own. We're in a small bubble of time, Jon, and I don't want any pressure coming into it."

"Pressure is the last thing I want! Okay, I really, seriously promise. No more talk of marriage or anything until you say the word!" His arms wrapped around her hips. "I'm not that old myself yet, you know. So yes, we have time. As long as you don't leave me!"

"I won't! Goodness, you're needy tonight! And all because Sal liked my fantasy!"

"No, it's more than that." The playfulness seeped out of his tone. "I've known Sal for two years now, and he's never that…kind. He has an acidic tongue, Sal. Something really dire or really special has to happen to make him soften like that. So yes, this worries me."

"Jealousy from Jon Stone. Wow."

"Hey, I'm just a regular guy inside! I worry like anyone else if someone throws his girl those kinds of looks! That doesn't change just because I'm famous!"

There he stood, the young rock star, the centerfold image, and he was pleading for love. It was almost more than she could take.

"Jon. I don't know what to say to you. I'm here, and I love you. That's all. That's all I can say, because it's the truth."

"Let's go to bed, my fairy maiden. Let me hold you in my mortal arms."

SHE woke before dawn, as always, and crawled out of bed. The sky was still gray, still asleep beneath its blanket of stars, and the ocean below was dreaming of eternity and the deep.

The stones of the trail through the yard felt wet and cold under her feet, and the jasmine petals drooped under the weight of dew. It was getting colder, even here.

It made Naomi think about how it would be in Kleinburg now. The leaves would have begun to turn, blooming into their autumn splendor. Like jewels, they would sparkle and shine under the deep-blue skies, and the breeze would be filled with earthy smells and the scent of wood fires. Sometimes when the wind was just right, a whiff of boiling maple syrup hung in the air. She'd always loved fall best, and gone riding every day, always early in the morning. Apollo loved to run across the lawn and up and down the long, winding drive to the road, wet grass spilling its sweet perfume as it was crushed under his hooves. They'd stop at the estate's orchard, and she'd pick a few apples for him, a treat he'd greedily welcome. The lake was so pretty in fall too. Wisps of fog would hang over it, and the sun would be lightening into golden cotton candy, with loons playing hide-and-seek in it, their calls echoing across the still water. Once she'd seen a moose. He had appeared out of the mist, a stately, huge beast, his head held high, his antlers carried like a crown, as if he was the king of the forest. Apollo had stood as still as a rock, watching the majestic animal wade into the lake, and they'd remained until he had swum across to the other side and vanished among the trees.

Later, as she told Owen about what they'd witnessed, he'd nodded sagely, and said yes, he knew that moose, and he was indeed the king of the forest.

"He's special," he'd said. "He doesn't let just anyone see him. You are special too."

SHE'D reached the gate and unlocked it, and slipped the key on her wrist. A while ago she'd exchanged the piece of twine it had been on for one of her hair bands, saying it was easier to carry around like that and her hands were free for her loot.

Amber, she'd told Jon that day—she wanted to find amber on the beach, that was her big ambition—and he'd laughed at her and told her there was no amber to be found in California, he'd never heard of that; but she insisted. There was amber on every beach, Naomi had said, and California was no exception.

"Maybe we should go north then," Jon had replied. "Maybe you'll get lucky in Oregon. Your chances should be better on those colder shores."

And she had envisioned those shores, with black sand and tall cedars, and surf that gripped her ankles with the icy breath of the arctic.

The beach was empty except for a couple of men walking along the waterline in the distance, their backs to her, hands in their pockets, their heads lowered as they talked to each other. They didn't seem dressed for the beach; one of them was in rolled-up jeans, but the other wore trousers and a white shirt, and he carefully kept away from the water.

Ignoring them, Naomi went down to the surf and let the tiny waves kiss her toes. The night had been calm, and so was the sea: Like a shiny mirror, it stretched out endlessly, waiting for the sun.

She found some shells, but they were either broken or boring, and only good enough to be tossed back into the water. A couple of stones blinked at her from the sand, and she picked those up and washed them, and put them in her pocket.

As always, she slowly followed the curve of the beach, her gaze downward on the debris. A couple of times she looked up to the hills, where the sun would rise any minute now and bathe the sky in rose and purple.

It happened when she was on her way back.

Those two men, they were coming toward her, and now they weren't strolling anymore but marching purposefully, their eyes fixed on her as if they wanted to nail her to the spot where she was standing.

Dropping the shell she had just picked up, Naomi ran up the beach and toward the gate, stumbling on the soft sand, cutting her foot on a hidden seashell. Out of breath, she fumbled with the key, her heart beating painfully from the run and her fear.

She managed to open the gate just before they reached her, slip through, and slam it into place. Still shaking, she turned the key and kept turning it in her frantic attempt to make sure that they couldn't follow her inside.

"Naomi," Olaf said, his eyes sad and angry. "Why do you run away from me? I'm your father, for crying out loud! When have I ever hurt or harmed you? Why are you running from me?"

She took several steps away from the gate and the fence. "I'm not going home with you." Her throat and mouth were as dry as old wood.

"Naomi. Do you know how heartbroken your mother is? You run away, you run all the way to California, and you don't tell us? Why in the world would you do this? What happened to make you do this?" Olaf's fingers gripped into the mesh of the fence. "And Seth here?"

Yes, there he was, Seth, only he didn't seem half as troubled as her father.

"You run, and you're as good as engaged, and you run off with a strange man? Have you no idea what a disgrace this is? Please come to your senses, Naomi, and come home with us." Olaf sighed. "We'll forget all this and make the best of it. I promise. But please come home with us now. We had to come here and try to meet you on the beach, because there's no getting near you otherwise; and I wanted to spare us all the shame of ringing Jon Stone's doorbell, asking for my daughter to be returned to me."

Seth still hadn't said anything. He was watching the exchange with the dry interest of a bystander who had nothing to do with what was happening.

"Jon can't return me to you, Father, because I'm not his property." The cup. And the tantrum, and the wall. Only there was no cup, no wall, and she was much too scared for a tantrum. Fleur's advice didn't help her here. "I'm not going anywhere with you. I'm staying right here."

"You don't know what you're saying." Olaf shook the fence. "Naomi, I can't begin to tell you how disappointed I am. This is what we get from you; after all the care and money we spent on your upbringing and education, you run off with a pop singer? Don't you have any self-respect, any pride? Is this what we get for letting you run free in Geneva? I'm so ashamed of you, I can't begin to say."

"I tried to tell you." A step back, and another, and she was almost hidden in the safety of the bushes. "I tried to tell you, Daddy, and I tried to tell Mama. But you just don't listen to me. You never listen when I try to talk to you. It's always 'Go buy yourself something nice, dress properly, look your best, remember who you are.'" I'm not even a person to you! I'm something that you need for your business, someone to groom to take over. But I don't want to take over, much less be Seth's wife. I don't want it." Somewhere at the back of her throat hung a sob, a big, messy lump of a sob, and she tried to swallow it. But it didn't work, and her next words came out wavering, smaller than she wanted. "Go away, and don't come back. I'm happy here. I'm loved for who I am, not for who Jon wants me to be. And I love Jon. Go away, Father."

The jasmine swallowed her, embracing her with its sweet scent.

Chapter Forty-three

"NAOMI!"

Hidden among the bushes, leaning against one of the cedar trees, she could hear Seth calling for her.

"Naomi, don't be stupid. Come back and let's talk. I've asked Olaf to give us some space; I told him we needed some privacy. Won't you come out and talk to me?"

That was the last thing she wanted to do.

"Please talk to me. I want to know what went wrong." Seth sounded like a dog barking at a cat up in a tree. "I accept that you don't want to marry me, but I'd really like to know why. I think I'm entitled to know why."

Carefully, slowly, she crept out of the bushes and back into sight; but she kept her distance from the fence, and her feet were firmly planted on the slabs of the path. Her hands were shaking so badly that she hid them behind her back, the key between them like a magical talisman.

Seth, seeing her, took a step away from the gate and nodded. "Okay, thanks for speaking to me. Now. Tell me what happened."

Naomi tried to envision Fleur. She made her image stand in the shade of the jasmine, nodding to her, encouraging, whispering instructions.

"Nothing happened, Seth. I fell in love, and I did what any woman in my place would have done: I decided to share my life with the man I love."

A short laugh escaped him, but he quickly cleared his throat to hide it. "Love? You fell in love with someone else? This?" His hand flew out, pointing at the garden, the fence, her. "You're infatuated with a rock star, Naomi, that's all. And he's taking advantage of you. Who wouldn't; you're sweet and young, and so lovely. I'm sure he was very happy when he saw how willing you were. But that's not love, Naomi. It's lust. It means nothing." He came closer, gripping the fence. "I don't care, you know. So you had an affair. I'm okay with that. But now it's time to go home and lead a normal life. Are you coming?"

Insults. He was insulting her, and he didn't even know it. For the first time ever she wished she had something to throw, but there was nothing, just some dried leaves, and stones. And she wasn't going to throw a stone at Seth and maybe hurt him.

"I'm not coming, Seth." Strange, it was strange, but she felt calm, clear, even cold inside now. The fear and the anger had dropped away, had snapped away from her panicked heart like breaking icicles, falling away with every word he had said.

"I'm not going anywhere, and certainly not with you. I tried to tell my parents over and over again that I didn't want to marry you, but they didn't want to hear it. And you, Seth." She moved closer, but not close enough to touch. "How wooden and dead can a man's heart be, not to feel if you're loved or not? How can you be so disrespectful to the girl you want to marry to tell her you have other women for sex, and that you don't desire her?"

"I didn't say that!" Beet-colored heat flooded his face, and it clashed with the red hair. "I never said I didn't desire you!"

"And you never said you did either." She was wishing for something to throw very badly now. "You never once told me that you love me, Seth. And I think I deserved that, just like anyone else. I'm more than just part of a business deal. I'm better than that, and I deserve to be told that I'm loved." Looking back over her shoulder, looking toward the house hidden behind the greenery of the estate, she let go of the air caught in her chest. Her heart flew along the path ahead of her and directly into Jon's arms. He'd be there, waiting for her, catching her in an embrace when she returned; and she'd revel in it, feel the love, feel the desire. She'd kiss him, she'd hold him, she'd whisper love words to him that he'd return; and all would be well.

"Yeah, I do love you. How could I not? We grew up together." Seth shrugged. "I always assumed it would be like that; we'd get married someday, and that was that."

Naomi moved forward to stand close to the fence.

"I love you," she whispered. "I love you with every thought, every breath I take, with every fiber of my soul. My heart beats your name; my lips say it like a prayer, like the only prayer I'll ever need. You're my world; you're the spirit that lives within mine."

"Uhm," Seth said, "Okay... I'm confused." Again he shrugged. "Why are you telling me this now? Didn't you just say you didn't love me? Are you..." He blanched. The blood left his cheeks as fast as it had invaded them earlier. "Are you being kept against your will? Is that it? Do you need to be rescued?"

It was too much. Bitter laughter welled up in her throat, and somewhere mixed into it where tears of anger.

"No, Seth. I'm not a captive. Or at least not in the way you want to think. And I didn't say those words to you. I was repeating to you what Jon told me last night, what he tells me all the time. Those are the words a girl wants to hear. Not something that begins with 'assumed,' Seth. Never, ever tell a woman that you take her for granted."

Her knees were shaking, but she ignored them. Something had happened, something had changed, and she felt free in a way she'd never felt before, not even when she'd gotten on that plane to Amsterdam.

"I've said all I needed to say to you," Naomi told him, and somewhere on the way up from her lungs those words mingled with the laughter. "You can go now. And take my father with you. I'm done with you."

She wished someone had caught this exchange on camera so she could watch it over and over again and remember how she'd found the strength to fight, and just when it mattered most. And how Fleur would love to see it, would love to see how once in her life she'd found the guts to face someone down.

"Right." Seth pushed his hands into his pockets, and stepped away from the fence and into the sand. "I don't think I deserve to be treated like this either. I think I deserve someone who loves me too."

He sounded like a disappointed child, like a chastised boy.

"Oh yes, Seth, you do!" And this time she could speak to him from the bottom of her heart. "And I wish that for you! I wish that you meet someone who loves you the way I love Jon, and the way he loves me. You really, truly deserve that."

The garden was calling, and the house. She could hear their tender whispers, could feel the comforting caress of the jasmine on her hair.

"I'll go now," Naomi said, and her mind was already racing along the path ahead of her and into the studio, where Jon would be waiting. "I have to go. He'll be waiting for me, and getting worried. I never stay away that long." Guiltily, she shuffled her feet. "I slipped out again without taking a bodyguard with me, and see what happens; I nearly get abducted. I should really listen to what Jon says."

"So you're okay? You're safe and happy?" He sounded like her old friend, like the Seth she'd known all her life.

"I'm very happy, Seth. I love my life; I love every single thing about it." That made her laugh. "Well, obviously not every part. The need for security hasn't changed; if anything, it's worse. But it's easier to bear when you know it's not because of you but because of the one you love. And here, in this house, in this garden, I feel like a fairy, like I've reached my haven. I'm loved here, and cherished."

"Okay then." His glance wandered to his right. "I'll tell Olaf what you told me. I'm not sure he'll give up that easily, but I'll suggest that he leave you alone. Are you okay with money? Do you need anything?"

That really made her laugh. "No, I don't need anything, and certainly not money. Go home. Find someone to love and marry. And don't let my father influence your choice. You're master of your own life. Good-bye, Seth."

And with that she turned and followed the invitation of the path, back toward the house, and Jon.

MUSIC floated toward her. Like a gossamer thread of light it floated among the flowers and the scents, following the trail of the white stones along the path, and when it found her, wrapped around her like the arms of love.

She let it carry her back to house, and into the kitchen, from where she could smell coffee and frying eggs.

Jon was there, barefoot, in jeans, his shirt open. His hair was wet from the shower.

"Babe," he greeted her, "you're back just in time. Look, I'm making eggs for you. There are mushrooms too."

He'd set two plates on the kitchen counter, and there was fresh toast on them. The butter dish was open, coffee steamed in the mugs. From the studio, music was filling the house. It was the demo tape they'd recorded at the studio: her words, Jon's music, braided into song.

"You were out longer than usual today," Jon said, stirring the eggs in the pan. "I was beginning to get worried. And you went out without security again, didn't you?"

"Yes." Naomi sat on one of the stools at the counter. "I know, and I'm sorry. Won't do it again. Today was a bit spooky. The beach was deserted; there was no one else. If someone had wanted to abduct me or something, they'd have had a good chance. I've learned my lesson."

He looked at her over his shoulder. "Are you okay? You sound weird, as if something's scared you. Did something happen?"

"Nothing. Nothing happened. It just occurred to me that I was being foolish." She picked up a knife and spread butter on her toast.

"You and your need for independence!" Jon came over and ladled egg and mushroom on her plate. "You make me worry all the time. I don't want anything to happen to you, Naomi. I can't even bear the thought. Please, baby? Please be more careful?"

"I promise, Jon." The rubber with the key was still around her wrist, and she pulled it off. It had seemed like a token of freedom to her, like the magical key in and out of her little kingdom. "I really promise."

He bent over the counter to plant a kiss on her lips. "You taste nice! Coffee and buttery toast, what an enticing mix! Maybe someone should create a perfume with that scent! Come here, kiss me again."

For a moment, breakfast was forgotten.

HE needed to go back to the studio, Jon said, piercing one of the mushrooms with his fork, and did she want to come? Or did she have plans for the day?

Sally, she'd promised Sally she'd go shopping for winter clothes with her, Naomi reminded him, and he smiled.

"Here." Jon got up from his stool and went to get his wallet. He pulled out a black credit card and pushed it across the counter. "Have fun, and don't worry about money, baby. There's more than I know how to spend. I think I've been hoarding it just for you." He smiled at her, his elbows on the table. "I love that thought very much. I want you to have fun, and I want to give you everything you could possibly want."

Naomi turned the card over in her hands. Her father had one of those too; she'd seen it often enough when it came out to buy her or Lucia clothes, or anything else they fancied.

"I really don't need anything," she said. "Everything I've ever wanted is right here, having breakfast with me."

"Naomi."

Their hands met across the kitchen counter and melted into a lover's knot.

Chapter Forty-four

"EVERYONE WEARS BLACK satin, Naomi," Sally said, and held up the rose silk dress, "but few can carry off rose the way you do. I think this color was created just for you. Why would you want to wear black when you can have rose?" She pointed at another gown. "Or that cherry red. My God, I love that color, but not on me. I need a brighter, more orange red."

"Yes, you do. Nothing with a blue tinge for you!" How she missed Fleur, and how she would have enjoyed this shopping spree. Fleur and Sally would be fast friends, cut from the same, sassy wood.

"Okay, I'll take the red" Naomi sighed. "Even though I really don't need an evening gown at all."

"Ah, but you will! Next week we're all going to that movie premiere thing; didn't Jon tell you? Typical male. He hates putting on a tux, or any suit at all, and he tries to ignore this part of the job for as long as he can. But not this time, oh no. Tomorrow I'm going to take him to get his hair trimmed, a manicure, new tux—the whole nine yards."

They wandered over to where the new winter collection was displayed, followed closely by the saleswoman.

"Valentino." Sally grinned. "I wonder if Jon knows just how expensive your taste is. Well, he'll find out when he sees his next credit card statement."

Naomi stopped in her tracks, opening her mouth, but Sally waved her away.

"Don't worry about it, Naomi! He really, seriously, can afford it. I know you probably have no concept of what's expensive and what's cheap, having grown up the way you did, but it's really okay." Tilting her head, Sally thought for a moment. "In fact, I think it's a good thing. I think it's good for Jon to have someone in his life who'll teach him how to move in the world of the upper class. He's a good boy, but he's not used to sitting down to a six-course dinner and using the right utensils, let alone glasses. That's something he can learn from you!"

"Those dinners are utterly boring."

Sally laughed. "I know they are! Well, mostly. But we have to go through them once in a while anyway."

"And I don't want to teach Jon anything. I mean, I don't want to make him think that I think I'm somehow better than him."

Sally blinked. "That was a convoluted sentence, if I've ever heard one." She shook her head when Naomi picked up a cream-colored cashmere twin set. "Nope, unless you want to wear a tweed skirt and pearls with it."

"I wear these with jeans," Naomi replied, "and not even my mother objects to it. And yes, pearls. Or rubies."

Sally burst out laughing. "You're really something else. And here I thought no one could teach me anything about fashion, ever. But you beat me. Okay then, cashmere it is. And do you have the rubies?"

"Yes." Naomi really liked the soft wool and the neutral color.

"Really?" Sally was peering at her closely. "Rubies? And what about the pearls?"

"I didn't bring those."

"I need a drink. And do you also own a crown?" Sitting down on the couch near the shop window, Sally waited for a response, her eyes open wide.

"Not a crown." Naomi handed the twin set to the sales woman and added another one in a soft, powdery blue. "A circlet, yes. Rubies and pearls. But it's in Geneva, in my father's safe, with the other jewelry." She turned down the corners of her mouth. "There's a lot of stuff there, and I hardly ever got to wear it, only when we went out to the opera, or some ball or function. And then my parents picked which one I could wear."

Sinking down beside Sally, she added quietly, "You have no idea how complicated and suffocating that life was. I had everything a girl could ask for, but it wasn't really mine. Everything I did was controlled, watched, judged." Her heart suddenly heavy, she hung her head. "They didn't see me, Naomi. They only saw the heiress, the asset, the chess piece in their schemes to own even more, get even richer than they already were. My only freedom was my friend Fleur. They let me visit Fleur, and hang out with her and my other friends. But it was always clear that I couldn't fall in love, couldn't go out with a boy, or heaven forbid, have an affair. No, the daughter of Olaf Carlsson would go into the marriage they'd arranged unsullied, a virgin. Anything else was unthinkable for their conservative Catholic hearts."

"And then Jon happened."

"Yes." It was painful, but Naomi managed a smile. "And then Jon happened. He burst into my life like a comet, so blindingly brilliant, so beautiful, and with the same dreams, the same ideas that I had." Her gaze strayed to the entrance as if she expected him to walk in on her, take her hand, promise her that she was loved, and safe.

"Well, you made him burst into your life, if I remember correctly." Sally nodded to the saleswoman and whispered that, thank you, yes, they had all they needed.

"I know." They rose together, exchanging a small, secret girls' grin. "I'll never forget that moment when I first heard his voice. It was like…it was as if he was reaching out, and his hand was gripping my heart, squeezing. It was the most exquisite pain, the pain of yearning, of sudden love and the sorrow of loss, all of it mixed together. I was mourning that I'd probably never meet him, and at the same time I was imagining dancing with him, making love to him."

Sally had stopped in the middle of the store to stare at her. "Wow, Naomi. You talk just like Jon. You sound like his echo. I can actually see him saying the same things, but to Sal or Sean. I'm beginning to understand how much you two belong together."

Back outside on the sidewalk, shopping bags in hand, Sally suggested lunch.

"But not at a noisy place. You'll see enough movie stars next week at that party to last you a lifetime, trust me. If it's okay with you, I'd rather chat."

"Someplace where we can watch life pass by," Naomi added. "I like those best."

SALLY took her to a restaurant where, she said, she'd taken Jon when he first came to LA. "You should have known him then." The memory made her eyes go soft. "He was the cutest kid ever. A little lost, a bit homesick for his family, but full of drive, full of power. The music was bursting from his ears. You could almost see the melodies floating around his head, like a halo. He walked into my dad's studio, began to sing, and that was it. He had his first record deal before he'd even finished smoking his cigarette. Jon is just so outstanding. A treasure."

"Yes." She wanted to turn around and fly across the city all the way back to the house, and straight into Jon's arms. The pull was so strong that Naomi had to press her hand against her chest to calm her yearning heart.

They were sitting on the terrace of a hotel where they could look down on the street below and the cars cruising past. There were a lot of people on the sidewalk, many tourists talking in different languages, but on the terrace it was quiet and shady.

"I've been thinking," Sally said after they'd been served their drinks, "I know who you are, Naomi, but I know you don't want Jon to know, or anyone else. I haven't quite figured out why yet, but since it seems to be working for you and Jon, I won't ask. I'm sure you have your reasons." She took a breath to go on, but Naomi raised her hand.

"If I told Jon, or Sal, or anyone here, things would change," she replied. "They wouldn't let me go anywhere without a bodyguard, and trust me, Sal would think of some way to use it to their advantage. Jon and a hotel heiress, lovers? How could Sal not use that? I wouldn't even be angry at him. But I don't want it. Lord, and my parents would come down on me like a rain of fire!"

The thought alone was enough to make her shudder.

"I know." Gently, Sally laid her hand on Naomi's. "Trust me, I know what you mean, and you're right. That's why I've been thinking. Naomi. That party next week. And the Grammy and the Oscars. I know you want to go, and chances are good that Jon will even be nominated for a Grammy. He'll want to have you there, right? I mean, that's why we bought a dress for you, and that reminds me, you need shoes and an evening clutch, and maybe a shawl. The nights are getting cooler." She plucked the little parasol out of the olive in her martini. "The problem is the red carpet. If you walk the red carpet with Jon, there will be a million questions. It won't take the tabloids twenty-four hours to figure out who you are. But if you appeared as, let's say, Sal's escort, no one would give a crap about who you are. It's just a thought."

Their lunch was served. Naomi had never seen a salad so fancifully decorated. There were things in it she'd never seen before, such as tiny mushrooms with very long stems, and flowers. It looked very colorful and very pretty.

"They're used to seeing me walk in with Jon." Sally shrugged. "I'm his label manager. No one cares or suspects. And they'll never notice you. And it would help you keep your cover."

The small mushrooms had an interesting, nutty aroma and were unexpectedly crunchy.

"But won't Jon ask why?" She pierced one of the orange flowers with her fork. It looked familiar, but she didn't know the name. Gardening had never been her strong point.

"I think we can easily convince him that it's a good idea to hide you for a while yet. He's very careful now, after that thing with that fan. If we tell him that it's for your safety, he'll be more than glad to let Sal escort you. And I don't even think it's a lie. It would be safer for you not to be recognized as Jon's lover." With dainty fingers, Sally picked a mussel from her salad and popped it into her mouth. Her fingernails were as red as a fire truck, and matched the red polka dots on her white dress. Those polka dots made Naomi smile every time she saw Sally. There was always at least one item on her that had them, even if it was only a hair ribbon.

"You were in love with Jon."

Sally looked up, grinning. "Of course I was! Who wouldn't be? But he wasn't in love with me. A bit infatuated perhaps, but that wasn't really directed at me but at what I am: the daughter of a record company owner. That was right after he got here, and he was a bit starstruck. It was over before it ever began. I like him a lot; I won't deny that. But seriously?" She picked a daisy from her plate and held it between glossy-nailed fingers. "Loving Jon is way too exhausting for me. He needs someone who adores him twenty-four seven. He's like that: a demigod, a comet with a very bright trail, the sun that blinds you. Sooner or later a girl would burn up in his fire. You're welcome to him."

"He's not really like that," Naomi muttered, blushing again.

"Yeah, he is. You don't notice because you're exactly the same." Raising her glass, toasting Naomi, she added, "Two comets clashing. I wonder what will happen: do we get a new sun, or a hell of a lot of stardust? Only time will tell."

Chapter Forty-five

IT WAS EASIER than she'd thought to convince Jon.

"Right," he said, "I hadn't even thought of that, but yes, Sally is right. I wouldn't want you in danger because of me! I want to keep you safe, and protected!"

The funny thing was that she didn't mind at all. There was a different quality to his worry about her, a care and attention about her as a person, as someone who was precious to him for her own sake.

He loved the new red dress but said he'd prefer to see her in the rose one she'd brought with her from Geneva. It had been hanging in the closet for so long now, a sad, lonely remnant of her earlier life, and he felt it was time to show it some attention.

Naomi argued that she didn't have the right shoes to go with it, the new ones she'd just bought were red satin and meant to go with the new dress, but he just shrugged and told her to go shopping with Sally again.

They were sitting on the roof garden, enjoying some Californian Zinfandel, watching the sunset. The evening was surprisingly cool. Jon had brought out the quilt from their bed and wrapped it around them.

Snuggled up, her head on his chest, Naomi listened to the rhythm of his heart and the heartbeat of the ocean. They seemed in tune, both slow, strong, steady, both beating for her.

"I'd like to call Fleur," she softly said./ "I'd like to invite her. Do you think we could take her to the party?"

Jon shifted and didn't reply right away. "How strange this all is. It's almost as if the moment we met, we stepped into an alternate universe where life is easy and fun, and I can live in fearlessness. After that thing with that girl, I thought I'd never be happy again, never breathe without tasting the sour tang of sorrow on my tongue. Then I go on tour, and there you are; and suddenly everything is light and sweet again, lighter and sweeter than ever before." His arms tightened around her. "You've changed everything. I feel like I'm living through you, as if you're my portal to a happier life. Yes, my heart, do call Fleur, and do invite her. It's time we opened our fairy paradise to laughter and the love of friends. Call her, and we'll take her movie star hunting."

"HELLO?" Fleur sounded sleepy and disoriented. "Do you know what time it is here, you crazy nut?"

Naomi had forgotten, and it made her giggle. The sun had just vanished into the sea.

"Fleur, come and visit me. Come tomorrow? Or rather today, for you? We're going to a movie premiere party in a few days, and I want you to come."

Through the phone, she could hear the rustling of bedsheets and Fleur moving. "Are you crazy? I'd have to jump on a plane like now. And I have to pack too!"

Her heart beating at the back of her tongue, Naomi said, "Ask my parents to let you use the jet. Tell them I want you here."

Fleur's breathing stopped. "Have you talked to them? Is everything okay?"

"Sort of." She didn't feel like explaining, much less thinking about it. "Just come. You'll love it."

"I'm not asking your father for any favors! I'll get on a regular plane; heck, I'd rather swim than ask Olaf for a favor! Favors from Olaf always come with strings attached. No, I'll pack some things now and find out when the next plane heads to LA. God, Naomi, do you have any idea how many hours on a plane that means? I'll be stiff and bleary-eyed, and in need of a spa day when I get there. And I sure as hell hope you have a pool!"

No, Naomi replied, laughing, they didn't; but there was the beach right outside the door, and it was still warm enough to go for a swim, and if she wanted, Jon could teach her to surf.

From where she was sitting on their bed she could see the ocean, still and covered in its slate-gray evening sheen. She hadn't been down to the beach since her meeting with Olaf and Seth. It had lost its attraction, and the fear of running into someone who had orders to abduct her, take her back to Canada, was just too great. Not even a bodyguard would be able to free her from those claws.

She wondered if Jon would come after her. She wondered if he'd come to rescue her if that happened, or would he just assume she'd run away again, just the way she'd run away from home to be with Jon.

The thought was so sad and so lonely that she had to swallow it before she could reply to Fleur, who was asking if they'd pick her up at the airport or what?

"Yes, I'll be there. Jon, probably not."

There was a pause. Then Fleur said, "Right. How weird. Do you ever have that feeling of living in two worlds, Naomi? One where he's a star and all public and stuff, and one where he's just the man you love, just another guy? It must be very weird. Like wearing the wrong glasses and seeing things double or something."

"Sometimes, a bit." She didn't tell Fleur that those two sides flowed into each other quite easily for her now.

"Bring an evening gown," she said, but Fleur had already hung up.

Turning, she looked at the rose gown hanging on the closet door and blew it a kiss. "Your fate is so much better now," she said. "Seth's grubby little palms will never touch you. I like that thought. I like it a lot!"

JON opened the quilt and his arms to her when she returned.

"So? Is she coming?" His lips touched her temple.

"Yes. Tomorrow. Which is today for her. I never realized how long that flight really was."

A chuckle escaped Jon. "It seemed endless to me. I wanted to be home and to show you the house. Couldn't wait to have you safely inside my walls so you couldn't run from me the way you'd run from your parents. And now that I have you I'm living in constant fear that one morning I'll wake up and you'll be gone, and there'll be nothing left of you, nothing. I'll walk through the house and search for a clue, but there won't be a trace. And however hard I search for you, I'll not be able to find you. That's my worst nightmare."

Naomi wrapped her arms tightly around him. "I can't imagine a scenario where that would happen. It would have to be something really, really dire. It would have to be so terrible that my world crashes. But I can't imagine anything that awful."

Silently, they watched pelicans patrol the beach, following the line of the surf in neat formation, their great wings beating a stately rhythm.

"Of course, if you fell in love with another girl…" she mused, "if I came home from lunch with Sally and found you in bed with another girl, that would be very bad."

"Your fantasy is running away with you," Jon growled. "Don't paint pictures no one wants to see."

She laughed, but he gripped her around her waist and pulled her on his lap. "Not funny, my dear, so not funny. And what if you fall in love with another man? What am I supposed to do then? What if you leave me because you fall in love with someone else? What then?"

"Jon, really." Shifting, she straddled his knees. "You have such a penchant for self-torture. Why in the world would I go and do that when I have you? I can't imagine being with someone else, or… or sleeping in another man's bed. That won't happen. No, if I leave you it will have to be because of you. Because you did something to make me run."

"Well then, I'll have to take care that doesn't happen, right?" His hands cupped her hips to pull her closer. "And I'll have to do everything I can to make you happy here, with me, so you don't want to run, ever."

"I think that's a good plan." She began kissing him, breezy kisses on his lips, barely touching them.

"Stop that," Jon whispered. "Stop now or you'll be ravished on this old couch if you don't."

"The bed isn't far away."

"IT'S impossible," Jon said later. "I can't make up a scenario that would make us break up. I just can't."

Naomi sat up, the sheet wrapped around her. "Well, since it

seems to be such a fascinating subject, let's try and make one up then."

"The strange girl in my bed doesn't count!" He reached out to her, but she shook her head.

"Okay then, no strange girl. Let me think for a moment."

The night wind blew over her naked back, making her shiver. It seemed as if the whispering fingers of foreboding, like a dark dream born out of the darkest part of the ocean.

"If you changed," she said, "if you changed into someone for whom fame is more important than the people who love you. If your craving for adoration grew out of proportion, and you forgot the difference between love and adoration. If you expected me to treat you like a star and not like the man I love. I think that would make me leave." She nodded to herself. "If you weren't *my* Jon anymore, but the centerfold Jon, the star on the stage all the time. That would make me run away."

"Baby, if that ever happens, I'll leave myself. I'd flee from that man even faster than you could. So it's an easy promise to make: I'll never be like that. See..." He sat up against the headboard. "That's the good thing about being a Brooklyn boy: You stay grounded. You remember where you came from, and how hard the road was. I can promise that easily."

He was beautiful the way he lounged there, naked, unashamed, secure in his body, secure in who he has.

"Well then, we can end this discussion." Creeping back up to him, Naomi pulled the sheet over both of them. "And we can talk about what we should do with Fleur. She's tickled pink to be invited to Jon Stone's house. She was the one who gave me your album, Jon. Technically, she introduced me to you."

"Well then! We'll have to give that girl the Hollywood treatment, won't we? Take her out to lunch where the stars hang out, tour the studios, get someone important to throw a party for her. Oh, and we'll take her shopping! I think Fleur will love Rodeo Drive." Groaning, Jon broke off. "That reminds me." He sighed. "A tux. I need a new tux for that movie premiere. Sally won't let me hear the end of it if I show up in the old one."

"And I can't wait to see you in it." The thought alone was delicious. "You do wear a real bow tie, don't you? Not one of those cheap snap-on things?"

"Heck, yeah, babe," Jon growled. "Nothing is as sexy as a man in a tux, a good, pleated linen shirt, gold cuff links, and a bow tie he can slowly pull open. Makes every woman swoon."

Chapter Forty-six

"THE GREAT THING for you about living in the US is that no one here knows, or even cares, about rich people in Canada. You picked a good spot to be invisible. There are so many pretty young girls in Los Angeles, no one gives a crap about one more." Sally lit a menthol cigarette and blew the smoke out the car window. "As long as you're not seen smooching with Jon anywhere in public, that is. I promise to help you keep your secret, but you have to do your part too."

"Thank you, Sally." Naomi breathed a sigh of relief. "I don't know how to thank you."

Sally waved her away, the gold lighter and her coral-red nails glinting in the sunlight. "No problem. As I said, I'll do almost anything to keep Jon happy and creative." She took another drag, but this time she forgot to exhale out the window, and the smoke spread inside the car.

Naomi coughed.

"You have no idea how tickled Sal and my dad would be if they found out. Every tabloid from here to Moscow would be carrying the story. It would be something like, "Super-talented rock star Jon Stone finds love among monied royalty." Sally's brow wrinkled up. "Something along that line. Maybe a bit more caustic. Or explicit. Anything for a good headline!" She patted Naomi's arm. "But there's no need to worry. It won't happen, because we won't let your secret get out."

"Thank you," Naomi said, the scratchy taste of cigarette smoke on her tongue.

They were on the way to the airport to pick up Fleur, and this time they were in the van escorted by two bodyguards from the record company. Sally had introduced them, but Naomi, frightened by their size and the guns showing under their suit jackets, had opted to forget their names immediately. She wasn't sure she wanted to know them. These men, if the worst thing happened, would have to be willing to die for her, and that was a burden she didn't want to shoulder.

"WE'LL have to tell Fleur to keep her big mouth shut," Naomi said as the van pulled up at the curb of the arrivals terminal. "She'll talk down the blue from the sky if no one stops her." Her head was beginning to hurt, and she rubbed her forehead. "I don't know what made me invite her. It was so impulsive."

Sally, rummaging in her purse for something, looked up. "You wanted to see a familiar face, Naomi. You've been here nearly two months now, and you're totally isolated from everyone you knew. I'd stay in bed and cry out my eyes if I was in your situation. Not even Jon would be able to help me over that sense of loneliness." She brought out a pack of chewing gum. "Which makes me wonder. Why did you run away? Was it really just because you fell in love with Jon, and he with you? That's no reason to give up everything else!"

Her heart was ready to break. "No. You're right, I did run away. They…" she didn't even know how to put it in words. "My father is a very business-minded man. The family business is his world, and all he really cares about, and I'm an important part of it."

They entered the terminal, and Naomi looked around. As a member of Jon's retinue, she hadn't passed through it when they'd arrived; the caravan of cars had whisked them straight from the hangar to the city.

"In his eyes, I'm not a girl with dreams and ideas of her own. I'm an asset, part of the business, a pawn to move into a favorable position. Which means into a marriage with someone who'll bring something to the Carlsson empire. He'd never have allowed me to become Jon's girlfriend if I'd told him, let alone come here to live with Jon."

Sally was staring at her, her dark eyes as round as marbles, the chewing gum unwrapped between her fingers.

Naomi shrugged, but with a bitter, suffocating feeling of defeat. "They'd picked a husband for me. I didn't love him. I ran away."

"Wow," Sally said, and then, two breaths later, again, "Wow. Now it all makes sense. And now I understand why you don't want anyone to know who you are. Wow, Naomi. I'm impressed! You have the heart of a tigress, to run away with Jon into the unknown."

"Not really."

They meandered toward the passenger exit. There were a lot of people milling around, staring at the announcement board, wandering across the space, some with flowers, some glancing at their watches in boredom, some carrying paper cups of coffee.

The security men were right behind them, but keeping enough distance to give them privacy and the illusion of freedom.

"It wasn't that hard," Naomi went on after they'd found an empty bench. "All I did was follow my heart." She smiled, reliving those moments in the Geneva hotel lobby. "I didn't have to think at all. It would have taken more courage to walk away from Jon."

"And here I thought you were just another infatuated fan." Stretching out her legs, Sally regarded her shoes. They were crazy shoes: sneakers with pink laces, bright green sneakers too. They clashed in an interesting way with the red panty hose she was wearing under her short jeans skirt. "But no, you really aren't. You freed yourself from a heavy load, didn't you? I don't know if I could have done that in the same situation."

Naomi smiled. "If Jon hadn't blasted into my life, I'd have married Seth eventually and settled down to a boring, secure, and predictable life. I'm not a fighter. If Jon hadn't begged me to meet him in Amsterdam, I'd never have done it. Did you know he gave me a ticket, and his private address, before he left Geneva?"

"Yeah." Sally's chin moved furiously as she chewed her gum. "Don't remind me. I threw a fit when Sal told me. I was ready to slap Jon for that. Idiot man."

The lights on the board blinked, announcing that Fleur's plane had landed.

"I love him," Naomi said softly. "I really love Jon. Life with him is so special, so different from what I knew. My stupid scribblings, and he thinks they're worth my weight in gold. He encourages me to explore my writing talent, pushes me to write more. Jon makes every day a wonderful day."

"Yeah, yeah. I know." Sally flicked her wrist at Naomi in cool dismissal. "It's okay, you can have him. All that creative mush is too much for me. I want to see him at the studio, pouring out new songs. And the way it seems right now, he does that better with you around than on his own. So be it!" She got up and pulled at her skirt, but it was a futile undertaking. Her legs were as visible as before. They were healthy legs too, well shaped, toned, sleek, and strong.

Naomi, watching Sally stretch and look around, was reminded of a fragrant rubber ball, something full of joy and energy, a curious puppy, or a bright-eyed squirrel.

She wondered how her parents would have reacted if she'd shown up dressed like that, in a scanty t-shirt and a skirt that hardly covered her behind.

How strange it all was. How limited her life had been, despite her family's wealth and the illusion of freedom she'd been given in Geneva. Her life had happened within precisely defined borders set by Olaf, and tolerated by her mother.

The exit gate flew open to release the first batch of passengers.

Excited now, Naomi moved toward the barrier. Fleur, she hadn't realized how much she'd missed her friend, or anyone from home. Even the thought of Olaf mellowed a bit for a moment as she recalled fun moments, moments when he'd forgotten about business and had just been a generous, loving father.

"I think," she said, "I think parents should love their kids for what they are, and not for what they want them to be. I hope I do better when I have kids someday. I hope I'll remember how it felt, trying to be someone I'm not, just to please my parents. They nearly succeeded, and it would have made my life torture forever after. I hope I remember that lesson and do a better job with my own children."

"Yeah well, you can. No one is going to stop you, Naomi. You're free of all that now." Daintily spitting her gum into the saved wrapping foil, Sally added, "And you don't even need your family's money? That album you and Jon are working on will make you independent. And if there are others, you'll be quite wealthy in your own right someday soon."

The album. Sally was talking about it as if it were the most natural thing in the world when for her, for Naomi, it was the most outlandish thought ever.

She was just writing songs with Jon, and his producers talked about an album.

It was as if she'd left Earth and landed on a different planet, in a totally different world where other things mattered, where her heritage meant nothing, something to be completely ignored. She was in a world where creativity mattered, where it was the most precious, most important thing, and she was part of it.

Her mouth open, her breath caught in her throat, Naomi let the feeling run through her. She was free; she didn't have to hide her need to write, a guilty secret she'd shared only with her red journal.

"I think that must be your friend," Sally broke into her tangled thoughts. "She looks like she'd be your friend."

Fleur was waving at them, holding on to a sun hat and her dangling purse, a porter pushing a cart with two large suitcases in her wake.

"Hello," she cried. "I'm here! Where is Hollywood?"

"Sheesh." Shaking her head, Sally put her fists on her hips. "Really? The same old cliché, and I bet she wants to see the Walk of Fame too. Damn tourists!"

Naomi didn't care. She flew into Fleur's arms, hugging her tightly, whispering, "I'm so happy to see you! You have no idea how much I missed you."

Fleur held her at arm's length. "Well darling if I remember correctly you couldn't wait to run away with your lover! And it had to be to a place on the other side of the planet. Of course. You and your drama, Naomi! You made me spend abysmal hours on a plane! And no proper French bread? And Californian wine? Who in the world drinks Californian wine?"

"I do!" Her heart was singing. "And it's lovely! Way better than that sour French stuff! Come on; LA is waiting for you!"

"LA, will you just listen to yourself! I swear you even have an

American accent now!" She stopped to pay the porter, but Sally had already done it. "And what do you eat here? Man, maybe I should have brought our cook. I'm sure you only eat American food too."

"A lot of Mexican. Jon's housekeeper is Mexican." Bubbles of mirth were forming in her chest, and creeping up into her nose and mouth. "You'll love it, I promise. How long can you stay?"

Critically, Fleur watched as her luggage was transferred into the van. "A couple of weeks, I guess. But then I have to go back. School starts." Pursing her cherry-red lips, Fleur regarded Naomi. "You look good! Tan and fit, if I may say so. The climate seems to agree with you. And the food. And the company."

Naomi, blushing, realized that she hadn't introduced her to Sally. She took a breath to do it, but again Sally was faster.

"I'm the label manager," she said. "I work for Jon. My name's Sally."

"Pleased." Fleur, shading her eyes with her hand, gazed out at the city. "Los Angeles, eh? Who'd have thought I'd come here to visit my best friend, a rock star's little lovebird?"

Chapter Forty-seven

SALLY TOLD THE driver to take them through Hollywood so Fleur could get a first impression of LA.

They drove past the studios, the Chinese Theatre, and down to Santa Monica beach, where they climbed out and took a walk down to the water across the lively beach.

Of course, Sally said, the beach in Malibu where Jon lived was much nicer, and not as busy, but if Fleur wanted to breathe in LA, this was the place to do it.

"I need those," Fleur cried when they were back on the promenade, watching the scantily dressed girls flit by, elegant and graceful goddesses weaving through the spectators like dragonflies hunting among reeds on their Rollerblades. They made their movements even sleeker, faster. Naomi felt the same itch. She wanted to be one of those girls too.

"Maybe we should all get them?" Sally was staring. "I haven't been here for too long! It does look like fun!"

"We need to get home." Naomi was beginning to feel uncomfortable out in the open for so long without Jon. She kept glancing over her shoulder, expecting someone to jump at her and drag her away, back to her parents. She was quite sure that Olaf wouldn't stop at hiring some thugs to do just that.

"This is such a fun place," Fleur said when they returned to the van and scrambled in. "I'm not surprised that you love it here! I'm surprised your old man doesn't own a couple of hotels on the beach."

Realizing what she'd said, she clamped her mouth shut so fast her teeth clicked.

"Yeah, that's something we need to talk about." Sally sighed. "Listen well, Fleur."

Naomi turned away her head, listening to Sally and Fleur laying out plans on how to keep Jon from ever finding out who she really was.

Anger formed in her stomach, silvery, flittering pieces of anger that danced in a wild whirlwind of shards just below her heart at what they were saying about her.

"Sweet," Fleur was calling her. "Innocent and fragile."

"And we need to protect her at all costs," she ended, with a deep sigh. "That's what I've been doing ever since we met. She walked into class at our school in Geneva one day, in that very unflattering navy school uniform, her hair in braids, her knees shaking; and I knew it would be my job to look after her. Naomi always needs someone to look after her. She's as gentle and as easily spooked as a fairy. I wish that girl grew some muscle."

"I have muscle," Naomi threw in, her mouth dry. All that silver floating inside the center of her body had sucked up every drop of liquid. "And I'm not frail and innocent. I can take care of myself just fine. I made my way to Amsterdam on my own, and I'm here now! I even sent my father away when…when…"

They were staring at her, open-mouthed.

"Your father was here?" Fleur asked. "Really? You sent him away? He went away? He let you send him away? That's hard to believe."

Sally was looking at her with carefully narrowed eyes, waiting for Naomi to go on.

"I was inside the garden, and the gate was locked," Naomi muttered. "But I had to run for it. He and Seth were there; they wanted to take me back to Canada."

"And what did he say? What did you say?" Fleur had gripped her wrist and was holding on to it as if she was about to drown in curiosity.

"The usual stuff. Business, blah blah, disgrace, ho-hum, marry Seth, bleh." Naomi shrugged. "I slammed the gate in their faces and told Seth to fuck off."

"Naomi!" Gasping, clutching her throat, Fleur blanched. "I've never heard you use that word before! We don't use that word! Oh my God, if our parents could hear you talk like that!"

Shocked by her own choice of words, Naomi slapped her hand

over her mouth. "I'm sorry," she mumbled through her fingers. "I didn't mean to say that! It just slipped out, I was so angry."

"Yeah, you meant to say it all right." Sally hadn't even blinked. "And good for you, girl. You've got some serious spunk hidden away under that flawless complexion! So what happened then? They just left?"

"Yes." Naomi shook off Fleur. I told Seth to take a hike." The anger in her chest dissolved and turned into a silken ribbon of easy breath. "He said he'd always assumed that we'd get married at some point, and that just blew my mind. I told him that yeah, that was just what any girl wanted to hear. And then I told him what Jon says, what Jon tells me..." She could feel her blood creeping up the skin of her face. "What Jon tells me when he wants to show me that he loves me. For a moment Seth thought I was speaking to him. It was hilarious." She wriggled her shoulders. "And he doesn't blush well. Redheads should avoid blushing at all costs. It clashes with their hair."

Fleur hiccuped in mirth, and Sally, a crooked smile on her face, shook her head.

"I told him to leave me alone for all time. And I think he accepted it." The thought made her sad all over again. "I think he was even sort of relieved. I returned to the house, and there was Jon, making breakfast for me. And everything was fine."

They fell silent. The van took them to Malibu, driving along the shore, the water always visible.

"You didn't bring an evening gown," Sally remarked as they pulled up outside the gate to Jon's residence. "You'll need one."

"Oh." Fleur fluttered her fingers through the air. "It's not a problem. I'll go down to the flagship store of the designer my dad works for and let them fit me with one. They'll love doing that. The daughter is wearing one of her father's gowns. Can't get any better advertising. What are you going to wear, Naomi? And where are we going anyway?"

Naomi didn't listen to Sally explain the event, or to Fleur's squeals of excitement. Her thoughts were racing ahead, to Jon.

"WOW," Fleur said. And then, inside the hall, again "Wow. I didn't expect this."

"So what did you expect?" Jon was coming out of his studio, the koa guitar in one hand, every inch the star. He wasn't in t-shirt and jeans but had dressed up for Fleur, in black trousers and a cream silk shirt. He almost looked as if he was ready to go onstage.

"You." Sally pointed at him. "Tux, my friend. Let's go! Give the girls a couple of hours on their own and come with me. We're buying you a new tux."

"Sally." Jon placed the guitar on the couch. "You're a pain in the ass, no mistake about it." He said it in a friendly tone, and Sally grinned.

"You and Naomi are having real issues with your language today. Your sweet little girl used the *f* word today. I swear, that was on my list of things that would never happen."

"Really?" Curious, Jon gazed at Naomi. "You must have been really upset! Is everything all right?"

"Oh, it was the..." said Fleur, and her eyelids fluttered in panic. "She was cursing the traffic on Sunset Boulevard."

"Aha." Jon looked from one to the other. "And what in the world were you doing there?"

Sightseeing, Naomi replied, putting her arms around him, rising on her toes to kiss him lightly, just some sightseeing. She had no idea why it had gotten to her, all that traffic on an otherwise quiet Wednesday morning.

"I'll show Fleur her room," she added. "Then we'll have lunch or walk on the beach while you're out with Sally."

Jon groaned like a teenager told to do something he really hated. "Can't you come too? I'd feel so much better if you were there. I might even enjoy it."

"Jon!"

"Babe, what?" On the point of letting her go, he again slung his arms around her for another kiss. "Are you blaming me for wanting you near me all the time? Really?"

"No. Of course not." Put that way, she couldn't resist his pleading. "But I can't leave Fleur alone here the moment she arrives, Jon."

"Yeah." He let go of her. "All right then. I'll leave you girls to explore the house and yard, and I'll go with Sally." He began moving away, but stopped in the doorway. "But Naomi. No excursions or walks on the beach without a bodyguard, okay? Don't take any chances."

"I promise, Jon." And it was an easy promise to make.

THEY walked through the house, opening all doors, peering into all rooms, even the niches under the roof, the turret, and the wine cellar. Naomi introduced Fleur to Amparo, who handed them coffee and some freshly baked cookies. They took them up to the roof garden.

"Ah." Fleur stopped when Naomi opened the door to the master bedroom. "Now here at last is a room that looks like you. Lovely carpet, Naomi, and what a lovely bed!"

Naomi ran her hand over the dark wood. She'd never told Jon how much he'd spent on it, and she wasn't sure if he even cared. It was so much better than the mattress on a wooden box that he'd had before.

"Here." She pushed aside the lace curtains and opened the door to the balcony and the roof garden. "My favorite place in the house. We've slept out here too. It's so calm and peaceful, and I love how I can see the ocean beyond the trees."

They sat in the big daybed swing, sipping their coffee, gazing out at the horizon. From far away they could hear the faint hum of the traffic on the highway, passing behind the estate on its way south and north. From time to time there was a siren, as if to remind them that the outside world still existed.

"I can't believe I'm here." Fleur waved at their surroundings. "Imagine, a guest in Jon Stone's house! Only a few months ago you didn't even know he existed. And now we're going to a movie premiere with him! You really did it! You caught the hottest rock star there is! You win, girl"

Naomi crumbled off a piece of her cookie to sprinkle on the broad stone railing, where a couple of little birds were waiting, watching her through bright, black eyes.

"That's not what this is about, Fleur." The song they'd been working on earlier today, just before she'd left to pick up Fleur, ran through her mind. Jon had sung it to her, standing near the grand, one foot up on the bench, the koa guitar on his knee. She'd led him through the lines, had patiently rapped out the rhythm for him on the lacquered wood of the Steinway when he stumbled over the words.

"These don't rhyme," he'd complained over and over again. "And I've never sung a song that doesn't rhyme before! There are no verses, there's no bridge; you're blasting all the songwriting rules to hell!"

"So let's blast them to hell," she had replied. "Why not give it a try?" And had swallowed in fear, waiting for his response.

"Right." He'd settled the guitar against his body and stood up straight, and taken a deep breath. "You're right. Why not? Let's go break some rules, Miss Geneva!"

And he'd done it, had sung through her lyrics, while she gave him the rhythm.

"You're teaching me, Naomi," Jon had said when he finished. "You're teaching me to be unafraid, to move away from what I know. You're opening up the world for me."

"WHAT'S it about then?" Fleur asked, watching the sparrows pick up cookie crumbs. "Isn't it about you being in love with Jon, and he with you?"

"Yes, but more."

The greatest love, it was the greatest love, Naomi wanted to say, a love that gave them the courage to walk new roads, try new things, together and on their own, because they knew someone was holding them, was supporting them, and was there ready to catch the other if they stumbled. She'd learned that love wasn't about staring into each other's eyes, using them as mirror. Love was about walking side by side, fearlessly taking on the world.

And it didn't matter at all who they were. Rock star, hotel heiress—those were only shells, and they'd broken them.

Chapter Forty-eight

"DO YOU LIKE it?"

She did indeed. She couldn't even begin to tell him how much. Jon looked even taller than he was, his shoulders straight and broad. He was well-groomed, smelling nicely of aftershave. His hair, neatly trimmed, fell in well-behaved curls around his shirt collar.

He gave his sleeves a final tug to free the cuff links from the jacket and straightened the bow tie one last time.

"Ready to go? The limousine arrived a couple of minutes ago." Picking up her shawl and purse, Jon held the door for her. "Excited?"

She nodded.

"I have a feeling you're used to this." His fingers trailed over her bare arm. "You're not half as excited as Fleur is, and she's the couture designer's daughter. She should be at events like this all the time, right?"

"It's different. We're going to see famous people!" Naomi tried to put as much enthusiasm into her words as she could. "And we're in Hollywood! That's exciting!"

"Well, technically we aren't, and the party won't be in Hollywood either, but in Beverly Hills." Jon gave her the shawl when she held out her hand for it. "But I realize that Europeans think LA *is* Hollywood, and who am I to argue? Sometimes it sure seems that way."

They walked down the stairs together and into the living room, where Sally, Sal, and Russ were waiting.

"So." Sal, buttoning his jacket, stood up. "I hear I'll have the honor of escorting you tonight. I get to pretend that you're in love with me and not the master."

"Yeah, just remember, Sal. *Pretend* is the key word here." Jon growled at his friend, and it made Naomi smile.

"I would've brought you flowers, but someone would've ripped out my throat with jealousy," Sal added, ignoring him. "But the way things are, you'll have to make do with my arm." Bowing to her, he held out his elbow, and Naomi hooked her hand in it.

"You don't have to do that just yet, you know." Stepping forward, Jon pulled her away and put his arm around her waist. "There's enough time for that once we get there. And don't you try anything, Sal. This is my girl. She's booked. Find someone else."

A shadow flew across Sal's brow. "Don't get your undies in a bunch, Jon. No one is taking anything from you. Just calm down, for heaven's sake. Let's have a drink before we go!" He went into the kitchen and came back with glasses and a bottle of bourbon. "Here, you pour."

They were waiting for Fleur. The sun was dipping toward the horizon, giving LA that special light that Naomi hadn't seen anywhere else: it was so soft, molten, that the sky seemed to turn to liquid under the sun's benevolent touch so it could better drip into the sea. It was the hour when the rustle of wind in the palm trees mingled with the song of the waves crashing on the beach and the birds saying good night to the day.

Most evenings they wandered down to the stone bench in the hidden arbor, their bare feet caressed by soft moss, their hair stroked by flowers, and sat there, watching the sky change from the rosy sheen of sunset into the feathery blue of dusk. They pointed out the stars to each other as they appeared in the growing darkness.

"Worlds, all of them," Jon would say, and Naomi would reply, "Suns, or galaxies."

Watching the night sky made her homesick for the clear winter nights in Ontario, where she and Olaf had gone out onto the terrace and watched the great wheeling of the Milky Way, and sometimes, when it had been very still, Naomi had been almost certain that she could hear the song of the galaxy as it turned and turned, and with every completed turn moved farther away from the center of the universe.

Too big to comprehend, Olaf had always said; and, shrugging, he'd returned to the house and warmth, while she'd stood, staring, trying to understand the incomprehensible, torturing herself with the ultimate question of what lay beyond the universe.

"I'll dance with you anyway." Jon, standing close behind her, whispering so softly into her ear that it was more a caress than something spoken. "No one can stop me from dancing with you once we're inside. You'll be the loveliest woman there tonight, I'm sure of it. All those silly models and movie stars, they're nothing compared to you. Nothing."

She leaned against him, her head under his chin.

"I can't bear to think of you being escorted by Sal. I'm sure I don't want to go at all. I just want to take you away to some secret place where I don't have to share you. Can't we just run away?"

"No. You can't spoil the evening for Fleur. I'm sure she's totally nuts by now, hoping you'll dance with her."

"And will I?" Jon laid his arm around her and pulled her a little bit closer. "Will I dance with Fleur and not with you? Not even one dance?"

"I don't know. Will you?"

He really smelled nice; the scent was a mix of cedars, sweet tobacco, and the ocean. It was tart, fresh, very male, very elegant.

"I don't think so," Jon said. "I think that right after the official part we'll take off for the beach. That makes more sense to me."

"Makes sense. But we can't. You're too famous now. You have to mingle and be a star."

Jon let go of her and turned her around so he could see her face. "Goodness. You sound like Sal; you're talking like a manager! This can't be my sweet love; this must be someone else." His voice was light, easy with banter, but it changed when he looked at her. "But you mean it. You know what you're talking about! What happened, Naomi?"

"Nothing, Jon. But I'm not stupid. I knew right from the start that I'd have to share you with the public, and tonight it starts." Her mouth felt like quivering. "I knew it would have to happen. You're who you are, and your career has just begun. We've been given such a wonderful time of grace. But now your audience wants you back. I love you."

"Baby, and I love you! And I don't give a crap about appearances and what's safer or better! Let the world know I'm taken!"

There was so much arrogant bravado in his tone that she forgot the sadness and smiled instead.

"You're such a goof, Jon Stone. No, we won't declare our love to the world quite yet! I think we can squeeze out a few more private months before that happens. And if it was up to me, they'd never know. I really don't want all that attention on me just yet." She made her hands creep up his back, under the fine tuxedo jacket. "Please can you do that for me?"

"Of course. You're very lovely in that dress, you know."

The rose dress, and it was going to an event that was so much better than the summer ball at the yacht club. It would dance with someone so much better than Seth too.

"I'm ready!" Fleur was dancing down the stairs as if it meant nothing to be in heels, and wrapped in ten layers of dark-blue silk. "Are we leaving? Sorry to keep you waiting, but I had to make a call."

"That's okay." Russ stepped forward, his hair charged and standing on end, as always when he was excited. "I'm pleased to meet you." He held out his hand, and Fleur, staring at it for a moment, took it.

"You're British," she said. "How unusual!"

"Not in Britain," Russ shot back, and she laughed.

"Right, then. Are we all sorted?" Sal opened the door to the driveway, where the big limo was waiting.

SHE hated it. She hated seeing Sally on Jon's arm, smiling into the cameras, answering questions, shaking her head when she was asked if she and Jon were an item, and adding, with a flirty smile, that you never know, maybe someday and then laughing her own words away.

"It'll be over in a moment," Sal said, his voice low. "Don't worry. No one talks to a Hollywood manager or the decorative girl escorting him. For all they know, you could be a professional, hired for the evening." He shrugged when she looked up at him. "Hey, this is LA. Everything is for sale, and everything can be bought. And one thing we have a lot of are pretty girls."

Fleur was ignoring the cameras, chatting amicably with Russ, enjoying herself immensely. She was like an exotic bird, even here among the colorful crowd. The dress she was wearing hung well on her, leaving most of her back bare, and a little too much of her chest too for Naomi's taste; but it looked grand and exquisite on her. Her long blond hair had been piled into a precarious nest of braids and curly strands, with a blue feather tucked into it. It quivered with every breeze and every movement, and Naomi wondered how it would be welcomed by those sitting behind her during the presentation of the movie.

"Who did you call?" she asked when they had to stop again and wait for someone in line ahead of them to be photographed and interviewed.

"Oh, home." Fleur waved at someone taking a snapshot of her. "And your mother."

Naomi couldn't move. She was certain that her blood had instantly turned into ice, into wood, anything that made breathing, talking, moving totally impossible.

"Don't look at me that way, Naomi." Fleur nudged her ribs. "Kiddo, I promised your mother to give her an unbiased report on how you're doing out here. I think she deserves that, don't you? That was all she wanted. She wanted to know if you're happy, well taken care of, cherished. When I told her that I was going to fly over, she begged me to let her know. That's all."

"You should have told me. You should have talked to me before you called her, Fleur."

Sal wasn't listening to them. He was chatting with Russ, and they had turned a bit away from them to smoke a cigarette.

"What's the big deal, Naomi? Nothing is going to change, and no one will tell Jon anything about you if you don't do it yourself. I'll be leaving in two days, and everything will go back to normal for you." Fleur shrugged. "Or do you want to punish your parents forever and ever?"

Jon's back was turned to them; he couldn't see her gasping for breath, fighting the panic.

"I just think you should have told me. It feels as if you've broken my trust, Fleur. I invited you here because I missed you, and because I thought it would be fun if you came with us to this opening night. But you came here as a spy for my mother! I think, yes, I really think you should have told me."

The luster had gone out of the day; she couldn't bear the thought of sitting through hours of watching a movie, a dinner, and some speeches until after midnight. She wanted to go home, lock the gate, lock the door, and hide in the bedroom, where no one would enter unless she asked them to.

"Well, I'm telling you now!" Fleur rolled her eyes. "You're such a drama queen, Naomi! All your mom wanted to know is if you're happy, if you're well. So I told her. So now she's relieved, and a lot happier than before. What's wrong with that?"

"Nothing. You're right. There's nothing wrong with that. You're right."

It was as if a door had closed, as if a heavy iron door had swung shut, she was cutting off everything that connected her to old friends.

One step, and another, she was moving away, into a smaller world, one that she had defined herself, that obeyed her rules. She could traverse her small kingdom in a few steps, and those always took her back to the same spot, the same hidden arbor with its stone bench, and always, there was Jon.

Chapter Forty-nine

NAOMI HAD USED every ounce of her careful upbringing and courtesy to get through the last two days with Fleur. Her heart was burning with disappointment and sadness. She didn't want to talk, she didn't even want to see Fleur, but there was no way to evade her and not make Jon suspicious at the same time.

To pass the time—and avoid having to talk—she suggested that they go sightseeing; visit a winery, an orchard, the San Diego Zoo, Chinatown and go Rollerblading in Santa Monica. And surfing, Sean and Jon could teach her how to surf, then she could go and try it on Lac Leman.

Jon had thrown her a long, thoughtful look and said, "There aren't any waves on that lake, darling." Which had made Naomi pick up her coffee cup and wander away from the table, replying that Fleur's father would surely be able to think of a way to make a few waves possible for his daughter. And if not, then she could ask Lucia.

Fleur, hanging her head, hadn't responded, and Jon hadn't followed up. He was too preoccupied with the new lyrics Naomi had given him that morning.

Sad, they were sad, he'd commented, and he'd wondered aloud why they were so sad; but she'd only shrugged and smiled at him, saying that sometimes memories were sad. After all, everyone was sad now and then; it was nothing special. Moods were like stones: you could pick them up, hold them in your hands, rub them against your skin; and if you wanted, you could toss them all away again, toss them into the vast ocean of forgetting and be done with them.

She'd looked at Fleur, saying this, and her heart had felt as heavy as one of those stones ready to be thrown away.

The movie party had flown past her just like the movie itself. She'd never been a fan of films with a lot of noise and crashing cars, and she liked disco music even less. There had been plenty of both that night.

Jon had been beleaguered, chased down, made to give autographs as if it was his last evening on Earth.

Things has turned surreal when the leading man from the movie came over to her and Sally and sourly informed them that he'd make sure always to invite Jon from now on, regardless of the event, since he always drew a crowd. Sally had raised her shoulders and replied that she was so sorry, but she was only there as an escort and had no influence whatsoever.

Morosely, they'd ordered another bottle of champagne and shared it, Naomi and Sally, both bored, and left to wilt at their table.

"That's what I get for meaning well," Sally had said, toasting Naomi. "Now we're both left to stew here." And shot a poisonous glance at Fleur, who was dancing with Russ and enjoying herself.

BACK at home, Naomi had excused herself and retired right away. Jon had come after her, worried, remorseful, apologizing; but she had waved him away, reassuring him that everything was fine, it wasn't his fault, she just had a headache from that terrible, noisy movie and the dreadful music.

"They could have played your music, and everything would have been fine," she'd complained from the shower, and almost meant it.

Jon had come into the bathroom, laughing. He'd still been dressed, except for his jacket. "My songs aren't really party music, sweetheart. I'm not sure that's a good idea." He'd came closer to peer over the shower partition. "I have to apologize, Naomi. This evening didn't go the way I'd wanted it to. I think Sally's idea for your safety isn't working. And it won't work in the long run anyway. Someone will see us together, pushing a baby carriage, or walking on the beach, or whatever." Shrugging, he'd began to unbutton his shirt. "And I have to admit that I don't give a crap. Why can't the world know that I've found my one true love? They should be happy for me, right, and not try to harm you? I don't understand people."

Naomi, her eyes closed so the shampoo wouldn't run into them, heard him sigh.

"It's as if first they want to make you successful and famous, and once you're there, their only goal is to bring you down again. Why else do I need to live like this, hidden away, constantly escorted by men whose job it is to protect me at the cost of their own lives if need be? And my love, my wife, she has to share this odd and scary life."

When she'd opened her eyes, he was sitting on the rim of the tub, his shirt in his hands, his head bowed.

"Why does it have to be like this? Why do I have to live two lives, to please everyone? Why can't I just be myself and still do what I love?" He'd been fiddling with his cuff links, plucking them out of the sleeves. "Even my own mother, even she treats me differently when I'm home. As if I'm a different person, as I've changed so much that I need to be treated like a stranger." Heaving another deep sigh, Jon had given her a thin smile and returned to the bedroom.

STANDING in the open doorway, Naomi watched Fleur pack her suitcases.

There was no room for the blue dress; it was hanging on the closet door, much like her own rose dress had done.

"You can have it, if you want," Fleur said without looking up. "Only I think you don't have the courage to wear it. You're only happy when you can hide and have your secrets, aren't you, Naomi?" Straightening, she turned. "Here's your chance to sort out everything in one fell swoop. Talk to your mother, tell Jon who you really are, and live your life the way you want to. Anyone can do that, you know. We're all entitled to live the way we want to. No big mystery here. Just say no to your father and be done with it."

"It's not that easy…" Naomi began, but Fleur waved her away.

"Of course it is. Not even Olaf Carlsson can force you to marry someone you don't love, not even he can make you live where you don't want to. You've got to understand that, Naomi! The only cage is the one you've built for yourself! We don't live in the Middle Ages, where a father could marry off his daughter, and she had no rights whatsoever! You could have said no anytime at all." Rolling up a shirt into a tight ball, she added, "I know your father isn't easy to deal with. But have you ever tried talking to him? Have you tried talking to your mom? Because all I can see are two heart-broken people who have no idea what's going on, or why their child ran away. I really think you should give them a chance, Naomi. I think they deserve that."

"You have no idea how my father really is." Naomi felt like crying, like slapping Fleur. "You have no idea, Fleur. I've tried and tried to please him, to do what he wants me to do. You're forgetting the business thing in your equation! I'm not only hiding from my parents, I'm hiding from the huge burden of being the heiress to that business. That, that is what I can't do, and won't do."

Fleur tossed the shirt into her suitcase. "So you're not really running from your parents but from duty?"

"Yes!"

Again Fleur flicked her wrist at Naomi. "And what keeps you from selling the whole damn thing once it's yours? Just sell it to the Hiltons or whatever and live happily ever after."

"You don't understand at all, do you?" Sadness. There was a lot of sadness, and a leave-taking she'd never expected to happen. "You're like a butterfly, Fleur, without any obligations, no strings attached. No one expects you to do anything; no one even thinks you can. You'll marry a rich man, wear your father's dresses, and have a new affair every week. You'll be the celebrated centerpiece at every party worth mentioning, and you'll have fun, fun, fun. And that's okay, I'm happy for you! But I'm not you!"

Closing the suitcase, Fleur turned her back on Naomi. "Very well. We've been friends forever, and I've always been on your side; and now you tell me that I don't really know you at all. That's bitter, Naomi. That's really sad, and very bitter... But if that's the way you want it, suit yourself. Go on hiding behind these high walls, and go on pretending that life can't touch you here. I'll tell you though, you're in for a rude awakening. Someday it will come, and then you'll need your family and friends. And I really hope someone will be there for you."

The morning sun was streaming through the open balcony door, pooling on the dark hardwood floor, floating over the silken sheets of the bed, kissing the flowers on the table.

So much care and love had gone into getting this room ready for Fleur. Naomi had bought those sheets herself, had made Sally go out with her, and had picked apricot-colored silk, Fleur's favorite. The carpet, and the paintings on the wall, everything had been chosen with Fleur in mind.

"I love you, Fleur," Naomi said, "I do. I've always loved you, and thought of you as my sister. I don't know what brought this on. I don't know why it would have been so hard to let me know that you were going to talk to my mother before you called her. That's all. I'd never have done such a thing behind your back. My loyalty is to you, not to your father or mother. To you. And I thought it was the same with you. That's the part that hurts."

Fleur sat down on the bed, her hands in her lap. "All I'm saying is that you're shutting yourself off from everything that meant anything to you before you met Jon." Her hand flew out, the gesture meant to encompass the house, the property, the beach, California. "You've made yourself a stranger living among strangers. You don't even really know the man you're living with! You ran away with a stranger, and now you're playing princess in a charmed castle. It'll break down one day, and that's what scares me."

Naomi took one step out of the room, and then another, until the hallway was around her.

"It was nice of you to come and visit." One more step, and she'd be on the stairs, and those would lead her down and into the studio, where Jon and his music were waiting. "I'm glad you had a few fun days here in Los Angeles, and I hope you'll have a smooth trip back home. Please give my regards to your parents, and mine."

"Naomi, don't be an idiot," Fleur called after her. "Are you even listening to yourself?"

"I'm listening to you. And what I just heard was that you either don't believe what you're seeing, or that you don't wish me a happy life. Both are pretty dismal. And it shows me that you can't look beyond the surface. This is not about hooking a rock star and being his playmate of the month. This is beyond what you'll ever be able to understand." Her hand on the bannister, Naomi took the first step. "When you're gone, the moment you're in the van and on the way out the gate, I'll return to the studio, and I'll be working with Jon on the new album. We'll work, Fleur, probably all day long. And tomorrow we'll take it to the studio, and Jon will record a demo. His music, my lyrics, and it won't be the first song either. You don't get what's going on here."

Defeated, Fleur shrugged. "Fine. Whatever. Call it whatever you like. As long as you don't burn all your bridges."

"Fleur." A breath of doom touched Naomi's cheek, settled on her shoulders like a big, black bird. "If Jon and I ever break up, if for some reason we can't go on together, nothing will matter. I'll be alone. No one, nothing, will be able to fill that chasm in my heart. Life will end."

"Drama queen," Fleur muttered. "Stupid, stupid." She sat up and glanced at her watch. "It's time. I need to leave for the airport. Could you please ask your musclemen to help me with my luggage?"

Chapter Fifty

SHE WOKE IN the predawn, when a cold breeze touched her and made her realize that Jon was hogging the covers.

When she tried to pull them back, he muttered and wrapped them even tighter around himself. Shivering, Naomi got up and dressed. It had become too cold to go out to the beach early in the morning in just a summer dress; she needed a jacket now. October was nearly over; driving downtown with Jon, going shopping with Sally, she'd seen the first Christmas decorations. How unreal they looked under the palm trees and the steady California sun. Her heart had tugged a little, trying to draw her back to Toronto, where they'd surely be tasting the first snow by now.

And Geneva, how lovely Geneva would look, with all the lights, and the smells of honey cake, roasted nuts, and mulled wine. Olaf had always taken them to the opera during the Christmas holidays, always after a lengthy discussion among the three of them, where Lucia opted for ballet, and he and Naomi for Verdi. They even had a synchronized groan that had made Lucia laugh every single time. Most years, they'd done both in the end, ballet and opera, and often in different cities. Ballet, Olaf had always said, putting down his newspaper and setting his glasses straight, could only happen in Paris. And opera, well, Hamburg was always a good bet, even though they'd started experimenting with the stage settings; and he wasn't sure he wanted to see *Rigoletto* with only a playhouse in the center of the stage and a ball on a string hanging from the ceiling.

"The setting," he'd lectured them, "should enhance the music, not distract from it. If Hamburg goes on with this modern crap, we won't go there again."

She'd loved those arguments. And she'd loved the outcome, when Olaf would pick up the phone to call his office and ask them to make reservations. "I'm taking my girls out," he'd tell his secretary. "Need to pamper them a bit."

Walking through the garden alone, once again alone and without a guard, the memory made her smile.

He'd sounded just like Jon then. He'd been a lot like Jon in those benevolent moments, when he forgot the business and his work for a few days.

Proudly, he'd presented them to the world, a woman on each arm, as he strode into a restaurant or theater lobby. Naomi had actually caught him looking around, smiling, to make sure that they were noticed.

SHE unlocked the gate and carefully slipped the band around her wrist. The sand was cool and damp under her bare feet; the warmth of summer had evaporated. The beach was settling in for the quiet days of winter. There were more people out; she was late. The sun had already risen and was shining, spreading a pale yellow across the hills and the town.

Out on the sea, a couple of big container ships moved northward, as slow as stones moving against the tide.

Dolphins were playing in the surf, and that almost made her turn around to go wake Jon, make him get out of bed to come, come quickly; and he'd shake her off, laugh at her, and they'd end up in bed together instead of on the beach with the dolphins. The thought made her sigh, and smile, and turn back to face the gate and the wilderness of the estate beyond it. She could almost see her love, could see it like a thread of light that led directly from her heart and along the garden path to where Jon was. It was entwined with his, another silver band reaching out to her; and where they met, where they wrapped around each other, in the places where words failed, there were sparks, little sunbursts, rainbow explosions, showers of diamonds.

So precious, such a wonderfully miraculous thing it was, this love; and thinking of Fleur, sadness gripped her again.

Fleur hadn't understood.

Naomi had told Sally what Fleur had said, had tried to find understanding and comfort; and Sally, gently rubbing her shoulder, had said, "You know she's jealous, right? You know she can't bear to see you with Jon, and Jon seeing only you. She can't understand why Jon Stone the rock star would prefer you, quiet, thoughtful you, to a woman as flamboyant, witty, and glamorous as her. She's drop-dead jealous, Naomi."

The insight had washed over Naomi like a cold shower, and Sally, her hand still on her shoulder, still rubbing, had nodded.

"There. I know how it hurts, believe me. You're not the first to lose a friend because she can't take the glory of someone else's success. It happens as often as a sunny day in Hollywood."

The sadness remained though.

THE high surf had washed up a lot of debris. Walking with her head down, Naomi poked through the seaweed to find her treasures. Her pockets were soon filled with stones and seashells; and a couple of times she even thought she'd found amber at last, but it turned out to be sea glass, rubbed smooth by years of dancing with the sea.

She'd carefully looked up and down the beach before stepping out, but there were too many people for her to feel threatened; if anyone came too close, if someone tried to grab her, she'd scream, and there'd be someone to come to her rescue.

When she'd reached the promontory she turned around, blinking against the sun, pushing a few windblown strands of hair behind her ears.

Her mother was thirty steps away from her.

Lucia hadn't changed at all. She was in jeans, which was unusual, but then again, Naomi hadn't often seen her on a beach. She was barefoot, which was even more noteworthy.

"I should have worn shorts," she said, coming up to Naomi. "No one told me the tide would be so high here."

"It's not always. Today the tide's very high for this beach." Naomi dropped the stones she'd been holding. Two steps, and she was in Lucia's arms, crying, sobbing like a child, breathing in the familiar scent of her mother's perfume.

"You silly girl," Lucia was saying over and over again. "You silly, silly girl. The heartache you've given me; and here you are, and you look as healthy as a horse, and as pretty as always. I was so worried about you"

"I'm sorry, Mama. I'm so, so sorry." Sniveling. She was sniveling like a baby, and it was so hard to let go of Lucia.

"I know, child, I know." Lucia handed her a tissue. "Why in the world didn't you say something? We never knew you were that unhappy about marrying Seth! I really thought you were looking forward to it!"

"But I tried, I tried, Mama; even the night before I ran away, I tried to tell you!" She was holding Lucia's hands in hers, pressing them, holding on tightly. "Don't you remember?"

"I do remember, and I thought you were joking. I'm sorry, Naomi. I never knew you were that unhappy. I should have listened more closely."

Suddenly afraid, remembering where she was, Naomi stepped back. "Is Papa here too? You're not here to take me away, are you?"

"No."

Together, they strolled along the beach, their feet in the last sighs of the surf.

"I've been in Los Angeles for a week now," Lucia said. "I came down here every day at dawn in the hope of catching you alone. But Jon was always with you. And I had the feeling that there was security too. I'm glad you're so well protected." She stopped to bend down and pick up a pebble. It was flat and black, with a white line running through it like a lighting bolt.

"Your father had you watched, you know. There were at least two private detectives following you around. And he's hired security for you. You're always watched when you leave the house, to make sure you're safe." She put the pebble into her jeans pocket. "He called the detectives off after they assured him that you were well and happy, and not being held against your will." She smiled. "Your father was so surprised when he read the report about that movie premiere you attended with Fleur. He couldn't stop laughing when he read that you were escorted by Jon's manager to hide you from public scrutiny. I think he really liked that. Jon Stone is a clever man." She paused. "So does he know who you are?"

"No. I wanted him to love me for who I am. To him, I'm just Naomi." Great, big boulders were dropping from her heart, big stones of worry Naomi hadn't even known were there. "I'm the girl with the lyrics. And I want it to be like that for as long as possible."

They walked, mother and daughter, side by side, pointing out shells to each other, laughing at the dolphins' antics in the surf.

"So," Lucia said after a while, and stopped walking.

"So." They were near the gate, and now that she knew, Naomi could see some men hanging around, one of them playing with a big dog, another one reading a newspaper, sitting on the sand, and a couple more were jogging up and down a suspiciously short stretch of beach.

"I'm not coming back home." There, she'd spoken the words, just like Fleur had told her to do.

"I know." Digging into her purse, Lucia brought out a wad of cash. "Take these. I know you won't take your credit card back, you obstinate child. But at least take this."

"I don't need any money, Mama." She wanted to sink into the ground with shame. "I really have enough; Jon is wealthy, and I don't need a lot."

"Take it, Naomi. Don't spend it if you don't have to, but take it, for my sake. It will make me feel a lot better to know you can just walk out of this house if the need arises."

The bills felt like embers in her hand. "What did Seth say?"

Lucia laughed. "Oh, Seth. He was quite impressed by you. Said he never thought you had it in you to put on a show like that." She shook her head. "I haven't seen him in a while. But it's clear that your father's ideas for succession have gone up in smoke. Seth has pulled out. He told Olaf that the thing was worthless to him without you. He really loved you."

"Well, he never said. He never told me once." It didn't change a thing. Naomi realized that it didn't matter at all. It was her own heart that was important.

"Yes, I know." Lucia again looked up and down the beach. "Well, I think I'd better go. Seeing you, seeing for myself that you're okay, was all that mattered to me."

Hesitating, her hand on the gate, Naomi said, "I'd ask you inside, but I'm not sure… It's so early. Jon is still asleep. Some other time?"

Lucia nodded. "Some other time."

"Mama. I'm so sorry."

"No, you're not, Naomi. You like your new life." A small smile undulated across Lucia's lips. "And it's okay. I remember only too well how I was ready to run away from my family to be with Olaf. I didn't have to, but I'd have done it." She sighed. "Okay then. I can return to Geneva now and work, and rest my soul." Ready to turn away, she stopped. "Call me from time to time, Naomi. Will you do that?"

Naomi nodded. "Yes, of course, Mama."

"And if anything happens, anything at all, if you need help, any kind of help, call your uncle in Kleinburg. He'll know what to do. Will you promise me you'll do that?"

She couldn't stop herself. Hugging Lucia tightly, Naomi promised to call, to ignore the security Olaf had ordered for her and let them do their job, and yes, she would call if she ever needed to be rescued. The thought made her laugh and shake her head, but she promised.

And Fleur. Could Lucia please call Fleur and tell her that Naomi loved her? Could she tell her that Fleur had been right; she didn't want to be a stranger to her parents, not at all, because she loved them.

Lucia smiled and nodded. "I'll tell her. She was devastated when she returned home, said she'd lost you, and she had no idea how to go on with life if you weren't in it."

"And she calls me a drama queen. So typical." Naomi's heart danced. She hadn't realized how sad a part of her had been. It was hard to let go of her mother. Her arms didn't want to move.

"It's all right, darling." It was Lucia who disentangled herself.

"Be happy," she said, giving Naomi one last kiss. "I want you to be happy. And call me."

"I will."

Lucia walked away, stopping a couple of times to turn back and wave; and Naomi waited until she left the beach, walking toward the street and vanished out of sight, the man with the dog following her.

The thick bundle of money in her hand, Naomi unlocked the gate and stepped into her little paradise.

The jasmine was calling to her, and the cedars…

…and Jon.

www.ingramcontent.com/pod-product-compliance
Lightning Source LLC
Chambersburg PA
CBHW020407260626
47156CB00007B/2272
9781941523001